A STORM OF DARKNESS

Timmy's heart almost stopped when he saw the black of sky cover the dog. Dish was simply swallowed up by the night, gone. Timmy got to his feet and raced to the spot where Dish had been standing. But he was gone.

Then he felt a drop of rain patter on his shoulder, then his cheek—except that it smelled twice as strong as the normal smell of thick copper rain—and when he went to touch the rain, he felt the warmth.

It was raining blood. . . .

GEOFFREY CAINE

CURSE OF THE VAMPIRE

DIAMOND BOOKS, NEW YORK

CURSE OF THE VAMPIRE

A Diamond Book / published by arrangement with
the author

PRINTING HISTORY
Diamond edition/May 1991

ISBN: 1-55773-506-9

Diamond Books are published by The Berkley Publishing
Group, 200 Madison Avenue, New York, New York 10016.
The name "DIAMOND" and its logo are trademarks
belonging to Charter Communications, Inc.

PRINTED IN THE UNITED STATES OF AMERICA

10 9 8 7 6 5 4 3 2 1

This book is dedicated with all my love and heartfelt thanks to Stephen, for he is the promise-come-to-pass of a dream: a wonderful son who is also a best friend who supports a strange writer-dad....

PROLOGUE

Since the dog had dug up those human bones in the open field an hour before, he had been acting like a wolf. He again loped away from little Timmy Meyers, luring the boy deeper and deeper into the night.

"Dish! You get back here, now! Dish! *Diiiiiishhh!*"

Dark as it was, Timmy Meyers moved on through the wood, panting, pleading for the animal to return when he suddenly came to a clearing. Dish crouched on the other side at the edge of the woods, glaring at him, his eyes shining silver in the moonlight, his lips pulled back in a grotesque snarl, baring teeth and gums. He didn't even look like Dish anymore. And there again was that uncharacteristic wolf's growl that seemed to bubble up and curl out from his gut.

Timmy feared the worst, that his friend of so many years was ill with something awful—rabies or something. Why else would he snap and bark and snarl at Timmy and the others? It all had to do with the bones.

Earlier, the boys had followed Dish to a hole he had begun digging feverishly and when they had seen the unearthed treasure of bones, they had gone a little crazy, all of them. They had dug out, kicked around, and toyed with what the earth had coughed up for some time before Dish began growling, snarling, and biting.

Then the others had run home, leaving him alone to find Dish. That had been back at the weed patch where he had fought with the

1

other boys. He wondered momentarily how far from that spot he had come; he wondered how far from home he was. He wondered how late it was and what his parents would do when he finally got home, way past dinner and curfew. But he couldn't just leave Dish, not like this, could he?

It was their fault. The other boys had taunted Timmy with the skull of some dead person that they'd dredged up when Dish had sniffed out the ugly find. They'd scared Timmy, made him back off and fall and look stupid and frightened. Dish was mad at them—not at Timmy—when he began to growl and snap like a wolf, just before running off.

"Dish, Dish, boy, come here. . . . Come on," Timmy now said. "It's all right, boy."

But it wasn't all right, because Dish began an ear-splitting, spleen-numbing wail that shook Timmy to his core, telling him that the dog was dangerous—that it was no longer Dish but something else, some alien creature in Dish's form.

The dog got up and made a step toward Timmy whose twelfth birthday was coming day after tomorrow. Timmy saw a slick, slimy substance draining down Dish's neck and front. In the moonlight it looked purple, but Timmy knew it was blood. Dish was hurt badly.

Timmy's concern for himself instantly melted and he went to his knees, opening his arms for his longtime friend to enter there. Dish took a tentative step toward him, his growl swallowing into a whine that almost sounded like the old Dish. But at the same instant, something dark and strange-smelling came down over Dish and made the dog disappear.

Timmy's heart almost stopped when he saw the black of sky cover the dog. Dish was simply swallowed up by the night, gone. Timmy got to his feet and raced to the spot where Dish had been standing. But he was gone.

Then he felt a drop of rain patter on his shoulder, then his cheek—except that it smelled twice as strong as the normal smell of a thick copper rain—and when he went to touch the rain, he felt the warmth. It was raining blood.

Timmy looked up, and in that instant of looking he saw two things: death in the form of blackness that blotted out a good section of the trunk of the tree, and Dish's lifeless body stretched raglike across a branch.

Fear turned Timmy to stone. The black tarlike mass engulfing the tree was feeding on Dish's slashed neck; suddenly it looked down with two piercing, fantastic, and bulging eyes at Timmy, transfixing him there.

It never let Timmy free from that moment on; it held him with its powerful, hypnotic gaze—the gaze of light at the center of total darkness. The creature held onto the tree, upside down, suspended magically there, until it swooped down. With a mild, interesting flutter-sound, like an army of moths, it came to cover Timmy in its darkness and enfold him in its bony, flinty-haired wings.

The child's wail began as a terrified plea and soon turned into a wail of animal madness—the squeal of a trapped, tormented boar. Or was that the crazed killer giving voice to his own delight? It was then that Timmy, while unable to recall his name or what he was, suddenly felt an attachment—a need—for the thing at his throat. Without it—should it remove itself from his throat—Timmy knew that he'd be dead, that all his blood would drain away like Dish's was doing.

In fact, he felt closer to *it* than he ever had to Dish. Timmy somehow knew that it knew; he had somehow communicated this to the monster that folded him into a fetal position and rocked him and held him by his feet, swinging safely with him from the limb so strong it defied gravity.

Monster. He loved it. He had to love it. Even as it was drawing his life away. For it made promises in his mind, positing them there for future reference, telling him that it loved him, too. . . .

—1—

Abraham H. Stroud was the only witness to the attack on the boy and his dog. Stroud didn't know the names or identifying marks or mannerisms of either of tonight's victims. He didn't know the boy's age or address, his favorite color, superhero, comic strip, toy, film or game show on TV. But he *did* know the boy would soon be declared missing and that Andover, Illinois, would be aghast and hard-pressed to find him.

Stroud knew he must do what he could but he must also be most cautious in what he said, did, and pointed to. He didn't relish the idea of his new neighbors thinking him the killer.

Abe Stroud's mind fought to regain access to the trance that was forcing him out like a melon through a tube. The trance he'd been in was not one he had expected or invited, induced as it was via a painful seizure that sent his body into a catatonic state—his only defense against the head-quaking, lightning cracks around the fissures of his skull.

He had been a long-distance witness to a brutal killer wearing black clothes, who had leapt from a tree to take the dog, slash its throat a second time, and then return for the boy.

Stroud saw hazy outlines and an occasional detail, his enormous body shaken and wracked with the convulsions of the seizure and the emotion brought on by what he was witness to.

He saw it all from the center of Stroud Manse, a pre–Civil War mansion made entirely of stone, its spirals, pinnacles, and columns creating a Mid-Western Stonehenge in the little community of Andover, Illinois. Some called the ancient house a monstrosity and hoped the "Andover Horror" would be torn down brick by brick, along with its ten-foot-high stone fence. Some said it'd been used as a fort during the Civil War, and many of its battlements had been built during that era.

Abe Stroud knew better; Abe Stroud knew many of the secrets of his family and of the house. Not all, but many. He knew that the original house had been built more than two hundred years before, and that the original foundation walls had been fashioned by stone carvers from a quarry that had torn a rift in the side of a prehistoric cave dwellers' graveyard. What had been done with the bones at that time had never been mentioned, but once his grandfather had said that the bones were ground up and used in the mortar and concrete that filled the cracks of Stroud Manse. Until now, until becoming the owner of the manse, Abe Stroud had never believed the story. Now he was beginning to wonder, as the walls seemed sometimes to groan.

It was not his first night as owner here. He'd slept here alone now for almost three months, and he had visited and lived here as a child between the ages of eleven and eighteen, some seven years. Even then he'd become used to creaking-wood voices, scratching-limb whining outside, doors banging in the pantry, steps crossing the girth of the halls. He was used to swelling window jambs that moaned in banshee chorus. The whistling dervishes out of thirteen bloody fireplaces he hardly heard at all. It was not the first time he had ever felt uncomfortable here, not the first time he'd ever felt as if there were eyes in the walls, shapes in the woodwork, hands reaching from above and behind him. Much of it was the space—so much of it. He was not used to so much space on all sides. It was enough to give anyone the impression that his every step was being shadowed.

If one allowed the imagination full reign here, anything was possible in the rambling old stone manse left him by his grandfather.

But tonight was the very first time he had ever seen or known of the circle at the center of the manse.

In a sub-basement, hidden and unopened since his grandfather had last seen fit to enter here, lay a sunken chamber filled with dusty instruments of torture, a kind of black museum. There was a rack for extorting confessions and a chopping block that could only serve one purpose. Smaller instruments of death

abounded, such as guns and knives, but the one that drew
Stroud's eye was a box of stakes, cleanly honed and shapely,
the dust recently blown off. Amid the awful collection of weapons there were a number of huge crucifixes and a collection of
ancient books on shelves stocked with skulls, jaw bones, femurs,
and oddities made from bone—such as boxes and clasps. Other
skeletal remains littered another wall. Ananias had said he was
something of an amateur archeologist, but what was all this?

Near the center of the chamber, alongside a desk and chair,
was a huge old red ottoman. Oddly, the room was in the shape
of a circle, and it was at the very heart of the house.

Like its owners, the house held its dark secrets. Stroud, at first,
and again now as he fought to fully regain control of himself,
was not at all certain he wanted to know more than what his
eyes told him. His great-grandfather had been a madman, he
knew, but a Gilles de Rais, an Elizabeth Bathory who fed on the
pain, suffering, and blood of helpless victims strapped to such
instruments as those housed here? It could not be.

And why all the old books in this cathedral of horrors? Great-
grandpa's reading room? Abe had stumbled onto this room and
this fear all in an instant, fully unprepared for it. The jolt had so
shocked him that he had sat down in the cobwebbed chair and
was just as suddenly in the realms of another world altogether—
the world that stress and the steel plate in his head controlled.
It threw him into the night beyond the protective walls of this
house, out on the still-wild prairie of the Spoon River Valley.
It placed him in danger, alongside a terrified little boy who was
out there now—or tomorrow, or next week, or next year—slowly
dying . . . unless . . . unless he could do something.

All the years he had lived with Grandfather here he had never
known of the circular dungeon. Now this place was his along with
the rest. . . .

It had been his first discovery—the circular room—and in this
room strange things happened inside Abraham H. Stroud, specifically in his heart and in his head. For now he knew there
was more truth to the old stories his father and grandfather had
told than he had ever imagined. Like the weird tales told by his
grandfather in front of the fire—lessons of a kind, foretellings,
concern and anxiety over Abe's future. He knew now the stone
walls and fences *were* really laid out by his great-grandfather not
to ward off marching armies of Southern anarchists during the
Civil War, but for the man's very neighbors for whom he'd had

a morbid fear. Perhaps they would one day discover his torture chamber and hang him from the nearest tree, or the highest turret of the manse, before burning it to the ground.

According to his grandfather's tales, Ezeekial Stroud had believed that some of his Andover neighbors were ghouls returned from the grave—that they were even stranger and more eccentric than he, in other words. One of his last written statements, on his deathbed, told of a nest of blood-sucking creatures that roamed the hills and gulleys, the river bottoms and graveyards of Andover, holing up by day in caves. He finished by calling other local citizens, some in high positions, grave robbers and body snatchers, pleading with his son to do to him as he had with all of Ananias's brothers' bodies upon their deaths—cremate his remains.

How Ananias's six older brothers had all died was one of the secrets the house wasn't giving up, but given the torture chamber, Abe Stroud wondered if he hadn't gotten the answer. A foul thought—that his own flesh and blood could kill six sons, Abe's great uncles, here in this hideous chamber. But Stroud had been a policeman and he had seen worse in Chicago when a woman drowned all of her children in the kitchen sink.

Ezeekial, like his son Ananias, and now Abraham Hale Stroud, had, according to the stories, unusually strong precognitive powers. In any event, the "curse/gift" gene, or whatever it was, seemed to have gotten the better of the old man in the end.

Abe often wondered if it would not one day get the better of him as well. On Ezeekial's death certificate was stamped the awful epitaph DEAD OF MADNESS. Apparently, no one ever knew just how mad . . . no one but Abe's grandfather Ananias, Ezeekial's seventh and only surviving son.

Ananias was but mildly gifted with unusual abilities—save for astrally projecting himself out of body. He'd sometimes "visit" to whisper well-meaning words of encouragement to Stroud when he was in the V.A. hospital, and later whenever he felt a seizure coming on, as if they were somehow psychically connected. Ananias had not gone insane but had died peacefully and quietly in his sleep.

Abe had nearly gone mad with grief and guilt when he lost his parents. He had seen the terrible disaster before it had happened, but not soon enough to alter it. As a child he had seen plane crashes before they occurred. When he tried on occasion to warn anyone in authority, he was put off and ignored, until it was too late.

But it was not until his own brush with death that he had truly become a gifted seer. Now what he saw he also smelled, and sometimes he garnered sounds and feelings and textures as if he could reach out and rub his hands into the visual scene in his head. Since his brush with death, along with the metal plate the doctors had put in his head, there was more to see and sense on the screen of his precognitive powers than before; it was as if the metal had electromagnetically charged what nature had already given him. Without the plate, he doubted that he could have received Grandfather Ananias on his astral calls.

Newspapers in Chicago had just begun to call him the "Psychic Cop" when he had left the force as a detective. He hadn't wanted to be treated like a freak because of his gift.

The gift was a curse for the most part, won when he was nearly killed in Vietnam. Part of his skull was gone, replaced by a less than perfect substitute—a thin anchoring of pressed steel that one expert at the V.A. claimed was causing inward pressure against the neurological center of the brain known to be most active during REM sleep and during ESP and PSI studies.

For some time he was a living, breathing, walking, talking laboratory for researchers at the V.A. hospital in Chicago, until he became tired of the role. Not waiting around for a second botched job on his head, he left the V.A. and, amazingly, plate or no plate, seizures or no seizures, he made it through the police academy and all those years on the street.

Tonight's images of the boy, the dog, the clearing, the trees, and the thing in the trees were clearer, more coherent and real, and so vivid as to send him into a paroxysm of fear and loathing—fear for the boy, loathing for the monster that killed him.

Thirteen years in Chicago as a policeman and he had never so clearly put together the details of a crime scene as he did this one tonight—a crime scene he had not ever been to. So real, like high-tech resolution, on certain details—like the bizarre twist of one large tree among the stand where the boy died; the fact a handful of marbles fell from the boy's pockets along with a jackknife he'd halfway opened in his defense before it, too, fell as the boy was lifted, feet first into the air. How the killer moved with such boundless ease up and down the trunk of the tree; how the dog looked so twisted and mangled where it dangled in the branches.

Tell a local cop a hint of such details and you'll be accused of the disappearance and murder, Stroud assured himself. Hell, a

Chicago cop would be hard-pressed to follow how Stroud arrived at such information. Besides, he was alone here. He had no alibi. He'd been in the dark realm of a black seizure brought on by the sudden pressure in his head—like an incubus had sat on him there—then the black world softened into images of children at play, and wound around slowly to the lost boy and his dog.

But it had taken two hours, long enough for him, in a "were-wolf" or "Hyde" form, to have left the manse, killed the dog and the boy, and returned.

But he was in the same clothing, his hands and shirt unspoiled by the innocent's blood. No, there was one other witness to the attack, and whoever the fiend was, he knew the Spoon River area very well. This fact made him most likely an Andover resident.

Again he got a whiff of the boy's fear in the form of perspiration and the odor of blood as it pattered down from the carcass of the dog onto him in a diabolical shower of red. He saw the dog mutilated in a satanic display before the boy's fear-filled eyes.

Then he saw the boy attacked in a similar manner.

Mutilated how, by what means? He hadn't seen or sensed the slightest hint of a weapon. He felt no menacing knifepoint, no axe or other cutting instrument of man's manufacture. Instead, he got the vague image of the talons of a bird of prey. It was impossible to tell exactly how the boy was attacked and how the dog met its end. They simply were covered by the inky blackness of the creature that moved in sync with shadow and darkness, up, down, around, and among the trees without a shriek or cry or warning rattle.

Passed on from generation to generation, Abraham had now taken possession of the Stroud Manse and its secrets (like this room that was both the center and the soul of the house). But had he really taken possession? Or had the house taken possession of him?

He felt weak, woozy, and defeated. He could not get back to the boy in the wood. He could see no more detail, hear no more cry or word, smell none of the odors, taste none of the flavors, feel no solid, scraping bark against his skin or coarse animal muzzle at his throat. He also was physically drained, the seizure ending in locked limbs. He fought to untangle himself from what appeared to be a drunken bout with himself, a grotesque sprawl that would make Dr. Jekyll never again turn to Mr. Hyde. Coming out of it was like surviving a plane landing on him.

He held onto the chair arm and levered himself onto the otto-man, knocking over a small table and the books atop it—books he didn't recall pulling down from their shelves. He propped himself up like a paralyzed man, his legs without feeling until he beat them with his fists where he sat on the dusty old ottoman.

"Radio," he told himself. "Got to get to a TV or radio." There were no such devices in the chamber. He cursed his unresponsive body and slow movements, but finally managed to find the door where he had entered and fought step by step to gain the main floor.

In ten minutes he learned of the news that had aroused every able-bodied man in Andover: a boy named Timmy Meyers was missing and presumed lost in the wood. Timmy was the second boy in two months to disappear mysteriously in the area. The other boy had never been found.

Stroud mobilized himself to join the volunteers to help in any way he could. With his police background alone, he was certain they'd welcome him along. Still, it would be the first time he'd meet most of his new neighbors, many of whom had already classed him with the reclusive Ananias who had not enjoyed the best of relations with many of Andover's 85,000 other residents. The Stroud fortune had been made in land holdings and real estate, and the family held deed to half the town who still paid land "tithes" to the Stroud Manse via the Manse Bank, which Stroud also now owned.

At the moment, however, regardless of the hammerlike jolt that streaked through his skull and the numbness in his limbs, the new millionaire rushed from the enormous house and tore down the paved path and out the iron gate which opened to the touch of his finger from his four-wheel drive Jeep.

It was nearly midnight, and tonight a small boy, helpless and alone out in the scariest forest in the whole damned state, needed all the help he could get.

—2—

The skull was so small it fit comfortably into Abraham Stroud's left hand. The poor light here made it difficult to tell if the seaweed mat atop the cranium was clinging roots that pulled out with the clay or desiccated matter and the last remnants of hair. Whatever, it clung to the skull like the last weeds on a sand dune.

It was the skull of a boy or a girl, perhaps fourteen, maybe fifteen. Impossible to determine either sex or age precisely, at least not here under the circumstances and conditions provided by the Andover Police Department. The flashlights were worthless and they hadn't a single field light or a generator to operate one. Chief Bill Briggs's only comment was that the County Sheriff's Office got all the funding. He also said, "If need be, we can run the four-by-four out and flood the area with the new floodlight we installed on her."

Almost a hundred volunteer searchers were scouring this and another area with crummy equipment. They were looking for a missing eleven-year-old boy named Timmy Meyers. Abe Stroud had come out feigning ignorance as just another volunteer who had heard the news of the missing child. He had been paired with an insurance salesman named Carroll. Carroll had almost stepped on the skull when his flash had picked it out of a clayey runoff alongside old Route 14. The eyes of emptiness had startled the man. But Stroud bent down to pick it up as if he had expected just this. Meanwhile, the insurance man did a bit of hyperventilating.

11

It wasn't every day that a man stumbled onto a skull alongside the highway.

"Don't fret, it's not the Meyers boy," Stroud had told Carroll. "Been here too long for that."

"How can you tell?"

Briggs was stumbling down toward them, seeing they'd picked something from the ground and that Carroll was distressed.

"If it was the Meyers boy's skull, it'd have flesh on it." Stroud saw now that the stringy matter clinging to the bone was a mix of roots and a last vestige of hair. The combination had created a macabre macramé only possible in nature, he thought. Carroll was staring at him as he stared at the skull. Neither man said anymore for a moment.

Briggs had seen and heard now, and he said with a bit of forced cock-sureness, "Professor, that might be right, but you're sorta presupposing the killer didn't *boil* it off!" Briggs's reference to Stroud as "Professor" was facetious, both a nod to Stroud's degree in archeology and a stinging accusation that Stroud was an out-sider.

"Je-Jesus," moaned Carroll. "With all you read about in the papers, things that happen in New York, Chicago . . . "

"Abe here's from Chicago," said Briggs.

"You never believe it could happen here . . . but it does . . . and then . . . "

"Mr. Carroll, I assure you, this"—Stroud pointed to the skull—"is not the Meyers boy."

Others began gravitating to them, hearing Briggs's brash re-marks, sensing Carroll's anxiety, seeing the man's labored breath-ing.

"What the hell?" Briggs turned and asked Stroud, "How do you know, Professor? How do you know it isn't the kid?"

"The teeth for one thing. Your description of the boy said he was missing two front teeth."

"Oh, yeah."

"Whoever this is, he's got all his."

Stroud, an archeologist and anthropologist, had been a lieu-tenant detective on the Chicago Police Force for some thirteen years. Prior to his stint as a detective and sometime undercover cop, he'd been a "grunt," a U.S. Marine in Vietnam. It was a war from which he had returned with two things other than his life: the Medal of Valor and the steel plate in his head. He sometimes felt that the steel plate had made him loco enough to become a cop and dumb enough to remain one for as long as he had.

Surrounded now by many of the volunteers gaping at the little skull, Stroud felt uneasy as he studied the contours. He revolved the eye sockets round in the light, turned the cranium and jaw upside down, staring down from the neck hole. Around him he heard the audible moan of men in close proximity to death. He knew they wanted him to say something to make it go away, and so he spoke his thoughts.

"This skull's been here for a long time."

"How long?" asked Briggs.

"That would take lab work to determine, but from the condition, I'd say a long time."

A whipping March wind sent a shiver along the base of the spine and through his body in pulsar fashion. He was unsure whether it was the chill, the skull, or the eyes of the others that made him involuntarily shiver. For a nanosecond he felt like the stranger and outsider that he was. Despite the fact his grandfather's fortune had kept the town alive when it would have died, they saw Abe Stroud as a peculiarity amongst them. Despite the fact he had often summered here as a boy before he had lost his parents in a car crash, and despite the fact he now owned the huge, elaborate Stroud Manse on Stroud Road along with six hundred acres of land and animals and stables and a fortune in stocks, bonds, and cash left him by his grandfather. Despite it all, he was an "outlander." And he'd likely remain so for as long as he remained.

"There's likely to be more bones hereabouts," Stroud told the others.

Again Briggs spoke the mind of the others, "How do you know that, Professor?"

"It's been my experience as both a policeman and an archeologist, Chief Briggs, that where you find one bone you'll find many more."

"Makes sense," mumbled Carroll, and some of the others agreed. Briggs worked to bring the center of command back to himself. He was calling out to men he'd known all his life, high school buddies and drinking pals, to fan out and begin a sweep off in the direction from where the skull had been found.

Stroud admitted to himself his surprise over the skull and what it portended. Skulls didn't just pop up out of the clay. In Chicago, it would have started the police off on an investigation that would most likely end in a raid of some cult group that had gotten careless with its toys. But here in quiet, sleepy little Spoon River Valley in southern Illinois? He had heard no talk of missing sheep or other livestock found gutted or beheaded, blood siphoned off. But he wasn't forgetting that such things happened. He'd keep an open mind, or try to, because the Spoon River area held what few fond memories Abe Stroud had stored away; even the suggestion that drug-crazed cult creeps were working Andover now made him angry. Everybody on the planet, it seemed, was going mad, everyone wanting a surefire, quick fix to nirvana. But nirvana turned out to be hell on earth. Could such crime exist here in his boyhood dream town of Andover? Were there drugs in every household drawer and every locker at Andover High?

But he was getting far ahead of both himself and the physical evidence to support such wild imaginings. All he had was a skull that had lain in a ditch beside the road and the image in his head of the missing boy he now knew was Timmy Meyers.

Stroud held onto the skull as if it were a treasure. The others began doing as Briggs said. Carroll looked to Stroud for his okay, and they moved off, going about the black forests in the moonless night, their flashlights as useless as dentists tools against the great pyramids near Giza.

He had often visited his now deceased grandfather here as a boy, and if he fought back the good, rich fun of those days with old Grandpa Ananias Stroud—going fishing, boating, horseback riding, camping out in the wood, and listening to the old man tell ghosts stories—if he peeled back that layer, he recalled vividly the other Andover. Walking about in the fog, the eerie bleak fields gobbling down the ineffective lights, Abe Stroud's memory opened further, allowing him to remember that Andover had always been *strange*. It was a place forever pervaded by a sense of imminent evil. The Spoon River itself was a black abyss by nightfall, and its course ran along the property back of the old manse. As a boy he'd stare out at it from the window on the third floor where he'd slept, a long, moving, giant eel. For the past three months he'd slept in that same room, now as a man. He'd watched the river but had forgotten that it was an enormous monster snake until now.

Breathtaking in its blackness, he once had believed anyone going into the Spoon at night was instantly taken away to a bad place. It was the spirits of land and water—forests gnomes and river demons combined—that had teased his boy's mind with misty

figures giving chase over the moorlike pasture that had enticed
him into the Spoon one night. He didn't even remember stepping
from land to water, nor who had pulled him out, or how he was
returned to the house. In fact, he hadn't remembered the incident
until now, searching for bones not six miles from the manse, in
what had begun as a search for a living boy who'd gotten lost
out here.

Now Professor Abe Stroud clearly remembered—unless the
metal in his head was causing havoc with his memories again—
that much of his fascination with Andover was a child's curiosity
about ghosts because *he had seen ghosts*. In his grandfather's
house, and in the wood around the great old manse. Like anyplace
inhabited by mankind, the place had its share of secrets. Even as a
boy, the place was pervaded with a kind of spirit life all its own,
as if the trees housed souls and the bushes hid body snatchers.

The skeleton crew of officials and the army of volunteers who'd
come in search of the disappeared Timmy Meyers, hadn't much in
the way of high-tech equipment, but they carried enough weaponry
to lay waste to twenty acres if the need arose.

Stories and rumors of grave-robbing, child-snatching warlocks
and witches abounded here, tales of dark and evil rituals carried
out in the dense, black under-forests that hugged the Spoon River.
Abe Stroud had paid little heed until now. He was not the boy
who'd followed apparitions into the black river any longer. He
was a veteran of two nasty wars, one in Vietnam, one in Chicago.
He was now getting on in years and had finally earned that degree
in archeology, and had remained with the University of Chicago an
additional two years to also claim a doctorate in anthropology. He
had no illusions about man or the horror of his past and present.

Stroud was a big man at a full 6'4", his gait measured in the
thoughtful step of a Henry Fonda or a Yul Brynner, but the
rough cut edges of his face, particularly the high cheek bones and
wide forehead were reminiscent of statues found only in big city
museums. Clint Walker in his TV *Cheyenne* phase came to mind
for a lot of people, except that Stroud's Indian blood came from
a Cherokee great-grandmother named Minnie Hale. His hair was
peppered with silver strands. His eyes were an icy steel blue-gray,
and they seemed to light on any object they came across.

Even as a young person Abe Stroud couldn't abide heavy
clothing, especially in a cramped area; he was often seen in
his shirtsleeves even on the coldest of days. At the moment he
huddled inside his parka just staring at the sad skull while some

of the men in the "posse" stumbled onto the burial site Stroud had predicted they'd find. Some were aghast at the number of bones the lights were now picking up.

It was a boneyard in the middle of a field back of the trees. From here the lights of the cars on the road were shut out.

Someone in the group called Turnip by his pals, a man who'd been drinking since the rescue effort began, shakingly said, "It's ahh . . . a burial site for the witches!"

"Oh, shut up, Turnip!" shouted Briggs, pushing through. He stopped suddenly at the sight before him.

But Turnip kept talking. "Place where they cast off *parts* they don't . . . u-use. I heard it's their way."

"Might be a blessing if it's so," said Abe Stroud, making them all turn and stare at him. It seemed the maddest comment anyone could make. When the professor of archeology realized how his comment had been taken, he said with deliberate emphasis, "A cult working the area would be a lot easier to trace than a serial killer who randomly stalks victims. Briggs knows that, don't you, Bill?"

Briggs cleared his throat and nodded and said, "The professor's right on that score."

Turnip said, "Hell, he's been right on every score, Briggs. Maybe he ought to be chief of police, or maybe he knows *too* much. Maybe he knew right along . . . "

Stroud stepped to within smelling distance of the hefty man called Turnip. Another man beside the sloppy Goliath made excuses for him. "Don't pay no mind to Glen, hell . . . he don't know shit, Professor."

"That's obvious," said Stroud, glad that Turnip was turned away by his friends who'd all come in a pair of pickups together. "Look," said Stroud, straight out. "In my bones I feel this isn't the work of a local spook cult. I've seen things like this in Vietnam and Cambodia, and I've seen some things in Chicago that sent me racing here when I got word about my grandfather's death."

"You mean his *will*, doncha?" said Turnip with a laugh that started a few of the others laughing as well.

Abe had expected such talk among the law-abiding, peaceful citizenry of the small city; it came as no surprise to him that men like Turnip would place a man like Abe Stroud on his top-ten list of the dangerous and circumspect. Small towns and cities thrive on backfence gossip, barroom bullshit, the extravagant and melodramatic, tall tales of flannel-shirted knights who overcame the obstacles of bringing down a deer with a telescopic lens or stories of the "one that got away." In Andover peace was not enough. Stories abounded about a Big Foot creature that roamed the nearby wood, of a hound from hell that occasionally made off with a cow or a child from a crib. There were rumors of twisted night people who lived for the pleasure of drowning others in the Spoon. Now Abe wondered if Andover wasn't about to get just what it wanted; he had the distinct feeling Andover wasn't going to be quiet any longer.

The Meyers boy's disappearance was the second in as many months. The other boy, Ronnie Cooper, aged eleven also, had his picture in every store window in town, on every fencepost and tree for miles around. It was as if the forest were abducting them. The thought made Stroud fearful. Suppose there was a Green River–type serial killer at work here? A serial killer who preferred little boys?

Other strange, oddball happenings might be chalked up to tavern talk. But now it seemed there was something in the wind that bespoke an explosion of horror, a disastrous stench like the smell of blood as it ripples up from a dagger cut. Abraham felt too old for this work, too old and too tired.

"Whole thing smells bad," said Briggs in his ear in a conspiratorial manner. "Closest crime lab of any real caliber is in Springfield. "S'pose we oughta get some of these bones over to Herman Kells over there. Herman'll put these bones in perspective . . . put 'em through their paces. Crime lab's the best 'round these parts."

Stroud was aware that Briggs was attempting to impress him with his police jargon. "What about sending some to a friend of mine in Chicago?"

Briggs looked dubious for a moment. Then he said, "Sure, sure. You got contacts?"

"Good contacts."

"You use my secretary, Mabel, for anything you need, Professor."

"Thanks, I'll do that."

Briggs then began shouting to his closest deputy. "Call out Magaffey, or is Banaker on this week? I can't keep it straight. Neither one of 'em much with M.E. work, but they're all Andover has," he said apologetically to Stroud. "Go!" he ordered his deputy. "Tell 'em what we got. Tell 'em to pack a lunch. We'll be here through noon tomorrow. And call Carl Dimetrios—"

"Dimetrios?" asked the deputy, confused.

"Yes, damn it!"

"Who's Dimetrios?" asked Stroud of Carroll who had rejoined them.

"Dimetrios operates the John Deere place out at Three Corners."

"Get us some heavy machinery out here, a backhoe maybe," said Chief Briggs to anyone within earshot. "It's my guess we got our own little Killing Field right here, Mr. Vietnam Vet." He directed this comment at Stroud. "What do you think?"

Stroud swallowed the comparison without pointing out to Briggs that it would take literally hundreds of thousands of skulls the size of the one in Stroud's hand to begin to put this dark little plot of earth in the running with Thailand, Cambodia, and Vietnam. "You can't go in there with a backhoe, Chief," he said, "not until we know what we're dealing with. Suppose this is an Indian burial mound we've stumbled onto? It could be a major archeological find."

"Give you something to do, huh? What other purpose would waiting serve?"

"It will give me time to determine the extent of the site and—"

"With a hand pick, on foot? Sorry, Professor but—"

"An important archeological find could mean a great deal to the history of the town, Chief."

"History never was my favorite subject; besides we got men out here ain't seen their families in over twelve hours, men who've got jobs waiting. Now suppose somewhere in all this is that boy's body, and the other one before him? We got to know now."

"But, Chief, these bones are old!"

He wasn't listening. Not a word more. He was off in another direction to give more orders to other deputies. Stroud watched him as he loped away, carrying his weight like excess baggage as if he had not had time to accustom himself to it. Briggs had been a basketball star at the local junior college, had gone on from there to the police academy, and had never been beyond Andover's limits except for the occasional excursion over to Springfield. He boasted of having traveled to St. Louis and Chicago once. He didn't particularly like or understand Abraham Stroud, and most likely agreed with Turnip's general assessment of the brooding former Chicago detective turned archeologist. Briggs, no doubt, could not understand why he'd given up the excitement of police work in a major city for the opportunity to dig holes in the ground.

Neither had Stroud gone out of his way to endear himself to the men of Andover. He never had a beer in a local watering hole. He was never seen doing anything beyond the gates of Stroud Manse where he preferred the company of the horses in the stable to that of most men. He'd never been seen on the arm of a woman in Andover. All strikes against him.

Briggs, by comparison, spent all-nighters chugging beer with friends and relatives at places like the Iron Horse Saloon, a place with a neon boot overhead and a fiberglass horse out front. It was located on a road—the old Combs Hill Road that ran alongside of the Spoon River for a stretch—that was morbidly referred to as Tombstone Highway for the number of drunk drivers killed going over a rail there.

Stroud picked among some of the additional bones that'd been uncovered. It looked to him like it was the work of some animal that had unearthed the remains. He was wishing again for more light when he found a long femur. It seemed too long to be a match for the skull, unless the youth had been exceptionally tall. He put aside the other bones and again studied the small skull up close. The eye sockets were huge and empty like the innocent look of a sad animal, like the living eyes of a South Vietnamese child he'd once seen in two parts. Her torso and brain were both still operating, as were her eyes, while at the same instant her soul was taking flight from war.

Stroud wanted to fling the damned skull away, but instead he doused the light, cradled the skull gently, and stepped back toward the trees that masked the squad cars and pickups on the roadbed. He wasn't aware that Carroll and some of the others watched him. Half of Briggs's people were here, the other half were out near Sagammon where another report had come from—a sighting of a boy alone walking the highway. Why didn't the same asshole who made the sighting bother to pick the boy up?

Abraham Stroud empathized completely with the lost boy wandering on the highway; the boy's situation pained him to his core. Abe's bones talked to him all the time—bones left broken and riddled with metal by a firefight that had left him a lost boy on a battlefield. He had lain in a field of dead in Nam; he had assumed he would die there. It had taken sixteen hours before someone on his side had found him amid the dead, and by that time he had spoken a long time with his bones and the bones of others. The little skull in his hands talked volumes which all amounted to a whispering complaint: "Desecration."

He suddenly turned to Carroll, abruptly saying, "You don't just pick up little skulls in weed fields; they don't grow from the earth the way rocks do."

Carroll nodded and muttered, "Agreed."

"Don't you see, Mr. Carroll? Someone, earlier, this way came . . . found this unusual *rock* and dug at it until it looked back at him. Curious, intrigued maybe, he picked it up, even carried it away from the other bones . . . dropped it where we found it."

"Got pretty far away before he tossed it aside."

Stroud's eyes bore into Carroll's in the dark with the skull between them. Carroll felt the thought in Stroud's mind leap across the chasm between them. "Kids?"

"Group of them, maybe? With a dog, maybe?"

"A dog?"

Stroud was instantly sorry that he'd mentioned the dog. If the locals knew of a dog that'd been with Timmy Meyers, no one had made a particular point of it. Yet, here he was, a relative stranger to the area, telling Carroll that the missing boy was accompanied by a dog. Information he had garnered through a hazy and halting vision. He didn't want Carroll or anyone else thinking strange thoughts about him, so he quickly tried to cover himself, dispelling the nebulous vision of Timmy's cringing below the sight of his dead dog, by saying, "Kids and dogs go together, as natural as pie and cream; out for fun, they stumble onto this bone field. Maybe one of them was Timmy Meyers."

"Lotta maybes. . . ."

Stroud stood and stared at the fog-bound field, trying to envision the scene. Who would these kids be? Where were they now? Were they friends of the Meyers boy who lived on a farm not so far from here? Could the boy have ridden his bike down here, or caught a ride behind another kid on a bike? A series of questions that led to questions which in turn led to more. The search for a missing kid had turned into an investigation of foul play. You don't bury a kid's skull in a wood far from any roads just because you want to save on the cost of a pine box, although Abe had met some Andover folk who might think it the prudent thing to do.

A van with bright lights sped toward them and seeing it, Stroud groaned. Briggs went for the camera van like a bear on the scent of honey. It was an election year. "Here comes Eyewitness 2, Your Neighborhood Crime Watch Channel!" he said, repeating the tiresome television phrase.

"Suppose John McEarn'll be with 'em," said Carroll flatly. "Went to school with the jerk. Guy's like an ant, the way he crawls over dead rats."

"What the hell's he expect to get here now?"

"Teeth. Briggs'll show him a lot of teeth. And he'll want shots of the bones, of course. Ratings wet dream, that's what this is for McEarn."

Stroud laughed lightly. It was the first time he'd so much as smiled this night. Carroll eased a bit himself now that he saw Stroud had lightened up. Someone among the searchers, all of whom had fanned out with lantern-size flashlights, shouted, "Over here! Some more! Over here."

Briggs stared at Abe Stroud as if he were the Wizard of Oz. He could not believe there was yet another bone pile. None of them could. "Christ, Briggs, stands to reason," said Stroud, marching off with Carroll who he took by the arm, directing the man toward his brand new four-by-four Jeep Cherokee. It had been his first purchase in Andover. Behind them they heard Briggs telling the newsman, McEarn, about the initial discovery of a single skull. Briggs made an ass of himself by stating for the camera that, "Hell, I thought it was just—you know—maybe a passin' hippie car from Arizona or someplace, just tossed it out with other trash."

—3—

Stroud placed the skull on the seat of the Cherokee and told Carroll to get inside beside it. Ray Carroll didn't know what Stroud had in mind, but he got inside anyway, checking out the Jeep's features, fascinated by it, saying he'd always wanted one, had promised himself he'd own one before he died. Stroud tore off into the ditch and up again on the other side, driving through the tree cover and out into the open field where all the others had raced to the new bone site. He hit his brights and flooded the field and the men on it, their shadows doing a dance of a distance of some fifty yards. "Throw some goddamned light on the subject," he said curtly as Andover men scurried to get out of his way.

"Jesus! Goddamn!" they alternately swore and threw dirt clods at the Jeep. Behind and now beside Stroud came the news van, anxious to get in closer, the wheels kicking up twice the loose soil that the Jeep had.

When Stroud got out, he didn't have to push his way past the others. The ones remaining in his way eased back from him, allowing him entry without a word. None of them knew Stroud well, since he'd just taken up residence among them three months before but they did know he was a tough man. It wasn't something he'd done, or ever said, not even backing down Glen "Turnip" Turner. Until tonight Stroud hadn't ever had to display it. It was just accepted when another man looked into his face and those hard, cold eyes. His eyes told others that he had killed men.

22

The man who'd found the additional bones was Ray Carroll's brother-in-law, Mitch Campbell. Campbell was shaken; like others here, he was a man with kids of his own, a hefty wife, and an even heftier mortgage. He worked for the city, road work, Stroud had heard. Like Ray Carroll, he became a volunteer because he always volunteered. When Andover had a completely volunteer fire department, both men were on it, as were many of the other men present tonight. In old junkers and pickups, Jimmys and Jeeps equipped with CB radios, they came from out of the seemingly empty night on a moment's notice: Andover's Minutemen.

"What've we got, Professor?" asked Chief Briggs, playing to the camera now rolling as Briggs kneeled into sight of bones half in and half out of the earth.

"Back off a bit," said Stroud. "Watch your step. Damn, whole area's covered with footprints. No way to reconstruct what went on here."

"Back off," Briggs repeated, "just a bit."

Stroud's thoughts raced ahead of him. He didn't tell the Chief or the camera or the others that the bones had something to say. Stroud studied them for longer than was comfortable to the camera eye. He studied them until his legs complained with cramps. He sifted through the dirt and pulled some out and stared and hummed to himself until everyone present was also uncomfortable.

Finally, Briggs said, "Well, whataya think, Professor?"

In a near whisper into the microphone, McEarn, somewhere over Stroud's shoulder, told the listening audience at home who Professor Abraham Stroud was. Stroud said tonelessly, "Chief, you can't bulldoze this area until—"

"Backhoe, son . . . backhoe. Don't intend to doze it over. Intend to dig and sift until we got the extent of the problem in our sights."

This sounded good to everyone present who agreed with verbal soundings.

"Just give me until sundown tomorrow," said Stroud. "I think this area is some sort of burial ground."

Briggs only scratched behind his ear.

Stroud said to the gathered men, "Do any of you men know who Timmy Meyers played with, went to school with?"

"Be my boy, Joey," said Carroll, "but—"

"Did you talk to him about the disappearance?"

"He came home late . . . didn't eat . . . wasn't feeling well . . . went up to bed early."

"Is it possible, Mr. Carroll, that he played with Timmy before dark? That he was the last person to see the boy?"

"We couldn't get him to say much when we asked him about it. Said he and Timmy weren't playing together anymore. You know kids."

Stroud knew some kids, but he'd never had any of his own. Still, as a cop, he knew how their minds worked, particularly when they were scared. He'd interrogated a lot of frightened kids during his time in Chicago.

"Would you mind, Mr. Carroll—"

"Ray."

"—Ray—if I talked with the boy?"

"He'll be asleep hours ago."

"It could help."

The insurance man nodded. "I guess . . . maybe . . . when I think it could be Joey out here missing . . . well . . . "

The unspoken truth was that any boy lost in these woods could be dead by morning. "Get into the Jeep and we'll go together."

Stroud began to make his way back around the Jeep when the TV floodlights hit him in the eyes, making him curse.

"What progress, Professor Stroud, has been made in locating the Meyers boy? What do the bone finds have to do with the boy's disappearance?"

Stroud grabbed John McEarn and lifted him against the side of the Jeep. "You have any idea what that kind of broadcast'll do to the boy's parents, you hemorrhagic ass?" Briggs and a deputy pulled Stroud away from the newsman before Stroud's fists got into the act. For a moment, Stroud felt like a cop again.

McEarn was shouting that he'd be sorry for his actions.

Stroud got into the Jeep and tried to calm down, taking a great breath of air.

"Rest of you men, we're not going to be able to do much here 'til daybreak when we can see what we're doing. Go on and finish your sweep for the Meyers boy. Leave any more old bones to us. Meanwhile, my deputies'll be with you," Briggs was saying.

Stroud and Carroll tore off, the Jeep backing out at full tilt, lights picking up Briggs holding up a skull to the TV cameras. Stroud cursed under his breath and grabbed for the skull he had placed on the seat earlier, his large hand wrapping around it in a protective cocoon. He stopped the Jeep and drove forward again, whirling alongside the chief, kicking up dust and whirling dervishes into the camera and his face. Briggs's interview was stopped. Stroud shouted out to Briggs, "Whatever you do, Chief, hold off on the goddamned heavy equipment until I get back."

Briggs was choking on dirt, wildly shaking his fist high over his head when Stroud's Jeep hit the pavement and raced down the tarmac. The black ribbon of the twisting highway had been neglected here for so long that even the center lines had become invisible. Stroud thought the road looked like the nearby river, two of a kind.

"Eerie, isn't it?" asked Ray Carroll of the bone field.

"Yeah, you might call it that."

"Never seen the like of it . . . outside the carcass room at the slaughter house."

"Slaughter house?"

"Sure, Andover's biggest employer. We hold the policy."

"What, like cattle? Beef?"

"Beef, yeah, but everything else, too. Sheep, pigs, veal when the season's on."

"Lot of bones there, sure."

"Bones are ground up for meal. Every so often somebody has an accident on the job. We cover the damages—workman's comp package, the whole shot. We have an inspection made once a year. Last time, I went along."

"How old's your boy, ahhh?"

"Joey, he just turned thirteen. Quite a boy. Won MVP for soccer this year. He's a good kid. Gets in his share of trouble, but a good-hearted kid like him, you won't find another—"

"Think he understands the importance of our finding Timmy?"

"Sure . . . sure he does."

Then how could he sleep? Stroud wondered.

The insurance man and the hard-edged archeologist continued on in silence toward Carroll's house aside for an occasional question raised by Ray Carroll.

"What do you think my boy can tell you?"

"Don't know till we ask."

"He won't know anything about the bones, I promise you."

"He may not."

"He likely doesn't know anything about the other boy's disappearance either."

"Maybe not."

"But you want to wake him in the middle of the night and ask him anyway?"

"I do. You can tell me no, of course, bar me entrance at the door, if you like, Mr. Carroll, but so long as you do not, I'm going to wake the boy and ask him some questions."

"I see."

Stroud caught sight of the grinning skull that dirtied the seat between them when they passed under the street lamp. *Make no bones about it*, Stroud thought but did not say.

They arrived at the Carroll house where all lights were out. Ray Carroll made a loud entry, purposefully rousing first his wife and then the children. He had several kids, two younger than the boy Stroud wished to question. Mrs. Carroll had to be restrained by her husband. She didn't want her son "interrogated" in the middle of the night. When Carroll tried to explain to her who Stroud was, the fact he was a former cop upset her even more.

"Darling," Carroll pleaded, "Abe's just trying to get at the truth."

"Joey wouldn't lie to me."

"No, I know that, but this isn't like cutting school."

"If your child were missing, Mrs. Carroll, you'd want everyone to cooperate," said Stroud firmly.

"You're that stranger that took hold of the Stroud place, aren't you?" she asked with a suspicious index finger pointed at him.

"I am the grandson, yes."

She nodded, her stare summing him up. He was from Chicago, therefore he was a mobster in hiding, more likely related to Al Capone or Bugs Moran than to old Mr. Stroud. And even if he was who he said he was, old Mr. Stroud himself had been an eccentric oddball.

"It could save a life," Stroud said.

Stroud was finally allowed a few minutes, but not alone with the boy. The mother and father stood nearby, staring pointedly at their son.

"Yeah," he said sleepily, rubbing his eyes, "we were all of us playin' when we found the bones."

"Now, listen, Joe," said Abe Stroud, "those bones—did you kids dig them up?"

"We didn't . . . sir, not all of us . . . and not at first."

Stroud studied the child's expression as he spoke and he believed the boy was telling the truth as best he might under the circumstances. "Joe, how did you boys first discover the bones?"

"Timmy's dog got at 'em."

Then Timmy did have a dog with him, and so the vision of the dead animal hanging limp over the child's amazed eyes was not merely symbolic or meaningless after all, thought Stroud. He swallowed this news with calm acceptance while Carroll said, "By golly, you said he'd have a dog with him."

Stroud gently told Joey to continue.

"Dish!" Joey near shouted it.

"Dish?"

"Called his dog Dish," said Ray Carroll.

"Short for Dishrag," added Joey, his eyes widening. "Ain't that funny?"

Stroud intentionally called the boy Joe. "Joe, did Dish find the bones and start tearing at them?"

"Yes, sir."

"And you boy's did what?"

"Tried to pull him away. First we didn't know what he'd run up on. We just wanted to keep going, but Dish wouldn't leave it alone. So, Timmy, he went back for him."

"Alone?"

"Yes, sir."

"But you all saw the dog was into a bone pile, is that right?"

"Some of the boys said it was old animal bones where a coon died or something. We didn't want nothing to do with it. Then Timmy went back for Dish . . . and he . . . and he . . . "

"He what, son? What did he do?"

"He snatched up the head with its hole eyes, trying to scare us when we come through the trees."

Carroll and Abe Stroud exchanged a look, Stroud glad that he'd kept the skull on the seat in his car. Eventually he'd see to it that the skull got a thorough going over. For a moment he flashed on Bill Briggs's toying with the other skull on TV. To Stroud the grown man's behavior was far more sick and ludicrous than eleven- and twelve-year-olds playing with the horrid mask of death deep in the wood.

"So, Timmy scared you all and you left him there?"

"No, sir! I wasn't scared. Some of 'em were, but not me."

Stroud calmed the child's indignity at having been called a coward in front of his father. "Sorry, Joe, I didn't mean you. But now, remember, Timmy held the skull's eyes up at you all and shouted something like *boooooo*! right?"

"He tried."

"What do you mean, he tried?"

"Dog, that dog, Dish."

"What about Dish?"

"He didn't like it, not a bit. He, he jumped onto Timmy's back and started growlin' at him, so Timmy threw the skull down, claiming it bit him, crying and showing his fingers where he said the-the skull bit him!"

Carroll's wife chuckled nervously, and Carroll said, "Boys . . . what imaginations."

"What happened to Timmy then, Joe? Joe?"

"He run off."

"Ran off? Alone?"

"Deeper into the woods."

"Really, and what about Dish?"

"Dish run right along with him, nipping at him like it was all a game. Dish was getting weird though."

"Weird?"

"Growly and snarly, like a wolf all of a sudden."

"What happened next?"

"Nothing."

"Nothing?"

"Nothing else happened. It was dark, and we . . . we knew we'd best get home, or get a tannin', so . . . "

"You all allowed Timmy to run deeper into the wood, while the rest of you went home?"

"Yes, sir," he replied, looking to his parents, tired of this game now.

"I think Joey's had quite enough," said Mrs. Carroll, a thin woman wearing a nightgown that hung limp around her small frame, glasses perched on her nose, somewhat plain and bitchy looking, Stroud felt.

"It really is late," said Carroll, weakly agreeing.

"Sure, sure. Thank you, Joe," said Abe Stroud to the boy. Joey Carroll just looked over his shoulder and gave the strangest smile Stroud had ever seen in a child his age. It was not snide or spiteful, but a knowing smile, as if to say in an old man's wink, "I know you've had a tough night, too." Then the boy was gone, and Stroud stood staring at Carroll.

"What do you make of it?" he asked Carroll.

"Make of it?"

"The boy's story."

"Sounds like boys at play to me."

"Sounds like something's missing to me."

"Joey's no liar," his mother defended him.

"No matter what mistakes he and the other boys made," said Carroll, "Joey wouldn't lie to us. He said he saw the boy before dinner, and that's the last he saw of Timmy Meyers."

"He's chosen to leave something out, or he has turned things about. Sure, there's truth in what he's saying, but there's also something else he's not telling. I can't quite say what just yet, but the boy's hiding something."

"For God's sake, the boy's only just turned thirteen. What dark secret are you looking for, Stroud?"

"Was Joey part of a group of boys who always hung together?"

"Hung together?"

"Did things together?"

"Yeah, what of it?"

"But Timmy—is he a part of Joey's regular crowd?"

"The Meyers family's new to Andover."

He was an outsider, Stroud realized now, like himself.

"The Meyers family's new to the area, but my son would not be treating a newcomer badly, Professor. I'm not sure I appreciate the tenor of your questions, nor the direction they've taken."

"Your son ever involved in an initiation rite with the group of boys he plays with?"

"That's out of the question!"

"Have you ever discussed it with him?"

"I have had absolutely no reason to do so! No!"

Mrs. Carroll was leaning into the doorway to the room where they stood, and for a moment Abe Stroud saw an intense spark of hatred blaze across her eyes, just before she said, "The hour is uncivil, Professor Stroud."

Something about the dog's behavior in the boy's story, for one, didn't ring true. Timmy's dog chasing him?

"I think it time you left!" she said and stormed off.

"Sorry, she . . . she's not normally like this, but it's got her upset, the whole thing. These missing children, and then she thinks of how close . . . how it might well have been our boy, you see."

"Sure . . . I see," replied Stroud. "Want a lift back to pick up your truck?"

"No, no . . . I'll fetch it in the morning." The predawn sky told both men that it was already morning.

"Fine. See you later then, and please, extend my apologies to Mrs. Carroll."

"Absolutely . . . and good night, Doctor Stroud."

Stroud departed the neat two-story brick house in Andover, the spin of his wheels sending a cascade of rocks bulleting up the driveway as he backed out. Alongside him, on the seat, the skull tipped over and was lying upright, staring and grinning at him, laughing at him, daring him to bend and kiss it.

Being alone with the damned thing wasn't as easy as being with Carroll and the damned thing.

"What kind of person had lived out a life inside this skull?" he asked himself. Only time and precise examination might provide the answers. He had to get head bone connected to the neck bone, connected to all the others, to show first that the bone pile, while it appeared a random dumping ground, housed whole people who were buried intact. The bones were very likely Indian, from a mound leveled at a much earlier date when the highway was built, and now eroded completely. The last scratch had been supplied by Timmy's dog. Stroud's services might be useful to Briggs and Andover. He knew enough about bones to shed light on the discovery. Still, his heart went out to little Timmy Meyers who'd most assuredly been teased, frightened, bullied, and shamed into running off with his dog who's snarly behavior was likely in response to the other boys' bullying and pressing the ugly little skull into Timmy's face. Stroud knew how kids worked. He had part of the puzzle. But some of the pieces might never surface.

— 4 —

His return to the scene of the discovery made him angry enough to kill. Carl Dimetrios had arrived, and had moved in with his yellow backhoe. Bones were being destroyed in the process, many lost in a mountain of soil that hadn't been here when Stroud had left with Carroll.

Stroud rushed to the backhoe and lunged onto the side step, snatching out the key. The machine came to a coughing halt.

"Son of a bitch, Briggs!" the Greek, Dimetrios, shouted.

Briggs rushed toward them with Dr. Oliver Banaker on his arm, shouting that Dr. Banaker was now in charge and that he had ordered the backhoe in.

"Nothing here to preserve, really," said Banaker curtly. "But if that boy was put in the earth here, well, the faster we dig, the better."

"You're a medical doctor, Banaker," said Stroud. "What the hell do you know about bones besides the ones you've set?"

"So happens I'm a bone specialist."

"Among other things?"

"I'm also Chief Medical Advisor for the police, Doctor Stroud, and frankly, I don't believe you have any say in this matter, since it is a police investigation."

"This is a grave site of some sort and you're devastating it!"

"Tell him, son!" shouted Dr. Martin Magaffey who came up beside Stroud. Magaffey was visibly put out, shaking with indig-

31

nation, his features pinched. Banaker represented the medical profession in Andover. Martin Magaffey—at an advanced age that caused him seizures during which he dozed off while standing, sometimes while performing an autopsy—was to be replaced by a man appointed by Banaker as soon as the one with the right stuff came along. "He would have to be a fool," Magaffey had confided in Stroud once, "a fool to take the putrid pay, the indignities, and the overwhelming tasks!"

Before all this had exploded in Stroud's face, he had been looking over the arcane system which had made Banaker Magaffey's superior. It was an odd mix of medicine and politics that smacked of the sort of horror that usually occurred whenever government and medicine crawled into bed together. Stroud didn't like it, but today's fiasco was real proof that Banaker only made evidence-gathering in Andover inexcusably muddled. Whatever happened to scientific police investigation?

"Banaker's in charge," Briggs said.

Stroud carried his argument over to Magaffey as the backhoe was churned up again. "You get Banaker out of it, and I'll see what I can do," Magaffey said. "If he's involved, I'm not! Sorry, son . . . just ineffective, whole damned process. Used to think that my having to report to the police chief as his underling was bad. This structure now, ten times worse. Banaker's a two-faced—"

He let it drop suddenly when from across the length of a hundred yards he looked up and saw Banaker's eyes riveted on him and Stroud. "He's wondering how soon he can get rid of me; look at 'im. Doesn't like your being here, either, if you'd like to know, Stroud."

"Likes to run the show, huh? Can't accept an idea not his own?"

"You got it." Magaffey, his wild thin hair lifting and falling with the A.M. breeze, laughed at this. "Sure . . . sure, and my mouth's got me into more trouble than anyone in Andover oughta have. I don't know. . . . Was a time Andover was a nice place to live, raise a family."

"You small-town lifers don't trust anyone, do you, Doc? Banaker's father started the clinic, didn't he?"

"His father wasn't like him."

"Fair man?"

"No, but at least he didn't pretend to be! Say what you will, Stroud . . . town's changed, and it ain't all for the good. Not no more."

"So, what do you think of the bones, Doc?" Stroud wanted very much to get the white-haired old gentleman back on course before he went on another tirade or had a bout with his dropsy.

"Bones is bones, some say. Me, I know bones, son. I tell you one thing." He came close and conspiratorially whispered, "These here bones've been buried twice."

"What?"

"You heard me."

"What do you mean by twice?"

"Not so damned loud, Stroud. Want that chickenshit Briggs, or that TV man to hear? Just what I said, damn it—the bones I've seen buried here aren't fresh. They've all seen better days."

"Some sort of archaeological find, you telling me? An Indian burial mound, maybe. I've seen the Cahokia find up north of here. Northwestern University, Dr. Treller."

"*Nooooooo!* Damn it, Stroud, how'd you ever get so far on your own?"

Stroud dropped his gaze, rubbed his unshaven face, and felt for some reserve with the old man. Maybe Banaker was right about Magaffey. Maybe Magaffey ought not to be working on important forensic evidence in such cases as this. Maybe he was senile as hell. Hard to say of a coroner.

The old man retained much of his sharpness, however, reading Stroud's expression and saying, "Don't look like that, Abraham Stroud, not in my direction. Hell, boy, I've forgot more about bones than Banaker ever knew. Calls himself a bone expert over at that spanking new technological wonder of his, but the damned fool hasn't even seen this. Looky here." The old man pushed a long femur into Stroud's face. "Hold this at the tip where it's been lobbed off—"

"Broken off?"

"Precision cut at the joint where the red marrow's found, you know, the spongy stuff? My guess'd be we won't find even a speck of it, not even in the microscope. Hell, Banaker could even put it under his goddamned whatchamightcall it—*ahhh, ahhh, eeee*lectron scope—and he wouldn't find a damned trace! Not a trace! My eyes and a friggin' flashlight tell me as much. Don't need no *eeee*lectrons telling me that."

Stroud stared at the femur for a moment. "Someone sliced this bone with a saw of some sort, near the joint—"

"With long bones," said the old doctor of forensics, "the marrow's all around the ends. Short, flat bones it runs all the way through, but these long 'uns like this and the arm bones, mostly filled with yellow marrow, not the red stuff where blood cells are produced, you see."

Stroud scratched behind his ear, and the old man told him that never helped anyone to think clearly. "Look, son, most of those bones in that pile?" The old man winked.

"Yes, sir?"

"Most of 'ems children's bones."

"Doctor, what are you getting at?"

"Christ, Stroud, most every bone in a child's body is chock full of red marrow, even the long ones! Children are factories for producing healthy red blood cells so as to build bones and teeth! Hell, a *Crest* commercial'll tell you that."

Stroud frowned at this. Nearby, Chief Briggs was directing Dimetrios to take his hoe to the second site. Many hundreds of bones had already been uncovered. Banaker wanted every one unearthed now.

"Let me get this straight, Doctor Magaffey," said Stroud over the roar of the machine at work. "Are you saying that these bones've been buried not once, but twice?"

"Be a third time after Banaker's through playing games."

"I've heard of *Twice Told Tales*, but twice buried bones?"

"It's a fact."

"How . . . how can you know that?"

"One thing, Abe, people's bones aren't supposed to be robbed of the goddamned marrow. Maybe that occurs in Chicago at some fancy institutes when some cancer patients leave their bodies to scientific study, but around here . . . people got funny ideas about their bodies going to science. They got the notion that if you're not buried with your heart and your head, you're most likely never going to find your way to the Pearly Gates."

"Superstition, you mean," muttered Stroud, studying the long femur bone at the end where it would have met with the knee cap. There was a definite cut, and the usual red earth, or powder, of dried bone marrow was missing. "It might just be that a carbon 14 dating on these bones is called for. For all we know—"

"They're old, Abe, but not ancient."

"It could be an Indian burial site, couldn't it?"

"None around here according to records."

"But records've been known to be wrong."

Magaffey nodded thoughtfully.

"If they are old bones, couldn't the marrow have just disintegrated years ago?"

"I guess Banaker'll see it that way."

"But you don't?"

"You've studied the bones of ancient cavemen, son, and they all retain microcosmic trace elements of marrow—or should."

"Well, what the hell explains the absence of marrow then, Doc? And what do you mean, buried twice?"

"Son, you know we're a small place, Andover . . . you know, you don't have to believe everything you hear, but do me a favor—"

"What's that?"

"Next time you go by the *Sentinel* offices?"

"Yeah?"

"Stop in, have a look-see at their back issues, particularly any stories about graveyard vandalism."

"I've heard rumors, stories."

"Bull. Rumors don't unearth bodies."

"Are you saying we've got a modern-day body snatcher on our hands? Grave robbers?" Stroud could hide his impatience no longer.

"Two cases unquestionably," replied Magaffey. His features assumed a frown of remembrance. In the old days, Martin Magaffey was the only man in all of southern Illinois in the field of forensic medicine. He actually had an M.E. degree, a rare piece of paper for any doctor. But he enjoyed a poor reputation, and seemingly made it poorer each chance he got. Stroud didn't know him well enough yet to form a complete judgment.

"Dirt was freshly dug, found that way by the family. . . . Both cases the graves of children."

"You order an exhumation?"

"No . . . tried to . . . wanted to . . . but nobody'd have it, not Banaker, not the families—"

"But you're the coroner."

"Small town, even the coroner's got to worry about re-election."

"Was Banaker here at the time?"

"The old man and the kid both. Father was mayor for a time. Didn't you know?"

"No, no, I didn't know."

"Anyway, nobody believed it possible. It was written off as graveyard vandalism, along with a few headstones that'd been turned over, and some chinked good with heavy tools, spray-painted with obscenities, that sort of thing. Nobody believed kids around here were industrious enough to make it the six feet under; said maybe they got a few feet and then decided it weren't worth it, and then just tried to cover it back over. I said—"

"Why would vandals make a show of covering it back over?"

"Exactly, but no one wanted to hear it. Families didn't want to believe it. One old-timer wanted an exhumation on his grandchild, but ahhhh, he wasn't the parents, and the parents wanted it left alone."

"This was all in the papers?"

"Nah, I mean, sure, but not half as much as ought to have come out did."

Dr. Oliver Banaker was coming toward them. But before getting to them, Banaker stopped to say a word to everyone he passed. It seemed that he exuded some magical force like an invisible aura about him that people wished to touch, either physically, through eye contact, or a shake of the hand. He seemed more politician than medical man, and in a sense, running the Banaker Institute in the city of Andover made him a politician. He looked polished and in charge even in his stylish casual wear selected randomly from his closet as he rushed to the scene of the discovery. Behind him, the backhoe churned up more bones and clayey southern Illinois soil. The sight outraged Stroud as the killing of whales would outrage a Greenpeace man.

Banaker was waving a map that was yellowed with age in his hand as he approached. Stroud studied Banaker's features in more detail than before. Certain physical characteristics seemed some-how more prominent now than before, such as the arching brow and confident, loping stride. He had a thick-boned frame and skull, the forehead protruding yet sloping back at the same time, wolflike in this aspect. His bushy eyebrows met over the nose, forming a long, dark line. The man's hair was tufted, crispy from too many applications of hairspray, perhaps? Banaker's triangular ears were large, as were the man's lips. His nose was not flat and large, but sleek and long like a bird of prey. He seemed an exaggeration of the species, but the eyes were luminous, lovely even, like the life-filled eyes of a pregnant woman. Stroud found himself fascinated with the man's gaze as Banaker spoke to them.

"Appears we've got an answer to our mystery, gentlemen."

"Is that right?" asked Magaffey.

"What we've stumbled onto here is a long-forgotten graveyard, Stroud."

"Taken over by the weeds," said Briggs, joining them. "How were we supposed to know? Have my badge for this."

Banaker held up a thigh bone and several times slapped it into his open palm as if he were a teacher and it was a ruler. The gesture was meant to bring home his point. "I wouldn't worry unduly, Briggs. It was, after all, unmarked. How could you know?"

"If you knew this, Banaker, why did you allow the damned machine in?" asked Stroud.

"I just received information."

A lame reply, but Stroud sensed Banaker was taking some macabre pleasure in all of this, despite the fact a graveyard had been razed and Timmy Meyers remained missing. Banaker said, "Besides, the way the bones were discovered, it appeared to be a dumping site! A potter's field for the poor and indigent. This explains the absence of coffins, headstones, and any semblance of a normal pattern as in other grave—"

"*Ahhhhh*, I see," said Magaffey thoughtfully.

Banaker took Stroud aside for a moment and said in his ear, "Been listening to our town octogenarian, I see. Take care, Doctor Stroud, and remember to take ample salt along with whatever the old coot tells you."

Stroud's dislike for Banaker had its roots in ancient history. Stroud recalled that his grandfather had had difficulties with a man named Melvin Banaker years ago.

"You've cleared up the confusion for us all, Doctor Banaker. The mixed bones, the fact they weren't properly interred."

"If the site is as old as I assume, no coffins of the era would have survived to date," added Banaker before stepping away again to speak with Chief Briggs.

"The old settlers' boneyard is four or five miles from here," countered Magaffey when Stroud turned to him.

"Perhaps there were two old graveyards."

"Not by my recollection."

"Potter's field, maybe . . . you know, for those who couldn't pay for a place in the usual way. How far does the other yard date to?"

"Early 1800s, maybe late 1700s."

Muttering to himself now, agitated, Magaffey stormed off. He'd taken some of the bones in hand for later analysis. For a moment Stroud stared after the old man whose frame was racked with arthritis, and whose legs were bowed. He looked the picture of an old eccentric, but deep inside the gnarled form and bedeviled brain there seemed, at least in Stroud's mind, a great deal to admire. When he turned to Banaker, he had the opposite reaction, and yet Banaker seemed to have made the only sense in the bizarre set of circumstances: an old grave site long forgotten and fallen into disuse. Take it a step further and you go the route of a group of people practicing a cult form of burial rites which requires the bones to be pitched one upon another, scattered about the earth in order for what? To keep them from reassembling and rising on dark and stormy nights? The bones of the young were intertwined here with those of the aged. Why? And what significance was there in Magaffey's observation about the missing marrow? And what of the old man's statement that had the bones buried not once, but twice?

Stroud was familiar with the literature of burial customs and rites in such places as Burma, Cambodia, Vietnam, Bulgaria, and even Transylvania and he knew there were still people in the world who observed the dead bodies of their loved ones for upwards of six months to ward off a takeover of the body by evil forces. He had studied and read of people who buried their dead twice, people whose custom it was to exhume the bodies of their beloved to check on their progress toward decay. If there was little or no sign of decay, then it was feared the soul had been trapped there by evil spirits, the body reanimated. It was the kind of superstition that begot ghouls and vampires.

Was Magaffey playing games with his twice-buried bones? Daylight and Banaker would sort it all out. His potter's field theory was good. It certainly explained away a lot in one fell swoop. But how did Banaker explain shallow graves in which the bones of the elders were mixed with the bones of the young after bleaching out the marrow?

Banaker returned to him the instant Magaffey disappeared. "You must be exhausted, Stroud. Sorry we must be meeting for the first time under such conditions, the missing boy . . . this business . . . sad. Of course, you may be assured that my team will be making determinations soon."

Stroud saw Banaker's *team*, a group of white-clad men and women so well trained they never spoke a word to the press, or anyone else. The only spokesperson for Banaker's operation was Banaker himself.

"Thank you," Stroud said.

"About Magaffey. It's time this town let the old man rest."

"What?"

"Magaffey's finished. Next city council meeting and he's history, like these bones." He slapped the thigh bone into his palm again.

Stroud saw before him a man who had sprayed and dried his hair before arriving at the scene, a man who was always playing to the cameras and said half a dozen indispensable words to the television cameras before and after he picked over a crime scene, and each indispensable word was vague enough to have no apparent meaning. While Magaffey's meaning was preposterous.

"May I?" asked Stroud, extending a hand out for the bone.

Banaker frowned but turned it over to the archeologist. Stroud searched for the break, or cut, at the ends where Magaffey had said the red marrow should have been. There were no breaks, however, and the bone didn't look quite the same as Magaffey's femur. Something about it looked different. Stroud wondered if he didn't need sleep, wondered if his mind was not trying to shut down on him. "Where'd you find this one? Same site as the original find? Or over there?"

"I pulled it from a patch of earth brought up by the backhoe. See the sheen of it? It was impacted in clay, a lot deeper than the others, much better preserved."

"I see."

"Lot of the others were broken, scarred, wearing down."

"Wearing down?" asked Stroud. "Decaying?"

"Happens in the mineral-rich earth we have around here."

"Does that mean, sir, that the bone marrow, too, could rapidly break down?"

"Sure, as I said, given the right minerals surrounding the bone, sure, but why do you ask?"

From what Stroud knew of soil properties, the bone appeared remarkably well preserved and so too then should the marrow. But he said nothing more to Banaker who began chatting with another neighbor.

Stroud stroked his stubble noisily and rubbed the throbbing back of his neck. He stared at Magaffey's beat up old Ford as the man drove off with a gunnysack of the bones. Nearby, some of Banaker's people were filling their own sacks—polyurethane bags of various sizes. These got labels and numbers to correspond to a grid of the site which they had worked out. They appeared to be scientifically expert; they looked like a team of archeologists at work, except for the white lab coats and white-to-transparent rubber gloves. One of them was a young woman Stroud had noticed earlier: name tag, Pamela Carr. She glanced in Stroud's direction several times as she worked. She seemed, next to the others, animated, although she did next to nothing in any truly animated way. It was just that the company she kept, Stroud thought, made her look like a jumping jack.

She was Stroud's height, but hardly his age. What, twenty-three, twenty-four? With him in his early forties any liaison between them in Andover would be considered scandalous. Stroud had always wanted to be considered scandalous. Might be a refreshing change from being simply thought of as dangerous. Perhaps danger was what prompted her curiosity; perhaps she had been warned about him and that'd served as a red flag. Who'd tell her such things? Her momma and pappa? Her minister? Maybe even Banaker? Something both odd and fascinating about her, even to the pallor of her skin. It might be what they called alabaster—it had a translucent blue tint to it. She must have been cultivating her long-flowing hair since 1979, he decided on the spur of the moment. Large, oval eyes, near Oriental in their dimension and those full black centers; enticing eyes, eyes that said more than most women said with their entire bodies. . . . Not that the rest of her wasn't gorgeous also, because it was.

In the predawn setting, in her tight lab outfit, the blue tinge to her skin was not noticeable to Stroud. She was either the best makeup artist in the world, or she wore no makeup whatsoever. Her naturally red lips were hers. The dark, mysterious eyes and lashes and brows were hers. Nothing artificial about this young woman. And the way she looked at him, making him feel alone with her. Or was he imagining it? Was he so beat that at the moment he might believe anything put to him, as he had believed for a moment that old Magaffey's missing marrow meant something? Something interesting and chilling about Magaffey. But for the moment, her eyes riveting him, he couldn't remember what Magaffey looked like, much less what the old fart had had to say.

She ran her tongue across her lips in a sensual show for him. Banaker must have seen this and he marched directly to her and set her straight, sending her back to work with a reprimand.

Briggs further broke the spell when he ambled up to Stroud, saying, "We ain't yet found the Meyers boy, but it's getting light now and we've got more volunteers coming in. Thinking now is, we're looking in the wrong place. Somebody sighted a boy back of the houses near Combs Hill Crossing, out past that old shack of a church they use over that way for black revivals. Taking some men over there to have a look-see. You've been here all night, Professor. Best get some ham and eggs over at the Starlite Diner, put it on APD tab, get some rest. Or . . . come along if you like. Suit yourself."

"Thank you, Briggs."

He was tired and hungry. He didn't want to admit defeat, but he wasn't as young as he once was. With Briggs gone, the Meyers boy's parents came up to Stroud. They'd just done a spot for McEarn's A.M. report, pleading on the local broadcast for the safe return of their child. Some people were convinced now that young Timmy, and Ronnie Cooper, were the victims of foul play—that it was either abduction for ransom or abduction for lascivious purposes.

Dave and Kitty Meyers were hoping against hope that Timmy was being held for the lesser of the two evils and that a ransom contact would soon be made. Stroud feared the worst. He feared the boy was dead. Feebly, he said to the parents, "Briggs, the other men . . . we're all doing everything we possibly can."

"We know that, Doctor Stroud," said Dave Meyers, a car sales-man in town. "But if you don't mind, we'd prefer you let Doctor Banaker and Chief Briggs handle things now."

Word spread like weeds here. The Meyerses had already gotten word that the outsider, Dr. Stroud, had gone to their neighbors, the kindly Carroll family, and had accused their son of Timmy's dis-appearance. Probably even before he'd returned to the old grave-yard site everyone from Magaffey to the last volunteer had heard the story of his brutal interrogation of poor little Joey Carroll, and how he had intimidated Ray and his wife.

It was enough to send him to the Starlite Diner to take breakfast there, a box of the scattered bones in the back of his Jeep. He ate while brooding about the imbecility of it all. He wondered if he shouldn't just return to the manse and leave Andover and its problems to itself. He ate alone, the few other patrons staring. When he paid his bill and got to the door he heard the waitress gasp at the size of the tip he'd left behind.

—5—

By noon, little Timmy Meyers remained missing. No ransom calls or notes, no articles of clothing found, no further "tip" calls coming in from people who thought they'd seen the boy flitting about the woods or alleyways around their homes, no nothing. All that Briggs might boast of was a cache of bones, too many bones to count.

Stroud packed some of the bones in a small crate, wrapped them with stuffing and Styrofoam, labeled the box to go to the excellent crime lab in Chicago with which he had always maintained good ties, and asked Mabel Stanica, Briggs's secretary, to see that the box get over to UPS for overnight delivery. Mabel worried about the cost being exorbitant. He snapped at her over the inappropriateness of her concern. Much later, around ten, when he crawled into bed at the manse, he was angry with himself for snapping at the blue-haired Mabel who'd been sniffling when he left the Andover City Police Station.

Overtired, his mind racing with images of the Meyers boy combined with the skull and bones the boys had unearthed like so many pirates playing at Peter Pan games, he rested but fitfully. His sleep was haunted by old Magaffey whispering of burials in sunken churches, ghouls beneath haunted lakes, of death-tolling banshees and sinister changelings. Magaffey's sunken and pinched face spewing forth a ballad of Baal, of specters and unholy creatures, dissolving into Banaker's legion of white-clads looking over him,

42

picking at his body with their probes and forceps, cutting at his cranium to peel back layers of skin to reveal his own artificial skull cap. This steel plate was approximately the size of a tea saucer in a child's tea set. Banaker's people poked and pried it from its moorings amid the bone surrounding it. Cut from its lodging where it covered his brain, they then simply held the steel plate up to ridicule and laughter. The entire operating theater was filled with spectators and the nauseous sounds of hilarity. Meanwhile, his brain lay exposed and palpable, subjected to taunts by cold implements, and it began to come apart like an overripe melon. There was nothing now to protect his head or the pulsating gray matter that rose and swelled and fell as the blood flowed through it.

The horrid image faded only when the tenderest of touches of a human finger was made. It was her touch and it healed the pain. It was Pamela Carr, leaning over him, pressing her body into his and magically closing the large, open wound with her mouth. Her mouth smothered him. He relaxed under her caress. His sleep calmed, and his mind focused on her to the exclusion of the worst night he'd spent in Andover since his arrival back in late November.

In moments he was whole again. He visualized himself a complete man and she had transformed the operating theater into a lovely white and silken bedroom. He watched her uncinch the white lab coat and it fell away in slow motion.

Beneath she wore only lacey underthings. Pamela raised her arms and invited him to take from her all he desired. The dream was so vivid, so real, he felt the firmness of her breasts, the fire of her lips and the force behind them. He felt the thighs as they wrapped about him.

The dream was like none he had ever experienced, and in it he became lost in her hypnotic hold.

"Jesus, Jim, leave it to you to get us lost in the middle of fucking nowhere."

"Will you take it easy, please?"

The car interior was lit as Maude Bradley tried desperately to locate County Road 17 on the map, but all the map offered were state and interstate roads. "How in the hell did we get on this road?"

"Should've stopped at that gas station when we got off the interstate and asked like I said."

"Now it's my fault. You get us lost and it's my fault, hmmmmmpf!"

"Andover's around here somewhere. Had a cousin who used to live in Andover."

"Lot of good that does us, Jim."

They'd gotten off the interstate to find a place to sleep since Jim was dozing at the wheel and Maude didn't drive at night. Now they were lost on one of those unmarked little pavements that was barely wide enough for two vehicles to pass—not that it mattered. They hadn't seen another pair of headlights for forty minutes. They had seen empty fields waiting for the corn to grow, they'd passed a slip of the Spoon River, going over a bridge, and they'd passed a graveyard that stood out in the moonlit glow of the early spring night casting out the faint message that where there was a graveyard there had to be a town . . . but where was it?

Now they were angry with one another and their frustrating circumstances. It was the kind of fix Jim Bradley always thought it took a fool to get mixed up with; the kind of situation that ranked with running out of gas, forgetting one's wallet, keys, or losing one's glasses. At the moment, he was so tired and sleepy that he couldn't even see with his glasses, and if Maude said one more word, he feared he'd explode.

"Hell with it," Jim announced, his protruding Adam's apple bobbing with irritation. "We'll just park it right here, and to hell with it. Curl up in the back—"

"Sleep in the car?"

"Yes!"

"All right . . . I guess. . . ."

"I'll sleep in front. Come daylight, we'll find the interstate easy enough."

"Wish I'd never heard of Sarah Giddings," she replied, crawling over the seat.

Jim and Maude Bradley were going to Sarah Giddings's third wedding. Maude and Sarah had been roommates in college, but like Maude, she hadn't finished, marrying instead. In Maude's case, she'd remained with Jim Bradley through the years. "Sarah's somethin'," Jim commented.

"You men . . . all alike."

"Oh, Maudie—"

"So Sarah's got long legs and a pencil-thin waist—"

"Don't start!"

"She's a vamp, Jim. Can't keep a man because she runs right over every man she's ever had."

Not like you, Jim thought but did not say. "I got to sleep," he moaned instead.

"Sure, honey . . . you get some rest now and things'll look better in the morning. Lock your doors."

They both worked to be certain all the doors were locked. "Thank God we thought to bring the car blankets," she said, spreading one over him and then herself. "Night."

"Night, Maudie."

An hour into sleep Maude felt the impact of something like a tree fall over the rooftop of the car. It made her sit up and exhale with a gulping scream. Jim was also awakened by the sudden impact of something hitting the car. Whatever it was, it had been heavy. The sudden pound was like the slamming of a door. When he and Maude opened their eyes, however, all their attention was on the strange fog that engulfed the car. He had seen fog over the river when they drove past the bridge before, but this was pretty far from there. Valley fog, he reasoned, but it was an unusual fog in that the windows hadn't become wet with condensation. They were clear, so clear you could see the swirls in the fog on the other side of the glass, swirls that spiraled and dipped and did little loop-d-loops. It was like looking through thick gauze.

"Fog," he said, having become somewhat mesmerized by the stuff.

"To hell with the fog! What was that noise? What struck the car?" she wanted to know, couldn't let it go.

"I don't know."

"On your tombstone! That's what they'll put on your tombstone! I—Don't—Know."

"Probably a tree branch."

"Can't you just get out and check?"

"It's over. . . . What's the use of trudging out in the dark and—"

"Flashlight is in the glove compartment. Hand it to me and I'll have a look!" she said in a tone that clearly challenged Jim.

He shoved off the blanket about him and smacked out at the button that popped open the little compartment, sending papers and a screwdriver to the floor. He snatched out the flashlight and turned it on and banged his shoulder on the door, forgetting to unlock it first.

"Christ," he muttered, "you can't leave it alone, can you?"

Before she could answer, he got out. Two feet from the car he was out of the eerie fog. It was bizarre. The fog seemed to be seeping from the tree under which they'd parked, and the car was rocking, literally rocking now, with Maude inside. He could hear her gulping and shouting as the thing bounced within the fog.

"What the hell . . . is going on?"

He flashed his beam up into the tree, the light slicing through the unnatural fog, the edges of light turning the stuff into a gooey, dripping substance. It was like looking through an egg held up to the light. Inside the huge fog egg something dark and large moved, shook, and began to take form. The outline became larger and larger as the fog decreased, sucked up into the black Goliath, until it just hung there at the end of Jim's light, enormous and black, a large, six-foot-long inky seed pod, just dangling in the tree.

"God . . . " he moaned. It was finally happening, and it was happening to him and to Maude. *Aliens* . . . aliens from another time and place, the fog some sort of protective covering, the seed pod the ship, and inside . . . *inside*?

Fascinated and fearful all at once, he went to stand beneath the looming black form in the tree over the car. The rear car door opened and Maude got out as if in a daze. She walked to the rear of the car and began climbing up the trunk and to the top, reaching out to touch the black conical shape there. She seemed as mesmerized by it as he, maybe more so.

"Maude, Maude," he cautioned. "Don't touch it, Maude."

She acted as though she could not hear.

"Maude!" he shouted, his voice echoing all the way down to the Spoon.

She reached it with her fingertips and said, "Take me. . . . I want you to have me . . . I do, I do . . . "

The black torpedo opened up and Jim fell back with abhorrence at the power of the wind that hit him like a whale fluke. Two enormous wings unfurled to take Maude in, stabbing her about the shoulders with talons that jutted out, and lifting her large frame into their folds. Jim saw the fetid eyes of the creature and they locked on him with enthusiasm. From its mouth flowed the fog, escaping with it was some dribbling material that was neither saliva nor blood. It plopped onto the top of the car just as the fangs sank deep into Maude's flesh. The creature took another more powerful gripping hitch with those fangs on Maude's throat and began feeding on her.

Terrified, Jim, knew he could not possibly save Maude; he knew instinctively that this creature that traveled by cover of fog, perched upside down in trees, had more strength and power in its smallest part than he had in his entire body. Jim hadn't a weapon on him, nothing beyond the Ford.

He threw down the light and leapt into the driver's seat, turning the key, burning the ignition when it did come on, tearing away from the tree. Tears streaming down his face, he saw Maude's ankles in the rearview mirror in the distance where she hung, lifeless, in the tree beneath the creature.

"God, oh, God!" He shook as he cried and pleaded, hitting the gas full throttle.

He tore back the way he came, rampaging over the little bridge at the Spoon River, rattling the timbers. He screeched tires at the hairpin curve that he'd taken at twenty just hours before. He saw a sign for a main road in the distance and blubbering, crying, he saw that he was going to make it out alive. Maude . . . there'd been no way he could've saved her, and had he tried, he'd be dead now, too. This way, at least, he could get help, return with weapons to the scene.

The road here skirted the Spoon, a deep ravine to his left leading to the silvery stream. He was doing eighty, eighty-five in a car that couldn't take it, a car with a four-cylinder engine.

A sign came up so fast he could hardly read it: ANDOVER—4 MILES.

Then something smashed into the car overhead, denting the top inward. It made him weave, almost lose control. Another powerful pounding rent the top just above his head. It was the thing! Finished with Maude, it was now atop the car, after him. He hit ninety just as the driver's side window was smashed in and his throat was gripped in a powerful vice. The grip choked off his air and suddenly snapped his neck.

The car careened off into the ravine with something large and black atop it, tearing out the human prey from the window, latching onto a passing tree just moments before the vehicle hit the water. The top where the creature had been lying seethed with an acidic smoke at the touch of the water.

Jim Bradley, neck broken, felt his limp body being heaved up and up into the branches of a gnarly tree, his last sensation the smells of pine sap and blood intermingling with the smell of an animal, a smell he had not forgotten since childhood, the odor of a nest of rats found beneath the old rotten boards of his father's tool shed. The last thing Jim saw was the humanlike eyes of the monster which had hooked itself once again upside down to the top of the tree and had hooked its prey up in the manner of a large IV, to feed on Jim's blood.

Only now did Jim realize that he had fallen prey to a vampire bat as large as a man.

—6—

News of a car going off the road at or near the Combs Hill Bridge
had the entire town's attention this day. It was towed out of the
water and into Andover by Bunnell's Shell Station, old Jacob
"Bun" Bunnell doing the hauling himself. Semi-retired, Bun still
enjoyed hooking cars out of the Spoon.

A group of interested bystanders were on hand both at the scene
of the accident and at the station when Bun finally towed in the
wreck. It was chock full of dents and rips, especially to the top,
as if it'd flipped over onto an enormous boulder. The windows
were all smashed up and the windshield shattered but holding.

"Crazy fool had to be doing a hundred," Bun told waiting
ears.

Whoever was in the car was nowhere near the wreck. John
McEarn's TV report flashed scenes from the salvage—the license
plate number and the car itself as Bun was having it cranked out
of the five-foot shallows of the Spoon where it curved away from
the bridge some distance down. Everyone was relieved that the car
had out-of-state license plates, and that it was an unfamiliar car.
The community had had its share of loss already. State patrolmen
on the scene were relieved that the old bridge had sustained no
damage. The car had apparently come careening off the bridge,
barely missed going over at that point, but the driver fought to keep
it on the road for another fifth to a quarter mile, one patrolman told
viewers at home.

Abe Stroud heard the report and shook off sleep to listen. He must've turned the TV on, but he didn't recall doing so. He didn't remember waking.

"Skid marks and tire trail where it dug up earth and rock tells the tale," said Sheriff Briggs, inching out the patrolman.

Crazy man.

Drunk.

Cocaine, maybe . . . all suggestions from TV reporter John McEarn.

Abe Stroud leaned on his elbows, trying to take in the information as it came over. McEarn was apparently doing this live. Stroud recognized the area as one very near where he and the others had stomped through the woods on the trail of missing Timmy Meyers.

"What about the body?" he wondered aloud, just as John McEarn's voiceover said, "Thus far the body has not been located. It is estimated that the swift current carried the driver downstream, and will possibly deposit her along the shore at some future date. It is not known whether or not there were any additional passengers in the vehicle. A lady's handbag was found on the seat, and police theorize the handbag belonged to the driver, but identification of the victim has not been released, pending notification of the family."

Stroud saw Chief Briggs hanging about, a look on his face that bespoke his confusion; or was he angry because McEarn hadn't interviewed him on air?

Stroud wondered if Briggs had a diver on his payroll, someone who'd go in after the body. If not, Stroud would put in for the job. He'd done it before, and while he did not welcome the notion . . . if there was no one else, he'd do it.

But for now, lying in bed, he still felt weary, his eyes still burning from tiredness. The stress of the last few days had taken its toll. He laid back, wondering if he should not get right up, shower, go into the city for breakfast and see if there was anything he could do. In addition to helping out with locating the body, or bodies, in the Spoon, he still wished to learn if anything new had developed in the Timmy Meyers search. Instead, he laid back, closed his eyes, and allowed the warmth and softness of the big bed to engulf him. He fell back into a slumber.

Stroud's mind drifted through the major periods of his life. Until he was eleven he lived with his parents who were very well off, his father being a physician and his mother being a computer engineer. They'd died in a tragic accident while he was left unharmed physically. The emotional difficulties he faced were helped by the love and devotion his grandfather had shown him. When he became old enough to be on his own, he began college at Northwestern University, quickly changing to the University of Chicago, most anxious to become an archeologist. However, with the growing hostilities in Vietnam, he felt duty bound to join the armed forces and so his education was interrupted. It would take him all these years later to finish what he had started, thanks in large part to the plate in his head and something deep within that told him he was only good enough to perform to someone else's orders—a sergeant's orders. So, he'd enrolled in the police academy, barely keeping track of his grandfather and never coming home.

It had been a period of aloneness and loss. Stroud began to feel the old man's aloneness and loss now, too.

Stroud Manse had the same, empty feel to it: the feeling of aloneness. The old place was dismal, oppressive, and Stroud wondered if he shouldn't simply put it on the market, take the best offer and sever ties for good and all, in order to start fresh.

Maybe it was a dream, or some hallucination brought on by his damaged head. Or maybe something literally came out of the woodwork.

Stroud had lain back just to close his eyes for a moment, still pondering how the TV had come on, and now wondering how it had gone off. He recalled no time when he had actually gotten out of bed or fished about for the remote to do either. Then his eyes locked on a shape, the stretched, taffy-pulled form of a humanlike creature in the wood grain of the oaken door across the room. It looked like a half man, half praying mantis until this image began to move.

He watched the image in the wood, knowing full well that if a man stared long enough at an object all sorts of bizarre tricks of the mind might visit him. Still, he stared and stared, unable to remove his eyes from the coalescing stick man who seemed to be trying to fight his way from the wood he'd become embedded in.

The haunted manse, so full of bizarre objects and memories, was, at this moment, outdoing itself.

Stroud threw his legs over the edge of the bed and in his underwear stepped toward the door tentatively, one hand extended to the milky, moving image before him. It could not pull free of the wood, but it sent out messages, not in a voice but through his brain, saying, "Leave this place. Leave this place."

"Who . . . what are you?" Stroud asked in a choking voice.

"Leave . . . before it is too late . . . leave."

Stroud turned to see himself still asleep in bed when suddenly he was shaken by the rattling ring of the telephone. The noise and the start instantly put him back together again, and he found himself rousing from sleep and the solid door still just a door. In its grain, if he worked hard at it, he could, however, see the faint outline of the image that had spoken to him in his dream. Unable to make head or tail of it, he grabbed for the phone and at the same time saw that indeed, somehow, the TV had been shut off.

"Sheriff Briggs, here!"

Stroud's ear was hurt by the man's loud voice. "Oh, yes, Sheriff . . . "

"Good news, Doctor Stroud! Good news!"

"Indeed?"

"The Meyers boy? He's been found, Stroud, and—"

"Found, really? Alive, you mean?"

"In one piece and alive, yeah! We got damned lucky, damned lucky. Course men like you and me, we always think the worst . . . but you can never tell, now, can you? Hard work pays off."

"What about the other boy?"

"Other boy? Oh, Ronnie Cooper?"

"Yes, did Timmy Meyers offer up any information about the other missing—"

"I really don't think the two cases are, you know, related. Anyway, Timmy's not talking. He's kinda in what you'd call . . . shock."

"Shock?"

" 'Fraid so."

"Where is he now?"

"Banaker has him under observation."

"I see."

"Best facilities in all the county."

"Yes, of course."

"That's right."

"Unharmed?"

"Narry a scratch on him. Physically, he's none the worse for wear. Emotionally, well . . . boy spent a rough night."

"Where'd they find him?"

"Up near Twin Bluffs. Hell, nobody was even lookin' up that way when—"

"Who found him?"

"Some of Banaker's people, on their way toward the Institute, found him wandering around, lost and cryin'."

"I see."

"Well, all's well that ends well, Doctor Stroud."

"But what about the other boy?"

"Lost cause, that one. Been too long in them woods. If anyone ever does stumble onto the body . . . won't be recognizable."

"Well . . . I guess we can all breathe easier."

"You bet we can."

"What about the bones, Sheriff?"

"What about 'em? Banaker's explained that to you, hasn't he?"

"Ahhh, the graveyard theory."

"Not no theory."

"Oh, right, city records . . . all that."

"Right. Well, rest easy."

I was, until you woke me, he wanted to say but instead replied, "Did your people get the package out to Chicago, the UPS package?"

"Hey, not to worry."

"Thanks."

"Thank you, Doctor Stroud, for showing such civic duty."

"No more'n anyone else would do."

He laughed lightly. "Your old grandfather would've sat up there in that house and done nothing, not a damned thing."

He hung up before Stroud could protest what seemed to him to be a slur against his kinsman. The man he had known would not have idly sat by while the entire town was on a night search for a missing boy. Unless the old man changed near the end. Unless his personality had altered.

The thought shook Abe Stroud along with the memory of finding the secret chamber below the manse.

It seemed, for the moment, that all the trouble that had rocked Andover and its people was contained now, wrapped up neat and tidy by Briggs and Banaker, as tight and proper as the package Stroud had sent off to Chicago for examination. So why was it so difficult to put it from his mind?

Something like a nagging whisper in his ear, so strong he felt as if someone were standing over his bed breathing into his ear, except that the exhalations were chilling instead of warming.

Something suggested itself to him and made him sit up in bed. He wanted to see and talk to Timmy Meyers.

Fifteen frustrating minutes later he learned by phone that no one was permitted near the boy, not even his parents, as yet. It seemed the boy's condition was far worse than Briggs had allowed. It seemed total isolation was necessary, according to Banaker, if the child was to regain his former strength and identity. According to reports circulating about the Institute, the boy had gone into a kind of walking coma, unable to speak or feed himself. Such a condition was typically brought on when the mind shut down in the face of unacceptable horror and fear.

Abe Stroud felt he understood the child's plight. He placed himself in the boy's position and he experienced the old wounds that had once threatened to lock him away deep within himself to emotionally bleed to death deep inside a silent frame.

Stroud got up suddenly, tossing the covers aside, but when he stood, he found himself in a cold, chilling, and damp circle. He involuntarily shivered and looked around for the vent which was allowing the chill in. But there was no vent and as suddenly as he'd touched on it, the cold spot disappeared. He shivered again and rushed to find a change of clothes, shower, and go into town for breakfast. He meant to be at Banaker's Institute to see the boy one way or another.

He got as far as the front door of the huge manse, where he was stopped by an elderly couple calling themselves the Ashyers who wished to become his house servants. "We served your grandfather in his last years," said Mrs. Ashyer.

Mr. Ashyer had with him a collection of newspapers—the *Chicago Tribune, New York Times*, the *Springfield Herald* and the Andover *Sentinel*. "With my compliments, sir," he said.

"If you will permit, Doctor Stroud, I will see to your breakfast," said Mrs. Ashyer.

"I . . . I don't know what to say," he replied. "How long were you with my grandfather?"

"Thirteen years. Before us, he had a lovely couple, did everything for the master. We . . . we worked for Mr. Gilcrest on his estate—now, in terrible condition. The place fell on hard times."

"Gilcrest?"

"On Barnstable Road, some distance from here, but within a half day's drive, and if you should want references—well, there is an address I have here you may wish to write, a previous employer, sir."

Stroud looked into the man's eyes, and then into his wife's. They were the picture of English servants, down to the unremarkable features and clothing, and yet there was a gentle light in their eyes and an aura given off by the pair that defied any doubts he might have about the couple.

"Tell you what. I'll have you on, and we'll see how it works out. But tell me, where've you been all this time? Why'd you wait so long to return to the manse?"

"We were told you'd be selling. We didn't know you'd be settling down here, and although Mrs. Ashyer and I felt as if we knew you—from what your grandfather related—we had no reason to believe otherwise. And with the promise of work upstate . . . "

"Didn't work out?"

"Afraid not, sir."

"Their loss, my gain?"

"You might say so, sir." He was charming and she was as demure and politic a woman as Stroud had ever met.

"You may move your things in. Take whatever rooms you had previously—or bigger ones, if you choose—and we'll see how it goes. God knows I could use the help, and perhaps you can tell me something about my grandfather's last days."

"Whatever we might," said Mr. Ashyer. "He was a grand old fellow, your grandfather."

"Thank you, I've always believed that."

"We heard about your part in finding the boy," said Mrs. Ashyer. "When we did . . . we knew you were like your grandfather."

Just the opposite of Briggs's view, he told himself. What could cause such contradictory opinions of a man's memory?

"I'll get right to work on your breakfast, sir," she said.

"I'll see to having our things brought out," he said.

Stroud accepted the newspapers and Ashyer's ushering him into a large chair in the den where his grandfather did most of his reading. Ashyer told him to relax and that all would be taken care of.

Stroud turned to the Andover *Sentinel* first, wishing to see what was written about the discovery of the boy. It was a sketchy piece at best, ending with a statement from Banaker predicting that the boy "would, in time, recover from his listless condition."

Banaker seemed everywhere. Stroud could rely on his being at every turn. Like gum on the shoe, he thought. It made him suspect the Ashyers now suddenly. Their having just shown up as they had, "infiltrating" the manse. Or was he just being paranoid?

Paranoia had over the years saved a number of lives, however, and, as a former cop, he knew this only too well. A woman might begin to suspect her husband was trying to poison her; a man might begin to wonder about someone he has seen shadowing him; there was enough family related violence to go around to make paranoia a useful trip. But when Mrs. Ashyer called him into the dining room the aroma of her bacon and eggs and coffee melted away Stroud's fears for the moment.

Stroud felt foolish sitting at the enormous table in the huge room dishing up his breakfast alone, however. There was enough room at the table for several football clubs or the men in his platoon in Vietnam. He pictured them all sitting about the table now with him, the ones still alive. As he did so, the empty chairs filled with the likenesses of the dead soldiers he'd fought with as well, and for a moment it was as if they were really in the room.

The spell was broken only when Mrs. Ashyer returned to ask if he would like more coffee or more food.

—7—

"I want to see the boy now!" said Stroud firmly to the nurse who had stopped him at the station moments before at the Banaker Institute.

"I'll handle this, Nurse," said Pamela Carr who stepped from the portal behind the nurses' station where she'd been reviewing some charts. Under the bright fluorescent lights her skin was as pale as alabaster. The light seemed to irritate her eyes. She wore soft blue dark glasses, offsetting the tinge of blue beneath the skin of her smooth cheeks. She was a tantalizing woman. He felt the instant attraction and fascination with her that he had felt the other night.

"Doctor Stroud," she said, "I am not surprised to find you here."

"I came to see the boy."

"I know that. You don't think that I thought you came to see me?"

She walked a few steps with him to the room where Timmy Meyers lay, according to the nurse on the main floor. She even gently pushed the door open for him to peer inside. But the room was empty.

"Timmy is gone. His parents took him home."

"But I thought he was in a condition of shock."

"Yes, well . . . even Banaker can argue for reasoning only so much in the face of parental concern. He gave in to Timmy's parents. They wanted him home. Doctor Magaffey convinced them that the boy would do better in familiar surroundings at this point."

"Magaffey?"

"Banaker was fit to be tied."

"I'm sure."

"At any rate, I'm sorry we couldn't have been more helpful to you, Doctor Stroud." She gave him a coquettishly warbling blink.

He nodded and smiled. "Yes, well—"

"There is an empty room here," she said, letting the door close behind them, "and an unused bed. Perhaps we ought to . . . put it to use?"

She began undoing the buttons of her lab coat. "I'm one of Doctor Banaker's residents. Don't have much time for socializing or small talk. You must appreciate that, being a soldier once."

She moved toward him, lifting his hand to her breast, pressing it into the silky finery below her top. She was firm and her heart pounded rhythmically. Stroud found her provocative and alluring and bad and a great turn on. He quickly covered her mouth with his own, feeling a power come swelling back at him like that of another man, she was so strong. He was pressed against the bed and she was clawing and climbing over him in animalistic abandon.

"Wait, not here," he tried to say, fearful for them both. Should she be found out, she could lose her job; should he be found out, it wouldn't reflect well on the Stroud name so carefully preserved in the community for generations.

"I can't wait . . . can't," she panted, moving over him, nipping at his neck, her lust virtually burning through their clothing and making him burn with it.

"Not here!" he said.

"Here, yes, now!"

"No . . . Pamela."

"No one will disturb us."

He pushed her away firmly. "I hardly know you. I . . . it's not that I don't find you attractive . . . "

She began a slow strip before him.

"But there're other things to consider."

"I've been considering your thing for some time."

Just then the door opened, making them both stare. It was the nurse who'd stopped him in the hallway. She was giggling, but managed to get out her message. "Doctor Banaker's on his way up."

"Jesus," moaned Stroud. "Later, Pamela. I'll call and we'll get together in a more private setting. How is that?"

She didn't say a word but her mouth was curled in an angry, frustrated snarl. "Bastard thinks he owns me," she said.

"Does he have reason to think so?"

"I suppose . . . once maybe."

Stroud straightened himself and rushed from the room before Banaker might make a scene. At the elevator he ran into the big man.

"So, you came to have a look at the boy?" asked Banaker as he stepped off the elevator. At the nurses' station the women were gaggling and whispering like so many witches over a brew. It seemed as if one of them had alerted Banaker to the danger Stroud presented him in respect to Pamela Carr.

Pamela came out of what had been Timmy's room and ducked discretely down another corridor, but the movement was not lost on Banaker.

"Guess I missed the little tyke," said Stroud. "Understand the parents wanted him to rest at home."

Banaker nodded, went to the nurses' station, and latched onto a chart lying open there. With a pen he jotted down a few items. "Yes, well, no arguing with a mother over her cub, you know. Despite the fact the boy should have remained in my care for observation another day, perhaps two, they took him home."

"Do you think he'll soon recover?"

"He has every chance of doing so. He would have a better chance in my care, of course."

"Of course."

"As it is, whatever happens . . . it's on the heads of his parents."

"What does that mean, Doctor?"

"That means that with the boy off these premises, he is no longer a concern of mine. They chose to endanger him further, thanks to Magaffey's interference, and so that is that. I am no longer feeling responsible."

"I see."

"You see? You see? Really? No, Doctor Stroud, you do not see."

He stalked off in the direction Pamela had taken. Stroud pushed for the elevator to return, and while waiting he felt uneasy. When he got into the elevator and turned around he saw that six of Banaker's nursing staff were all standing in a state of frozen stares at him. Their eyes bore into him and he felt a shock of vulnerability. The doors closed and the car began to move down, his head disoriented and dizzy from the bizarre exchange.

He then heard the faint whisper in his head, the same muffled, struggling voice that had fought its way from the figure in the wood that morning. It was no longer warning him off. It was wailing, "Baaaaynaaaaakoooooorrrr."

Stroud hadn't cared for the Institute or Banaker: each reminded him of the V.A. hospital in Chicago—cold, clinical, antiseptic, inhuman. These were the words that leapt readily to mind. Stroud wanted only to get back out into the cold rush of the morning breeze, the light and air, to fill his nostrils and pores with the stuff of life.

He panted to himself, "Got to get out of here." He felt the old darkness creeping in around him, seeping into the pan of his brain like acrid, spreading grease, seeping through the crack no doubt left unsealed between his skull cap and the portion made of metal now—left unsealed by doctors who were either inept, no good, or interested in experimentation: to see what would happen if they did so.

The creeping dark he was familiar with was like a slow-moving fog that infiltrated on soft paws, stealthily, as if it had a mind and an evil intent. He felt it in every nerve ending, felt it make his skin cold and sweaty, felt it climb to the nape of his neck until he welcomed a dead faint, an old-fashioned blackout, anything but this overwhelming feeling of weakness and fear.

He must find a quiet place, a place where no one could see. It was an ugly affliction he didn't wish to share.

He found a stairwell, not even knowing how he had gotten from the elevator to the enclosure. He didn't feel it when the seizure finally struck and sent him cartwheeling down a half flight of stairs into an uncontrollable jerking and kicking out at his inner demons.

One V.A. medicine man had claimed the seizures would one day kill him. Once or twice, on the job as a cop, his partner covering for him, he came close to dying, but not from the seizures so much as from the bullets that could strike when he was in one of his seizures. He'd learned to detect the early warning signs. He had learned to prepare by placing a plastic wedge—a wedge riddled with his teeth marks now—across his mouth to bite on. He had also learned to go with the seizures; there was no gain in fighting them.

He had learned that the seizures, while unpredictable, were often brought on during extremely stressful situations, or when he was most frustrated. It was one reason to end his career as a police officer.

A V.A. shrink had called his seizures self-induced sadomasochistic behavior, which meant he was fucking himself over for some sick reason having to do with the fact that he had lived when so many of his friends had died. Stroud told the shrink to shove his theories up his Freudian ass, saying at the time, "We both know bloody well that enemy shrapnel, followed by a team of military surgeons working some 'friendly fire' of their own, screwed up my head *twice*! I've had little say in the matter, much less *sado*masochism. You and the U.S. brass are worried about where I might point the finger, whether or not I'll get a good lawyer, so you come in here shoveling shit. I didn't cut myself or beat myself *before* I entered the service. Why would I begin now?"

That had silenced the psychological approach to the problem, but the seizures had never been silenced.

Typically, when he came out of a seizure, he found he was twisted pretzel fashion; typically, he'd have to unknot his cramped fingers and toes, frozen into gnarls. Sometimes his abdomen was wound round opposite his chest; legs and arms were akimbo. Throughout his seizures he was aware of himself to the degree that his physical pain and contortion were brutal, even sadistic. He often felt that some devil in Satan's army had been given his case file and been told to get Stroud. But the mind was busy with horrors of its own during the seizures—images of past horrors and sometimes images that terrorized but meant nothing to him in and of themselves, as if they were the fragmented fears and terrors of other lives.

But this time it went differently. He felt a power or force not inside him, but around him, holding on, gripping and struggling with his limbs and form. But it was a benevolent power, a reassuring touch. There was an odor along with the touch and it reminded him of his grandfather's pipe smoke.

He saw no one, heard no voice over him, only felt the pressure and force and touch in many directions as hands held his seizure in check, so to speak. It was the oddest sensation of all: this touch, strong and sure, of many.

Then his mind was clear and he was standing—*standing*! He'd come out of the seizure on his feet! It was not to be believed.

He must surely still be in the grip of the seizure, hallucinating. Hallucinating positively rather than negatively for a change. Yet still, it was a hoax concocted by his mind to hang onto his dignity.

But everything he touched was solid and real, including himself, and he was on his own two legs walking down a corridor. It was a dark corridor but there was a light at the end and from behind the light he heard mirthful people at what sounded like a birthday party. Someone was singing an unfamiliar song, something ages old, Gaelic perhaps, in an ancient tongue for sure. He tried to pick out the words, but other voices drowned out the singer.

Laughter, raucous and bawdy, came from behind the light.

Had the elevator car taken him into the subbasement of the building, opening on a dark and claustrophobic corridor? Perhaps he'd never gotten off, never found that stairwell? He distinctly recalled pushing the lobby button, but maybe someone had called for it at this level first, so he had zipped by the lobby. Maybe.

End of the hall was the light behind the doors of the morgue.

End of the hall there was raucous laughter coming from behind the doors.

This troubled him. It was more than the sick humor of residents tossing livers and spleens. It was a party. No morgue he had ever visited was noisy. Occasionally the coroner's lab was noisy, but never the morgue where death blanketed the walls with its presence.

"Can I help you?" The voice so startled him he almost jumped. Silence swept through the place now as if those behind the doors knew he was here. He turned to face a white-coated younger man with acne over his neck and dark circles under his eyes.

"I seem to have lost my way."

"Haven't we all?"

"Yes, well . . . Doctor ahhhh—"

"Cooper," he said, looking over his glasses. "Are you here to give blood? The blood drive is over but—"

"No . . . well, I mean . . . frankly, Doctor Cooper"—Stroud wondered if Cooper was any relation to the boy named Ronnie who'd not been as fortunate as the Meyers boy—"I was just looking for a way out."

"Stairwell is to your left, elevator's behind you," he said, the dark eyes shining white in the dim light. He looked like he might well be a drug user, so dark were the circles about his eyes.

"Any relation to the little boy who was lost?" Stroud asked.

The dark eyes glazed over with tears and he clamped down with his teeth in an effort to control the sudden trembling of his chin. "My . . . my son. Bastards killed my son . . . didn't leave anything behind."

"Who? Who killed your son?"

"Who? You don't know?" He was beginning to sound like a madman.

"No, I don't know."

"Then . . . you're not supposed to be down here."

"What?"

"You have come to give blood?"

"No."

"Always a good thing if you come here, to give blood."

"Doctor Cooper?"

"Who is it you're talking to, Cooper?" came another voice out of the bleakness. Up stepped a long, lithe fellow with a pair of menacing eyes that were enough to send Cooper through the double doors of the morgue where most of the noise was coming from. Stroud recognized some of the sounds: hideous laughter, a machinelike sucking noise, a water hose. The air was thick with the smell of blood as it pummeled out through the big doors when Cooper rushed through.

"Who're you?" demanded the tall physician before Stroud now.

"Me? I'm a friend of Doctor Banaker's."

"Friend? I'm Dolph Banaker, Doctor Banaker's son."

"Oh, yes, he's told me about you," lied Stroud.

"This area is off limits to all but Banaker people," he said firmly. "From what I see . . . " He let it hang, as if he wished to say more. " . . . you don't have clearance to be down here."

"I meant to find the lobby and got down here by mistake."

"You lost your way on the stairs?"

"The elevator brought me down."

"Impossible. The elevators used by staff come down here. None of the others do."

"I tell you, I just got off the elevator."

Dolph shook his head at Stroud as if he were a blithering idiot. Then he did a remarkable thing. He took hold of Stroud and stared into his eyes, sending an electriclike charge through him, attempting some sort of hypnosis. Stroud sensed danger and knew what was happening to an extent. Somehow he felt a resistance to Dolph, a repugnance. Something about the young man smelled bad, smelled of decay. Stroud's mind fought his in a tug-of-war there in the corridor, a war for control.

"Dolph!" It was Pamela's voice that broke the spell. "I see you've met Doctor Stroud. I have been searching for him. Your father is consulting with Doctor Stroud on a case. We must hurry, Doctor Stroud. I can't imagine how you became so lost. Please, follow me."

Dolph Banaker watched them disappear into the stairwell. A story up, she said, "How did you get down here?"

"No one seems to know."

"You must get out of this sector unseen. Doctor Banaker is not going to like this if he hears, and he will."

At the door to the lobby he turned to face her. "Will you be all right?"

"Of course."

"Your job, I mean."

"Intact . . . don't worry. They can't do any more to me than they already have."

"Where can I reach you later?"

"I'll call you." She kissed him passionately, saying into his ear, "I've never thrown myself at a man like this before. It's just something . . . something about you . . . I . . . I need . . . your strength . . . your power."

He kissed her in return and she then pulled herself away, rushing up to the next floor.

With that he stepped out into the lobby, grateful for the light streaming in from outside. It was so strong that some people milling about disappeared in it, fading into the glare. He rushed for the exit and went through the revolving door, his own head spinning with the experience.

Still he had not seen the boy.

Still the image of laughter and frolic in the morgue disturbed him.

—8—

Another night passed and Stroud was beginning to believe all the mystery of his seizure-induced vision, the turmoil and hell of the missing boy and the bones—all that had come before now, including the passion between Pamela Carr and himself—had been imaginings born of a fevered brain. Pamela hadn't contacted him. And as for the incredible incidents of the past few days, Andover acted as if nothing had happened. The story was dropped from the papers after the boy was found, nothing said about the bones. People here went about their business as if it had all been perfectly normal and the outcome just as expected, and yet it could not be so. Abraham Stroud had too much faith in himself these days, despite his tormented cranium, to relinquish the ideas set in motion by that first night when the boneyard was discovered. And he for one was not about to forget the condition of those bones and what Dr. Magaffey had said about the bone marrow.

He could not simply dismiss it from his mind.

He telephoned Dr. Louis P. Cage in Chicago. He'd sent the bones to Cage. Cage couldn't possibly have any answers for him, yet, but he wanted to impress upon his old friend that this was no ordinary cache of archeological artifacts, that these bones might have something to do with a series of strange disappearances in the community. Dr. Cage was one of the foremost authorities on bones, an archeologist and anatomist, he'd done a great deal of work for the CPD in reconstructing features over skulls in order

65

to identify the previously unidentifiable victims of homicides.

Cage came on line the moment he learned it was Stroud. "Stroud, you get tired of reading *GQ?* How's the easy life down in southern Ill? Come on, out with the truth! You're bored outa your friggin' brain and you want to go to Iraq with me, screw the war over there, right?"

"Cage, did you get that package I sent two days ago, UPS?"

"What package?"

"Look around. A box filled with bones from me with a letter of explanation."

"Hey, we open it as it comes in, Abe, you know that."

"Then you didn't get it?"

"Nada."

He blew out a long gush of air. "I'll call you back."

"Abe!"

He hung up and telephoned Sheriff Briggs. Finding him out, he talked to the deputy, a man named Stanley Kisner. Kisner looked around and found the box in back, came back on, and said, "Musta got mislaid."

"Goddamnit, Deputy, that package is important!"

"Got some of them bones in it, right?"

"Yeah, right. Now, you hold it there and I'll come get it myself."

"No need to come all the way in for it. I'll ride it out to your place, Mr. ahhh, Doctor Stroud. My patrol starts in ten minutes and I'll be up that way."

"I want it sent out to Chicago, not sent to me!"

"Oh, ho, I'm sorry. Can't read . . . sorry. I see that now."

"Just hold it there. I'll pick it up and get it to UPS personally."

"Hell, I know those guys and I can get it rushed for you. Take it by there myself, Doctor Stroud."

"I can't trust you to do that, Deputy."

"You sure can, sir." He hung up.

"Damn it!"

Earlier, he'd stopped in at the Meyers place to ask after the boy, wondering aloud why the dog was never found.

Mrs. Meyers visibly shivered at the words as he neared her. But Mrs. Meyers wouldn't allow him past the threshold. She wasn't out and out rude about it, but she made it clear that she didn't want the boy disturbed. She put it rather oddly, however, and it stuck in Stroud's mind.

"No one's welcome here for now, Doctor Stroud. 'Preciate what you done, but no one's welcome."

It reminded him of Mrs. Carroll's protectiveness with Joey a couple of nights before. But there was something else here, something Mrs. Meyers's frail gray eyes revealed, something to do with terror. He was reminded of scenes in old movies in which one family was cut from the wagon train due to the fact their wagon carried diphtheria or smallpox. It appeared to Stroud that no one but himself had come by the house to offer help with the boy, until he saw Dr. Magaffey's old battered vehicle come over the rise.

"I'll just talk to Doctor Magaffey," he said to Mrs. Meyers who promptly disappeared inside the ranch home.

Magaffey got out of his car clattering the doors, struggling with his bag. "You're looking in on the boy, Stroud?" he said.

"Would if I could, but—"

"Ahhhhhh, parents have closed in 'round him so tight they're chokin' him off from everything, good and bad."

"Meaning you and Banaker, in that order?"

"Well, Mr. Meyers asked me to come out. Told his wife to expect me. Says the boy's . . . I don't know . . . acting strange, yet."

"Something's happened to him."

"He's gone through a difficult time."

"People tend to deny and deny and sometimes it just makes it worse, doesn't it? It's as if none of it has happened, for a while, and then it crashes down on you again. I know."

"Hard won experience. Got to let the Meyerses take it as it comes; they've got to learn it for themselves, son."

"And as for the still missing Cooper boy, not a peep."

"Life goes on like the rushing river it is . . . like the Spoon, Stroud, not stopping for man or God. Hell, you should know that."

"Why do you say that?"

He looked incredulously at Stroud. "By God, you're old enough and smart enough to know."

"I'd like a look at the boy."

"Sure, come ahead. I'll get you past Mrs. Meyers."

"She and her husband suddenly began to treat me like the enemy, for some damned reason."

"Single man, taking an interest in a young boy, what do you expect?" He laughed at his own remarks as they made their way up the steps and into the house. Mrs. Meyers stared at Stroud, her features agitated and she did not relax when Dr. Magaffey said, "It's all right Mrs. Meyers. No one's going to take your boy from you. I give you my promise. Do you have any coffee?"

She hesitated but finally started away, saying she'd make some.

Stroud followed Magaffey into the boy's room, a foul stench filling his nostrils as it passed from the doorway into the rest of the house. "What the hell is that?"

"Dressing needs changing," said Magaffey.

"Dressing? I wasn't aware the boy was injured."

"A might bit. Something wild out there got at him, scratched a hole in his chest, neck and arms. Looked like he was dragged; skin abrasions over a good part of his body."

"Christ, maybe he ought to have been left in the hospital."

"Oh, he's healing fine. No doubt of that. You know how boys are. Bounce right back, 'cept for this mind thing. Look at 'im."

Stroud did just that. Timmy was a round, little roly-poly boy who had lost a lot of weight quickly, his skin hanging loose on his jowls. He was sitting upright in bed, but Stroud got the distinct impression it was a position he'd been placed in. It was very dark in the room.

"Turn on a light, will you, Stroud?"

Stroud did so, twisting a button on a lamp with a Batman motif. The sudden light didn't even make Timmy squint. He just stared ahead of him as if he saw something clear across the room that commanded all of his attention.

"Anybody ask him any questions about what happened to him?" asked Stroud.

"Sure, everybody has, but he won't speak."

"How long will he be like this, Magaffey?"

"No way to know." Magaffey gently began the work of replacing the bandages. Stroud saw that one of them was wrapped completely around the boy's neck. Magaffey took each off very carefully, slowly and with care not to cause any pain, replacing them as he went. Magaffey was right, much of the stench from the wounds was filling the room. The skin under the bandages had been filleted in great streaks where the wounds appeared in three separate but uniform gashes on each of the boy's sides, as if he'd been lifted up on meat hooks. The lines were too perfect, too neat to be caused by anything in nature, unless the boy had happened onto a bear or a panther, and unless the animal swiped at each of his sides at exactly the same spot and with exactly the same intensity.

For a moment, Stroud imagined a man capable of such horror, using some sort of pulley device to rip in an upward movement, the deeper part of the gash being at the lowest point of entry. Magaffey, being both an M.D. and an M.E., must surely have seen the same thing that Stroud saw.

"What do you make of these wounds?"

"Forest animal got at the boy."

"Sure, sure, Doc."

"Bit him in the throat," said Magaffey, undoing the throat bandage. "Boy's lucky to be alive. I figure he went limp on the . . . the—"

"Bear?"

"Bear, yeah, and it took him for dead."

The boy was pallid, near white, skin tinged by yellow and a few splotches of blue-white. "Lost a lot of blood, gashes like that . . . and still he found his way out. Some kinda kid."

"Miracle he survived."

Stroud wasn't sure he believed in miracles, however. He himself had lived when he was within the tight vise of death. He'd *gone* while lying out there on the battlefield, spirit lifting off the corpse, looking down at the carcass amid all the others, about to rush away toward an intense laser beam of light pinpointed at the end of an enormous cavern. He started toward that light when something blocked his way. Something tugging insistently, tearing him from the direction he'd taken. A medic had intervened; end of miracle.

Magaffey revealed the neck wound and it was startlingly small, yet it still gleamed with droplets of blood. "Can't for the life of me stop this bleeding here."

The blood obscured the wound. Stroud inched in closer for a look. Magaffey sponged and for an instant it stood clear: two deep puncture marks had cut a jagged, unclean trail near the jugular, close enough in fact that a layman might believe the jugular had been severed, in which case the boy would've bled to death.

"Have you measured these puncture marks, Doctor Magaffey?"

"I have."

"Well?"

Magaffey had the instruments for such measurements, but they were typically used on a corpse. "Nearly three millimeters deep."

"Christ."

"Like I said, a bear. Only a bear or a panther has incisors long enough to've inflicted this wound."

"Teethmarks?"

"Most assuredly fangs, yes. Curvature of the wound points to a set of real choppers."

"And not a trace of the dog?"

"None. Dog likely sacrificed itself so the boy might save himself. Ought to find that dog and bury him proper."

"Yeah . . . yeah."

For a moment Stroud's eyes locked onto the boy's and he did a tug-of-war with the staring, bug-eyes, but the boy was having none of it. Stroud wondered how he could keep his eyes open for so long without so much as a blink when Magaffey suddenly sprayed eyewash into each. The boy didn't flinch or move a muscle, not so much as an eyelid. The eyewash followed a tear down Timmy's cheek until Magaffey wiped it away.

"Must've been horrible for the boy," said Magaffey.

The new bandages on the wounds along with Magaffey's own time-honored poultice, the unusual odor of fetid flesh, and whatever Magaffey had concocted to place on the wounds took on new strength. Stroud's eyes watered from it.

"What the hell've you got on that wound, Doc?"

"Herbs, some old provincial medicine . . . nothing like Oliver Banaker would apply, I'll guarantee."

"You're sure you're doing the right thing, Doc? Taking him outa the Institute and—?"

"Hold on, there. The parents pulled 'im from there, not me."

"At your urging, I'm sure. Could go bad for you if the boy doesn't, you know, get better."

Magaffey threw the bundle of used bandages stained with pus into a wastepaper basket he'd brought in with him. He stampeded his things together, and just before he was about to make for the other room, he said, "Come over to the window here, Stroud. Pull back the drapes."

Stroud frowned but did as instructed. He realized only now why it was so dark in the room. The windows in the boy's room had been boarded over, nailed down, and as Magaffey replaced the drapes, he told Stroud that the parents were having bars installed.

"To keep the boy in?"

"You tell me, Mr. Know-it-all." Magaffey stormed from the room, insulted.

Stroud took a final glance at the boy, the bars, the condition of the room, and he inhaled the last of the foul air before he rushed out after Martin Magaffey. Magaffey knew more than he was saying, much more. He halted the old black doctor at his beat up car.

"We searched all over that area for the boy and could not find him," he said.

"Found a boneyard instead," said Magaffey. "Peculiar one at that."

"The boy's'd been playing among the bones earlier, Doctor."

"So Mr. Carroll informs me."

"Then how'd he get so damned far on foot? It doesn't make sense, doesn't add up."

"So, your arithmetic's getting better, Doctor Stroud. Twin Bluffs is a piece from there. Not too bloody far from your old place."

"You got in to see the boy, despite the fact Banaker had him . . . had him . . . "

"Under close guard."

"I was going to say intensive care."

"I got lucky," he replied.

Had help, Stroud's mind told him, but who? Pamela Carr, someone else at the Institute?"

"You convinced Timmy's parents to take him out of there."

"I might've."

"You got them thinking the Institute was no place for him. That you could take much better care of him here, at home."

"Are you a clairvoyant, Stroud?"

"You forget, I was a detective."

"Detectives read minds?"

"Sometimes."

"Well, the Meyers are good folk, and frankly, they were feeling a bit betrayed by Banaker. Strange thing to feel betrayed by a man you put all your trust into. I think Oliver plain lost them all by himself when he refused to allow the parents near the boy."

Stroud nodded. "I can understand why they'd become upset with the man."

"I told the father about the boy's physical condition," continued Magaffey, his head shaking with the memory. "Didn't want to upset the lady any more'n necessary, but Meyers, he told her and they made the decision to bring him home. Simple as that."

"They had no idea about his condition before that?"

"They were told of his mental condition, the trauma state, but nothing of the physical condition."

"Routine hospital screw up?"

"Or willful withholding of information, Stroud? Which you prefer? Parents were allowed to see the boy but only from a great distance, through glass, and he was in a darkened room."

"But why would Banaker lie to the parents?"

"Says he was trying to get the more dangerous problem under control and was avoiding any infection possibilities with the wounds by keeping people out."

"But you got in. How?"

"Hell, I'm the boy's family physician for one thing, and Doctor Sidney Cooper was on watch, and Sid isn't completely taken in by Banaker, either, and—"

"But what did Banaker have to gain by . . . by lying to the parents?"

"He was stalling for time, I suspect. Wanted to present them with a whole kid, so that when the cameras flashed on the boy as he exited Banaker Institute it would bring in more funds, more faith in the mighty Banaker legend he's created around himself and that place."

Magaffey sounded bitter. "He certainly seems to orchestrate his every move," said Stroud. "That's for sure."

"Orchestrating me out of practice."

"Provides a lot of jobs for the community."

"Most of Banaker's people aren't Andover born nor bred . . . most've come from the outside . . . but I suppose what with the linen that goes in and out, the dirty jobs and the scut work, he does employ a lot of people. . . . yeah . . . progress . . . "

"And yet he plagues you?"

"Son, he plagues you, too."

Stroud laughed at this. "You read minds, too."

"You forget. I knew your grandfather. You're a lot more like him than you realize."

Stroud studied the dark little man's eyes for some sign of meaning in what he'd just said and he found Magaffey studying him back. There was a long moment of silence between them. "Most people in Andover have nothing kind to say about Ananias Stroud."

"Abe . . . Abraham Stroud." Magaffey grasped his arm and squeezed tightly. "Most people have no idea in their heads about your grandfather, nor how much this town owes to him. He gave a good part of himself up in sacrifice to Andover. So, don't you listen to the fools and the Glen Turnips, all right? All right?"

Stroud felt compelled to say, "Thank you, I'll keep that in mind."

"Commit it to memory," the old man said with a wide, missing-tooth smile as he got into his automobile.

"Doctor Magaffey, have you had time to examine the bones you took from the field?"

"I have."

"And?"

"All my original hunches are now on record, but my place, my lab, was broken into last night—"

"What?"

"And all the bones, the records . . . all of it gone."

Stroud thought of the UPS package that had gone undelivered. He got a fleeting flash through his mind, a bulletin. The bones still remained undelivered and Dr. Cage in Chicago would never see them. The sheriff's deputy, and perhaps Briggs himself, would see to that.

As if reading his thoughts again, Magaffey said, "Son, Banaker has a saying that aptly fits our situation with respect to the bones, and although it's rather an old and oft misused truth, here it fits: Let the dead bury the dead."

He started his engine, but Stroud held onto his frail arm, stopping him from leaving. "Doctor Magaffey, what advice did you give to Timmy's parents?"

He looked as if he might just drive off, but finally he said, "Abe . . . Abe . . . Abe . . . I told the Meyerses what I'd do if the boy was mine. Same advice your grandfather would've given them, save for one other option, uniquely his own."

"What option was that?"

"We may talk about it sometime . . . but not now."

"I'd like to know more about my grandfather."

Magaffey laughed. "You will, son. The longer you stay in that house, the more you'll unearth . . . trust me."

"All right, what advice did you offer the Meyerses?"

"I'd take Tim as far from this area as possible, preferably to another state, over across the Mississippi River, to be certain."

It sounded like the worse kind of quackery and superstition. "To be certain of what?"

"Whatever got the boy isn't finished with him, hasn't *used* him up. Whatever got the boy'll come back for him."

Stroud was beginning once again to think Dr. Magaffey had something rattling around in his brain worse than Stroud's own metal plate. "But, Doctor—"

"Don't but me, Stroud! Christ, it happened the same damned way to Sid Cooper's kid! Same damned way!"

Magaffey's engine revved.

"You can't seriously think that some animal—"

"Creature—"

"Creature—whatever—got at the boy and has enough sentience to plot against the boy? To come back specifically for Timmy Meyers."

"Damn it, it knows where Timmy lives. Knows how to get at him. If the Meyerses would just take him across the line, across the water . . . maybe he'd be safe . . . maybe."

Magaffey tore off, leaving Stroud standing there with the realization that Magaffey's herb remedy and poultice smelled most strongly of garlic. He also recalled the huge crucifix above the boy's bed. Was that, too, a medical prescription of Dr. Martin Magaffey's?

Christ, it seemed the whole town was going crazy and that Magaffey was leader of the pack.

Maybe it was something in the goddamned drinking water. Maybe it was the shadow of science fiction cast with the towering Banaker Institute facility at the edge of the city which on a map stood directly opposite Stroud Manse. Twin Bluffs, where Timmy was allegedly found, was somewhere in between. Narrow strips of highway connected the three points, almost like a preordained triangle. He imagined he could go to a map and draw the triangle in red and that it'd be perfect.

Nothing was stacking up. Teetering, tottering information that threatened to keel over at the slightest touch, but nothing with foundation beyond what seemed outright lunatic reasoning on Magaffey's part. Still, why did Banaker so thoroughly isolate the boy, even from his parents? Why did he lie to them? What had he been up to? Why did his actions—so apparent and acceptable to the community at large—disturb Stroud? Why? Why? Why? The question became a mantra for Stroud.

— 9 —

Mrs. Elizabeth "Kitty" Meyers looked through the living room window once more to see if Stroud had left yet. Dr. Magaffey had left them alone with Stroud, apparently trusting the strange huge man, allowing him into their home without so much as a second thought. But Magaffey could be wrong about Stroud. Stroud's grandfather was believed to be one of them, and now that this man lived in the same house, reputedly haunted by the dead, surely it made no sense to allow him near the ailing boy. Suppose he deposited something in the room that might further "contaminate" Timmy?

God, oh, God, she thought, wishing Stroud would go away when Stroud did just that. "Thank God," she moaned, and downed what was left in the glass she'd held at her side. The Valium was as much needed as the alcohol, she assured herself, but the events of the morning were too much for her to bear alone, and now she feared for Timmy's life as never before. She cried unstoppable tears as she went back to Timmy's sickroom. Next to the phone in the hallway, she saw that Stroud had hastily written down his number and a curt message to please call if Timmy's condition changed.

She went at the note with a vengeance, tearing it to shreds and casting it about the floor. A look in on Timmy told her that his condition wasn't about to change, and that perhaps they'd made

75

a mistake not leaving him in Dr. Banaker's care, and that maybe Dr. Magaffey didn't know what the fuck he was talking about, and that her weiner of a husband had better take some action now or she was going to go stark raving mad.

She bolted from Timmy's unseeing stare and raced to the phone in the hallway, tripping, and knocking it over. She located the console and pushed for her husband's work number. How dare he go about the day as if it were just like any other; how stupid of him to leave them alone at a time like this.

"Dave! Dave, damn you come home now! Now!"

"What's the matter, Kitty? Is it Timmy?"

"Just get home!"

"Has he come out of it? Is he talking?"

"Christ, Dave! We've got to pack the car and get the hell out of Andover as fast as we can! Before nightfall!"

"Kitty, now calm down. I got the bars on order and the men'll be coming to install them on the windows as soon as—"

"Fuck the bars, Dave! I want out!"

"Kitty!"

"Out! Out, now! Or I leave and take Timmy with me!"

At Dave's place of work everyone in the showroom could hear the irritation at the other end of the line, and the other salespeople and customers stared.

He whispered angrily, "You've been drinking all morning, haven't you?"

"What else can I do, damn you, Dave, I mean it!"

"The bars are on their way!"

"Bars won't stop them from getting Timmy back!" she burst out, crying, pleading. "You know the Cooper boy disappeared twice, and the second time—"

"It's not the same, Kitty. Old Magaffey's being foolish to think—"

She wailed. "Stroud was here."

Dave fell silent, shaken at this news. Banaker and others had told him some strange tales about Stroud's grandfather, and the stranger to the area had shown up just about the same time as the Cooper boy disappeared.

"Stroud, at the house?"

"He came right in. Magaffey said it would be all right, but Daaaaaavvvvveeeee, suppose it isn't all right? Suppose—"

Dave didn't say it but he was thinking it. Suppose Timmy was a victim of some bizarre torture chamber inside Stroud Manse, and suppose Stroud meant to be certain the boy could never speak to accuse him again.

At the other end she was pleading for understanding. "Magaffey let him in; what could I do? I tried to keep him out. I didn't welcome him in."

It sounded bad to Dave. "Jesus . . . Jesus, God . . . "

"What're we going to do?"

"Calm down."

"They'll come for him, and we won't be able to stop them."

"I'll call Ray Carroll, let him know—"

"Carroll? Your brother-in-law spent a lot of time with Stroud, Dave!"

"Good God, Kitty, we can't go suspecting Ray of . . . of being involved in Timmy's disappearance."

"We can't trust anybody! No one."

God, she was sounding on the edge. "All right, calm down . . . calm . . . got to think."

"Christ, Dave, there's not time to think left! We've got to move fast!"

"Get hold of yourself!"

There was a knock at the door that Dave heard through the line. "Has he come back?"

"I . . . I don't know." She'd frozen in place, sprawled about the floor with the phone in her lap.

"Briggs, Mrs. Meyers . . . Mrs. Meyers? Come to look in on you and the boy. Your husband, Dave, asked me to come by earlier, but I got tied up. . . . Mrs. Meyers?"

"It's Sheriff Briggs, Dave," she said in a hoarse whisper. "Did you send him?"

"No . . . no, I didn't."

"He says you did."

"Stall him, honey. Keep him at the door. Don't let him or anyone near Timmy! You understand?"

Dave Meyers slammed down the phone with a resounding bell chime replying. He started out, his boss shouting that if he left it was the end of his job. Meyers returned, ignoring Mr. Blanchford, and dialing for Ray Carroll as Blanchford repeated his threat in his ear. "Ray! Ray! Son of a bitches want our boy, Ray!"

"What's this? What're you talking about, Dave? Can you slow down and explain?" asked Ray Carroll from his insurance brokerage office.

"Could be your Joey next, Ray. We're surrounded by them."

"Calm down, Dave! Dave! We . . . you don't know that. There's no evidence all that crap Magaffey fed you and Kitty's true!"

"Christ, Ray! If I didn't know better! Maybe Kitty was right about you."

"Right about me?" Carroll was completely confused by now. "Dave, I want you to take a deep breath, think about what you're saying, and—"

"Ray, don't patronize me!"

"I'm not!"

"Like hell, you're not. You think I don't know how this sounds? It sounds looney-tunes, I know, but my kid and Kitty are at stake and—"

A double clickety-click on the wires stopped him from speaking for a moment. Ray heard it, too, but said nothing beyond asking Dave Meyers if he were still on the line.

"Dave, your son is safe! He's alive! You and Kitty ought to be kissing the ground, for Christ's sake, but instead—"

"You . . . Kitty said you might be one of them!"

"Shit, Dave! Nobody—repeat—nobody is out to get Timmy! Or you, or Kit! Nobody."

"They're there now, at the house! Briggs, Stroud!"

"Just checking on the boy's progress is all, Dave. . . . Dave?"

But Dave was gone, tearing from his place of work to home. He'd been a fool to trust the old man, Magaffey, and his concoctions and lotions. Nothing would stop these Satanists and fiends from finishing Timmy off. Dave and Kitty Meyers had become convinced that some of the very men who'd put up a mock show of concern and an all-out effort to locate Timmy had in fact been the very devils who'd kidnapped and tortured him into his present condition. They had heard tales of a witch cult operating in and around Andover, tales that spoke of men and women who'd graduated from sacrificing goats and dogs to little boys and helpless women. They'd talked to Dr. Cooper who told them about how he had lost his boy, Ronnie. Cooper had told them that they had been lucky, that he'd never get his boy back alive.

It had been on Dr. Cooper's suggestion that they rush Timmy from Banaker Institute, that it was not a safe place. He also told them they must trust no one, that half or more of the population of Andover could not be trusted.

Dave hadn't wanted to believe it. But now, Kitty was frantic. She might do anything. He wondered if they were both going mad in the effort to salvage what remained of their son.

At home, in his lonely, too large, hauntingly cold old inheritance, Abraham Stroud wondered if he shouldn't just call Cage back in Chicago and take him up on the Iraq trip. There was more going on in the Middle East than unrest—there was a fantastic dig going on that had uncovered ancient mummies and gilded coffins and curses—lots of curses—to those who dared disturb the Assyrian kings and queens found there. Cage was going at the end of the month, and he'd invited his former star pupil to go along with the team he was putting together at the behest of the Iraqi government. Thus far, Stroud had put Dr. Cage off because he had no idea how long or complicated the settlement of the estate would be. Now, the strange goings-on in and around Andover and most assuredly the bone find here had complicated things further.

It would be a simple enough thing to do as the rest of Andover chose to do: stick his head in the sand, go about his business . . .

He went out to the stable where Lonnie Wilson, a half retarded, huge man who'd never left the manse, staying on to care for the horses that he loved, asked after his health. Lonnie had Star, the big brood mare, prepared. All that Stroud had to do was get in the saddle. Riding helped clear his mind, helped him make decisions.

"Fine, Lonnie," he said, "and how're you?"

"Cou-couldn't be-be-be-better, sir. Beau-ti-ful day."

"Yes, it is, Lonnie. Thanks for getting Star ready."

"Yow welcome."

"Want to ride out with me?"

"Naaaaa, too much to do here."

"Suit yourself, Lonnie."

He turned once to see that Lonnie was waving him off still, a huge smile on the big face, his blunt Wellington boots cutting a ridge in the earth where he kicked out in an habitual and rhythmic digging.

Stroud was gone all of an hour and it pretty much decided for him that he'd call Cage back—not about the damned "marrowless" bones, but about Iraq. Cage needed the funding he could bring to the expedition now, as well, and why let such a friend down?

Ashyer was waiting at the door for him, however, the telephone extended to him. "Mr. Carroll of the town, sir."

It was Ray Carroll. He was concerned about the Meyerses. They'd taken their son and all three had left Andover. They'd left their house standing open. Carroll characterized it as *fleeing*.

"From what are they running, Ray?"

"I don't know. Got it into their heads that Timmy was no longer safe here. Got it into their heads he'd disappear a second time, the way Ronnie Cooper did."

Stroud flashed on Magaffey's seemingly harmless presence at the home, and he wondered what the old man had been feeding to the terrified couple. "Tell me, Ray," said Stroud. "How much do you know about the Cooper incident? Was it similar?" Stroud recalled what Dr. Cooper had said, that the "bastards" had done his kid in. What bastards? Who? Was he generalizing about the rampant childnapping that seemed for the past year to be sweeping the country as the latest in crime? Or had he meant something more specific than that?

"Naw, not really. Ronnie got odd with his father all of a sudden."

"Odd? How?"

"Afraid like."

"Afraid of his father? How many kids aren't?"

"Exactly, but Ronnie just took to running away."

"I see. Anything else similar?"

Carroll thought for some time. "Matter of fact, come to think of it—"

"Yes?"

"Kid came back the first time with a lot of scars on him, cut up pretty badly. Word had it he'd fallen from a cliff. Least he was found below a bluff."

"Anything else you can remember?"

"He wasn't the same."

"Wasn't the same?"

"I mean, he was, like, withdrawn and bedridden after that. Never showed at school. They were sending books in. Parents said he'd contracted pneumonia, but nobody ever saw him after that."

"Wait a minute, Ray—"

"Yeah?"

"Are you saying he wasn't held at the hospital until he became well? That he—"

"Coopers reacted just like the Meyerses. Snatched him from

Banaker's place too soon. Ronnie just never got better, and then one night we were searching for the kid again, but—"

"But he was never found."

"Right."

"Like Timmy's dog."

"Huh?"

"Nothing."

"Oh, yeah, the dog, Dish," Carroll said.

"So where do you suppose the Meyerses have taken Timmy?"

"They got family over near Springfield. I have a suspicion they headed that way. I locked up the house for 'em. I thought it was just Kitty, you know, but I get this weird call from Dave . . . seems to have been spooked by your and Briggs's visit to the house."

"I was in the company of Dr. Magaffey, not Briggs."

"I see. Look, we maybe will have to finish this talk later. I gotta go."

"Ray!"

"Yeah?"

"What do you say we take my four-wheel tonight and look for that dog?"

"Sure, sure. About eight okay?"

"Deal."

Whole portions of the old manse had been shut down to conserve on energy, Abe Stroud supposed. He remembered that his grandfather had closed down the enormous, unused ballroom, for instance. The big ballroom was located at the north end, overlooking the Spoon where it forked around a plot of island the old man called Huck Finn's Island, but it really had no name. The old man had just told him it was Huck's Island because they'd read Mark Twain's novel together and it seemed a fitting tribute to the clump of trees out there.

Abe got a burning desire to look in on the old ballroom and peer out through the floor-length windows that stood opposite Huck's Island. The wraparound porch stopped short of the north end. To go out on the veranda there, he'd have to pass through the ballroom.

The Ashyers whispered between themselves when the key was finally located among a cache of keys on a large jailer's ring in the pantry. Stroud wanted to find the doors that fit each key, and he figured he had the time to do so if he stayed in Andover. He still had not called Merton Cage regarding Iraq. Something was holding him back.

The Ashyers seemed agitated at his opening the ballroom, making him even more curious about the place.

They kept up a constant chatter, taking turns.

"Mr. Stroud never allowed anyone into this room."

She said, "Something about a murder having been committed here once."

"Just an old story," he added with a nervous laugh.

"Mr. Stroud believed it," she added.

"Who was supposed to have been killed here?"

"Your great grandfather, Ezeekial Stroud."

"But the death certificate said death by madness."

"We really don't know the particulars, sir," said Mr. Ashyer, his tone clearly telling Stroud he wished to say no more.

The reserved couple seemed to be working out very nicely, and Stroud's suspicions had been considerably chased away by the cheery nature of the two and how they seemed to enjoy doing things for him. Still there remained about the couple a strangeness, a deep sadness even.

"I'll just have a look about," he said, and disappeared into the ballroom alone.

The electricity had been cut to this area. It didn't stand to reason that the place was shut down due to his great-grandfather's having died here. Even if he had been shot or knifed in this room, the furniture and fixtures alone told Stroud that the place had been opened and used in fairly recent times. His grandfather had made use of the room before he had shut it down.

The room was expansive. At its center was a lovely crystal chandelier. But its dazzling beauty refracted the weak light coming in through the thick red velour drapes through a blanket of cobwebs. The furniture—tables, settees, chairs—was covered with yellowed sheets with an inch or two of dust that flew up at the touch, creating a ghostly cloud that whirled like so many misplaced atoms, until the particles finally settled like sediment at the bottom of a spring.

One swirl of dust leapt up at his side as he moved past the table a bit too energetically for here; the current of air coming off him disturbed this place. He looked into the swirl of dust as it created a fairylike presence. It seemed there was nowhere in this house he did not see the spirits of his forebears, for through the swirl of dust particles high over the mantel his grandfather was staring back at him. It was a portrait he'd forgotten but now remembered as always being here. It was not his grandfather but his great-grandfather, Ezeekial Stroud. He looked so much like Ananias that it was uncanny. Standing before the picture as a boy, he'd never seen the resemblance.

He also saw in the stern, hard gray eyes something of himself. He recalled having been frightened by those eyes when last he stood in this room, and he now heard his grandfather, angry with him for having come into the room. It had been off limits to all but his grandfather even then. And his grandfather would come and sit amid the collected dust and stare for hours at the portrait of his father, Ezeekial. One night Stroud snuck down and heard the old man talking gibberish to himself in the room, talking to the painting that Stroud now felt compelled to reach out and touch.

It was layered with dust, but somehow those eyes of Ezeekial Stroud, ever watchful, surveyed the entire ballroom with his unerring, penetrating stare. Right through the veil of dust, right through the years.

Stroud shook himself and went on with his journey across the hardwood floor to the windows where he expected to see the river and the island. He pulled back the drapes, causing a rain of filthy dust to engulf him, making him sneeze.

"Christ, this place needs cleaning!"

The damage done, he pulled back the drapes to reveal the floor-length windows, amazed to find eight-foot-high wrought-iron bars outside them. The gate around the windows was crisscrossed with spider webs, leaves, and blown grass, obscuring the view of the river and the island.

"What the hell . . . bars?" Stroud turned on hearing a noise behind him. Deep in shadow on the other side of the room, some-one stood and an eerie, unreal whisper said, "Abraham."

It was a voice like Ananias Stroud's voice, but that was impossible.

Stroud rushed at the corner where it came from but there was no one there, only a cold emptiness. When he looked up at the picture of Ezeekial he realized that Ezeekial's eyes were on him, that in fact, no matter which way he moved, from right to left and back again, the ancient eyes seemed directed at him.

"What's the meaning of these bars?" he asked aloud and instantly felt foolish.

Ashyer pushed open the door and said, "Did you call for me, sir?"

"Ashyer, were you just in here?"

"No, sir."

"Those bars," he said, pointing to the windows. "What can you tell me about them?"

"They've always been there, sir . . . since I've been here, anyway."

"But why bars on just these windows. If you're going to put bars on windows, shouldn't you do it for all the windows? At least on the ground floor?"

"Doctor Stroud," said Ashyer, "at one time all the windows on every floor had bars about them. Your grandfather was having them all barred but the job wasn't quite finished when he passed on."

Stroud nodded. "Thanks, Ashyer."

"Not at all, sir, now if you like—"

"I'd like to look into getting some cleaning men in to completely sanitize this place. Like to restore it. Will you see to it?"

"If it is your wish, sir."

"It is, Ashyer . . . it is."

—10—

Abraham Stroud wondered about the bars on all the windows and the coincidence of those planned to be installed over Timmy Meyers' windows.

What did old Magaffey know that he did not know? Why was the old man reluctant to speak his mind completely and freely? Why did he speak in riddles? Were the bars here at the manse erected to keep people in or keep people out?

Ashyer had left him—a walking mystery himself. The damned house was filled with mysteries—so many in fact he felt he might live a lifetime and never discover them all, certainly not uncover the meanings behind them all. "Sort of like life itself," he concluded aloud to the watching eyes of his great-grandfather.

Stroud returned to the window covered with bars taller than himself. He opened the windows inward, studying the workmanship of the bars more closely. He wiped away clinging nests of leaves and webs of debris as well as spider webs. Even in the dark, the intricate pattern of spears and crosses that had been created by the craftsman was impressive. It was the kind of work he might expect to find on the gilded ships of the Edwardian era, or perhaps the first grand houses built in New York or Chicago at the turn of the century. Simply beautiful wrought-iron work in thick, powerful proportions.

The tops created a wall of spears garnished with metal leaf outcroppings on either side of the spear point. A third of the way and midway up the spears there was a series of ornate, old world crosses of the type seen in the more orthodox Catholic churches, particularly Greek and Roman. They might even be copied from an ancient era, he thought.

In a dark, heavy-handed, old world way, the bars had a beauty of their own.

Stroud had four, maybe five hours before his planned outing with Ray Carroll. He decided he must put the time to good use and concentrate on Stroud Manse. He must, he told himself, learn as much as possible about the house and its history—bars and scars and skeletons and all. For instance, the strange covered old helicopter that sat in back of the stables on its own pad. Whenever he went near it, the feeble-minded stableboy, Lonnie, became agitated to the point of crying.

He needn't go to the library to search. Stroud Manse had its own library, several in fact. His grandfather had a business area in a den down the hall from where Stroud was sleeping. He had still not been able to take the old man's master bedroom on the floor above, continuing to like the cozier, smaller bedroom where he had slept as a boy, and which he had equipped with video, stereo, and TV equipment as well as an aquarium recessed in the wall. But the old man's bedroom was yet another library, the walls lined with books.

Then, too, there was the circular room in the bowels of Stroud manse, the books there apparently the oldest and the most used, treasured, and valued. Stroud hadn't had time before to peruse them, but now maybe it was time.

Dr. Oliver Banaker paced before his staff, who were assembled in the briefing room reserved for the dissemination of information vital to them all. But today his message was short and to the point.

"I am aware of the problem and who is at the root of it. With this man Stroud in our community, we must be doubly cautious, people! You all know what his forebears have done to our kind—set us back years when this man's grandfather destroyed my father."

Pamela Carr spoke up, her concern the same as most present. "Doctor Banaker, can you put an end to . . . to the killings?"

"It has been done. Worry no more on that score."

"Then, perhaps Stroud is no longer a threat," she suggested.

"He is of a kind, just as we are, my dear. . . . No, he lives to threaten us. Stroud's coming is no accident. On the contrary, it is very much by design."

"But if we just left him alone, and if the . . . the terrorizing is ended—"

"Pamela, the man is dangerous to us. No two ways about that. So long as he remains in that house, living near us . . . he poses a threat. Think of all that would be lost if we were exposed now? What would happen to Banaker Institute? Our research?"

"Not to mention your precious food sources," said Dolphin Banaker. "I can't believe you allowed him to roam freely about the hospital, Pamela."

"I had nothing to do with that!" she protested.

Dr. Cooper, the newest member on staff, searched about nervously, expecting Dolph to make some remark about his encounter with Stroud near the morgue, and here it was.

"And you, Cooper, chatting with the fiend in the corridor outside the morgue. Christ, why didn't you just invite him in for a better view?"

"You're the one who told the interns they could have at it with old Mrs. Lowenthal! It wasn't proper, Doctor Banaker! She wasn't fully prepped and here they come tearing in. Your son's got everyone breaking the rules! Hell, Oliver, she was still alive . . . hell."

Banaker's back stiffened and his eyes glowed with anger. "Dolph has been trying everyone's patience lately . . . but then, is not that the mandate of youth? To test the boundaries, push back the perimeters? He is a bit wild, yes . . . not unlike myself when I was younger. I expect great things from Dolphin, people. If something should ever happen to me, he will carry on my work."

Dolphin gave Cooper a cold, animalistic glare from across the table. Spoiled devil, Cooper thought. Pamela feared for Cooper. One day the weaker man who still pined for his lost boy would be devoured by Dolphin. There'd be no place at Banaker or anywhere else for Cooper.

More important than Cooper, or Dolph, or Banaker himself, however, was the work.

Years of painstaking study and literally hundreds of thousands of man-hours had gone into the research and education of the "family"—Banaker's euphemism for what they were.

At Banaker Institute everyone was regarded as part of what he jokingly called the "Corporeal Family." Everyone at Banaker shared the same blood. Fed from the same vats that purified and strained the fluid of life. The Institute's true work was not in patients and billing, but in carrying on a race so alien to most humans that some very wise forebears of the race had created children's stories and fiction around them so that they might continue to thrive and multiply. But no one had done as much for them as Banaker and his father before him. Banaker had uncovered secrets that made living among human beings virtually second nature to members of his family. They could come and go, day or night, as they pleased, without fear of detection or harm, as from the otherwise killing rays of the sun. No longer a problem, thanks to Banaker research, and the special genetically altered mix of Banaker blood plasma.

But now all their work—everything Oliver Banaker stood for—was jeopardized by the recent spat of killings and near killings that had erupted like a plague epidemic in the community. No one in the family seriously doubted that it was one of their own. Reverting back to the old ways, one among them had done the horrible deeds that could expose them all.

Outbreaks such as these had occurred before. They all knew the thin line each of them walked. Any one of them might fall prey to the ancient desire for fresh and hot and pumping blood taken from a cowering victim. Any one of them . . . maybe even Banaker himself.

All of them knew the real meaning behind the much touted Devil of Andover, the black panther creature that was carted out every so often in the neighborhood to explain away the unexplainable, the unspeakable.

Everyone who worked at Banaker knew the dark secret. All of them had the lust and craving. It was in their blood, so to speak, to become such a creature as the one who'd taken the Cooper offspring, and more recently the Meyers boy, as well as the couple from Missouri.

The people from the "Show Me" state, Pam mused, had been shown. . . .

"So, we all know the consequences. What is at stake here? Peace, my children . . . peace and cohabitation in our little corner of the planet! Our forebears were wiped out, literally made extinct . . . but we are making a dramatic return . . . rather like the gray whale, I'd say. Then for one of us to go rabid on the scent of man, for the sake of our god, people . . . Is a moment's passion worth all the risks to your fellow family members? Not to mention the several hundred disease organisms contained in the blood of mankind. AIDS is rampant. The most disturbing new development in our Andover Devil is that *this one* appears to cannibalize on our own kind! As attested to by . . . by—"

Cooper suddenly bolted from the room, unable to hear anymore.

"Cooper, Doctor Cooper!" said Banaker.

"I'll drag the wimp's ass back here," said Dolph, about to pursue.

"No, no! Let him go, Dolph."

"But, Father!"

"Dolph! Sit down."

"I'm not a dog you can order around, Father!"

"We will speak of this later, young one!"

Dolph's color raged in his face, his huge nostrils flaring in and out, but he said no more.

Pamela saw the leer on Dolph's face when he caught her staring at him. He flexed his huge biceps and planted his elbows back on the table.

His father continued the weary speech. "Do you wish to trade all you have in this place for one moment of passion? Take that message to your children as well." He saw that everyone had stopped listening. "Very well," he said with a sigh. "See to your duties, everyone, and continue to set the fine example you do to the others."

Everyone began to depart.

"Oh, Pam, if you will. I'd like a word."

She held back as Dolph, holding onto the door, looked back inside at his father and Pamela. He winked at her and disappeared. "I have a special task for you, Pamela, and forgive me, but I will be asking much of you."

She knew he had wanted her to flirt with Stroud, and now she knew he wanted her to take it further when he said, "You're happy here, aren't you, Pamela?" He didn't expect or want an answer. "When is the last time you . . . *had a man*, Pamela?"

"I swear to you, Doctor Banaker, I'm not the one. I swear to you—"

He laughed. His laugh was so full and resounding it filled the room. "Please, Pamela, I don't for a moment suspect you of being the cause of our, and Andover's, problem."

"Oh?"

"Now, answer the question."

"The question?"

"When was the last time you *had* a man?"

She swallowed hard, feeling it was a test. "You . . . you have my records."

"Must I go to the trouble?"

She shook her head. "When I was eleven. It was just after you *had* me."

"A long time. . . . Do you remember it?"

"Very much."

"Pleasantly?"

"Somewhat. I was . . . you know . . . awkward, afraid . . . unsure . . ."

"First time, a joy. Suppose I told you I wanted you to do Stroud?"

She shivered at the suggestion from intense agitation and an overwhelming desire to do exactly as he asked, but if she did so and somehow it was misconstrued by the others . . . wouldn't it come back to haunt her? Suppose Banaker needed someone to take a fall? Suppose Banaker knew who the man-eater really was, but he didn't want him caught and punished? Suppose he needed her as a scapegoat?

"Calm all your fears, Pamela, please." He knew what she was thinking. He had that capability. He had more power than any of them. "It's Stroud I want. I owe his family a great deal, you see. I owe it to him to give you to him."

"When?" she asked.

"Tonight . . . tonight. He'll welcome you into his arms and you'll take his life—all of it. No holding back, Pamela. No storing him away somewhere for later drams; no show of pity; no turning him into your fucking pet, all right? All or nothing. What do you say? It could get you moved up on the ladder here. I happen to be most influential, you know."

She also knew he did not tolerate mistakes or failures very well. "What if he doesn't, you know, welcome me to him?"

He laughed again. "What *man* could resist you?"

"But if something happens to—"

"Get him for me, Pamela," he said sternly, his eyes freezing her in place. "Kill Stroud."

There were levels in Banaker's "family" just as there were in any family, a natural pecking order. There were the weak drones at the bottom rungs, most like zombies, some of whom worked out of the brain-dead condition to improve their status—especially if they followed Banaker's prescription for improvement: his Pire

Regimen. It started with ox blood and iron and ended with human blood, large quantities of plasma and his secret ingredient. Some were content to remain as they were, however, acting as gofers and go-betweens, never acquiring full status or recognition in the "Pire Family." Others were hard-working, and then there were the *driven* like himself—few and far between. His father had been driven. He was obsessively driven, never sleeping, always at the helm of his empire. But Dolphin he worried about.

Dolphin's mother was gone and the loss had shattered the boy. Dolphin's mother had died at the hands of Ananias Stroud, trapped by him outside the sleeping place, dissolved in the then killing rays of the sun. Dolphin never understood the reasons until he was older, and he still did not fully appreciate the benefits of research that had armed him and his kind with additional resistance to such things as light.

"You and the others," Dolphin had shouted at him once, "you're just becoming like *them*! More and more like humans every day! Where's the dignity and heritage in that, my father? Safety . . . all you think of is safety so you might hide in full view of them."

Banaker had slapped his son hard across the face and the boy had stormed out that night. The next morning he hadn't returned, had holed up somewhere he would not discuss, and the newspapers told of Dr. Cooper's missing son.

Cooper had been a remarkable project himself. He was one of them, but he had married a human and they'd sired little Ronnie. It was not a first, as it had been accomplished in the distant past, but it was rare. The attention showered Ronnie over the years had caused a jealousy to build in the much older but vulnerable Dolphin and Banaker knew that Dolph hated Ronnie and his father.

With the Meyers boy's disappearance, Banaker feared the worst—that one of his kind had broken ranks . . . and deep inside he feared it was Dolph. He'd gone to him after the Meyers incident had gotten the attention of the city. He had pleaded with Dolph to deny it.

Deny it, he did, but Banaker didn't believe him. He followed Dolph when he stormed out this time and he found the Meyers boy and his dog, both looking dead, hanging in a cocoon spun of the ectoplasmic vomit of his species, at the back of a cave filled with bats.

Dolph had drained the dog completely. But the Meyers boy was still breathing, just barely so, but breathing. Banaker had the boy hours before he released the news, bringing his blood supply back to normal, but he hadn't been able to bring him from his shock, nor did he completely wish to.

That morning he had confronted Dolphin with the evidence. Dolph shouted and kicked for some time before he finally settled down to listen to reason, to the fact it meant the salvation of their species. "And for that any price, any price is worth it, Dolph! You must know that!"

"Yes, I know . . . I know."

"Then why? Why're you doing this?"

Dolph couldn't look him in the face. "I . . . I get urges, Father . . . urges that I can't control."

"Ronnie Cooper was only half human, Dolph!" he had said with a groan. "He was one of *us.*"

"I didn't do Ronnie!"

True, he hadn't found Ronnie's body. Nobody had.

"Then why the Meyers boy, why?"

"The kid found the bone field, the one where we buried all the used bones for your goddamned extractions."

"Then you only made a bad situation worse! And you just used it as an excuse, Dolph! An excuse to become a man-eater. Don't you know I know what's in your heart, your mind?"

"I got a right to know what it's like! Damn you, Father, damn you and Grandfather and the Institute and the research and all of it!"

"Don't use that tone with me!"

"What're you going to do, cut back my rations? I don't want any of your goddamned freeze-dried, prepackaged plasma!"

He took hold of the boy and, with his power, all that the ages had given him, forced Dolphin into submission before him, a thing he did not wish to do. "I don't wish to humiliate you, son . . . but if I must."

Dolph felt the power and the pain exerted on his body and mind by his father. It was excruciating, the pain of the grave, pain of hunger, eternity without a drop of blood.

"Now, son, let's talk openly and rationally, the way a father and son should. You know, your having my and your mother's genes and blood, you realize you are one of the few fullbloods left among us? That while others've become vampires, son, *you were born a Pire!*"

"Yes, Father . . . you've told me."

"Is that it . . . just testing your power? Trying your wings, as they say?"

"Part of it. Just never tasted the real thing before and now that I have . . . "

It truly was not difficult for Banaker to understand Dolph's improprieties and uncontrollable urges. Even now, as old as he was and as workable as blood substitutes were, he sometimes felt a passionate desire to abandon science and the future of the species for an orgiastic night of debauchery and blood—real blood from a real man—to become again the man-eater that his forebears were. It was more than an urge, it was instinct and a driving force from the deepest part of his black soul.

He understood the wild boy for he himself had indulged in the old ways some thirty-four years earlier when he was about Dolph's age. And, from time to time, he'd gone on "business" trips, picked up hookers in bars, and had feasted unashamedly on them in such places as Washington, D.C., where the last AMA Convention was held. To his knowledge, the bodies were found but not autopsied; who autopsied hookers with needle tracks up and down their arms and one large one on their necks?

His most foolish acts had, however, been accomplished here in Andover. It'd been the year of his rape of Andover, reaping in his human harvest. It had been his first but not his last taste of the real stuff. He'd gone on a madcap, bloodthirsty rampage; much of his anger, rage, and passion had been, he determined years later, directed at his own father—to get back at him for being his father, he supposed. Even vampires had psychological difficulties and dependencies.

Now Dolphin was repeating the cycle.

The father-son thing; a vicious pattern.

Dolph's little improprieties were meant to bring his father down along with Andover—to his knees. All the young fool was accomplishing, however, was to draw a too bright spotlight of endless questions down around the Institute.

"It will end, Dolph. You must get control of your inner urges and purge yourself. Meantime, the only help for it is the substitute, the enriched blood plasma I give you, son. You must understand: you must care for the rest of the family."

Dolph only frowned. Perhaps he didn't care a fig about the others of his kind; perhaps he was just too young and too spoiled to understand, to fully appreciate all that his ancestors had built here in sleepy little Andover. Perhaps Banaker had raised a sociopathic vampire son. Perhaps Dolph liked the hunt and the taste of blood too much to ever give it up? What then?

"Maybe I'll just move out on my own," he said sullenly, looking to his father for a reaction. "Get a place in Springfield, St. Louis, maybe . . . or maybe Chicago."

Banaker knew what he was doing. He knew that Dolph was taunting him. Dolph knew he wanted him to take charge of the Institute one day, manage things so that Banaker could plunge back into research. Such talk as what Dolph threatened now was designed merely to tear and rend Oliver Banaker's heart. For half a second, Oliver felt what his own father must have felt at such moments with him.

He would not provide the boy with the tools to destroy him, however, and he'd be damned before he would show any sign of weakness before Dolph. He merely said, "Do as you damned well please, Dolph, but you will not expose the rest of us to annihilation by your stupidity and arrogance. And should you . . . should you further do so—"

"You'll what? Kill me?"

"If that is what it takes, yes."

"You don't have it in you!"

Banaker stalked out on his son this time to the boy's insulting chorus: "You don't have the guts, Father! You don't have it in you, because you drink that milkshake crap at the Institute!"

He turned and rushed at his child, his form turning into a black missile that slammed into Dolph, knocking him over. Dolphin opened his eyes to the enormous, salivating mouth and fangs of his father as they clamped down on his neck, rending a portion of the skin and beginning to drain his blood. Dolph countered by shape-changing even as he was being held in his father's grip, the fangs pumping the life from him. As each changed into his true form, a wind swept through the house, blasting everything in its path. The unfurled, black wing-tip of the struggling pair cut walls and broke mirrors in their path.

Suddenly Banaker returned to his human form, spent. His son lay beneath him, the speed with which the attack had been launched had left him weak and wounded. Dolph, too, had returned to his former self.

"Lie there in your own blood, Dolph, and think about it! Think about it real hard. I want an end to this business you've been carrying on out there!" He pointed in the general direction of the doorway before he stormed through it and was gone.

That had been just after recovering the Meyers boy, but just before the incident at Spoon River. Banaker knew his little "talk" had failed.

He also knew that others in the family were beginning to suspect Dolph—nothing that anyone said directly to his face, but little things, like the way Dolph was being treated lately, and the handful of anonymous "tips" sent Banaker's way. If things were allowed to continue, not only would exposure be a problem, but Dolph could become the victim of a violent end from the others. All it would take was one among them to lead the horde. Like a lot of fathers, Dr. Oliver Banaker labored under a mix of love and anger, pride and disappointment in his son.

—11—

Had Ananias Stroud, like his father before him, ended his life an insane man?

It was a question that Stroud could not avoid, not any longer, not standing here surrounded by the trappings of lunacy that filled the weird, circular chamber at the heart of the stone manse. Stroud had only known his grandfather as a gentle, caring and peaceful man who had died in his sleep. The evidence against this image had been steadily growing since Abe had taken possession of the manse. First the Ashyers' cautious revelations, his discovery of the barred windows and the circular room, its bizarre furnishings, and the old man's secret library of arcane literature dealing with such esoteric hints as how to keep the dead from rising; all this, along with the information about Ananias' own father, Ezeekiel, having died a madman . . .

It gave him a shudder. Perhaps it was a genetic tendency toward madness or brain disorders, and here he stood, a man given to seizures, visions and chronic ghostly stirrings thanks to the metal band-aid in his head.

The question of his grandfather's mental state at the time of his death had now become overwhelming, inescapable and demanding. Had the grand old man become bitter, detached from reality, warped? Had that warp skewed his sense of morality and decency, turning him into a wicked, sadistic monster who inflicted pain on others? It did not seem possible, and yet before Abe's eyes, all around this room, lay the incontrovertible evidence.

Abe had come again to the center of the house, into the circle of rock where he had run his hand over the dust and cobwebs on a restraining instrument of torture. He'd been sitting here in the comfortable reading chair with a stack of what he now realized to be the old man's books, trying desperately to understand the meaning of this chamber.

Many, if not most, of the books were yellowed with age, their pages dotted with the holes created by feeding micro-organisms. Some pages fell away at the touch, flying from their bindings as if attempting to escape him.

It was a damp, chilly, large room; the air seeped in although no vents were visible. It seemed to be coming from all sides, seeping through the solid walls that were below ground. It reminded Stroud of underground springs he'd made dives in at a constant seventy-two degrees year round.

He had come by way of Great-grandfather's bedroom, somehow familiar with the route now that took him through a closeted room there, into a wardrobe and out the back to a spiral of stairs that descended into the bowels of the place. The descent made him think of Dante's *Inferno* and of the personal descent into his own black soul where fear and hatred lay alongside him on that battlefield in Vietnam.

He lit his way with an oil lamp that hung on the wall for the purpose, and once at the bottom and inside the ghastly prison, he found other lamps and torches set in the wall. Nothing artificial here.

At present it was a relief to sit and study the simplicity of a roach that skittered into his vision. It ran the gauntlet of mortar between the fieldstone blocks. Cracks in the mortar revealed the fact that earth on all sides was pressing and straining against the circle. Green to gray to black scales and barnaclelike lichens grew on the walls, living, dying, peeling off, ingested by the roaches and other insects, and finally replaced by their sunless, lightless progeny.

It wasn't the most pleasant of places in the manse.

Not even the Ashyers seemed to know of it, or so he thought before he began reading from the various books he'd pulled down from the shelves along one row of the ancient oak shelves. The bookcase itself looked as if it had made an ocean voyage from Europe several centuries before. How it came to be here was yet another mystery. How and why the old man had such books in his possession as that entitled *Life, Death and Demonic Possession*, published in 1692 by an Austrian Monk named Adolph Stroud-Nuebauer in a London press, was yet another mystery. But the conclusions Abe had been drawing from what he saw at every turn seemed no mystery any longer.

A notation in the margin of the book by Stroud-Nuebauer marked him an ancestor. It was one of a thousand notations made in the margins of this and other titles that spoke of a dark preference in reading matter.

Sex Worship, Encyclopedia of Spirits and Vampires, Revelations of the Dead, The Book of the Warlock Race, and an invaluable first edition of *Dracula* graced the oak bookcase. These shared space with titles published in the fifties such as Seabrook's work on vampires and Tobin's *Spirit Guide.* More recent books had also been acquired and housed here, books of a more scientific nature: *Psychism and the Unconscious; Mind, Flesh and Spirit; Transpowering; DNA and the Double Helix as Lifeforce; Hannibal's Medical Compendium,* and *Gray's Anatomy.*

There were also some papers in a manuscript holder which constituted what seemed a series of mad ramblings on magic and protection of oneself through magic and ritual. These were in someone's hand, perhaps his *grandfather's.* Given his final mindset his handwriting might have changed. But he could not be sure of this.

The notations in the margins of otherwise flawlessly kept first editions, such as *Dracula* by Bram Stoker, were, however, in Ananias's unmistakable hand; and here, his remarks were unmistakably those of a madman.

Encircled by the eerie, almost talking, almost dripping-with-blood instruments of torture, he read the rantings of a man gone insane. The old man had apparently spent his final days pouring over books dealing with vampire outbreaks and attendent vampire practices and destruction. *And* how to rid oneself of the demons. He had read of vampires in Bulgaria, Somalia, Rumania, Ireland, Judea, Asia, Russia, England, Jamaica, Haiti, the West Indies, Burma, New Zealand, Kenya, Brazil and other South American locations, as well as Canada and America in a book entitled *Vampires on the Continent.*

One account told of the Kwakiytl Indian tribe in British Columbia who were flesh and blood eaters.

At the front of the famous Stoker novel about the most infamous of vampires, Dracula, the old man had scribbled two urgent messages that leapt from the copyright page proclaiming the book to be a hundred years old:

> This is not a work of fiction, but a collection of diary entries and direct recollections of the parties involved in the incidents of 1897.
>
> Careful reading tells that on destruction of the vampire that Mina was pregnant not with J. Harker's child, but that of Count Dracula!

"To carry on the bad seed," Abe said aloud in the room.

His voice bounced about as if in echo, but in the echo he thought he heard Ananias's voice say, "Yes . . . yes . . . "

He closed the Stoker book in a mood of complete sadness at the condition of the old man's mind at the time he had exited this life: fevered and fearful and ranting. He'd died in his bed upstairs peacefully, Stroud had been told. Peacefully, no, he did not think so.

Stroud carefully opened a pamphlet-sized book he had pulled down earlier which now begged to be opened, a book entitled, *Disinterment of Suspected Vampires.*

Stroud could hardly believe the prescriptions and detailed recipes for spotting, unearthing, trapping, and destroying the beast. It sounded like the worst witch-hunt drivel. The eerie words on the pages were couched in the most dangerous tone—that of the believer, or religious fanatic. To Stroud it was the type of thinking and language that allowed the birth of the Spanish Inquisition, the blossoming of the Third Reich, and such world renown mistakes as Vietnam. Fortunately, few people believed in vampirism and so failed to become adherents of the faith that fought vampire practices.

He now scanned the "characteristics to be determined on exhuming the body of a suspected vampire from the grave." The peculiar list read:

1. Are a number of holes (about the breadth of a man's finger) in the soil above the grave?

Always conclusive, Stroud thought.

2. Does the revealed corpse have any of the following:
A. wide-open eyes

Again Stroud was skeptical, thinking, *it happens even at the best of funerals*.

B. a ruddy complexion
C. no (or few) signs of corruption
D. nails and hair grown as in life

Stroud shook his head over this last one, knowing that nails and hair continued to grow after death on every corpse.

E. small livid marks on the neck

"Ahhhh, yes, the infamous Devil's mark where the satanic beings feed on the corpse," Stroud told himself aloud, his voice reverberating round the room. "Must remember that." Then he did remember the small livid red marks on Timmy Meyers's neck.

As an anthropologist and archeologist, he knew a great deal about human myth and legend and the propensity to vent fear and frustration through magic and mythmaking to explain away the dark—both the dark of the night and the dark of the soul. And yet, he also knew that within every legend, myth, and parable there lay a grain of truth, sometimes more than just a grain.

"No . . . no," he told himself. The boy was attacked by some pervert, and then released to stumble away. Andover hid no worse horror than the psychotic who looked and acted just like anyone else in town until nightfall. But then his eyes fell on the large supply of stakes, both metal and wood, that the old man had put up here. Stroud's eyes continued on to the pain-making tools and instruments of torture that encircled the large body rack, and the medieval chains along the walls. It was no Nautilus room; and given the old man's proclivity for fantastic reading, Stroud's police mind was at great odds with his boy's memories of a gentle, caring old man. Was it the lot of mankind, that anyone in the race could fall prey to the evil within?

Here, now . . . at the heart of the old house stood the relics and artifacts of the old man's secret self, a side not even his worse critic might have guessed at. Sitting in the old man's chair he heard the screams of anguish of some poor devil in the past who'd been coaxed and cajoled this way. Given the old man's money, any number of scenarios was possible. Hell, he may even have paid people to endure suffering for him to watch from this very chair where Stroud now sat.

Such a prostitution was infinitely preferable to the idea of the old man's abducting and drugging children or helpless women. Suddenly the chair began to feel like the chair of Satan, the room the property of the Devil.

In his loneliness, had old Ananias—with Abe never giving it a thought—turned to Satan for solace? For answers in a vain effort to find salvation through that darkest of corridors? To extract torturous cries to reach satanic ears in the lowest reaches of hell? In an abomination of raising voices to the Antichrist?

He shuddered where he sat feeling suddenly very cold. The thoughts he was entertaining were unbearable, so unbearable they were moving him toward another seizure. He must block the horrific images and mad ideas if he were to block the black out.

He fought desperately to sustain his consciousness, however, wondering in the back of his mind how the Ashyers fit in. How had they not known of the old man's strange proclivities and activities here in the middle of the place? They must know something. He knew he must get out of this horror chamber to avoid the seizure, he must fix on some more powerful notion than the terror of this place if he were to succeed. He concentrated on the Ashyers. Concentrated on how they procured the helpless victims brought to this terrible place. Concentrated on the living culprits, concentrated on how they could be brought to justice.

He concentrated on the whispering voices in the walls here. Some were plaintive echoes of the tortured. Some were pleading. None were laughing; none were taunting. Then he thought he heard the Ashyers clear and controlled, calling him out. He thought of Ray Carroll and the thin tie he had with his new neighbor. He thought of the deal they'd made, above in the real world. Ray was likely on his way to the manse this moment.

The spoken reason: to locate Timmy's unfound dog, to have a look at the body they expected to find, for clues. There was some other reason they'd search tonight, some unspoken need. What had it been?

He kept getting the image of Timmy's dog ruthlessly killed after being used. Used how? To lure Timmy deeper into the trap? God, a marginal notation his grandfather'd made about vampires *using dogs* in just such a fashion had passed his eyes this night. Where had he seen that notation? No, no . . . he told himself. That's madness, that's a hole he didn't wish to stand in—the brink of a volcano ready to erupt. Instead he wanted the door to this place, the stairs leading out, and the very real world of light and solids above. Besides, there were people waiting dinner for him. There was Ray on his way. People were counting on him up there. The real world, he told himself, needed him. He must pull himself out from this place and these crushing feelings and the threat of his steel-plate seizure. He must. He must. . . .

And he did. He found himself outside the horror chamber in the secret passageway which led from the old man's bedchamber through his wardrobe and up several flights of stairs. He still had no idea in his head how he had found the chamber the first time.

When he emerged, the Ashyers treated him with a mixture of curiosity and staid reserve, a kind of pretense, he decided. He could almost hear them thinking: *Just like his grandfather, isn't he?*

But Mrs. Ashyer simply said, "We looked for you, sir, but could not find you anywhere. Supper'll be just a moment. I'll have it warmed for you, sir."

"In the kitchen, Mrs. Ashyer," he said.

"What?"

"I'll eat with you both in the kitchen, if you don't mind."

They stared at one another. "Oh, no, not at all," she said after a reluctant moment.

It was, after all, his kitchen. And he dearly did not want to eat in the mammoth dining room alone again.

The meal was good, warming and wholesome, a credit to Mrs. Ashyer. All these things he conveyed to them. He also said that they were becoming indispensable.

At the same time he wondered anew just how indispensable they'd been to his grandfather. They must know of the secret room and the secrets kept there for so long.

After much blushing and denial that they were anything but mediocre servants, Ashyer said, "Oh, I've found a chap to do the cleaning. Jack Trell and Company. They'll be out in the morning, sir."

"Splendid, splendid. I hope they bring more than a dustpan and broom."

Someone came on the intercom from the gate out front, back-scatter behind Ray Carroll's voice. "Doctor Stroud, it's me, Carroll. Got a couple friends to join us, if you're ready?"

"Open the gate, Mr. Ashyer," Stroud told his man.

"But, sir—"

"Let them up."

Ashyer pressed the reply and said into the intercom, "Gentlemen, please, drive up to the house."

There seemed some reluctance to do so, but finally Ray Carroll's crowd came through and the light indicating that the gate was open went off again.

"I'll be out late, so you folks just relax tonight, do what comes natural, take in a movie, whatever, okay?" he told the Ashyers as he busied to join Carroll and the others.

"Sir," said Ashyer, stopping him suddenly.

Stroud saw eye contact between the married couple as if they were sharing a psi message between themselves. "What is it, Ashyer? I'm in a rush."

"Has anyone spoken to you, sir, about the . . . well, about the Andover Devil, sir?"

"The what?" Stroud felt a lump rise in his throat, sure they were referring to what the townies must've been calling Grandfather Ananias at the end.

"Sir, there's been cattle and sheep—that sort of thing—slaughtered around here on occasion, and this latest thing with the children disappearing . . . well, you're determined to go out in those woods, sir, but we . . . Mrs. Ashyer and I are . . . worried for you, sir."

"Don't worry about me, please."

"There is something out there, sir. Your grandfather, sir . . . "

"What about my grandfather?"

"He knew it, sir. . . . He had a run in with it once. Returned here in a very bad state, sir. . . most bloody."

"When did it happen?"

"Many years ago, sir. . . 1966. After that it seemed to have gone away, but now . . . now it seems to have returned."

Stroud took in a deep breath of air and pulled on a favorite fedora and a hunting vest with some padding and casings for extra shells. He took a shotgun from the rack in the gun room, Ashyer following him about now, saying no more. He also took down a powerful rifle with a night scope on it.

"Not to worry, Ashyer," he told the other man. "I'm very good with this."

Outside, he tossed a water canteen into the back of his Jeep, along with a sandwich hastily put together by Mrs. Ashyer, and a thermos of coffee.

Stroud carefully placed the guns in safety holsters on each wall of the Jeep doors. All the while, he was being introduced and re-introduced to the men Carroll had brought with him. Stroud recognized faces from the hunt of the other night. There were, counting himself, only four men. Much better than the mob of the other night, so far as Stroud was concerned.

"One of you men want to ride with me?" he asked the others.

"Stroud," said Carroll, "we're all here family men with kids. We . . . we're all worried about our kids."

"Don't believe the official spiel given out by Briggs and Banaker, that all is right in the Andover world? Now, why do I not find that hard to believe?"

"Take that car accident the other day," said one of the men, Herman Curtis.

"What about it, Mr. Curtis?" asked Stroud. "What's it got to do with anything?"

"They said there was a woman in the car, but the only body found was a man's."

"They located the body of the driver?"

"Yeah, and none too pretty a sight."

"Broken neck," said Phil Loomis who was getting into Stroud's Jeep now. "Terrible gashes from having gone through the windshield."

"Not the windshield, the side window," Carroll corrected Loomis. "Odd way to get thrown from the car."

"And white . . . Jesus . . . never saw such white on a man," added Curtis. "I was happening by when they pulled him outa the water."

"White, huh?"

"Bleach white."

"Like clean paper," said Loomis.

"Water does that to a body," said Carroll.

Stroud knew there was some truth in what Carroll said, but the body hadn't been in the water long enough to turn it so thoroughly white as these men were describing. On the other hand, men looking on death created horror out of it.

"Looking still for the woman. She'll show up. Spoon always delivers 'em up, sooner or later," said Carroll.

"Sounds like there are a lot of accidents along the river," said Stroud.

Carroll nodded. "We get our share all right."

Stroud got in and revved up the motor. "Maybe we oughta be looking for the woman instead of the dog."

"Briggs and the State Patrol have it covered," said Carroll, whose vehicle lurched and turned out of the circle drive before Stroud Manse. Stroud tore out after him, leaving it to Carroll to pick the jumping off point when the land vehicles would leave the road and start over rough terrain.

Beside him, a near useless twenty-two carbine in his hands, Loomis lit up a cigarette and began small talk.

"Hear you were a cop in Chicago? Hear you were in Nam? Is it true you're staying on in Andover? People figured you'd sell out quick and never look back."

"Loomis."

"Yeah?"

"Where you from, around here?"

"Grew up in South Bend, Indiana. Moved here about . . . going on six years now. Wife and kids—got three. My boy and Ray's are best of friends, inseparable. Tell you this, I'd go nuts out of my skull if my boy just disappeared like the Meyers kid done and the Cooper kid before him."

"Any other disappearances, before the Cooper kid, I mean?"

"Naw . . . nice place to live before all this . . . 'cept . . . " He became quiet.

"Except what?"

"I heard something about some disappearances in sixty-six."

There it was again, 1966.

—12—

The night search churned up a lot of ground, but in the end the men were forced to face the fact they were wasting fuel and their time. At one point Loomis wanted to know why the goddamned dog was so important to Stroud. Stroud replied succinctly, "I'd like to have the dog to study. The markings on the boy were unusual. If the same animal got at the dog, maybe an expert could tell us what this so-called Andover Devil actually is."

"Oh, so you've heard the legend," replied Carroll.

"My house servants told me something about it."

"Well, I'm for callin' it a night," said Curtis, yawning.

"Andover Devil's been blamed for every poisoned cat, every lost dog, and slaughtered beef in the county," said Carroll.

"You get a lot of that?" asked Stroud, taking a pull on a bottle of Jack Daniels that Loomis offered up. "Cut up beef, I mean."

"Just passing hobos, bums on bikes. They'll kill a whole cow for one night's steak," said Curtis.

"We haven't tried the caverns," said Carroll.

"Caverns?" asked Stroud. "Oh, yeah . . . seem to recall that there are some caves and caverns hereabouts."

"They're a long ways from here, Ray. The boy was found in this area. How'd he get all the way over here if his dog and he were attacked way over at the caverns?"

"I don't know, Loomis. Just thinking out loud."

"It's past midnight now," said Stroud. Maybe we'd better call it a night, Ray."

"Hell, the night's young," said Curtis.

"We'd best head back," said Carroll. "The wives'll be worried as it is."

"You sure are trussed up with those apron strings, Ray!" said Curtis, laughing good-naturedly.

Loomis piped in with, "With what Ray's got at the end of those apron strings, Curtis, you'd better believe he ain't goin' far."

Stroud felt the friendship among these men. They were good men and like himself they'd been confused by the Meyers event and the Cooper incident. They were afraid, but also afraid to show their fear; showing it, just talking about it made them jumpy. Denial was their mainstay and defense. Stroud understood such men. He'd served with such men in Vietnam.

"Let's pack up then."

"Tomorrow maybe we'll get an earlier start, get out to the caverns," said Carroll, "have a look around there for any signs of the dog."

It had gone unspoken among them—they weren't here for the dog; they wanted nothing more than to locate Ronnie Cooper's remains. Stroud still believed that if there was a beast out here in the surrounding darkness, a man-eater that got its jollies from terrorizing people, that the beast, unmasked, standing naked, stripped to its skin, would be of the human variety. Most beasts were.

Stroud drove back to the manse alone, as the others all lived in a cluster of homes in a subdivision in Andover aptly named The Hamlet. They were just down from the Meyers place which faced an empty field that led to another and another until one came to the interstate. It was in one of these fields that the bones were uncovered. Stroud wondered what was being done to restore the graveyard and if it would be done haphazardly by contractors with backhoes or properly by concerned citizens of the Andover Historical Society.

He was almost to the manse when suddenly a red convertible sports car cut in front of him from nowhere, blocking his path, making him screech to a halt. In his headlights he saw that it was Pamela Carr and she wasn't wearing a white lab coat. She'd done a full one hundred and eighty degrees, dressed in a black evening gown with teasing red bra straps peeking through.

She got out of her car seductively, letting the door close behind her. She moved toward him with a look in her eye that meant he was hers. Her long colored nails curled up at him, inviting him out.

Stroud shook his head and got out of his Jeep. "Unbelievable . . . unbelievable. How long've you been waiting for me to come by here?"

"Talked with your Mr. Ashyer. He told me you'd be late. I don't mind waiting if it's for a good thing."

God, she was fast. He liked it on the one hand, but he had only known hookers in Chicago and Vietnam to be so forward, and for this reason he wasn't completely thrilled by her. And yet her eyes held him as they did that first time their eyes met, and when she reached out to him he didn't feel strong enough to fend her off. He wasn't sure he wanted to.

They embraced just standing there between the car and Jeep on the empty expanse of road, alone. But Stroud didn't feel alone; he felt as if they were being watched. Was this all some sort of elaborate setup? Who was out there, just beyond the reach of his eyes? He could almost hear them—*them*—it seemed to him there were hundreds of eyes trained on him and Pamela as she worked her body into his, nipping at his chest where she'd torn open the shirt.

"God, you drive me crazy," she told him in a husky voice, the odor of musk rising off her like that of a wild animal. "Can't stand it any longer," she told him, dropping to her knees and tearing away at his fly.

"Christ, Pam, not here . . . not like this," he protested. How damned horny was she?

He pulled her to her feet, returning her kisses, suggesting they go to his place. She blanched at the idea, saying she couldn't wait a moment longer. She lit into him again and he held tight, troubled, feeling as if she were on something. Again, the faint whispers in the darkness all around them. Was it the wind through the trees?

God, she was taking his clothes off piece by piece.

Whispers . . . distinct whispers, as if an audience were watching. Then he wondered about Curtis, Loomis, and Ray Carroll; might they've doubled back to follow him at a distance? Maybe they'd come to a halt when he did, and were now inching closer and closer for the floor—or *road*—show.

But just then all his questions were answered. He now saw the cause of the whispers and rustling. He saw a bevy of black-winged southern Illinois rodents rising on battling limbs to nearby treetops.

It was too dark to see from where they originated, but there were countless numbers of the feeding little beasts fluttering and flapping wildly, romping on the air currents after insects. Bats . . . bats fleeing into the night from nowhere. There had to be a nearby cave in those ridges in the distance. He thought of the old song *The Night Has a Thousand Eyes*.

She smothered his mouth with hers, tearing out his tongue with hers, biting it, drawing a taste of blood.

"Rough sex," she whispered in his ear. "You like it rough? Like me to nip you elsewhere? Want to feel it? Feel it?"

"Pamela," he said, trying to get control of her.

She dropped from his mouth to his throat and sank her teeth into his neck at the curvature where it met the right shoulder. The pain was instant and yet over as quickly as the intense flash of a camera. And then it was good. She was on him and he wanted her to be on him. She was sucking savagely at the punctures, salivating and making a rubbery-lipped noise as he, passive and blank, lay back under her weight with feelings of intense pleasure and pain, light and dark, good and evil mingling all in one. It was a sexual act like none he'd ever known, violent, shattering, and somewhere deep within his mind Abe Stroud wanted two things: he wanted not to stop her and he wanted her to kill him with her intense desire for him. No one had ever made him feel this way: so wanted, so needed. She made it clear to him that he, and he alone, nourished her need. . . .

Faint . . . fainter . . . faintest and *nothing* with a smile on his lips . . . strong, powerful, ex-Marine, ex-cop, she reduced him to nothing, and he welcomed the reduction.

Then everything went black.

It did not need to feed. It had not come to feed, only to watch with the enormous eyes of the wolf from deep within the cover of darkness. It had plenty of nourishment and did not require more. Tonight's hunt was of another kind. Tonight it watched the men in their machines, crisscrossing its territory, coming so close to it that it could look down on them with a sneer, smile, and think of them as future meat grazing upon ground that would belong to it forever.

At one point it grew tired of watching the hunters until it felt a sudden deep sickness from within, a fear that came whenever Stroud was near. It hadn't at first realized that Stroud was with them, but now it knew.

The form of the wolf was replaced quickly by that of the rolling green fog that it created of itself—its essence. It was the essence of decay, the same essence that fed the great many crawling creatures on its own body—the hangers-on. It fed these bloodsuckers with its own supply of blood, was mother and father to them. They'd spawned inside it: ticks, worms, weevils, fleas. The insects reciprocated in a variety of ways, spreading disabling and sometimes mesmerizing diseases to humans which in turn helped it to feed itself. It was as symbiotic a relationship as nature—*or the unnatural*—had ever devised. It had stood the test of time.

White worms that were spawned at the rectus, created of its organs, and a constant reminder of what it was—a being that defied death—also enjoyed being fed when it caught its prey. They then helped in cocooning up the leavings where it hung them in caves.

The one that spawned all such maggots, of course, was the ruler of all darkness, the thing itself—the Andover Devil, Banaker's own creation gone awry, the one part of him that he'd been unable to control.

It toured the night in its cloak of fog, skimming over the earth like a spirit, perching over the Spoon and running its ethereal atoms along its course, ruler of all that it surveyed. It knew of Stroud as the name had been passed through the generations of its forebears as the cause of much calamity. It must see Stroud dead this night, and for this it had come hunting.

When it happened on the puny humans with their guns and landrovers, it hadn't at first felt Stroud's presence. When it did, it was as if it could feel a pounding of several blows to its most vital organ, the heart, kept alive by its unquenchable thirst for blood—the heart revived from death and created from death in this case. Its parentage had been pure-blood vampires, which made it the child of death. Death had made love to death and it was spawned. Now it was here to take from life, to feed on life. But Stroud worried it where it waited in the dark. Stroud made it fear for its own existence.

It had raced from Stroud's party, not wishing to force an encounter, knowing that Stroud was strong and that he possessed magical means and capabilities that could penetrate its otherwise impenetrable strength. Why not leave Stroud to Banaker? To Banaker and to the lovely Pamela Carr?

But even if it left Stroud to this certain end, it wanted to watch. So it had perched high in a tree to do exactly this. The fog of its being had coalesced into the winged creature that was larger than any bat ever depicted by human naturalists or human imagination. And so it hung there, suspended, sightless. The eyes of the minions living upon it searched the night as it searched with its echo-location equipment.

It became confused when Pamela took Stroud in her embrace, for its side to side sonar received the message back that she'd broken off her attack! It located Stroud on the ground and she doubled over on the road. It was confused. They should be locked in Stroud's death throes together, she taking his essence into her. But something unforeseen had occurred. Stroud had worked some magician's trick to dislodge her from the hold she had on him and he was now crawling away from her, wounded but still very much alive, his body in roiling spasms.

It waited, sent out more echoes. She was, it could tell, aware of its presence but unsure just which of her kith and kin was watching.

It held on, patient, waiting . . . waiting . . . fearful of interference at this time for more reason than who Stroud was.

Then it began to receive images, movement down there on the road to Stroud Manse. Patience, it told itself, patience of demons.

—13—

When Stroud awoke, he was in the ditch beside the road, face-down, rough, sawing blades of grass cutting at him, a cold chill in his bones and a feeling of aloneness in his heart. But he heard and felt the patter of many living things around him, from insects in the undergrowth to screeching birds awakened and taking flight. Rushing life in disarray, flapping in all directions, including the skies: *the bats*?

He moaned with the internal weakness he felt. It was as if he'd gone consecutive days and nights without sleep or rest, so drained was he. It was as if he'd given back to back transfusions.

He sensed he was alone in the ditch, left for dead. He tried to turn himself over but his arms and legs were twisted and gnarled. At the same time, he didn't have any goddamned strength in his limbs.

With force of will rather than muscle, he rocked himself in the high grass until he turned, his legs cascading open like budding flowers. His hands hurt, his fingers were pinched and crossed. He'd been hit by his infamous seizure while Pamela was making love to him.

"Damn . . . oh, God . . . no," he moaned. The bite to the neck, the sudden vampire attack she made upon him . . . all a sick vision brought on by his own lunatic mind.

But when he opened his eyes she was there, *standing* over him, not kneeling, and her tone was like that of a truck driver.

"Goddamn you . . . you bastard . . . what sort of disease do you have? Is it contagious? Well, is it? You might've warned me! Do you have AIDS, Stroud? Do you, damn it? Oh, my Lord . . . my blood's contaminated, isn't it?"

"No, Pam, I don't have AIDS, and you can quit worrying about your blue blood. Will you help me up, please?"

"You went . . . you went crazy. Look at the bruises you brought up on me." She showed him her elbow and knee where they'd been scraped. "I thought you were going to hurt me."

"More likely to hurt myself in such a seizure."

"Seizure? Is it . . . you know . . . a hereditary thing?"

The question made him think of the mad Ezeekial Stroud and of his recent discoveries about his Grandfather Ananias as well. "I think, Pamela, we'd better call it a night. Don't know about you, but I . . . I kinda lost the mood."

She nodded and he saw vomit alongside the pavement, vomit that looked unnaturally bloody and yellow, almost like afterbirth, there on the roadbed. "I got a little sick," she mewed.

"I'm sorry." He wound up apologizing to her now as he got into his Jeep. "I should've done this to begin with," he told her, revving up the engine and cutting around her sports car, driving down, and then out of the ditch where he'd been lying. He stopped short just the other side of her car and backed up to shout, "Not that you're likely to need it, or take it, Pam, but I'm going to give you a bit of advice."

She was getting into her car at this point. "Advice?"

"Go a little slower in your next romantic adventure; you know, give a guy a chance to ask you to dinner, maybe pluck a rose for you, take you home to a cozy fire and an upstairs bed."

"I'm sorry, Abe . . . "

"You going to be safe? Get home all right from here?"

She laughed at this. "I'm a big girl."

"So I noticed."

"You're sure now . . . it's not a blood disease?"

This returned him to the anger he'd felt on waking to find her more concerned with her scraped elbow than his condition. She could no more love anyone than a boa constrictor loved anyone, he realized, knowing he did not want to see Pamela Carr ever again.

Abe's wheels burned rubber on the old paved road as he raced for the confines of Stroud Manse. Maybe it was a great deal safer behind bars there; maybe Grandfather Ananias had ought to've left the bars up all 'round the place.

Stroud momentarily wondered just what kind of doctor Pamela Carr was going to become after her residency at Banaker Institute. A medical professional so completely ignorant of the symptoms of AIDS, not to mention her morbid fear, was unusual. And yet, as a cop in Chicago he'd known many a nurse who'd dropped out of the profession out of just such fears. But this did not explain her revulsion at the convulsions she'd witnessed in him to the point of becoming physically ill. She'd make a lousy physician at best.

The iron gates of home came into his view just as he drove through a wave of fog. Stroud reached up to his throat, feeling something thick and damp clinging there. The white, maggoty leech that he touched there and which now discolored his hand with a red trail curled up and died. His neck was bleeding from a painful, deep incision of some sort. Pamela had cut him and had left him the bizarre prize of the leech.

The mad, convulsive fit that Dr. Stroud had gone through had both terrified and revolted Pamela Carr. One moment she was on the rhythmic sway of his blood as it flowed into her through the tubes at the center of her fangs, and the next he was twisting out of her control. He had overpowered her with bruising blows and kicking. She had been completely unprepared for his sudden surge of strength, as if he were immune to the hypnosis of the vampiress.

She now feared the consequences of not having dispatched Stroud as Dr. Banaker had wanted. But it was not her fault, she silently counseled herself. She'd only just begun the deadly transfusion when he, in a blind rage, reacted in so startling a manner as to throw her into a paroxysm of fear. She'd heard tales all her unnatural life of human disease and decay and how disease was spread among Stroud's kind. Suppose his convulsions were the symptoms of some dreaded disorder, and suppose even a vampiress like herself could catch it? According to Banaker, the vampire gene had been suffocated by human disorders, diseases that caused the introduction of aging into the lives of vampires, for instance. Banaker told cautionary tales, and he knew the history of his kind. He explained that those born to vampire parents were purer of heart, purer of the contaminates of mankind, than those, like her, who had not been born a vampire. Pamela had been *made* a vampire by Banaker, who had reclaimed her from an early grave, sharing his vampire genes and his vampire blood with her beautiful, young form.

Some vampires, like Dolphin for instance, believed since a vampire was by definition a walking dead, that no disease could touch him, that he was immortal by virtue of being a vampire. *Nothing could be further from the truth.* Vampires were given to severe depression and a weakening of their energies, and like addicts, the only cure was a blood binge.

It was, according to Banaker, through the arrogance of the race and the arrogance of such youths as Dolphin that vampires had become near extinct, because they had had their bloodline diluted over the generations, and infected by the host of human disorders that accompanied living in the midst of their prey.

A creature of Satan, feeding on carrion that was tainted, no less than a bird that swallows a diseased insect, might survive, but over generations and generations, the chemistry of the vampire had slowly given way to human frailties. One of these was *aging*, a problem Banaker was frantically attempting to correct through a research project the U.S. government had no idea it was funding.

Although the aging process in a pire was far slower than in his human counterpart, the days of vampires who lived to see successive generations come and go, were gone. Unless Banaker could succeed in fully restoring the primal vampire gene back to its original state.

As for vampires like her, Pamela's bones had grown and she had reached maturity only through the miracles wrought by Banaker. She was dug from her grave as a child of nine, dead of meningitis. He had literally raised her from the dead, creating of her not a vampire born of pire parentage, but a bastardization of his kind. Yet, he had always treated her as if she were a daughter, until now . . . until Stroud had arrived. Now he had used her like a whore.

Banaker had frequently warned her of the horrid possibilities of feeding directly from the human host, that she must feed on the elixir distilled at the Institute, where the blood was fortified with the vampire strain, screened and tested and purified. She'd never fed on a man like Abraham Stroud before, a man going into an epileptic type of seizure in the throes of her passionate vampiric embrace. It had so shocked her.

It had therefore been natural for her to instantly let go of the bite, repulsed by the twisted human form at the other end.

These thoughts and more weaved through her mind as she pictured herself in Banaker's office the next morning trying to explain the unexpected end to the evening. She went toward her own car, preparing to leave. The red was a purple under the cover of darkness, the white interior a soft beige. She was given the car by Banaker, her mentor and her "father." Pamela Carr's headstone still stood at the Andover Memorial Gardens Cemetery on Dunne near Sycamore, on the outskirts of Andover. Sometimes, when she'd visit she'd stand before the tombstone and read the chiseled lettering and wonder about the little girl who'd died so many years before. The headstone read:

> Susan Marie Muncie
> Beloved Daughter
> 1947—1956

Beside this headstone were other people named Muncie, Susan's parents. Pamela was drawn to the spot even as a child, although none of the others had ever told her that Susan Marie Muncie and Pamela Carr were one and the same—at least in body. No one needed to tell her.

Her life was the life of the recycled body. It was not so cowardly an existence, after all, and the torturous hunger was controllable, so long as she got her supply. And she got that supply, like all the others, from Banaker. She owed her life to Banaker. There was no failing him . . . and yet, she had failed him miserably tonight.

She opened her car door, but the sound of a beating wind made her look up just in time to see the massive black cloud blotting out the sky overhead. Her inner sonar told her that it—he, Banaker—was coming for her.

She must either face him here, like this, or flee. She'd failed him most certainly, and she expected his wrath, but she did not expect his punishment to come in this form and so swiftly. Why had he chosen to approach her in his most sinister and threatening aspect? When a vampire concealed himself in a black fog created via the cold breath stored in its lungs, it was *stalking*.

It came like an animal, creeping toward her. It intended to show itself as it truly was: a huge, carnivorous bat with hard, unseeing black eyes, peaked ears, and fangs twice the size of any snake's—a creature blessed by Satan, that picked its way about with sonar so accurate that it could reach down with its massive talons to rip off her head or hoist her to its mouth to slowly drain life from her.

Was this Banaker coming?

But he had worked so tirelessly and long to create a community of Pires who could live in mutual harmony and peace with humankind, going undetected among them. She thought of all the grueling years of service that she had spent in helping fulfill the goals of Banaker's Institute, thought of the years of lab work, searching endlessly for better and better blood additives, preservatives, and substitutes. She'd been there when the discovery came on withstanding sunlight. She recalled the experiments with the cross. She helped on fund raisers and drives, and saw to it that the monies were diverted instead to the study of rare blood disorders and poor strains among her kind, and how to improve the stock. She recalled the breakthrough in the DNA lab. They'd been testing a theory of Banaker's: that bone marrow held many of the ingredients for vampire needs. Banaker was proved right. He'd been ecstatic for days over the discovery.

Once this discovery was made, all the Pires in a position to help were summoned to do so. They then went about the process of accessing the human bone marrow—throwaway stuff at death— to support the colony as never before.

Banaker was working toward the day when his brethren could live on a self-replicating supply of his blood elixir, eliminating the need to ever again feed off mankind. He believed that Pires could prosper if they were independent of the human race, and it could be done through careful generations of gene splicing. In his quest, Dr. Banaker had had to unearth literally hundreds of bodies in order to extract the marrow from the bones. He preferred the bones of children because these carried the most marrow, but he and his crews, working among the surrounding graveyards, were not above taking the bones of any long dead human, including the parents of Susan Marie Muncie.

But Banaker's Institute provided a safe haven for the Pires' study; it provided the distillery and distribution center for Banaker's elixir. Human patients provided much needed raw materials. From time to time, the morgue provided a place to party, a place to vent off steam and primitive emotions and needs. The "venting," as Dr. Banaker called it, was helped along by a vagrant body coming in off the street.

So why was he risking everything now in a wanton, cannibalistic manner, going about a feeding frenzy that was leaving Andover in shock at the disappearances of children and others? Why was he now coming for her?

No time for further speculation, she threw up her own defenses, beginning with her own inner vibrations—a nerve-center antennae. It began quivering warnings both inwardly to herself, and outwardly to her would-be attacker. She bared her fangs to the threat. This display also showed the crawling, white worms that lived on her gums and below her tongue. She snarled and began to metamorphose, knowing she hadn't a chance now of fleeing in a car or on foot. Her shape began to change as her eyes met those in the black fog now directly over her.

She dispensed with any hope of creating and hiding within her own fog. Her only hope now lay in evasion and speed. She felt the familiar bumpy, ribbed furls of skin peel away from her back, arms, and legs, bursting and splitting the tight dress she wore. Small coarse hair sprouted from every pore, covering her body. Each of her fingers and thumbs elongated, the bone going elastic and hollow for speed, for the duration of the change. She feared, as always, that her internal organs would burst like her clothing with the difficult task of change required in the cellular structure. Her skin became leather under the dark mat of hair. Webbed folds of rubbery skin spread in sheets between distended, high-knuckled fingers. Each finger was now the length of her former forearm.

She lifted into flight, but it was too late as she was suddenly hit from out of the fog by a thousand bats. Was Banaker controlling them? She screamed as the multitude of lesser creatures took delight in effecting their thousand bites, drawing blood from so many wounds at once that she was quickly weakened. Her vampire body was carried along by the throng of bats feeding on her.

Each plunged its small incisive hole in her, each took its fill until she was blanketed with them. They then dropped her, as if on command, and she plummeted in her weakened condition until the powerful thud of her weight against the earth knocked her into stupor which was, mercifully, without pain.

Bruised and broken, her tough skin was now matted with blood from a thousand rabid bites. She reached out for something solid to take hold of in her attempt to pull herself to her knees. But she could feel nothing.

Punishment had come swiftly, surely. She prayed it was over, that Banaker had had his evil fun. She felt now the rents and gashes to her face acutely, although she bled from every part of her body. She lapped at the red tears of her wounds in a pathetic attempt to replace her blood as quickly as it was fleeing. But the weakness and the numbness were too much to overcome.

She soundly cursed Banaker. "May the God of the human, the God of Susan Marie Muncie, damn you, Banaker!"

With this curse she lay back on her broken wings and her eyes locked on the conical, black form that hugged the treetops over her. There he was, the Andover Devil, controller of mist, shape-changer, the thing that spanned life and death itself. Here was Banaker, the evil genius, the marvel of evolution that had been born of a creature like himself.

For a flashing instant, Pamela remembered her other life with her true parents. It had been a short life, but one filled with love, cut short by a childhood disease. She realized for the first time that her new life was a sham, that the eternal life Banaker had led her into was not eternal after all. It was in fact moments away from coming to a torturous end.

Yet, somehow, she was at peace, feeling relieved that it would be done. It was as if some greater power lie on the other side and was now extending a gift to her. She couldn't move, but she reached up, not for Banaker, but for the gift she saw shining beyond him. She *felt* for the first time since her natural death— truly felt. All this was going on deep within her even as the creature moved in closer, preying on her while attempting to convince her that this was, after all, what she wanted in the first place. It was trying to wrench her from her gift and the dreamy thought of life after death after life again, was trying to manipulate her affection to center on it. But she refused it this last bit of emotional carrion.

It took her anyway. . . .

Only at the last minute, as it took her in its great talons, did the broken Pamela Carr see that it wasn't Banaker who had done this to her. It closed her off to her senses then, as it, too, partook of her blood. As it lifted her into itself, the membrane of skin extending down from its wrists stretched around her, creating a cocoon. Other fingerlike talons formed struts for the larger talons, and these stretched back to the trailing edge of the membrane. Only the thumb remained free, an enormous knuckle, peculiarly human in quality and appearance. A kind of keel lie along the creature's breast bone, serving as an attachment for the large muscles which flapped its wings.

With elaborate, translucent ears, the ribbed cartilage was laced with scarlet blood vessels. On its nose there stood a spike used to direct the sonar sounds it made.

Through echo-location it had found her and now took hold of her. Like a shrew, it emitted ultra-sound waves which bounced off its prey. It had known precisely where Pamela was at all times, and that she was one of its own kind.

At least, it thought as it was feeding on her, she was *partially* one of them. Her parents hadn't been vampires.

A successful hunt had ended with its having lifted its prey from its talons to its fangs, once again, quenching an age-old hunger, a hunger that came with birth, the genes, heredity. The feeding caused momentary blindness in the bat creature. In order to feed, it must shut down its mouth, and so shut down its "eyes." It fed in its own darkness when its fifty-million-year-old larynx must be put on hold.

Pamela's eyes were wide. She had recognized him in the end. He drew her deeper into his folds, holding her lovingly and firmly against himself as he continued to feed the hunger. His prey had relaxed into that catatonic state that insured his feasting would go on and on.

The creature now spewed out a wet, elastic string of matter from his mouth. The gummy, white stuff stiffened in the air and on contact with his prey. As if wrapping a mummy, the creature worked with the shape of Pamela's body to encircle it with the hardening material. He meant to truly cocoon her for future feedings.

All in all, it had become a fruitful night. Now only if he could put the name Abraham Stroud out of his mind.

—14—

Dr. Martin Magaffey paced the sitting room at Stroud Manse, anxiously awaiting Stroud's return. The Ashyers watched him pace. All of them drank tea, but none of them actually tasted or enjoyed it. Magaffey was obviously distraught and fatigue had almost kept him from coming the long way out here, but his brain was brimming over with what Dr. Cooper had left in his hands.

"You're sure of your findings, Doctor?" asked Ashyer getting up to guide the older man to a sofa chair.

"Where the hell is Stroud?" replied Magaffey irritably. "If I sit down, I'll go right off to sleep."

"We can wake you, Martin," said Mrs. Ashyer kindly.

He ignored this and answered Mr. Ashyer instead. "I was all day at the Banaker Institute. Ananias was right to suspect the Banakers all those years. Warlock he called the old man, sorcerer."

"He finally settled on vampire," said Ashyer with a shiver.

"Only now we might have the proof, Ashyer, don't you see? Supplied to us by Cooper!"

"But how did Cooper come by this so-called proof?"

Magaffey took in a deep breath and told them how he had spent most of his day searching for the body of a man named James Bradley. "As coroner of Andover, it's my job, for God's sake. Bradley was pulled from the Spoon some six, maybe seven hours after his car went off into the river. He'd come off an embankment

121

at a high rate of speed according to the police report. I . . . I was not sent for."

"Briggs thought it routine, perhaps."

Magaffey laughed at this. "Briggs's mind is routine." Magaffey continued, afire. "What bothers me is how the whole matter's been mishandled. Any sudden or mysterious death, hell! any accidental death, is to be placed in my care! Not the goddamned morgue at Banaker Institute!"

Mrs. Ashyer tried to calm him with a buttery word and more tea.

But he would not be calmed. "The attending physician did an autopsy and hadn't bothered to call me in; nor has a report of the findings crossed my desk!"

"Highly irregular," said Ashyer.

"Lately, my friend, it has become all too common. But this time, I wasn't going to let the bastards—sorry, Mrs. Ashyer—keep me from my duty. I went there demanding to see the body and the report. For some time it was 'lost!' Paperwork didn't exist on the corpse. They kept me waiting for over an hour before the paper appeared—hastily got up it seemed to me. I never did see the body there—it was already gone—and I felt like the focal point of . . .well . . . a conspiracy."

"Where had the body gone?"

"Carl Hoff's Funeral Parlor downtown, *Christ*! By now the place was closing, but I found one of Hoff's people and was told the body was being prepared for transportation to Bradley's home by mid-morning tomorrow, at the request of the Bradley family.

" 'Don't do a damned thing to that body until I inspect it!' I told him. 'The body is from this moment confiscated by the Office of the Coroner.'

" 'But it's finished, Dr. Magaffey,' the man said.

" 'Finished?' I asked.

" 'All but broke the Perma-Glow machine down on him. Mr. Hoff said it was a rush job.' " Magaffey scowled at the memory.

Ashyer shook his head. "So, they removed all the bodily fluids, the blood, so any autopsy you might perform would be useless."

"True, but they can't cover marks and gashes. I inspected the body for these, and I saw marks I have not seen since . . . since Ananias came in that night from the caves."

The Ashyers fell silent, looking across at one another.

"If I could somehow hold onto the body, but Banaker and Hoff were called as I was looking over Bradley's wounds—deformities, actually . . . like those horrible rents and tears that had maimed Lonnie and Ananias. I knew I must flee or quite possibly face Banaker and Hoff over the body that they meant to be a 'rush job.' "

"You then went home?"

"With a few photos and scrappings from the dead man, yes." He showed Ashyer the photos, but Ashyer handed them back with a visible shiver, not wishing his wife to see them.

"And that is when Cooper came to you?"

"I was in my lab when the bell rang. He asked to come in. He seemed a bundle of nerves, but how could I tell? I was shaking for my own reasons. I didn't easily welcome him in. Cooper seemed afraid to stand out on the doorstep. He had a small leather case in his hand."

"The vial? It was in the case?"

"Yes. He opened it under the light and I had an almost instinctive dislike for it as the light hit it when he held it up. I felt certain he'd brought it as a poison for me to drink, to please Banaker."

"Tell us, in detail," said Ashyer, "what happened next?"

Magaffey was fatigued by the long, arduous day that had become an even longer night. He was drained from the many run-ins he'd had with Banaker and his people, and the royal runaround he'd gotten when investigating the whereabouts of the body dragged from the river.

Magaffey was also very shaken and fearful since the visit paid him by Dr. Cooper. Magaffey's brief talk with the Ashyers must now convince them that they must all confide in the younger Stroud everything they knew.

Magaffey thought of Dr. Cooper's peculiar visit to him in the night. Cooper had come to him with a strange vial filled with an admixture of blood and bone marrow, and a genetic substance which he was deliberately vague about. Dr. Magaffey told the Ashyers all this. Cooper had called the stuff Banaker's lifeblood.

Dr. Magaffey had taken the vial in hand, and he had held it up to the intense light there in his laboratory. It did not look like blood, but rather like thick tomato soup or even jello. Aside from the consistency, the color was a deep, near purple, the way red looks in the dark.

"It's the fountain of youth, eternal life," Cooper had then muttered under his breath.

"It looks like bile," replied Magaffey.

"Think of it! Has Oliver Banaker aged a day?"

Magaffey had noticed as much over the years, but he had remained skeptical. "Why're you here, Cooper? Why've you brought this to me?"

"I . . . I . . ."

"Did your boss send you? Make a fool of the old nigger? Is that it?"

"I have . . . my—"

"Why're you being so helpful, so cooperative, Cooper?"

"I have my reasons!"

"Your boy? That's your reason?"

"*Yes!*"

The look of pain creasing Cooper's features at that moment could not be falsified. Magaffey was fearful of pushing the man any further, and yet, he was confused by Cooper's motives, and he wondered what Cooper had to gain by discrediting Banaker, and why'd he direct his anger at Banaker? Had Banaker something to do with the disappearance of Cooper's son? Magaffey had looked up to see that Cooper was on the verge of a suicidal depression. He'd gone steadily downhill since the loss of his son—what in the old days the boys called being "on the skids."

Magaffey had gotten numerous favors out of Cooper recently, such as getting in to see the Meyers boy. Cooper had been equally mysterious then about his reasons, but it all seemed a vendetta of sorts against Banaker. Banaker had lost grace with at least one of his flock.

"I got to get out of here now. Place is dangerous for me," said Cooper, who'd lost weight by the day and was a walking skeleton, totally emaciated, pale, bone white.

"I quit taking the stuff," he said to Magaffey as if reading his mind. "Fighting the cravings . . . fasting . . . not long for this place, Doctor. Pam Carr . . . "

Magaffey instantly picked up on the sudden shift in his tone. It was one of fear. "What about Pamela?"

"She was put on Stroud to . . . to . . . "

"Seduce him? By Banaker? Keep him engaged, huh?"

"She's gone now."

"Gone? Gone where?"

"Left, gone . . . won't be back."

"Left Andover?"

"I'll be next, but I'll choose my own way out."

He then left abruptly, leaving the old man with the vial, an elixir that represented all that Banaker Institute had worked for over the years, according to Cooper. He'd hinted that test animals and human test subjects had died for the drink that gave Banaker and others a chance at godhood. He'd hinted that his son had died for Banaker's sins.

How much Magaffey could believe in the bereaved man's words, he was not sure.

He would hold his conclusions for later, after a look under his microscope at the thick, dark fluid in the vial. To keep it from contact with the air, he'd use a specialized slide that was created for such instances to keep a substance germ-free.

Under the slide he saw a teeming variety of cells that resembled those of human blood, but the white corpuscles were a dim, ghostly brown and the red corpuscles were a dark burgundy. A third viruslike cell impregnated the others with a dousing of inky fluid like miniature octopuses sending out blasts of ink, turning the corpuscles, both red and white, into some new, unrestrained cell that forged a bond. It was like nothing in nature he had ever seen, except for some slides a veterinarian had once shown him years and years ago of a bat's blood.

He then saw that the specimen was becoming superheated under the intense light of the microscope. It reacted very much like the blood of a cold-blooded animal.

He then tested it in the presence of oxygen to see if Cooper was telling the truth. Using only a pinhead dot of the elixir, he forced it onto a white cloth on a lab table. It burst like a firecracker, turning the cloth to flame. Yet, it had none of the properties of an acid.

Magaffey didn't know quite what to make of it. He tried to imagine the effects of swallowing this stuff. It made him think of Jekyll and Hyde. He wondered if he dared experiment on himself.

Given his age and the "little problem" besetting him, an elixir of youth was most tempting. But he had read Hawthorne's tale of the roomful of fools who'd gotten their hands on such an elixir and turned back time only to make the same sordid and idiotic mistakes they'd made the first time around, and so decided to withhold such a dram from himself, and his own bone marrow disease.

Instead he cocked an ear to the door outside his lab. Someone was puttering around outside. His secretary and nurse had long gone and he was in the building alone. He fought the fearful notion that someone from Banaker Institute had followed Cooper here, and was now prepared to retake the fluid at any cost—including an old fool's life. Magaffey knew no other way than what was normal for him, however. Despite the fact there were two other avenues out of the lab, one to a telephone and the other to a fire escape, he did what Martin Magaffey had done all his life. He pushed through to the outer offices with a barreling cry, "Who the hell's lurking around out here!"

It was Cooper, returned. But now he was again rushing quickly out the door. He'd left a note on the desk but it had taken leaflike flight in his haste to get away. Magaffey had seen the man agitated before, but now his entire body was quaking; he was literally shaking in the manner of a junkie denied the succor of his habit. Had Banaker turned him into a guinea pig, using the strange, brackish fluid? Was Cooper coming down hard? Did he need someone at his side, observation?

Martin Magaffey raced out after the man but he was gone, swallowed up by the dark of midnight. It was uncanny how he'd disappeared so thoroughly, as Magaffey had a view of the street that was completely clear of obstruction. The only thing he saw and heard was the faint shadow of a flying rodent! A bat! Magaffey hated the things, and for good reason. This particular one squealed a faint stuttering cry before it dashed itself through some unseeable crack in the fabric of the city's skyline. The thought of an Andover bat in his own attic made him shiver.

He returned to his offices and almost stepped on the paper that'd flown from the desk. He picked it up and read Cooper's shaky handwriting:

> By the time you read this I'll be gone. Nothing matters to me anymore, not here, not without Ronnie. The bones were dug up for the marrow. The marrow is needed to make Banaker's bloody drink.

The bones, the missing marrow . . . Magaffey rushed to his file on the tests he'd run and the conclusions he had come to on the bones. He'd hidden the copy of the results before the theft of the bones and his original paperwork. In some bizarre way, things were beginning to take on a strange shape. It harkened back to the time when Ananias Stroud was alive. It terrified old Martin Magaffey. Not so much did he fear for himself as for Andover and the valley and beyond; he feared for his own eternal soul, and he feared for those of countless others.

• • •

Fatigue had overcome Magaffey when Abraham Stroud found him asleep in the drawing room surrounded by the Ashyers who looked as though they were at a wake.

"You're home, sir!" said Ashyer, causing Magaffey to stir in fitful sleep.

Stroud could almost hear Magaffey's dream; he certainly sensed the man's stark, lurid hatred of himself.

Stroud silenced Ashyer with a finger to his lips, staring at Magaffey, trying desperately to understand the strange, troubled black doctor.

Then he began to see images as if playing on a screen in his mind. Somehow he was in telepathic agreement with Magaffey's torment.

In the fitful sleep there on the chair, images of the past flooded into his and Magaffey's mind like water. Was it the house at work again, the ghosts? Had they somehow learned to use Stroud's distorted brain to send messages through from beyond?

For a brief time he and Magaffey were one. Magaffey's awful dream was his awful dream, and for the first time he understood Magaffey.

Maybe he'd chosen to forget, to look the other way, not daring to confront the truth before now. But what good did it do in his sleep? And how was he to tell the younger Stroud that he, Magaffey, was at least partially responsible for the death of his grandfather?

Maybe if he'd been stronger in the past, tougher, maybe the calamities of this year would not have occurred . . . maybe. He thought of the injection he'd given Ananias Stroud on his death bed, an injection meant to relax him, allow him to rest and rebuild his considerable strength. But the drug had only served to weaken him and destroy what defense he had left against the creature then stalking him, a creature bent on the elder Stroud's destruction.

They'd found Stroud outside at the riverbank, his body lifeless, the marks of evil on his throat. The door to the enormous estate had been flung open, and a trail where the victim had been literally dragged from his bed and dumped onto the hoar frost to be bled to death was clearly visible. Not so much as a drop of blood had remained in his body. Yet, there was no blood in the house, none on the stairs, none around the body. But Magaffey had told no one of his autopsy findings, writing out the cause of death as natural.

At the time, given the conditions, he'd thought it best, even if it was cowardly. What else could he have done?

Lonnie Wilson had overnight become a lunatic, a stark, raving, madman. Ananias Stroud had, with the help of Ashyer, gotten Lonnie to Stroud's dungeon where the poor devil was lashed to a restraining table and imprisoned.

Magaffey had been on hand the night they'd returned from their final battle with the devil. They'd returned in the battered, sputtering helicopter with its twisted metal frame and broken glass. Old Stroud was already bitten at the throat by the monster. Magaffey—agitated, weak, and drained—had given Stroud the sedative against his wishes. He'd thrown Magaffey out, shouting foul words and calling him a traitor at the door. It was the last time Magaffey had seen his friend alive. He had looked remarkably robust and very like his grandson, despite the white hair, spectacles, and slight stoop.

Magaffey was trying to understand all the fragmented pieces of the puzzle, trying to once again recall all that Ananias Stroud had said about vampires when he suddenly awoke with a start, his eyes going directly to Abraham Stroud. Their eyes locked and it was as though the old man knew that Stroud had been rummaging about in his mind.

"You're very like your grandfather, you know," he said to Stroud.

Stroud remained skeptical about the old man. As for the man's nightmare—just images and items in a troubled mind. And yet he did believe that this old man standing before him actually felt guilty at having had a hand in his grandfather's death.

The Ashyers looked on like a pair of worried parents, their eyes going between the two learned doctors who seemed to be caught in a staring match.

"Your neck, Doctor Stroud!" said Mrs. Ashyer suddenly on seeing the swollen report of Pamela Carr's bite. Mrs. Ashyer went white with the discovery. Ashyer stepped closer, inspecting the wound as his wife rushed out for bandages and water. Magaffey, too, was aghast at the sight.

"It's nothing," said Stroud, still staring into Magaffey's eyes, still rummaging about his brain for answers. "Only a scratch."

"Scratch, hell!" said Magaffey. "It's a wound, son, like the Meyers boy's wound. How did you come by it?"

"I don't recall," he lied. "Some insect or parasite I picked up in the woods," he continued, holding out the white worm in his palm as proof. Any other explanation would sound too much like madness, he believed. "Must've picked it up when we were hunting."

Ashyer was shaken at the sight of the worm. Mrs. Ashyer dropped the warm water bowl she'd brought in.

"What is this?" asked Stroud. "It's only a goddamned parasite of some sort."

"These people have some idea where it came from, Stroud," said Magaffey. "And so do I."

Stroud held it under the light, scrutinizing it more closely. It looked like a man's thumb, as it was fat on his blood. The skin-colored creature was without eyes, moving in a mindless, sightless world of its own. It's mouth was the business end for it looked like some sort of sucker, like the vacuum of a lamprey, the eel that attaches itself to a fish and drains it of its blood, only to move on to a new host.

Stroud thought the three of them were behaving like guilty criminals under the lights of an interrogation room. He was about to ask what the creature meant to them when he felt the heat of the worm as it suddenly exploded into fire in his hand under the light. He instinctively sent the miniature fireball across the room, shaking off the burn to his hand, shouting, "Damn it!"

Ashyer rushed to where the fiery worm had landed and stomped it out of existence.

"We have much to talk about," said Magaffey to the stunned Dr. Abraham Stroud. Mrs. Ashyer wiped away at his neck wound, cleaning it of encrusted blood. The indents of two holes stared back at her like eyes out of the past.

"Yes, we have a great deal to talk about, Doctor Magaffey."

"I'll make us some more tea and coffee," said Mrs. Ashyer.

"Look now at the wound on your throat, Stroud," said Magaffey, "and tell me . . . where have you seen that kind of wound before?"

Stroud went to the mirror across the room and stared at the cleaned wound. He flashed on Timmy Meyers and recalled Magaffey's peculiar method of dealing with the boy's illness. The similarity between the two wounds was undeniable. It was nearing three in the morning, but there would be no sleep tonight. Tonight, there were just too many questions that must be answered.

Magaffey told Stroud all that he had told the Ashyers about the Bradley body and Cooper's visit to him, and the unusual elixir that Cooper had left him to scrutinize under his microscope. But Stroud was anxious to hear about his grandfather from Magaffey, and as Magaffey began the history lesson, the gaps were filled in by the Ashyers who, as it turned out, knew much more than Stroud had had any notion of.

Magaffey began with the night Ananias Stroud died and, reluctantly, the part that he had played in his demise.

"He was too far up in years to have been about that night. He had held out a hope that you, Abe . . . that you'd one day return to become a part of the fight. He said that he sent you repeated messages to come."

Stroud swallowed the rich black coffee in his throat. He recalled the succession of letters, but he had been too ill and self-involved at the time to seriously consider returning to Stroud Manse. Besides, there'd been no sense of urgency in the letters, only a request here and there to see him again. "I did not know the nature of his need," he said simply.

"For years he spoke of the fiend out there," said Magaffey, pointing toward the window.

"Called it a vampire," said Mrs. Ashyer.

"He claimed it had offspring, progeny everywhere," said Magaffey. "I listened to most of it politely that night as I ministered to the old man's wounds. I'd humored him up to this point, but here were actual wounds that he and Lonnie Wilson had returned with. He had several of these . . . these white parasitic worms crawling about his neck as well, Stroud. Gruesome sight. He insisted on capturing them and putting them in a preservative for later study. I . . . I don't know what's become of them."

"Where had they gone that night?"

"To the caves."

"The caves?"

"Along an embankment on the Spoon at Three Forks Road, he said. He said it was the monster's lair. Of course, I believed he was quite out of his mind, and so, without further consultation, I . . . I administered a sedative . . . to get him under control, you see."

"The helicopter was ample evidence he was telling the truth, Doctor," said Ashyer, interrupting.

Mrs. Ashyer added, "Lonnie was the pilot."

Stroud wondered how much of this he was expected to believe.

"The helicopter hasn't been touched since that night, sir, if you would care to inspect it," said Ashyer.

"Bank on it, I will. But for now, Doctor Magaffey, tell me all that you know about my grandfather. Was he insane?"

"Insane?" shouted Ashyer. "Your grandfather was a wise man, our protector! And with him gone . . . "

"He came to symbolize hope for the Ashyers, the only one who might counter the fiend that had once victimized Mr. and Mrs. Ashyer here," said Magaffey.

"We have him to thank for our lives," said Mrs. Ashyer. "We were with him for thirteen years, and when he died, we feared staying on here, certain that we would be the next to die."

"Ananias brought us back," said Ashyer mysteriously.

"Brought you back?"

"From the dead."

"From the dead?"

"Literally," said Mrs. Ashyer.

"It seemed to Doctor Magaffey cruel, even inhuman what your grandfather did to us, but it was necessary to make us feel again, to awaken us from the coma that the monster had induced in us. Your grandfather found us in the grip of slow death, and he brought us back," explained Ashyer. "He did so with the mechanisms in that torture chamber of his. He shocked us back into life."

"We were on the brink of death," his wife continued. "He somehow found us in the caves . . . he and Lonnie brought us back here and saved us. After he knew we'd be okay, he called in Doctor Magaffey for us. Later that same night, he went back for others, and that's when he and Lonnie encountered the creature and Doctor Magaffey was called in for medical assistance to your . . ."

"The chamber? The instruments of torture, you all know . . . you've seen these?"

"After that night, the Ashyers told me their story, and they showed me the circular room. In this room he administered what the Ashyers have come to call a 'healing pain.' "

"He brought us around to our senses!"

"It was the most beneficial balm he might have given, don't you see?" asked Mrs. Ashyer. "We were without sensation. We were comatose, yet we were aware of ourselves. The jolt of suffering and torment he induced was necessary in order to revive us! The same as you slap a newborn or pump water from a drowning man!"

"The venom of the creature acts very much like the stunning poison of a snake," said Ashyer, "to lull the victim into a state of unfeeling and uncaring in which there can be no struggle. The victim is rendered helpless to fight back."

Stroud thought of his encounter with Pamela Carr once more, his blackout and her subsequent anger. She must have taken his fit as evidence he was immune to her bite. Could it be? Or was he going mad? "I don't know what to think anymore," he said, standing and pacing.

"Think well of Ananias, son. He was a good man," cautioned Magaffey.

"His intentions were of the highest, sir."

"Road to hell is paved with good intentions," replied Abe.

"Damn it, son!" shouted Magaffey. "Don't you see, he had to use perverse methods—chains, straps, electric shock—anything to wake these people from the sleep of death? Hell, boy, they were found in *cocoons*."

"Cocoons?"

"Cocooned up in a thick spider's web of silky wax that this thing creates somehow."

"He had to cut us free, fly our bodies back here, and wake us from the dead," said Mrs. Ashyer.

"Sada and Jacob, here, owe their very lives to your grandfather," said Magaffey, going to him, pleading. "He removed them from the monster's grasp both physically and mentally. I know of no other man who could have so intervened with such courage, using his hands in such a *reversal* of goodness in order to keep these people from walking straight back to the caves and into the monster's grasp. Who else would have gone after them? Who else would have restrained them with straps? Beat them? Cut them? Shocked them?"

"Torture . . . for   the   sake   of   good . . . sounds . . . sounds . . . "

"Fanatical? Mad?"

"Yes, damn it, like the goddamned Inquisition!"

"Exactly!" Magaffey countered. "Exactly what I said at the time. And here was Ananias himself in dire distress, himself attacked, losing blood by the second, and what do you suppose he was doing? No answer, huh?" Magaffey paused for effect. "He was seeing to Lonnie Wilson's infection. He strapped Wilson down in that chamber and ministered to his needs in the only way he knew to combat the infection."

"You saw this?"

"No, I did not. I saw very little until it was all over, until I saw your grandfather dead. Ashyer here told me no sedatives, and so did your grandfather, but I'm a medical man! What choice did I have, seeing him in the state he was in. I was certain he was on the verge of a heart attack. So, I gave him a sedative . . . quite a strong one . . . and . . . and he died that same night."

"It was the worst thing you could have given him," said Ashyer with a decided edge to his voice.

"Under normal circumstances—" replied Magaffey who was cut off by Mrs. Ashyer.

"There was nothing normal about that night! He needed to feel his pain, to feel the anguish and to be disgusted by his wounds and the things crawling on him."

Magaffey dropped into a sofa chair, his head down, saying dejectedly, "I put him to rest . . . with a single injection."

Abe felt the older man's anguish deeply. "How long've you been carrying that around?"

"Since the night of his death."

"Why are all of you telling me all this now? Why did you wait? You might have at least warned me somehow, about the chamber, instead of letting me stumble on it and begin to think the worst."

"You would have thought us all mad, Abe," said Magaffey.

"Explain to you why your grandfather kept a torture chamber in his house?" said Mrs. Ashyer. "Just how?"

"Explain it to me again."

Magaffey said, "Some people your grandfather did not get to early enough. They were listed as disappearances and he was left with their remains. He might well have been arrested for what went on in Stroud Manse. To this day, some of the locals believe that somehow Stroud Manse is closely connected to the various disappearances—and so it is. But I tell you, the Ashyers are living proof that, if located early on, victims of this cave-dwelling Andover Devil can be saved. The torture chamber was not created for torture, but revival. He took people in Timmy Meyers's condition, and he literally shocked their minds into resuscitation."

"Then why didn't you bring the Meyers boy here for this unorthodox treatment?"

"The parents thought I was quite mad when I suggested it. They also thought you were somehow behind the entire incident."

"Some of the victims welcomed death to the half life the creature's venom had placed them in," said Mrs. Ashyer. "I know that I did."

Ashyer took up the story. "That night he and Lonnie raced from the caves, having been surprised by the vampire creature. The thing gave chase and crashed through the bubble of the helicopter, attacking each of them even as your grandfather beat the thing with a huge iron cross. Both men were scarred and bitten by the time they got down. The helicopter itself still bears the marks, sir."

Stroud tried to take it all in. He asked Magaffey to tell him once more about Cooper's visit. Magaffey did so, but this time he pulled a manilla folder from his black bag. "My findings on Cooper's serum, or whatever the hell it is. Look it over for yourself."

Magaffey allowed Stroud time to take it all in before continuing. "It has no properties useful to humankind so far as I can determine. It prevents no illness, cures no ills; it is merely a blood substitute similar to plasma but without plasmalike qualities—much more like animal blood than man's."

"What sort of animal blood?"

Magaffey swallowed. "Rodentlike, batlike, except there's something more. It's . . . quite volatile. It is not red on contact with oxygen, but a dark syrupy color which begins to burn—much like your worm friend a while ago—on contact with God's air. Texture is thicker than blood."

"Now we have a motive for Banaker's involvement in grave robbing," said Stroud as he took in the fact that the elixir Cooper had given over to Magaffey was in part bone marrow.

"Earlier, using the bones taken from the site, I determined that the bones were from the young, the old, the in-between. Some had spent sixty years under the earth . . . others a fraction of that time," said Magaffey. "These were the findings stolen from my office, but as you see, I had retained a copy in the event something should occur."

"What exactly does this bone marrow liquid do for Banaker?"

"I don't pretend to understand it completely but . . . but, I have reason to suspect that Banaker and the Andover Devil are one and the same! That Banaker is your grandfather's enemy, your grandfather's vampire!"

"Do you really believe that?"

"Whether I think so or not, does not matter. But Christ, son, Banaker thinks he can feed his blood craving with some sort of bone marrow cocktail he's cooked up in his lab, and that's close enough to vampire behavior for me!"

Stroud thought of the series of coincidences that resulted in no findings on the bones unearthed, and now this. He thought of the Meyers boy and the ones before him. He thought of Pamela Carr and their first encounter, her mesmerizing allure for him, her porcelain skin, and how oddly cold her touch had been. Had she just happened across his path or was she sent to seduce him into death? His hand went instinctively to the mark she'd left on him.

"So, Doctor Magaffey, what is it you want of me?"

"Your help."

"How?"

"I want to kidnap a body."

"What?"

"Bradley's body . . . take it out of Banaker's control. Get it to Springfield, maybe . . . have the forensics lab there check it out."

"But you said it was already prepped for a funeral. An autopsy would show nothing."

"We don't know that."

"But it's most likely, at this point."

"He has marks on his throat like those on yours, and he has the long terrible gashes to the shoulders. It can be shown that no automobile accident could cause such marks."

"Then *what*? What will you have?"

"Then come to the caves with me, if you don't believe me!"

"The caves? You know where these caves are?"

"I believe so, yes. Your grandfather was very specific about them."

Stroud thought of the missing Mrs. Bradley, Cooper's boy, the dog . . .

"How far are these damned caves?"

"Hour and a half by car."

"Ashyer?" said Stroud.

"Yes, sir?"

"Is this chopper you mentioned, is it operational?"

"I believe so, sir, yes."

"Is there fuel?"

"An ample supply, sir."

"Break it out. I flew for a time. I'll pilot us there, Doctor Magaffey. We'll get there in a quarter of the time."

"I suggest we arm ourselves, Stroud."

"With what do you suggest we arm ourselves, Doctor Magaffey?"

"We can start with some of those iron stakes that your grandfather had made when he put the wrought-iron gates and window coverings around the manse."

"You know a lot about this place, don't you?"

"We have to trust each other now, son."

Stroud thought a moment, nodded and said, "You're certain now that you know the location?"

"We can be there in fifteen minutes if you can get that old bird off the pad."

"Don't worry about that. Just show me your proof, Doctor Magaffey."

"Knowledge is a curse, Stroud . . . you'll find that out soon enough."

—15—

The other side of the stables the helicopter sat on the pad below a huge tarp. It had a sad appearance there, like an old '48 Chevy gone out of use. When Stroud pulled back the tarp he saw the reason why. Two to seventy reasons why, actually. It was an old machine for one, the type of army issue used in Korea. It was ugly in its crude green metallic fashion. Futhermore, it had seen combat and had endured metal fatigue to its superstructure, and the windshield was sporting a larger than fist-size hole on the passenger side.

While it was a two-seater, it had cargo space behind. As Stroud worked the tarp up and over with what little assistance Magaffey could lend, peeling a zipper down the side to round the shaft of the rotor, he saw into the cargo bay. The sight stunned him, and at first he thought the boxes were of the type that carried munitions. This was before he realized they were coffins.

"Christ, what's this?"

Magaffey simply said, "They're empty. Your grandfather used them for transporting . . . ahhhhh . . . incidentals."

"Incidentals?"

"Just think of them as pine boxes, Stroud."

"What sort of incidentals?"

The slow-witted, huge stable hand suddenly appeared at the other side of the cargo bay hatch, his eyes wide and his entire weight quivering at the sight. "No . . . no . . . no!" he stuttered and waved his hands. "Don't do-do-do-dis! No, Doc-tor Strow! No!"

The big man was terrified, looking over his shoulder, fear showing in his eyes, eyes that darted around at every tree, every bush, every rock. He then tore off for his small stable boy's house like a frightened child.

Stroud chased after him but Magaffey shouted, "Never mind him, now! We haven't time for Lonnie Wilson."

Stroud still found it impossible to believe that Lonnie had ever piloted this machine. Stroud said, "I'm not even sure we can get this thing airborne. Look at it." He wiped away the mass of spider web that had attached itself to his palm moments before Lonnie had appeared.

"What do you propose, Stroud? We wait for Sporty's Pilot Shop bulletin to show up in the mail and then we order a new one? Christ, son, we don't have time, not if we're going to hijack Bradley's body. It's at the funeral home now being prepped by Carl Hoff's people. Banaker released it to Hoff—"

"I'm not so sure I want to be a part of your plans of body snatching, Doctor."

"You will, Stroud! You will when you see the evidence in the caves."

Stroud stared at him for a long moment, still wavering between belief and disbelief. "You really believe that we'll find something in these caves of yours?"

"You'll see, son . . . just wait."

"What do you hope to find there?"

"Remnants . . . remains . . . "

"Remains as in people remains?"

"People, missing women, children."

Circumstances seemed to be plying Stroud's mind with nonstop horror that was stacking like reams of paper images in his mind, threatening an overload. "I'll reserve my judgment," he said, knowing it sounded pedestrian.

"I'm sure. You have much to sift through, put in order," said Magaffey kindly. "But there's no time to lose."

"Be that as it may, Doctor, I'm not budging until you explain these damned coffins! You knew damned well they were back here—knew it all along! Didn't you?"

"Son, Carl Hoff is one of Banaker's stooges; the funeral parlor is secretly Banaker's! I'm certain of it now."

"Is that supposed to shock me?"

"I hope so."

"Old man, coffins in the back of a chopper are a vet's night-mare. You might've warned me!"

Magaffey shook his head and raised his shoulders simultaneously. "The coffins are empty, Abe."

"And as for Banaker," Stroud continued, "how he chooses to invest his cash is his affair."

"But it's not just the funeral home, son."

"What're you saying now, Doctor Magaffey?"

Magaffey's hands went into the air. "Hell, Stroud, he's placed people—"

"Placed people? In jobs, you mean?"

"Jobs in key places."

"Key jobs in key places?"

"Staffed hospital emergency rooms with his people."

"That's not unusual for—"

"Paramedics, blood-drive vans! Gives new meaning to the word blood drive! And . . . and cemetery workers, and funeral homes, morgue attendants! To be close to the supply!"

Stroud believed Magaffey was sounding once again like a para-noid madman. "Look, let's take it one step at a time, Doc. Frank-ly, I don't even know if we can get this thing off the ground."

"But you haven't tried."

Stroud's fist came down hard against the hull of the helicopter, causing something inside to fall with a metallic thud—a crowbar. The noise clamored and reverberated between the two men.

"I'm sorry, Stroud," said Magaffey. "About the coffins . . . I'd forgotten."

"One step at a time."

"Can you get it in the air, Doctor Stroud?"

"I have to do some checking up front."

With this Stroud left Magaffey alone to stare at the three coffins in the cargo bay.

Ashyer had brought the needed fuel and Stroud had found a toolbox in the rear where his eyes once more took in the gruesome sight of the pine boxes. Hanging from one metal rack in the rear there was also a shoulder bag filled with the metal stakes fashioned by his grandfather. It was dark, and the work by flashlight hampered them all, but soon Stroud revved up the motor. The machine died at once. The second attempt caused a quaking, shuddering throughout the structure. Stroud had never heard such a rattle before. The third attempt brought on the rotor overhead with chugging, coughing and sputtering, but suddenly it kicked in.

Ashyer got clear of the machine. He stood biting his upper lip and, beyond him, almost hidden from sight, Lonnie Wilson also saw them off. Neither man wanted anything to do with Magaffey's scavenger hunt through the caves. Stroud could not blame either man, and he still wondered if he weren't being led around by a madman and his accomplices.

Still, the bird rose smoothly and leveled out, sending trees to bend in its wake as it soared past, and the exhilaration of flight brought an excitement to Stroud and a feeling of doing and action which he had longed for this night which, so far, had been filled with frustration. He didn't speak to Magaffey who was strapped in the seat beside him. He concentrated on the controls.

Magaffey, too, fell into silence as Stroud did another visual check of the fuel gauge, horizontal, and tachometer. He wasn't about to veer far from the pad until he was certain the craft was safe.

"You trust this thing?" asked Magaffey, his knuckles white where he hung onto his seat. He was staring straight out the front where the bubble glass had been smashed, ripples and lines leading from the hole in a spider's web pattern.

Magaffey had been telling the truth about the helicopter. It had no doors, but there were rents and tears in the metalwork, even in the hinges that had once held the doors on. Someone or something had done battle with the machine. An image of his grandfather going at it with a sledge hammer popped into his mind, but some of the marks didn't compute as signs of a madman wielding an oversized hammer.

The helicopter circled Stroud Manse like a bird of prey. Magaffey said, "Enough time wasted, Abe. I'll direct you now."

"Lead on, Doctor."

The helicopter groaned with the sound of a disturbed animal waking from a long sleep. Stroud gave her full throttle, however, and soon she flew with a gentle touch. Stroud found himself having fun as he maneuvered upward, then left. They were soon out of sight of Stroud Manse.

Everything was somehow in working order, despite the gashes, rips, and battered condition of her outer hull, and despite the wind that whipped through the all but open cockpit. Abe allowed for the additional drag. As they neared the caves, Abe found they were following the silvery ribbon of the Spoon River below. In his mind he tried to relate the condition of the bird to those wartime relics he'd seen in Vietnam. He had seen helicopters with twisted metal supports and even damaged rotors manage to get home safely, but he still wondered about the torn hinges and missing doors. What kind of strength could have managed this feat?

"There! There it is!" said Magaffey, suddenly alert and agitated and pointing to a stand of dead trees that flourished with bare branches atop a knoll along the river. As they honed in on the place, Stroud saw that it was a barren rock, hardly a weed capable of life at the top. But it was surrounded by woods on all sides.

"Going to be a tight landing."

"Can you do it?"

"Believe so."

The approach required a wide swing in from the left. On approach, a pocket of upsurging wind swept them into an unwanted tilt. He had to fight the air for control of the craft. The struggle reminded him of his short-lived experience with helicopters on the police force. Up drafts in the city were a constant threat. In a moment, however, he was setting her down gently atop Magaffey's caves.

"We'll need a few items from the back," shouted Magaffey over the rotor as it wound down.

Stroud dared not ask what items the old man wished to have. He simply followed and observed as the old man picked his way over cable, boxes, rope, picks, and spades that littered his way to the three coffins. Magaffey stopped at the tool chest and inspected it for items he'd need. He reached into the dust on the floor and pulled out a crowbar, placing it beside one of the coffins. He pulled out a cross-shape tire iron and held it up to the light, humming and saying, "This should do nicely." He pulled forth a claw hammer and then a screw driver, tossing it to Stroud. From a hook overhead he pulled forth a tattered old brown leather bag that was filled to the brim with the same metal stakes Stroud had found in the secret room in the manse.

Stroud, frowning, held one of these up to the light filtering into the helicopter. "What're we going to do, stake a claim? Pitch a tent? Start an archeological dig?"

"These stakes were made special by your grandfather. At their centers, son . . . Doctor Stroud . . . there is a shaft of pure silver."

"Silver, really."

"Help me pry the lid off one of these coffins."

"Doctor Magaffey—"

"Please, Stroud."

Stroud shook his head but bent to the work, realizing for the first time by the effort that the box was not empty. It was weighted down quite heavily. "Hold on, Doctor Magaffey."

Magaffey loosened his grip on the crowbar. "What is it?"

"What's inside these boxes?"

"Just earth, dirt."

"Dirt . . . you have any idea how damned heavy dirt is? No wonder liftoff was so rocky. Look, you want to tell me what's so special about three boxes of dirt?"

"This earth came from consecrated ground, earth that has never been desecrated, earth your grandfather had blessed and purified by the Holy Father in Rome."

"The Pope?"

"It was one of his weapons against the monster."

"What'd he do, throw it in the vampire's eyes?" Stroud once more had become skeptical.

"He laid people like Mrs. Ashyer onto this earth and it somehow began the healing process to bring them back."

"Back from the cave that we're going into?"

"Back from the dead, damn it! Now, can we carry on?"

They readied the coffins, loosening each, and true to his word, Magaffey showed Stroud with a flourish that all that each held was ordinary dirt. "Sterilized, of course. Neutral. No organism can regenerate in it. It is not anything like your ordinary cemetery earth." The old black man lifted and sifted the earth in his hands like an old pirate enjoying his booty. Stroud watched this action and the look of determination on Magaffey's face before he asked a question.

"No microbes, nothing?"

"As inert as moon dust. It's a real disparaging thing for a creature that is lice-ridden and carries disease and leeches—"

"Leeches?"

"Yes."

"What sort of leeches?"

"A worm . . . eyeless, white . . . just like the one you had on yourself earlier. Your grandfather had several in formaldehyde in jars."

"I've seen no such jars," said Stroud.

"Ananias sent several out to labs where there were friends he could trust, for study. But here, let's dig around a bit and maybe . . . maybe . . . "

In a moment, rummaging about the tattered boxes and paraphernalia, Magaffey came up with a vial of yellow-brown liquid. Beneath the liquid floated an imprisoned white maggot the size of a man's pinkie. It looked like some ancient life form specimen frozen in time.

"According to Ananias's findings, this little beast has the capability of keeping your blood and mine running freely, as it nibbles away at any attempt the human body makes at healing by way of coagulation about the wound. It doesn't create the wound, mind you, it merely keeps it free of interference so that the true wound-maker doesn't have any difficulty syphoning off what it wants in the way of your blood, Doctor Stroud."

He involuntarily shivered at the recollection of the live one on his throat, feeding at the wound. He then realized fully, for the first time, what Pamela Carr was. He told Magaffey his suspicions and the old man had no difficulty accepting them.

"So, are you still worried about her safety and whereabouts?"

"Whereabouts, yes. As for safety, yes, also—mine."

"Take up some of those stakes, in case we need them. And come along. Who knows, we may find Miss Carr, yet. Oh, and bring the tire iron."

Stroud picked up the dusty, tattered bag of the silver-core metal stakes, the hammer, and the tire iron. He noticed the crucifix around the old man's neck as he allowed it to dangle atop his shirt now.

"Do you think that will help?"

"Can't hurt. As for you, use the tire iron. It forms a large cross. If you are threatened, hold it out firmly at any attacker. Bring the shovel. We'll need it." He himself lugged the pickax over one shoulder.

Stroud was beginning to wonder what he'd gotten himself into. "Why didn't they just take Bradley's body, if all of them are vampires? Why the charade at an autopsy by Banaker and a funeral parlor once over?"

"Appearances, don't you see? Banaker has built an empire from the remnants of his father's legacy here in Andover. His father was somehow superior to others of his kind, able to mix in with humankind on a level never before achieved. They somehow have learned to withstand the light of day, for instance. The white worm cannot, perhaps, thus its numbers have dwindled, but it has found living quarters on their bodies, in their orifices. But Banaker learned the secret to combating the sun's rays, how to cast a shadow, a reflection, all in order to go unseen and unnoticed among us. What mayor, what doctor only seen by the community at night could possibly inspire confidence over curiosity?"

"Medicine, research, the Institute," said Stroud.

"Exactly. While they're superficially studying sickle-cell anemia and all manner of human disease, they are in fact financing vampire research which has culminated in a bone marrow cocktail that acts as a substitute for preying on the likes of you and me."

"But then why the massacres? The attack on my grandfather, and against the children, Bradley, his wife?"

Magaffey shook his head. "The substitute doesn't work for all their numbers, perhaps? Perhaps a sect of them, a splinter group, wants raw meat? A wolf among the sheep? A rogue vampire among Andover's sedate crowd? I don't know. But I do know they are here, and they are infiltrating at an alarming rate."

"If even a fraction of this is true, then my . . . grandfather did not die a madman?"

"Ananias Stroud was one of the sanest men I ever knew, up to and including the end."

"And he died of wounds inflicted on him by . . . by this thing that lives in these caves?"

"The wounds, yes . . . the last time he took the helicopter out, as I told you."

"Let's go."

They had to climb down and the going was slow and difficult for Magaffey. Dawn had turned into day; it was nearing eight-thirty. Birds were aflight, some crows cawed in the distance, an angry swallow screeched inches from them, protecting her nest just overhead.

At the water's edge they heard the slap of beavers at work and Stroud thought he saw his favorite of the animals dive beneath the surface of the Spoon—an otter. Life surrounded them as they came full turn at the bottom of the bluff and stared into the gaping mouth of one of hundreds of openings dotting the bluff. It was like an enormous sponge, holes of every size and shape leading into its black depths, creating a maze of unfathomable proportions. Swiss cheese came to mind, and Stroud wondered how the cloth of sand, so tattered and riveted with air could possibly hold the weight of the bluff, the enormous trees, the helicopter and the two men who'd moments before set down upon it.

They stepped into the stifling darkness where not so much as the passing breeze entered, their lungs quickly filling with a mordant, choking stench.

"Smell it?" asked Magaffey.

—16—

Dr. Oliver Banaker was furious with his son, Dolphin. The talk had netted neither one of them a thing. Dolph had now destroyed Pamela Carr. How Banaker knew this was unimportant, he just knew. It came in flashes, as if he could sometimes see what Dolph saw. At first the visions coming to him in his resting time were discarded as a vampire's nightmares, but as they grew in intensity and feeling, so, too, did the message that the images he was receiving were telepathic, as if forced on him from another psyche. Dolph wanted a confrontation; Dolph wanted him to catch him and reprimand him, much as a human child might. At first it all seemed too incredible, too senseless that his loving son would crusade against him in an attempt to bring him down.

Pam. Dear, sweet, dumb Pamela Carr had let him down, but Dolphin Banaker had betrayed him.

Where in god's name was she? She'd been due back hours before, and he had waited with mounting impatience in the enormous, gray concrete fortress of the Andover Mausoleum, which stood over a maze of underground tunnels here in the Andover Cemetery. It was here, at the mausoleum, that his kind could come together in a relaxing atmosphere, to not worry about keeping up their guards, to spend some hours without fear of detection. The crypts made convenient beds, coffins filled with pires at rest and sleep; not that they couldn't sleep in the coffins in their basements, but there was something about the vampire nature that made it imperative at times to be close to the dark recesses of caves and the graveyard shadows here. They were, after all, a gregarious lot, given to feeding in packs, but there was also a spiritual side to them which hungered for the old ways, the ancient practices, the haunts of the ancestors, and the mausoleum provided this along with its sanctuary from the human community at large.

The gravediggers, the cemetery custodian, they were all vampires, and they kept things tidy and secretive here. They were largely responsible for the network of underground tunnels that'd been dug below the cemetery, radiating from the mausoleum at its center, a kind of escape hatch against a day when they might be discovered.

Banaker had worked tirelessly, like his father before him, to place pires in positions of authority, and easy access to blood supplies, from policemen to paramedics to priests and funeral parlor people. Except that they weren't people.

So many vampires now wore white lab coats that it was almost humorous to think that the colors they preferred they could only wear here, at the mausoleum, so as to fade in with the night and the shadows. But by day it must be the uniform of the profession. Daylight had once made it necessary that all vampires go about their work during the dark hours, but with Banaker's perfectly remarkable pharmacy of genetically altered blood elixir, all that reliance on night was a thing of the past. And yet there remained a magnetism about the midnight hours that lured them out, and so Banaker had created the town's first and only mausoleum. It was a place of refuge and contemplation and vampire dreams.

Almost three hundred vampires now wandered in and out of the cemetery and its mausoleum on any given evening, secluded as it was by topography and the fearsome superstitions of the humans who rarely came here in the night. When they did, there were the doors of the mausoleum and the tunnels to scatter to.

The only human who had seen through the veil of secrecy Banaker had wrapped his people in was now dead, but the man's grandson was alive, and he lived in Stroud Manse.

Had Stroud somehow overpowered Pamela? Had he seen through her charade? He was a shrewd antagonist, like his grandfather, no doubt, and quite knowledgeable about vampires, possessing the capability and the know-how to destroy them. Banaker shivered as he surveyed the cemetery where pairs of vampires wandered about the stone slabs and trees, some finding comfort in one another, sharing intimacies. It was difficult and draining for him to use his ancient power of telepathy, but he concentrated on Pamela and her whereabouts, making a concerted, powerful effort to *see* her and what she was doing and who she was with.

He imagined she was Stroud's prisoner, perhaps trapped in some manner, her body impaled by one of his grandfather's awful instruments of torture. He imagined her hanging by a thread to what little life remained in her dehydrated form, cut off from any blood source. He imagined her begging for a drop of Stroud's blood. Completely, totally helpless, in great pain and anguish, her life seeping away like a melting ice cube, she was absolutely helpless to save herself. This was why she had not returned. She was trapped . . . held against her will, bundled up, tied, restrained in some barbaric manner, drained to the brink of death. Her mind had shut down, his telepathy told him. He could not reach out to her mind any longer, but there was someone with her. Stroud? No . . . someone else . . . one of her own kind . . . a vampire . . . a brother . . . her brother . . . Dolphin.

He pondered Pamela Carr for a time. He had groomed her from childhood. She'd been like a sister to Dolph, although they were not blood related. She'd been taken from her grave and given rebirth in the manner of the old ways; whereas Dolph was the child of Banaker and his vampire wife.

This dawn found Banaker saddened and disappointed. First with Pamela Carr. He was certain that she'd betrayed him after all the years of nursing her along, pampering her, showering her with life and vigor and a place in the vampire community that neither her education nor her talents warranted. Now this—to fail him when he most needed her.

She'd been due back hours and hours before to meet him at the enormous gray concrete fortress of the Andover Mausoleum. Where most of his kind kept crypts. It was preferable to the old caves far out of town, and much more convenient to the Institute where most of them worked. Others had been carefully placed in jobs where they could easily access human blood. Most of the network had been set up by Banaker's father before him. Some of the pires worked at funeral parlors, others in the autopsy rooms of hospitals from Andover to Springfield. Others worked at the Institute as paramedics and doctors. Today, thanks to Banaker, the vampire could live and work among the humans with little chance of detection.

The only man who had seen through the charade was now dead,

but his grandson was alive and living in Stroud Manse.

The huge mausoleum afforded a safe place to lie down among the "sheep" in plain sight. Meanwhile, Banaker, like the others here, maintained homes in Andover for appearance's sake. It worked fine so long as no suspicions were aroused. He owned the mausoleum and the caretakers were his kind of folk. Filled to capacity, it housed the entire community of pires, some three hundred now, and growing.

When Pamela did not return, he at first feared she had somehow been won over by Stroud, overpowered by his magic and his charms, and quite possibly destroyed by the man. Then he began receiving the images, horrible and unrelenting, of the way in which she was dispatched. He got a sense of her holding onto life at this moment by a mere thread and her body dehydrated to the point of complete and total helplessness. He knew she'd been drained to near death, and her mind had shut down, and that she was being held somewhere at this moment: cocooned in the ancient manner, stored for later feedings by Dolphin, her brother.

"Damn him, damn my only son!" he cursed. Dolphin was more of a threat now than Stroud. Dolphin would continue until they were all exposed, and as strong a race as they were, when exposure came it meant great liability. They were hopelessly outnumbered. Banaker foresaw a time when they surely would outnumber the humans, but that was far in the future.

It could only be resolved one way. Dolph must die.

Banaker pushed closed the crypt he'd been lying peacefully in and, with others looking out from their crypts, he dissolved into a fog there in the marbled hallway. The fog seeped through the locked doorway and out into the lawn. Aside from Pamela, another pire was missing from his crypt—Cooper. Banaker wondered what Dolph had done to Cooper.

Violence had become a thing of the past for Dr. Oliver Banaker, an unwholesome and unwanted historical tentacle which he'd believed to be severed with his incredible discoveries: the DNA matrix, the bone marrow protein, the drink that made them free of the dependence on human cattle to feed upon. All great gifts to his inhuman race. Gifts built upon the theories expounded down through the ages of his race, theories about blood.

They had come so far, too far to allow any one individual to destroy such progress—even if that one was his son.

Everyone left in the mausoleum sensed his distress and knew

the cause. They all had children of their own, or soon would.

Banaker ascended on wing now, his dark form like an animated night cloud, moving with the surety of a bat toward an old, familiar hunting ground. He wasn't so sure, however, that he could kill Dolphin. Certainly he had the power, but did he have the courage and the heart?

Dolphin Banaker sensed his father's approach and it made him lift his incisors from the flesh showing through the cocoon that dangled from the ceiling of the cave. The meat must be covered with the cocoon to keep the smaller bats from feeding on it. Dolph regurgitated a thick mass of white to beige waxy silk from his stomach, a substance supplied him by the parasitic white worms that lived inside him. He saw Pamela Carr's right eye frozen open and glaring back at him through the gauzy stuff, but he was certain she could no longer feel a thing. Not that it mattered a great deal to him.

As soon as Dolph removed himself from the upside-down Pamela Carr and the protective shell around her, his position was taken up by a multitude of ordinary vampire bats. Their numbers were so great that they blotted out the cocooned form of the female vampire. The effect was of a number of bats resting comfortably over the sides of a stalactite, a natural phenomena. And everyone knew that vampire bats had recently taken up residence in southern Illinois from the sister states across the Ohio; they just didn't know *what* attracted them to Andover.

Dolphin wished to pick the time and place of any further encounters with his father. He had no love for his father or the others of his species, due in main part to what they'd become. In fact, it disgusted him. They had the potential for such power and instead they spent their days and nights languishing about as humans, mimicking the cattle they ought to be lords over! It made no sense to Dolphin, not in the long run. And he believed that he was winning some of the younger pires over to his side. Just the night before, he'd led a small band of them into a neighboring county where they'd fed for the first time in their lives on the living, warm bodies of a family in a deserted farmhouse. They'd fed so ravenously and zealously that there was nothing left to store in the caves. They'd left the emptied containers of their four bodies there in the farmhouse for friends and neighbors to find and wonder over.

His father called it reckless endangerment. Dolph called it

instinct and drive, desire and will, and, in the last analysis, *freedom*. He wanted only to be free to be what he was. Taking that brown substitute for human blood invented by his father was a blasphemy against their kind and no one, not even his father, knew of the long-term effects of that shit. For all the great Oliver Banaker knew, it was turning them into a bunch of eunuchs and passionless humans! Look at Cooper, he thought, going to Magaffey and spilling his guts to a human. Wasn't that proof enough that the blood substitute turned their kind into fools and imbeciles?

Besides, there was nothing—nothing—like the real thing. Nothing like the taste of blood. Nothing like the feel of the struggling beast he attached himself to, and the feel of helplessness as its life was slowly drained away. It was power of the most primeval and ultimate kind. It was the source of Dolph's joy and reason for being. It was his heritage and his right. And, if need be, he'd fight to the death to defend it. If need be, he'd kill his father for the right to feed as his ancestors fed.

But he must fly. He didn't wish to be cornered here where there was little room for maneuverability and escape should he require it. He rushed for the high-ceilinged, open cavern at the center of the caves he knew so well.

He'd played here as a boy. . . .

"Smell it?" asked Magaffey again as they trudged into the mouth of the cave.

Abe Stroud did smell it, an odor of decay but more than decay— like the stench that explodes forth when the corroded lid of a septic tank is pried loose, only more so. It was the odor of defecation, but it was also the odor of flesh and blood and urine and earth commingling. "What the hell is it?" asked Stroud.

"Follow me."

Stroud began to doubt the sanity of this quest; he began to doubt Magaffey's intentions, his wild stories, all of it. But then they came to the source of the odor. "Careful with the flash. You hear them?" asked Magaffey. "One false move and they'll descend on us."

Stroud's light picked up the fact the ceiling of the cave was moving; it was crawling with bats of several different species.

"Fruit bats don't live in caves," said Magaffey. "Most of these are insectivores, but some are vampire bats. Shine your light down in that direction."

Stroud, loaded down with the shovel and the stakes, did as instructed. His flash illuminated in one corner of the chamber an enormous pyramidal dune of bat droppings that spread wavelike across the cave floor, rising in one area to eight feet.

"Some indication of how long they've been here," said Magaffey matter-of-factly as Stroud's flesh began to crawl.

"Where're we going?" he asked Magaffey who began to trudge over the dung heap. Underfoot was a glistening, moving carpet of cockroaches and maggots feeding on the droppings. The heavy stench of ammonia rose from the frenzied feeding.

At the top of the largest of these hills of life they found the larger vampire bats roosting in narrow, horizontal clefts in the rock. As Stroud's light hit them, some detached themselves as others merely began to lick the slick membrane between their fingers that formed their wings. Some swept past them, their wings brushing Stroud's face. Still others just hung there, twisting their snub-nosed faces and beady eyes with frantic nervousness.

Beyond these Stroud could see thousands and thousands more. They seemed packed as thick as heads of grain in a wheat field, except that they were upside down. As the alarm among them moved through the pack, it seemed a wind passed over them. Their blind eyes needn't tell them, for their sonar had detected the intruders. They erupted in panic.

Desperate to escape, they rocketed outward as if of one mind, forcing Stroud and Magaffey to their knees amid the insects. But instead of racing out into the light where the men had entered, they directed themselves deeper into the caves.

"Follow them," said Magaffey, getting to his feet.

Very soon they came on a large, open cavern. In this main chamber a torrent of the black creatures circled overhead. They seemed penned by fear of the unfamiliar daylight outside and terrified by the presence of the men. They became one vast eddy, beating the air with frantic wings.

Their sonar was beyond human ears, yet the lower components of their squeaks created a strange cosmic rustling. The already suffocating atmosphere was made worse by the heat created from the thousands of racing bodies. Stroud and Magaffey were spattered by their angry droppings. There were several thousand bats, as thick as snowflakes in a driving gale, circling around and around their heads, flying at such speeds they must all be using their sonar. Stroud wondered how they kept from jamming one another's signals, how they kept from colliding with one another.

Their capabilities were beyond science and technology. He was momentarily entranced by the dance of creatures that predated man by eons.

Their huge wings beat steadily now as long skeins of them kept a level, purposeful course across the huge cavern and out through another tunnel. As they exited, they left behind several pods of resting bats that seemed to be covering the stalactites in an attempt at gaining the moisture and coolness there.

"Some bats have taken to feeding on meat, Stroud."

He turned to look into Magaffey's eyes. "Vampire bats, I know."

"Some prey on roosting birds, some take frogs and small lizards, and one species is reported to feed on *other bats*."

"I thought they just sucked the blood of animals, like feeding at a horse's throat, penetrating the vein."

"Some do that as well. An American species even manages to fish, Stroud. Remarkable adaptors, actually. At dusk the fisherman bat beats up and down over ponds, lakes, or even the sea. The tail membrane of most bats extends down to the ankles. In the fisherman bat, it's attached much higher up, at the knee. So, the legs are quite free. It trails its feet in the water, talons I should say—hooked-shaped claws. When they strike a fish, the bat scoops it up into its mouth and kills it with one powerful crunch of its teeth."

"You seem to know a lot about bats."

"I do now. The most specialized of the bunch is the vampire bat. It lights on a sleeping mammal, say a cow or even a human. Something in its saliva contains an anticoagulant, so that the blood, when it appears, will continue to ooze for some time before a clot forms. The vampire squats over the wound, lapping the blood. It flies by sonar . . . the reason dogs are seldom attacked by them. Dogs are attuned to very high frequencies. They can hear them coming."

"What does all this have to do with Banaker and—"

Magaffey grabbed up the flash and fired its light at one of the pods of remaining bats—the stalactite just over Stroud's head. Stroud instinctively ducked when the maddened flock erupted in a whirlwind, beating past them. When Stroud straightened up, he saw that the light revealed a stalactite that was translucent and in the see-through stone was the form of a human being rooted to the ceiling by its feet, its head nearest the swelling dung heap on the floor below it. Stroud, aghast at the horrendous sight, thought of fossils and whole skeletons and even completely preserved bodies in arctic ice. The facial characteristics were indistinct, blurred by the webby, cottony, slick, and icy-looking covering. Whoever it was, she—for the hair was dangling and long—had been drained of all color. She was as white and as still as stone sculpture.

"What . . . what is it, Magaffey?"

"Once your grandfather found the Ashyers like this, in one of these caves."

"Who . . . who is it?"

"From the appearance, I'd hazard only one guess: Pamela Carr."

"Cooper lied to you."

"Cooper said she'd *gone*. That might've meant anything."

"We've got to get her out of here."

"We can later, Stroud. She's already dead. Look at her."

Stroud refused to believe it.

"She was one of them, and this is her punishment."

Stroud was weakened by the thought and the sight. Then he realized there were other bats on other clinging stalactites all about this chamber. He grabbed up the flash and attacked the other bats with the light. Each group in turn revealed a cocoon with someone or something in it. One had been eaten away by the bats, and all that remained were the desiccated parts of a dog—Timmy Meyers' dog. Another revealed the remains of a boy long since dead—Cooper's son. There was a large woman in a third, also long since dead, now the fodder of the smaller bats. Finally, there was one that had movement inside, although faint and barely noticeable.

They scrambled to this one and Stroud tore away at the sticky, slimey substance that imprisoned the occupant. He ripped and pulled with the end of the pickax he took from Magaffey until a naked, frail white arm fell out, the hand reaching out to them, a murmur of anguish welling from inside the bubble the monster had built around the body of Dr. Cooper.

"Get him free, keep working at it!" Stroud shouted to Magaffey. "I've got to try for Pamela." He raced to the first cocoon, tearing away at it until her eyes shone from deep within the complex maze of tissue and web, telling him in no uncertain terms that she was beyond help. He rushed back to Magaffey and Cooper.

Cooper's feet were entangled at the top of the waxy tissue, twisted round and round in the fiber, attached to the ceiling wall as if by glue. They now had the bottom of the pod open and grabbing him around the chest, Stroud heaved and pulled to free the smaller man.

It worked and Cooper, dripping with a salivalike substance that was milky and semenlike in color, wobbled on his legs, unable to hold himself up. Stroud felt the weakness, as if his limbs were water draining off the man. He'd wasted away to frail bone and loose skin, some of it loping in folds as he moved, reflecting the fact he was not quite human, that he had folds of skin between his arms and back that if extended would form *wings*. The sight made both Magaffey and Stroud back off instinctively. As Cooper tried to stand on his own, tried to right himself, he looked like a bat struggling with extreme dehydration. There was a sheen in his eyes that told the men that he was blind to them, and his lips curled into a puckering O. He "saw" them only when he sent forth echo-locating, high-frequency sound waves. He also located the pickax where Stroud had left it half buried in the earth beside the now crushed cocoon.

"Cooooooooper?" asked Magaffey. "Is . . . is it you?"

Cooper replied with a piercing screech as he threw what was left of his body onto the upturned pick, driving it home exactly where his heart was, dumping what remained of his life fluids over the ugly instrument of his death. Cooper's body then began to visibly disintegrate, rotting before their eyes and poofing into an acrid smoke and chemical residue in the dirt.

"My God!" said Stroud.

"We'd best pray to God there aren't others encamped here now," said Magaffey. "We must race from here, now, Stroud, now!"

"But we can't do that!"

"Now, before it is too late, before we are gathered up as fodder for these vile creatures! Hurry!"

"We have the proof we need in Pam Carr's body—preserved as it is. Proof that the vampire species exists! And here are the drained bodies of two humans. With this big woman, who's most likely Mrs. Bradley—all of this—we won't need that body in town."

Magaffey slowed his retreat from the cave, turning, the light outlining his shaking form. He nodded thoughtfully. "Of course, you're right. We must get what we can into the helicopter."

"We can use the coffins, the sterilized dirt. If we can get Pamela Carr into one of them, it may preserve the body, keep it from the sudden onset of decay Cooper's went into."

"The cocoon obviously has helped us in this. We would have done well to keep it intact."

"Let's get her out to the chopper first, get her nailed into that coffin." Stroud saw only a vestige of the erotic woman he'd been attracted to in the mesh of silky white cocoon covering. Like Cooper, she was hideously deformed and decrepit-looking, her limbs like those of the bats—sticklike and scant. Her skin was loose and flapping with the movement of the cocoon as they picked their way over the dung hills in the dark. Only the light at the end of the tunnel provided any sliver of pleasure in their minds. It was the work of ghouls and grave diggers—necessary, but brutal to the senses.

—17—

Banaker's approach to the caves showed full well that Stroud was here. It had been no false fear he had had of the powerfully built grandson of the man his own father had done battle with, and he himself had done battle with. Here, like a nightmare from Banaker's past, stood the ugly helicopter—machine of his father's destruction. His father and he had canvassed the machine as it raced from these very caves that night, blotting out the sky to those inside, terrifying them as the helicopter raced for Stroud Manse. Banaker's talons had gone right through the window and he saw that the hole was still there; he'd clutched the elder Stroud by the throat, tearing at his jugular. The pilot had frozen in fear at about this time, just as the copter was settling onto the ground, when suddenly Banaker's father was somehow caught up in the whirling cross overhead, sucked into the rotar, and twisted and torn into pieces before he could counter the devastation with a change of his shape. Banaker's father was killed, mangled beyond help, his blood spilling from so many wounds and rents he could not be saved, not even by his physician son.

Now Banaker hovered over the terrible instrument of that night's work, knowing that in the caves another of the Stroud brood—*those who had chased his kind and destroyed his kind throughout history*—was here to kill Dolphin. Ironic, he thought, that both of them had come for the same purpose. On the other hand, this new threat from outside the family could have a positive effect, could bring father and son together, to finally unite them against their common and ancient foe. How ironic, he thought.

Dolphin, like Stroud, *was* nearby. Banaker could sense him, waiting, watching, animal-like in his crouch and crook, about to spring on his unsuspecting father. Banaker had to get to the boy, knock sense into him, and together they'd get Stroud and in the triumph of sharing that auspicious moment, Dolphin would be accepted back into the fold and his sins forgiven. He expected Dolphin to attack with all his wiles, but Banaker felt he could overcome the boy and set him to right thinking at last.

Banaker drifted in a cold fog through the side of the hill and into the cave where he saw that Magaffey was with Stroud and that the two of them were taking something from the cave—the body of Pamela Carr. It enraged him to see what Dolphin had reduced her to. With the passing of the two mortal fools, he went closer to inspect the spotty remains of Cooper. He saw Cooper's boy—just a rack of bone inside the cocoon now. He saw the Bradley woman and the dog. The scene had a strange double effect on him. It made him sick at what Dolphin had done to endanger them all, and sick at seeing proof positive of his cannibalism toward his own kind, but also it made him salivate with the memory of fresh blood coming warm out of the living flesh. The memory had an odor attached to it, the odor of coppery blood, and in the recesses of his vampire mind he also recalled the effusive feeling of strength, well-being, and comfort in taking the power of another living being and infusing oneself with this power.

Sure, there were trade-offs to being able to live more peaceably and undetected among the humans; at moments like this, he understood Dolph's needs far more than Dolph might imagine.

Where the hell was the boy? There wasn't much time if they were to stop Stroud and Magaffey returning to Andover with evidence of vampires living among the sheep.

He formed into the bat creature he was. These surroundings, so far removed from the Institute and even the mausoleum, were for him a coming home. He flew deeper into the bowels of the myriad of caves in search of Dolphin. As he did so, he sent out radiating mental pleas to his only son. Along with his telepathic distress call, he forwarded his unique and unmistakable echo-location radar. Dolphin had a clear shot at him now, if he wished to attack.

"We must hurry," said Stroud to Magaffey.
"Don't you think I know that?"

They'd placed what was left of Pam Carr inside one of the coffins, nailing it shut. Supposedly, the neutral earth would destroy all vermin, parasites, and other creatures that went into the making of this vampiristic femme fatale. They were now backing from the cave with the heavier body of Mrs. Bradley, drained white, very dead, but still quite human in appearance. One could not say the same for Pam Carr.

"I sense something nearby, Magaffey," said Stroud, "something watching us."

"Perhaps we best make this our last trip."

"The Cooper boy's remains might go a long way to prove our case."

"Agreed."

"And the Meyers boy's dog. The fact they all came from this same cave."

"Right enough . . . then we'd best continue."

They placed Maude Bradley into the second coffin of sterile earth, banging home the lid, before returning to the cave for the two smaller bodies. "Mr. Bradley's body is by now embalmed and on its way out of town," said Magaffey. "I had no idea we'd run up on this lot. My intention was to show you a cache of bones below some of the bat droppings—human bones. The devils've become more active than ever."

As they neared the remaining bodies they heard a rumble of falling debris deep in the cave, followed by billowing clouds of dust-smoke and a high-pitched squeal, almost piglike, of something in pain. It froze Magaffey and Stroud had to shout at him, "Grab the dog! I'll have at it with the boy. Magaffey, do as I say!"

"What the hell was that?"

"Never mind! Go!"

"Son, we'd better run! It—this thing—it can outrun your granddaddy's helicopter."

"Move along then, move, Magaffey."

They rushed, stumbling and getting off the filth-ridden floor. In each man's mind was the fear of being caught and cocooned by the thing that had fed on the poor devils who'd slowly died here—both human and otherwise.

"Last time Ananias took off from here the damned thing chased him in the air, attacked the chopper while it was still airborne, nearly causing it to crash and burn. You saw the damage it sustained."

The men retraced their steps, dropping tools and lifting them as they went. Magaffey clutched the pickax as if it were a magical sword to be used against the thing that Stroud sensed more and more nearby. Stroud held tight to the boy's body in one hand, the tire iron in the other, wondering what use it would be against such a monster. Over his shoulder, he'd slung the stakes, and attached to his belt was the hammer—all dubious weapons at best.

Magaffey had the light now, but suddenly it went flying from his grasp, throwing them into darkness at the precise moment an enormous presence, like a rushing wind, knocked them both over as it passed. Stroud felt something physical flutter by his head and he smelled the animal stench of the wings in the dark. It felt like the largest bat in the cave.

Stroud had dropped the tire iron, and the small body fell aside as he searched in the total darkness. Magaffey was blubbering, "It's him! It's the thing! Oh, God, God!"

"Get the light!" said Stroud, seeing it wheeling about, creating a strobe effect on the wall, some enormous black shape blotting out the wall up there near the ceiling. There was no mistaking the beating and rustling sounds of bats, but this time the sounds were somehow amplified, larger.

Again the men felt the power of the creature that swept by like some prehistoric bird of prey. It took Stroud a moment to realize this was a *second* such monster.

Stroud floundered about the vermin-ridden earth until his hands found the large tire iron that represented a cross. *Superstition perhaps*, he thought, but he had very little else to guide him now. At about the same time Dr. Magaffey got control of the light and he bravely shone it on the two mighty man-sized bats atop the cathedral of the cave battling one another. It was like a fierce war between two dinosaurs. Whole sections of the wall were caved in by the force of battle. In the light Stroud caught glimpses of the ugly talons, the incisors, the batlike features about the head and face and the skeins of dark skin between the bony, elongated fingers that stretched the length of a man's arms. The sacklike, agile skin was unlike Cooper's only in the color, his having gone near white.

The snouts of the two battling creatures suddenly turned on the light, their blind eyes feeling the heat of it, their mouths punctuated in circles to send out the telling message that two animated objects besides themselves were in the cave. Magaffey shouted at Stroud, "Hold up the tire iron, boy! High!"

Magaffey's light, hitting the tire iron, created the shadow of an enormous cross cutting a swath across the two creatures, searing their hair and skin, the resulting odor like singed wool. The cross had the effect of catching the creatures by surprise and temporarily disorienting them, especially the one nearest Stroud.

"Back out now, Stroud. Leave the kid!"

"But—"

"Do as I say, damn it! Hurry back this way, now!"

Stroud felt paralyzed but he forced his legs to move while his arms were extended, his grip on the tire iron firm. The stronger of the two batlike creatures swooped below the light and came at Stroud, knocking into him, sending him tumbling. The force was like being kicked by a mule or a shotgun. Stroud came up with a bleeding forehead and he heard Magaffey screaming. The attacking creature had him by the collar and was lifting him off the ground. Stroud dove for the ax the old man had dropped and sent it piercing into the creature's lower portions, a kind of dangling pair of fleshy feet. The talons were located high up, on the wingtips, just as those of a bat might be. The feet were also equipped with claws. The ax drew blood and the instant result was that Magaffey was dropped.

Stroud saw the second creature diving toward them and he held up the ax, readying to swing at the thing's chest. It appeared he had a clear shot with the powerful stakelike end of the ax when the second of the monsters flew headlong into its brother, averting it from Stroud's sure swing. The swing almost sent Stroud falling to his knees when he missed.

Suddenly, the place was silent, the creatures licking their wounds, hiding in a crack in the darkness. Stroud helped Magaffey to his feet and together, slowly but firmly, they backed toward the light and the freedom it represented. In a moment, they were clear of the cave, but they expected an attack from all sides and above on the bluff where the helicopter waited.

Dolphin Banaker had fallen to the floor of the cave in a weakened state, fluttering about the dung hills and white worms, his mind racing with the fearful thought that his injury would lead to death. He'd thought himself immortal. He had never felt fear in his life, and he had never felt weak. This feeling of strength draining from him by the second as if it were fluid, as if his blood had turned to bubbles and gas and was escaping through his pores, shocked him.

In the distance—or might it be closer—he "saw" his father's shape, just managing strength enough to send out the signal that located him. His father was pursuing Stroud. Dolph feared being left alone with all the odd sensations of this moment.

The combination of battle with his father and Stroud's shining cross that seared through his flesh while leaving his father virtually unharmed, amazed and terrified Dolph.

As he lay there, sensing his father's hesitation at the mouth of the cave, he knew two truths: his father was not what he had always believed him to be, but rather a gallant foe of the human race after all. And, he knew that if his father destroyed Stroud now, leaving Dolph alone with his heart-draining, blood-draining fear and weakness, that Dolph would die of his wounds.

He "saw" his father turn at the cave mouth, returning his echo-location "stare". Dolph knew in that instant his father's decision was made and Banaker turned and started back toward Dolph.

But Dolph, floundering and weakened, wondered if the old bat was coming back to aid him or to put a final end to him, if he thought destroying Dolph was more important now than destroying Stroud.

Dolph felt his insides withering with the thought and amid the pain of inability and the awful imprisonment of weak and useless limbs, he vomited. Whole colonies and eggs of the white worms came up with blood. He was bleeding internally; somehow Stroud's magic had cut right through to his organs and the parasites that lived within him had begun to feed on him! Had his father not been there, he'd be dead by now, destroyed by Stroud and Magaffey using a flashlight and a tire iron! It seemed unthinkable, unbelievable, yet, how many times had his father told him about the old enemy?

His father, using the new miracles of science and medicine, had so improved his own resistance to such ancient weapons, he had barely been affected by them. Banaker had merely been amused at the crude display, while he had succumbed to it. There was wisdom in his father's plans, and in his "cure." Dolphin needed the cure now, but even more, he needed his father to know that he had learned his lesson well, and that he deserved a second chance.

Dolph, with all that he could muster in the way of energy, transmitted this thought to his father as the wide-eyed bat man approached him with a look that meant either fear or hatred. Dolph was too weak to tell. He had spent all his energy signaling and transmitting.

Banaker swooped over him and lifted him in what seemed a steady, smooth, powerful action. Without a word he demanded Dolph to "Take of my blood, now! Now!"

Dolph and his father were in flight for a deeper part of the cave, a larger chamber, and while in flight Dolph sank his teeth into his father's neck, drinking in the other's power. Banaker came to rest with his son at just the area he expected to be below Stroud's helicopter. He allowed Dolph a moment more of sustenance before he forced himself away from the boy, his bat shape dissolving into a fog that filled the cave.

Dolph felt stronger and he knew he would live on, thanks to his father.

–18–

Dr. Martin Magaffey's bleeding had continued nonstop, and the extent of the wound, covered in the coagulating blood and the dark folds of the man's own skin, made it difficult to determine exactly how deep the gash went, and how much blood he'd lost. Magaffey was in a near coma. Stroud, bearing up against his weight, helped him along the difficult path upward to where the helicopter and escape awaited them. Twice Magaffey foundered, his entire body going slack, and finally Stroud had to lift him up in a forearm cradle to carry him along. Along their path, sharp gray wooden stakes created a trail anyone could follow as these objects fell from Stroud's shoulder pack.

Magaffey moaned once or twice before passing out altogether from the shock of the wound. Stroud's mind raced with what to do with him, where to take him for medical assistance, and who could be trusted.

They made the steep climb and Stroud rushed to strap Magaffey's limp form into the passenger seat. He then raced to the pilot's position, tearing away the now empty but confining bag that'd carried the stakes, tossing it into the bushes. A glance down the slope informed him of the surprising fact that they were not being pursued by the disgusting creatures. He climbed hastily into the cockpit and prepared to take off without worrying about the usual safety checks. He did all this just as a dark rush of moldering fog seeped from out of the cracks and earth just ahead of the craft, as if the caves were spewing forth some vile gas. Molecules seethed and whirled from out of the earth, rising up and over the cab of the helicopter. It was an unnatural fog, like nothing Stroud had ever encountered.

"It's the creature, Stroud! It can control its own shape!"

Stroud turned over the engine but it only whined in response. The dark cloud was gaining thickness and an ever-increasing hold on the chopper, some of it seeping into the rear and through the broken window when suddenly the engine kicked into life and the rotar blade was given full throttle, exploding the ominous fog and scattering it so thoroughly as to weaken it completely.

Stroud, Magaffey, the chopper, and its contents were up and away. Just before takeoff, Stroud had pulled down a flare gun and was now clutching it, ready for anything.

"Be damned if I'm going to wind up like Cooper and Pam," he said between clenched teeth. But Magaffey was mercifully unconscious. Stroud wondered if he'd use the flare gun to explode the old machine with him and Magaffey and the evidence aboard rather than face the slow death the vampires had in store for them.

Banaker and Dolphin stood on the bluff now, the helicopter a far-off blur in the sky, going for Stroud Manse. Dolph wanted to give chase and destroy them now. Banaker held his son in check saying, "Patience . . . patience, Dolphin. The important thing at the moment is us!"

"Us?"

"You and I united in a common battle against a common enemy: Stroud. We will beat him down, the last of his line, and you, my son, will know what to do with that promising future."

At this, Dolphin stared at his father whose ankle was bleeding profusely. Dolphin bent to look at the wound, and he lapped at it. "It's a bad wound, Father," he said.

"I've got to get to the Institute, warn the others, gather our forces."

"Yes, of course. The brightness of the sun has me weak," confessed Dolph. "I must get out of it. I confess, there are some great benefits to your blood substitute."

"You were hurt more badly by the cross as well, son."

"Yes, I know."

"So much I've tried to tell you . . . you had to learn on your own."

"The hard way."

Banaker hugged his son to him. "One good thing about Stroud's being here. He's brought you back to me."

"I'm sorry about all the . . . the wrongs . . . about Cooper's kid—"

"And Cooper, and Pamela."

"But Cooper went to Magaffey and told him about us."

"What? When did this occur?"

"Last night."

Banaker nodded. "Of course, you did the right thing, son."

"And Pam . . . well, she failed miserably with Stroud."

"I suppose there was no other way for Pam. She was never quite completely one with the family . . . nor Cooper after his son's death."

"No sir, no . . . they weren't."

"I trust now, at last, you have finished, however, with feeding on your own kind! And with endangering your kith and kin."

"I have, Father . . . and I know I need your elixir."

"If we are to combat Stroud and win, yes, you do. But just as important, now, son, you realize you will one day be the head of the colony—what you do will determine the future of our species on Earth. That's what's at stake now."

Dolphin put his arms around his father and they parted there, Dolph going back to the dark of the cave while Oliver Banaker rushed for the Institute. He must be ready for Stroud. Dolph would join him at nightfall and together they would put an end to Stroud's hideous line.

Banaker wasn't overly worried about the items Magaffey and Stroud had removed from Dolph's lair. Their evidence would amount to nothing quite shortly, just as Cooper's body now amounted to a watery spot on the floor of the cave now being consumed by maggots.

Magaffey still had not come to when Abe Stroud landed the helicopter, intact, on the weed-infested pad back of Stroud Manse. They were greeted by Lonnie Wilson who, for the first time, was showing a fascination for the whirlybird, his eyes and hands caressing the metal monster. "Help me get Doctor Magaffey up to the house, Lonnie!" cried Stroud over the sound of the rotars which were still churning down.

"Yes, sir, Mr. Stroud!"

"Good man!"

Stroud jumped down and came around to help with Magaffey whose wounds startled Lonnie. "It's all right, Lonnie. He'll be all right if we can get him into the house!"

Lonnie grabbed onto Dr. Magaffey's lighter frame and lifted him bodily onto his shoulder, saying, "I got 'im."

Stroud watched as Lonnie hurried off with the doctor. He glanced at the cargo hold, full now with the incriminating evidence against Banaker, wondering what he might do with it. He imagined himself flying it into Andover and placing it on the steps at City Hall, or at Chief Briggs's feet. Briggs had been unable to safely get away a simple UPS package. What would he do with Pam Carr's remains, those of the Bradley woman, and the Cooper kid?"

The corpses required a thorough examination in the best and most sanitary conditions; they required Magaffey's attention and perhaps Banaker's well-lit, well-ventilated, sterile operating rooms, if a safe and useful autopsy was to be performed. The facts, such as they were, must be documented. Not only for his and Magaffey's safety—to prove their innocence in the deaths—but for the next time, for the future . . . and all those millions who would never otherwise believe it possible, either now or in the future.

But what were the chances of gaining Banaker's own medical facilities to prove him—along with most of his people—a vampire? Not bloody likely.

Stroud didn't want to let the evidence out of his sight. He could not understand why Banaker had allowed them to escape with the damning cargo, unless he hadn't a clue about their ability to maintain the condition of the evidence, or unless he intended to regain it later. Leaving it unguarded even for a short while could prove foolish, but all that Stroud had on hand to guard it with was the flare gun. And as for the condition of the evidence—sterile earth or no—the microbes seeping into the coffins via air were at work already on the corpses—unless the cocoons prevented this. However, the cocoons had rents and tears in them, particularly Pam Carr's.

Enormous, smouldering storm clouds rumbled in from the west, threatening to blot out the sky with blackness. Stroud had seen them from the air. Andover would, in a matter of an hour, be covered in darkness and rain. Banaker and his kind, if folklore could be believed, controlled the power of the wind and created such storms. Within that mighty storm cloud may hide hundreds, if not thousands of them, all come to descend on Stroud Manse, to reclaim what was theirs.

Abe was tired, spent from his battle with the man-sized bat creature he somehow knew was Banaker, one and the same. Something in the unseeing, cold bat eyes, something in the makeup of the creature, and all the knowledge brought him by Magaffey before dawn—the unbelievable tale of the Ashyers and Lonnie Wilson, the way his grandfather had died, and finding the bodies of Pam Carr, Cooper, and the others associated with Banaker encrusted in egglike sacs. It all pointed to Banaker and the insidious nature of his so-called Institute. He recalled the ghoulish behavior of the men in the morgue that day, and the strange suspicions Dolph Banaker had exhibited.

He knew he must somehow get to Banaker Institute unseen, that their only chance to reduce the odds against the human population of Andover was now to somehow decimate the population of the vampires. "It's either them or us," he said aloud—a phrase often repeated in the jungles of Southeast Asia during his years there. This was no less a war.

Lonnie returned for him, and Banaker had to plead for his help with the coffins. Lonnie didn't want to go near them, much less touch them.

Stroud took firm hold of the shaking man's shoulders. "Lonnie! Lonnie, it's important! It must be done! I need your help, Lonnie."

Lonnie, trembling, stepped up to the cargo bay and stared inside. Stroud thought he would bolt away any moment, but he caught him when he tried to do just that, blubbering and tearing away from Stroud's grasp. "Damn it, Lonnie, just grab hold! It won't hurt you, I promise! I promise!"

"Yer granfadder promised, too . . . but it got me! Bit me!"

"But you're alive, and he's dead, Lonnie! He saved you and lost his own life doing so!"

"I can't!"

Stroud struck him hard across the face, and Lonnie went down to his knees, further frustrating Stroud. "All right, all right, Lonnie. Get up to the house and bring me my hunting rifle."

"Won't do no good against them, Doctor Stroud."

"Just do it! And tell Mrs. Ashyer to call Ray Carroll to come out here. And . . . and tell Ashyer to come out here to give me a hand with the coffins. You got all that, Lonnie? Lonnie?"

"Yes, sir . . . yes, sir," he said, ambling off like a child soon to forget.

"Hurry, Lonnie!"

Lonnie quickened his pace. Stroud could still hear his wasting of words and blubbering nonsense as he made his way to the house. Soon, Ashyer rushed out with a rain slicker and two hunting guns instead of the one Stroud had requested. Ashyer readily bent to the work of removing the coffins from the cargo bay and onto the ground. He took an end and the three trips to the house were accomplished at about the same time the storm broke, sending mad sheets of glasslike rain over the land. Looking out the door from Stroud Manse, Abe thought it looked like midnight. Inside, he found it to be three P.M. He and Magaffey had been a long time at the caves.

"How is Doctor Magaffey?" he asked Mrs. Ashyer.

"He's asking for you, sir, but I think he needs a good rest. That . . . that scar on his neck is very bad. He needs true medical attention. I did what I could, using his bag."

"Thanks, Mrs. Ashyer," he said, their eyes meeting, telling him that she did not blame him, but that she knew the cause of the calamity.

"What're we to do sir?" she asked. "I mean, if they . . . if they come?"

"Stupid question, woman," Ashyer said to her. "We fight for our lives, or we take our lives. Right, Doctor Stroud?"

"I pray it will not come to that."

"But they're surely amassing against you, sir," she said.

"They are." He rushed to Magaffey in the parlor where he'd been lain out on a blanket hastily thrown over the ottoman.

"How're you feeling, old man?"

"Like the poor guy who was nearly cut in two in *The Pit and the Pendulum*."

"Banaker's talons were like a pendulum the way he slashed across your neck."

"Tried to take my head off, I figure. Lost feeling to parts of my left side . . . fingers especially, tingling all the way through my arm. First time I ever had to prescribe for myself anything stronger than aspirin."

"You're looking a great deal better than when I put you into the helicopter."

"I don't remember that."

"Rest now."

"Rest, how?"

"You can't put pressure on that wound; it'll burst and you'll bleed to death, you understand, and I need you right now, so just rest, please!" he shouted.

"Sure, sure, son."

Stroud frowned. "Sorry, but I mean it, Magaffey."

"Sounded like your granddad there for a moment. Look, Abe, what're we going to do?"

"Right now, we sit out the storm. I've got some thinking to do."

"Thinking won't do the trick, son. *Action*. We need to take action." Magaffey ended with a cough that racked his frame. Neither his color, which was ashen, nor his inability to speak without long hesitations, nor this coughing looked good to Stroud. He did need medical attention, but the only medical attention in Andover was Banaker's kind—and that kind no one needed. Little wonder most of the patients who checked into the Institute never checked out. What a clearing house and convenient conversion center. Take in the weakly human at his most vulnerable, when he is easy prey, and either feed on him or turn him to doing your bidding. How many people in Andover, in how many different walks of life, had been converted by the likeable, politic Dr. Oliver Banaker?

He thought of Timmy Meyers in the hospital—revived by Banaker's bone marrow concoction, perhaps? Or had Magaffey gotten the boy out before that stage of his development toward becoming a full-fledged vampire? They might never know, but if they came through this alive, and if the Banaker people were put down, then a search would have to go out for the Meyerses, and Timmy would have to be brought back and tested. A simple blood test would be evidence enough.

"I won't be long, Doctor," Stroud told Magaffey.

"The bodies? The evidence?" he wheezed.

"Safely in house at the moment. Placed it in cold storage. We have a walk-in freezer here."

Magaffey nodded his approval before he closed his eyes and died. At first Stroud thought he'd just gone to sleep, but immediately after he sensed it. The old fellow was gone. *Noble old man*, he said silently to himself before informing the Ashyers. Ashyer and he placed the body in the freezer with the others.

"You know, sir, they won't rest until everyone at Stroud Manse is dead," said Ashyer glumly before leaving him alone with Magaffey once more.

"I'm sorry I did not listen to you sooner, Doctor," he said to Magaffey's corpse before closing the door on the dead.

He felt he had so needed Magaffey's counsel. Magaffey knew about the properties of the bone marrow drink. He would know how to go about "poisoning" the vampires' supply, stored, no doubt somewhere at the Institute, just as the vampires themselves were stored throughout Andover. Exactly where, he could not be sure. He went to the circular room, only half hearing Mrs. Ashyer tell him that Ray Carroll was on his way this moment, anxious to assist.

In the quiet of the torture chamber, Abe Stroud mulled over his dilemma. He'd brought with him Magaffey's papers on the Banaker *Bloody Mary*, as the old man called it in his report. The properties were those of a super-charged blood plasma with the added ingredients of an unknown genetic material and bone marrow.

Stroud guessed the unknown ingredient to be a *vampire gene*. Banaker was into genetic splicing. He'd taken the best of human blood and the best of vampire blood and had created a new strain of the liquid of life. "The life of the flesh is in the blood," he said, quoting Leviticus 17:11. Stroud knew a lot about blood from firsthand knowledge. He knew that there was nothing in nature that had so profound an emotional effect on people as blood—unless it was the human skull. For blood could cause a person to faint, make his head reel, while at the same time irresistibly attracting him. At the same time that it inspired disgust, nausea, and a desire to murder, it amazed and fascinated. Some police shrinks believed that the underlying motive behind sexual murder was nearly always the desire to shed blood and not the desire to cause death. Some nut they'd caught after a series of murders one year in Chicago had killed people only so he could wipe their blood over his skin in the honest belief that to do so would keep him ever young and ever strong.

The Banaker family had learned medicine and modern technologies enough to know all of this and much more, to use the genetic coding of their race to infiltrate that of the human race, and to become as close to normal people as possible. Banaker had taken the medium of blood to create a new class of vampire. The gods and demons in Ancient Babylonia and Greece, according to the superstitions of the time, were attracted to the smell of bloodshed, especially to the bodies of the violently slain. In which case, Stroud thought, Satan had had a field day in Vietnam, and was now having a merry time in Andover, Illinois.

"From the emanations of shed blood," he heard himself saying as his thoughts became words, "disembodied entities—*spirits*— build up appearances and become visible."

He could not believe the thought that next crossed his mind, and yet he needed counsel—he needed the counsel of his forefathers, of his grandfather! And there might be a way to gather Ananias's ghost here, to him. The way was clear, but it was also *ghoulish*. It might also backfire. Could he do it? he asked himself moments before bolting off for the bodies in the freezer upstairs.

When he stormed upstairs, shouting for Ashyer to help him transport all the bodies to the central chamber, Ashyer hesitated a moment and asked, "Are you sure, sir?"

"I am certain. Let's do it."

At the same time the intercom announced a peeling of thunder outside, followed by Ray Carroll's voice. "Let him through, Lonnie!" Stroud told Wilson, who stood at the controls.

When the door opened for Carroll, Stroud and Ashyer were hefting Magaffey's body down the hallway.

—19—

Ray Carroll was aghast at the sight before him, his eyes telling the story, telling the others his immediate thoughts as if they were thrown up on a screen: he had stepped into a madhouse where the inmates had already done considerable damage. He thought he was witness to the murder of Dr. Martin Magaffey.

"Carroll!" shouted Stroud when he realized what must be going through the man's mind. "We need your assistance and help, perhaps the help of your friends, anyone in the town you know whom we can trust. Magaffey's been killed by vampires."

"Vampires? Vampires? Are you crazy?" Carroll was more than a little skeptical and he held himself firmly at the door which was ajar, rain pelting in, puddling about his feet where he dripped on the tiles.

"Doctor Magaffey, Bradley and his wife, and others, all murdered by creatures that, for lack of a better word, are vampires, yes!"

"Vampires? Stroud, that's . . . that's just madness to say that Doctor Magaffey was killed by vampires."

"A colony of them living in Andover! There's no time to explain. Suffice it to say that Banaker is one of them, most likely the leader. I have irrefutable evidence that this mutated race of demonic creatures does exist, and if you will come with me, I'll show it to you."

"Evidence . . . irrefutable . . . ."

173

"Yes, Carroll! The Meyers boy, the other disappearances, all stem from the fact that Banaker's Institute is a haven and a feeding ground for ghouls, vampires, whatever you wish to call them! I know it's hard to believe, but Magaffey had proof that they're feeding on the unearthed remains of humans, using bone marrow as an ingredient to insure the strengthening of the mutated gene that created them in the first place."

Carroll found a chair and literally fell into it. "I . . . I knew there was something strange going on, but Doctor Stroud, I . . . I find this hard to accept."

"Come with me then. Trust me long enough that I might show you the evidence."

He nodded. "Yes, of course. I'll follow you." Carroll glanced again at Magaffey and the throat bandages, soaked in red.

Stroud said to Ashyer, "We'll get Doctor Magaffey to his destination in a moment, Ashyer. I'll be right back."

Stroud showed Carroll the way to the walk-in freezer, explaining how Magaffey had come to him with the elixir and had convinced him to go with him to the caves where they'd been attacked by batlike creatures, the size and density of human beings. Carroll remained skeptical, just as Stroud expected, and he hesitated at the door to the freezer. He had seen ice crystals forming on Magaffey's body outside. He didn't relish the idea of being locked in the freezer and left there to die a slow death by the madman Stroud. He indicated that Stroud should go first. But he remained reluctant, standing at the doorway, even when Stroud stood on the far side to peel back a blanket that'd been placed over the pod that contained what remained of Pamela Carr. He only came closer when Stroud asked him to do so.

Ray Carroll seemed to have gone white, all the blood draining from his features. He seemed claustrophobic and was visibly shaking, either from the cold or the horror of what lay on the block before him. A second cocoon, that containing the Bradley woman, lay nearby, and this, too, gave rise to a gasp from Carroll.

"This is not the handiwork of any madman, Ray! Ray, this material, this pod is tightly woven like the silk of caterpillars. I know it makes no sense to you. Makes none to me either, but Doctor Cooper was inside one of these too and—"

"Cooper? Cooper from the Institute?"

"He was still alive when we cut into the cocoon."

"Oh, oh, my . . . " He looked faint now, as if unable to get air. His gaze over Pam Carr was long and sad. "And you say that Banaker is . . . is responsible for . . . for this?"

"Banaker, the others at the Institute, Pam here, Cooper, they're all of another race, a mutant race which our forefathers called vampires. I don't know but Magaffey studied the properties of the bone marrow drink and he concluded they've got what science nowadays calls a . . . a jumping gene—"

"Jumping gene?"

"Ahhh." Stroud shook his head, knowing he was on shaky ground. "Jumping gene, pieces of DNA that move about the chromosomes, parasites that actually live inside the DNA that trigger mutations. Magaffey was going on about it for some time before we got to the caves, something about the natural and unnatural order of evolutionary process. At any rate, here is the result."

"So, the cold storage is to protect the evidence, I see."

"Without the pods, who'd believe us?"

"But what about Magaffey's body? Where are you taking it?" Carroll was almost out the freezer door, unable to take anymore, it seemed. Stroud didn't press him any further, allowing him to escape. Outside, he shivered and spoke of how uncomfortable cold places made him. But Stroud sensed that it was not the cold at all, but the pods and their ugly contents that made Carroll visibly ill and shaken, despite the fact he made no reference to being aghast or uncomfortable over the pods or the poor souls inside them. His white face told all.

Stroud thought it odd at first, but the man's mind was being asked to take in so much at once, Stroud knew he must be patient with Carroll. "Now that Doctor Magaffey's gone, I need you with me, Ray."

"Sure, sure, Doctor Stroud. I've seen enough to convince me."

"Can you get us additional help?"

"Additional help?"

"Yes, any moment, I believe, we're going to be under attack here by . . . by them."

"I see. Yes, let me get on my CB, see if I can raise some of the boys."

Stroud recalled how many men had come on the double when the call went out for the Meyers boy. He felt a little comforted in knowing they'd soon have the help of neighbors.

From the freezer, they returned to Ashyer who'd patiently waited for help with Magaffey's body, Lonnie Wilson still useless in this regard. Ray Carroll passed by the mirror, his reflection turning eerily and shakily in and around on itself as if the image were one on a computer screen that was not getting enough power to it, but only Lonnie Wilson saw this.

"I'll be right back," Carroll announced to the others before disappearing for his truck and the CB Radio.

Lonnie watched him intently from the window but the darkness seemed to gobble Carroll up. At no time did Lonnie see the light of his cab go on.

Stroud and Ashyer continued with the work of removing Dr. Magaffey's remains to the circular chamber by the most direct route. Stroud was calling for Lonnie and Mrs. Ashyer to gather up some foodstuffs and blankets, saying they must all seek the shelter of the circle. It would act as their "bomb" shelter from the creatures that sought to take them from Stroud Manse.

Mrs. Ashyer raced to comply with Dr. Stroud, but Abe had to scream again at Lonnie who seemed mesmerized at the big bay window beside the entranceway. "Wish we had the bars back up," he was saying when he turned to look down the hall at Stroud and Ashyer trundling off with Magaffey's body.

"Two more trips," Stroud told Ashyer.

"Sir?"

"From the freezer to the chamber."

"The . . . the cocoons, sir?"

"Yes, Ashyer. We must keep them in our sight at all times."

"Mrs. Ashyer, the boy—ahhh, Lonnie, sir—are terribly upset by them, sir."

"That can't be helped. We must do what we must do, Ashyer."

"Yes, sir."

They laid Magaffey across one of the slabs in the torture chamber. "Shout to Lonnie to get the doctor's bag and bring it down, now! I'll meet you at the freezer. Where the hell's Carroll?"

Stroud and Ashyer did the work of removing the other two bodies which had remained draped in their respective pods. These they placed against a wall as far from the chair and ottoman and bookshelves as possible, Stroud feeling that the evidence could simply be ignored by Mrs. Ashyer, Lonnie, and all of them, if covered with blankets. More blankets were brought in for their comfort. It was dank and chilly here, and the rising hurricanelike attack may take hours.

Ray Carroll returned, drenched, the rain having plastered his hair to his scalp. He explained that it was difficult getting anyone out in a storm such as this, and that he dared not attempt to explain the true nature of the problem over the airwaves, primarily because no one would believe him and consequently no one would come. He had, however, reached some of his closest friends who were driving up this moment to assist.

Carroll asked, "Is there anymore I can do, Doctor Stroud?"

"If you care to put your life on the line. They're coming for us, the whole lot of them. I cannot promise you anything beyond that."

"Surely you have weapons to combat them with."

"Come along, I'll show you what we have."

Stroud led Carroll through the twisting maze that led to the central chamber where he balked at entering as he had at the freezer. "Where are we?"

"This is where we will make our stand. If we remain in the rooms upstairs, they'll destroy us all."

"But if there's no way out . . . "

"Nor is there any way in, if all goes as I plan."

Stroud knew of a passageway out along an underground tunnel, but it would seem foolish to place oneself on the bat creature's turf. They seemed to know every cave and every underground passage intimately.

"What's to keep them from diffusing through in a fog, Doctor Stroud?" asked Ashyer.

"Only these walls and my grandfather, I suppose," he said enigmatically. "Everyone now, into the chamber. Carroll, you as well."

The moment Carroll stepped into the circular room he became agitated. His eyes fell once more on Magaffey, whose fatal wound now lay open, the bandage spread like an opened handkerchief now over his chest with the odor of blood rising to fill the room. He also saw that the cocoons had been, in his absence, removed from the freezer to here. He was once more so shaken, his body began to quiver as he tried desperately to maintain his manly composure. Stroud understood why he was so uncomfortable and offered a word.

"Trust me, this is all very necessary."

"Trust you?" he asked, his eyes meeting Stroud's. "Trust you to be like your grandfather, you mean? Maybe Banaker was right about you, all along . . . maybe you're—"

He didn't finish his sentence as suddenly Lonnie Wilson, coming up behind him, stabbed Carroll between the shoulder blades with a hypodermic needle he'd fished from Dr. Magaffey's bag. Stroud rushed to snatch Lonnie away and pull out the needle, half drained of the fluid inside. Lonnie had filled the needle with God knew what.

Mr. and Mrs. Ashyer looked on in stunned horror as Ray Carroll wheeled, reaching for the center of pain. He raced from the confines of the room, clawing his way up the stone stairs, Stroud shouting after him.

"He's one of them!" Lonnie was shouting as Stroud raced after Carroll. On the stairway, amid the shadows there, Stroud saw Ray Carroll's form change before his eyes. His human body turned to an elastic outer shell that ripped through his clothing, and from his back burst a pair of thick wings made of dark hair and skin attached to his true limbs, bony arms with extended fingers. His features became ratlike and the eyes went from sight to nonsight as he sent up a silent-to-the-human-ear screech to alert his fellow creatures to his present location. Stroud saw the familiar pucker beneath the snout as the thing that Carroll had become sent out its pealing, high-pitched distress call.

Stroud raced back for the circle where he grabbed a weapon of his grandfather's making, a long standard pole at the tip end of which was a metal stake. The Ashyers and Lonnie Wilson looked on as he took the lance and went out once more in pursuit of Carroll.

He hadn't far to go, however, as Carroll's body came tumbling down to the bottom of the stairwell at Stroud's feet, apparently dead, as it began to wither and age and liquify and finally crumple into dust before the excited stares of everyone in the chamber.

"He's killed him. Lonnie killed him," said Ashyer in stark amazement.

Stroud heard the thunderous roar of the others as they tore down the door and crashed through the windows upstairs. The others heard the commotion coming from above as well, the Ashyers huddling together like frightened children now, Lonnie staunchly at Stroud's side, taking the lance from him and saying, "I knew when he went to his truck that he was one of them."

"Good man, Lonnie," said Stroud. "He was casing the place, and if we'd left the bodies in the freezer upstairs, they'd have gotten them, including Magaffey's." Stroud then kicked at the dust that was Carroll and shoved the thick, dungeonlike door to the chamber closed.

Stroud rushed to Magaffey's bag, taking Lonnie with him, asking, "What did you put in the hypodermic needle, and how'd you know it would kill Carroll?"

"Doctor Magaffey told me to stay away from it once," he said, innocently. "Once when I was asked to bring his bag along." Lonnie brought out a small vial of the stuff marked SUCCINYLCHOLINE.

Stroud knew enough about medicines to know that most, given in too great a dose, were poisonous. Succinylcholine apparently was no good to the average vampire, and was perhaps the best hope they had, should they live to use this new knowledge past tonight.

Overhead, the manse sounded overrun by the creatures tearing through it in a rage, unable to find what they'd come for, searching every nook and cranny. Stroud's time had become much too limited for explanations to the Ashyers or to Lonnie for what he was about to do.

Another thunderous crash like a gale force wind overhead made Mrs. Ashyer weep in fear. Her husband saw to her. "All of you," said Stroud, "must not under any circumstances leave this room, and you must obey me to the letter if we are to survive. You know to what extremes my grandfather had to go to save you from becoming one of them. Now, my friends, I'm here to save you once more, but you must do as I say without hesitation or question. At times I may not be able to speak, and you may see some terrible and frightful sights here tonight, but you must have faith, faith in me, faith in my family, my grandfather, and faith in God that we will beat these demonic creatures. Are you all in agreement on these items?"

"Yes," said Lonnie, showing that he intended to maintain his newfound courage.

The Ashyers nodded their agreement.

"Good, then take these knives I procured from the kitchen and open Doctor Magaffey's wound further."

The Ashyers looked at one another, swallowing hard. Lonnie bit his lip. For a long moment no one said anything.

"In order to gain the help of Ananias Stroud, we must sacrifice some blood here. Will it be ours, or Doctor Magaffey's? If it is ours, then it will be too late, and nothing my grandfather's ghost can do to help us can come in time. If we further spill Doctor Magaffey's, if Ananias's spirit is likely to come and we can gain his help in all of this, it will be through the spirit of Magaffey's blood."

"How do you know this will work?" asked Ashyer.

"I don't."

Everyone in the room, listening to the approach of the vampires, sensing their presence on all sides, began their own approach toward Magaffey's body.

Stroud began a mantra, using the resonant sound of his grandfather's name, calling for his spirit to be with them in this hour of greatest darkness.

"Ananias, Ananias, Ananias . . . "

The others chimed in. First Lonnie, then Ashyer, then his wife.

Outside, the walls seemed to be shaking, the stones ballooning in and out, as in an earthquake.

Twenty vampires careened through Stroud Manse, knocking over anything in their way. Like a natural force, the power of the creatures sent them through walls and doors, tearing away hinges, sending chandeliers toppling along with furniture; glass cabinets exploded with the high-frequency sound waves emitted by the creatures. Smaller, scavenger bats raced about wildly along with their hosts like pilot fish accompanying sharks. They stormed everywhere, having learned that the cocooned bodies of Pamela Carr and the Bradley woman were not where Ray Carroll had said they would be. Banaker sent telepathic messages to the others, some of whom were sharp enough to receive, while others, fearful and distrustful of the night's work and the sudden new turn in policy adopted by their master after all these years, flew from the scene and back to the safety of their roosting areas spread around the city of Andover. But most feared Banaker and through this cord of fear, he held them to him.

"Find Carroll," was his message, "and bring him to me."

It was Dolph who found Carroll's remains, surmising that Stroud had once again overpowered one of their number there on the stone staircase leading to what seemed nowhere.

Banaker looked over the damage with a mix of fear—the sight of one like him being reduced to ash—and hatred. "He is here, just on the other side of this door," said Banaker to the others. "We need only break it down, and we have him."

"I'll beak it down, Father," Dolph communicated to his father. The others backed a little away as Dolph, his energies fully recharged now, attacked the door. His entire power went at it but Dolph literally bounced off it and hit hard against the stone stairs at his back. He had not even touched the door. Some invisible shield around it had stopped him.

Dolph was stunned no less than his father and the others who witnessed this. Inside the room, they could hear the chanting, and they could make out Stroud's voice.

Stroud had been wise to manuever himself and the others here. Banaker was frustrated. Even if he could get the legitimate authorities out here now, point to Stroud as a fiend, showing the evidence of Magaffey's mangled body as proof, Stroud still held onto the cocoons which would then expose him and the others. It was a stalemate, unless his people could find a way into the sealed room.

He set his army of vampires to the task of searching for weaknesses in the invisible armor of the place. He sent some to attempt to come in overhead, some from below, others in another direction. It was at this time he realized that he had some defectors in his ranks. These he cursed and noted, in order to deal with later.

Three hours later the vampires continued pounding from all sides, some changing into spiders, frogs, and fog in an attempt to seep into the room in one fashion or another. As rats they failed as well. Banaker finally put all of his effort into gaining entrance by becoming smoke to burn his way through and choke his enemies to death. He felt weaknesses in the walls where he worked, small chinks that allowed particles of him to seep through. He was only partially through the magic circle Stroud had sent around himself and his people when he realized that Stroud and the others were not alone. He did not see it so much as he felt it: the definite presence of Ananias Stroud.

The sensation so shocked him he pulled back as if touching glacial ice. Vampires liked cold, but despised places below a certain temperature for they could be frozen up in such places for eternity, neither wholly alive nor dead. It was for this reason he'd had to rip away the freezer door before the others dared enter it. Carroll himself had come out quivering and blubbering about it when he'd gone in and come out again with the information Banaker requested of him.

Not even the bone marrow elixir had been of any help in combating freezing temperatures on vampires, but not for lack of testing at the Institute.

And now Stroud had gotten in touch with his dead forebears, a thing no vampire, not even he, could ever do. The ghost, or soul of a vampire simply did not exist. All that a vampire might count on in the way of immortality was in this life. It was the one true advantage *they* had over *his* kind, Banaker believed.

The others sensed Banaker's feelings of hopelessness, and more began to disappear from the scene. Banaker feared Stroud, and they all knew it, and now he had two Strouds to contend with, and they all knew it.

Dolphin had disappeared with the others, and Banaker felt quite alone in the bowels of Stroud Manse, and quite vulnerable as he thought of eternity without a soul, and as he thought of all that he and his father before him had accomplished here that only a Stroud could take from them. For the first time in his life Banaker felt truly afraid. And the others, sensing this, were leaving him. Apparently, even Dolph had gone, Dolph who had promised to give up his life to defend his father's right to lead the colony.

Banaker felt like a broken, unfeeling object as he left Stroud Manse, the shambles all around him looking like the work of a devastating tornado. Outside, the darkness was strangely calm and the old world seemed to mock him.

—20—

Inside the circular chamber Stroud conversed with his grandfather's apparition which had risen on the vapors of Magaffey's blood. It was a silent conversation, a talk between two minds, as the others saw nothing and heard nothing beyond a whispering sail of wind in the sealed room and a coldness like standing below an air-conditioning duct.

Stroud saw and heard distinctly however, as Ananias dictated some truths to the inheritor of the manse and all that went with the title.

There were, apparently, all manner of nasty creatures the world over, some of which had taken up residence in Andover, others of which were halfway around the globe. Abe Stroud was told that he alone had the capacity to detect and put an end to such creatures as the vampires of Andover which had sprung up around the elder Banaker and now his son, to be passed on to yet another generation of blood-eaters.

Ananias's form transmitted all this and more to Stroud as the others continued the chant, and continued to draw more blood from Magaffey's body. Ghoulish as it may seem, the old black doctor's body was being made to serve just as Magaffey himself would have it serve under the circumstances if he could speak. With that thought, Ananias showed Abe Stroud that Magaffey's spirit was here, too, with Ananias.

"Friends in death as in life," he said in that resounding voice that rolled around the coils of Abe's brain.

Abe then saw Magaffey's ethereal form alongside the fading one of his grandfather, the old black face calm and smiling and nodding as if to indicate that he approved.

Ananias's apparition then returned in strong focus and said, "You already know what to do, Abe. You know where to go."

"No, I do not," Stroud replied so strongly he shouted aloud. "I need your guidance."

"At the hospital," he said, "when you saw the blood bank, remember."

It wasn't a question as in *Do you remember?* Ananias drew out the blacked-out memory from inside Stroud's head, somewhere the other side of the steel plate there. Stroud saw in his mind's eye the clear picture of himself a flight above the morgue, staring in through a door marked BLOOD BANK. It was Banaker's well-lit, modern facility and the place where his food supply was processed, stored, and kept.

"Of course, that's our only hope," said Stroud over the chanting. At about this time he saw consternation pinch his grandfather's features, and he, too, sensed Banaker's presence. He smelled smoke and saw it seeping in at the wall through a crack. The shield of safety around them seemed to be eroding, when suddenly the dark fog retreated and was gone. Banaker . . .

Stroud turned again to his grandfather, but he, too was gone. There was not so much as a sensation left in the room to tell he was ever there, nor for that matter anything but the smell of blood, and something unappealing, sickening to the senses coming from the corner where the cocoons were.

The chanting stopped and the people in the room felt a new presence. All around them there was silence. Had the vampires given up so easily?

"I've got to get to Banaker Institute," Stroud told the others. "You'll be safe here until I return." Stroud took up the bottle of S-choline from Magaffey's bag. "I hope this is enough."

"I'll go with you, sir," said Lonnie.

"Are you sure?"

"Yes, Dr. Stroud."

Stroud nodded. At about the same moment, they heard something like a tear, a rending noise below the blankets where the cocoons lay. Ashyer snatched away the blankets to find a vampire in full form gnawing at the Bradley woman's pod, injecting some venomous white worms onto the surface of the woman. The creature had already done this to what remained of Pam Carr, and the worms were destroying what was left of her. Some had long before gotten into the insides, and the body was becoming a milky waxlike substance that smelled to high heaven, right before their eyes.

The vampire that had succeeded in gaining entrance had done so in some unknown form, and had secretly taken its time to destroy the evidence against its race. Stroud instantly reacted. "Lonnie!"

Wilson snatched up the lance with the stake at the end and Stroud caught it as it sailed to him. Stroud approached the slavering creature that was now spitting up the white maggots, its unseeing eyes trained on Stroud nonetheless, its snout sniffing wildly, the mouth puckering in the now familiar O as it moved with Stroud's careful movement.

Stroud was trying to get it to move away from the others. He poked at it menacingly with the stake. It snatched at the stake with its deadly talons. One sure swipe and it would break the lance in two. Stroud jabbed at the eyes and slit one, the blood coming to the pupil but not slowing the creature that grabbed hold of the lance and snapped it in its bite like a twig.

Lonnie was fighting with Magaffey's bag, trying to get the hypo and the S-choline solution, perhaps their only chance. The bat was just about to dive straight for Stroud, destroying him instantly, when it suddenly began whirling around the chamber along the ceiling, taunting them, as if telling them now they were all trapped here with it, and it was going to devour them one at a time.

Mrs. Ashyer screamed which seemed to heighten this one's fun.

Stroud ducked as it came at his eyes, the talons like those that had killed Magaffey going for his throat. Stroud dove and came up beside Lonnie who'd nervously dropped the S-choline–filled hypo which skidded across the stone floor and shattered. The beast now landed over Magaffey's body and began, like a bird of prey, to pick over it, scratch about it, and dig at the wound. Stroud saw his chance. Grabbing the bottle of S-choline, he tore off the lid. He then doused it over Magaffey's wound just as the monster lapped at the dead man's blood, taking in some of the S-choline with it.

The thing reared up almost instantly, a gurgling sound came from deep within it, followed by a smouldering gas that it belched, turning it into a dragon of sorts. Perched over Magaffey still, it gave the appearance of a gargoyle as painted in medieval texts. If not a gargoyle than a vulture with bat's eyes and snout, winged by virtue of a membrane of skin that stretched between talons of each hand, its body covered in coarse, ratlike hair.

It lurched forward over Magaffey's head and onto the floor, reeling, bubbles bursting like small explosions within it, until suddenly its chest constricted about the heart area and was suddenly matted with blood that spurt forth where the heart had exploded.

A stake through the heart, Stroud thought, but coming from within, not without. As the creature lay there in its death throes, its face metamorphosed into that of Dolphin Banaker and back again, and then began the process of decay as had occurred with Ray Carroll, until there was less than enough dust left to sweep from the floor.

"Damn, that stuff works great," said Ashyer. "We've got to get more."

"Magaffey's office, the pharmacy, maybe," suggested Mrs. Ashyer, who clung tightly to her husband.

"There may be more of them out there, above," she said, "just waiting for us."

"She's right," said Stroud, "though I don't sense any more near. Dolph Banaker's reeked havoc on our proof for the outside world. If Banaker learns of this, we're finished. I've got good reason to believe he controls the police."

"What're we to do?" asked Mrs. Ashyer.

"Our only hope is to salvage what we can of the evidence—"

"Cold storage?" asked Ashyer.

"You can bet the freezer upstairs is destroyed," said Lonnie.

"Then we find another."

"Andover Cold Storage. Fred Watts owns it. We could call him, meet him there," said Ashyer.

"No, no . . . we can't trust anyone now. We can only trust the people in this room," said Stroud.

"Are you saying that all of Andover is . . . are . . . are those things?" asked Mrs. Ashyer.

"Not all, but they've infiltrated so well, like Ray Carroll . . . how do you know without a blood test, or a cc of this S-choline?"

"Why do you suppose it . . . it burst their hearts?" asked Ashyer.

"I don't know, but Magaffey told me—"

"Magaffey?"

"Yes, he . . . he was here a moment before. He says the vampire's tissue, being that of a dead person, has high concentrations of S-choline already. Any additional and it triggers it to go mad in the monster's system."

"Sounds exactly like what happened all right."

"Lonnie and I'll take the pods to Andover Cold Storage, find a place for them there. We'll take Magaffey's remains as well. We'll stop by Magaffey's offices for more of the S-choline. Then we'll pay a visit to Banaker Institute."

"Please," said Mrs Ashyer, "take great care of yourself, Doctor Stroud."

"Count on it if we can arm ourselves with this liquid stake of Magaffey's."

His entire life, Dr. Oliver Banaker had perceived himself to be both a brilliant scientist and the quintessence of his race; he had come to think of his life as having meaning both before and after he had come into being, the product of the sexual union of two vampires—his father and his mother—both of whom had died at the hands of vampire hunters led by Ananias Stroud. Banaker had little memory of his mother, but he had always been told by his father of her beauty, grace, and intelligence. She, like his father, had been gifted. He had performed his entire life under the belief that his life had been predetermined, that the sexual union of his parents was part of a master plan; this plan was set in motion by the god of all vampires. He was a gift to his race. His son was to be the continuation of this bloodline and god-given course, to someday overtake the humans, out-number, and destroy them in order to become the master race. His mind had always overcome obstacles placed before him. He had made wonders and miracles through medicine and science that no one of his kind had ever done before. He had begun to believe in the dream to the exclusion of all else, including his son. And now, deep inside the pit of his vampire soul, he felt the pain and anguish of his inability to help his dead son.

He realized at the moment of Dolphin's death that the boy had remained behind, that he hadn't run from the battle, but rather hid there and patiently waited for Stroud to let down his guard. At the moment of Dolph's death he felt the blow that killed him, felt it physically as well as psychically.

Stroud had killed his son. Bastard vampire killer had killed his son. . . .

He rushed for the Institute where he expected to find the others huddled in their morgue beds, cowards and sheep. He needed the sheep now, however. He needed their numbers, idiots and all, to combat Stroud. He needed for them to draw on their instinct to survive at all costs. He himself had paid the dearest price. And with it his hatred for Stroud rose and rose and rose.

Stroud loaded his Jeep with Magaffey's bag and his own AK-47 assault rifle, hand grenades, and anything else he had in his arsenal, much of which he'd collected while on the force by way of confiscation. With his newfound wealth he had added a bazooka to his collection. This, too, he loaded into the Jeep as the others helped Lonnie Wilson get the pods out to the helicopter. The plan of operation was going into effect immediately. If they waited for another nightfall, they knew the vampires would return with two-fold strength, and what little evidence left them—now beginning to leak from the pods—would be gone forever.

Stroud tore around to where the helicopter was being loaded. Ashyer, still in his black butler's attire, and Wilson, still looking the role of a simpleton, appeared not much of an army. Mrs. Ashyer had remained in the gutted and destroyed house going about the first tentative steps to put things aright again. When they had come up out of the underground circle—the psychic bomb shelter as Stroud had come to think of it—they found a scene of devastation where bats, large and small, had knocked over everything that was not nailed to the walls. Sofas and tables were overturned, expensive vases, paintings, and glass were everywhere. An occasional small dead bat was found. The lone items left untouched were the huge painting of his great-grandfather in the ballroom where everything else had been shattered, including the chandeliers, and a portrait of Ananias over the mantel in the drawing room. Stroud found this significant. He knew now that Banaker and the others feared the Strouds as they feared nothing and no one else.

Thanks to his meeting with his grandfather's spirit, now he understood this completely and perfectly. He had always had a penchant for fighting evil; it had always seemed his special talent, found deep within himself. Now he knew the why of it, that it was in his genes and his makeup, and that perhaps God had set his family to this task. Little wonder that the ghost of Ananias Stroud was upset with him for having still remained unwed and without a child. Who would carry on after him in a world rife with the demonic, the cruel, the evil and the vile? Who would act as predator to the snakes, if not a Stroud?

In the hard seat of the Jeep, surrounded by tangible, physical evidence of the so-called real world, Stroud had moments when he wondered if he truly believed any of it, if he had not simply hallucinated his grandfather's spirit and that of Magaffey's there in the magical room. All that baloney about the circle protecting the soul. That although there might be danger to the body, their souls were safe while they remained within the safety of the inner circle. The circle chamber had the double function of concentration and protection. It was akin to the church, the mosque, the synagogue, and its ancestor was Stonehenge where a former Stroud had vanquished a former vampire colony.

Stroud knew now that the circle, at least in his head, had stood for the microcosm and macrocosm—both infinity and the focus within infinity. According to the disembodied voice of his own ancestor, it was the Akashic Egg—*the egg containing the spiritual ether.* It was the consecrated sanctuary, the barrier set up by ritualized, amplified willpower.

Maybe it was just a psychological aid. Even on that level, Stroud had to concede that it was a valid and effective one—that the church was just as much a manmade environment as the circle. Man always feels both holier and safer on consecrated ground, even though it is only he who has declared it so, by whatever criterion he might recognize. Certainly the Ashyers, Lonnie, and Stroud himself had felt the power of their combined wills when they had miraculously held back the hordes of vampires, and had they been stronger in their faith, perhaps Dolph Banaker could not have broken through.

I left Chicago for this? Stroud asked himself as he stared at his motley little army. He said instead, "Are we ready, Ashyer? Lonnie?"

"We are, sir," said Ashyer.

Lonnie nodded and swallowed hard. The cargo bay now held the pods. "See you at the rendezvous point," said Stroud. "Follow the route we agreed on. Use your weapons only if you must. Remember your prime directive."

Stroud then tore out for Andover and Magaffey's old place before going to the Banaker Institute. It would be daylight in a few hours. He hoped that his plan had a chance.

Sheriff Bill Briggs sat up, the muscles of his face twitching uncontrollably. He lifted off the slab he liked to sleep on. It wasn't as posh as the mausoleum where all the muckety mucks slept, all the guys in cozy with Banaker, but it beat the hell out of the morgue at Banaker Institute. His big problem with his digs was the distance between here and the Institute, should he want for more blood. He thought the Bloody Mary Banaker had concocted was a hell of a lot easier than roaming about all night hunting for prey, and years ago he'd gotten sick to death of cattle and horse blood, which Banaker said was the cause of his neurological disorder, why the tick kept coming back. The only thing that calmed the tick was a good replenishing of his food supply. But he, like most here at the communal sleep warehouse, had run low. He'd have to drive over to the Institute, display his card, and the broad there would have to punch it up on computer to see if he had had his monthly ration or not, and then and only then could he get more of the good stuff.

He pulled on his uniform pants over his human form and brought the folds of his skin under control and tucked them away with the shirttail. As an afterthought he pulled on his gunbelt and gun. Alongside his slab was a cardboard box with an address on it for Chicago that couldn't be read due to the ice crystals that had formed over the thing. All around Briggs there was a fog, an ice fog. In the fog were hundreds of others of his kind at shaky peace with the world, enjoying the much needed rest after the useless trashing of Stroud's in which they'd gotten nowhere. Here, in the cold, they could shut down their palpitating minds and hearts just far enough to sleep the sleep of the dead, to awaken refreshed and energized, so long as the temperature was a comfortable 22° F.

It was nearing dawn and Briggs marveled at Banaker's liquid miracle, the agent that made it possible for all of them to rise as the human's did with the sun instead of the moon, to cast a shadow, and barge in unbidden onto the premises of even the most faithful human who that day bowed his head to his so-called god. Banaker's elixir made it possible for them all to cohabit the earth with humankind until which time as they would take over.

Dolph Banaker'd nearly ruined everything, and now with another Stroud to contend with every pire knew that the fate of his kind lay in what would happen in the next twenty-four hours.

Briggs ran his hands through his hair two and three times, mussing it into a semi-combed pile atop his head before slipping on the police cap that distinguished him as sheriff. It had been a stroke of genius for Banaker and his father before him to place pires into politically powerful positions, and positions of social prominence.

Briggs went through a door with a sign on it for NEPTUNE FROZEN FOODS. He stretched when he got outside and he felt uncomfortable in the heat after the cold environment of the indoors.

He lit a cigarette, the light illuminating his face which was covered in ice, a white maggot frozen there at the crook of his lower lip, and over his head the large letters of the building read ANDOVER COLD STORAGE.

Briggs didn't like—couldn't even taste—cigarettes, but it had become part of his human persona, along with the dumb act, which he quietly told himself wasn't all an act. He knew he wasn't so smart as Banaker, but he also knew that Banaker wasn't so smart as he thought he was either. Seeing Banaker frustrated by Stroud tonight, Briggs wouldn't've missed it for the world.

Briggs located his unmarked car in the lot, heaved a sigh, feeling his bursitis inflaming. He slid into the car with some difficulty, feeling stiff yet, and then drove for Banaker Institute. On his way he called into the office to ask if there was anything he should know about. Dispatch said all was quiet, except for the ruckus out at Stroud Manse. Briggs and the dispatcher laughed heartily together over this joke. Dispatch voice was Deputy Tyler and he said, "Rumor has it Dolph Banaker never came back."

"Shithead, punk! Probably up in those fucking caves again, probably doing somebody right now!"

"You want me to send somebody out there, Chief?"

"No, no . . . but I tell you, Tyler, I'm b'ginning to think Dolph Banaker's our big worry, not Doctor Abraham Stroud."

"Yes, sir."

"Just can't get Banaker to see that."

"No, sir."

"Tell you, if I thought I could get away with it, I'd see that boy dead myself. What he did to the Cooper kid and the Meyers boy—and now I hear Pam and Doctor Cooper. *His own kind!*"

"Yeah, now that's sick."

"Best let Banaker deal with it."

"Sir?"

"You got Whiley and Buttrum over at Magaffey's place still?"

"All-night watch, yeah, but they're grumbling like hell."

"Let 'em grumble."

"Yes, sir."

"Over and out, Tyler."

"Yes, sir, good night, sir."

Briggs cut off communications and grumbled to himself. "Night hell. Night's over and I got to get a drink."

-21-

Abe Stroud didn't know who could be trusted any longer, but he hoped that his plan would give him some instant answers. Magaffey's place was an old Victorian home with a shingle out front. He'd maintained an office on the ground floor for general practice since setting up practice in his home town in 1954. His living quarters were above. He'd had little interest in grass and outward appearance, and so, as with his dress, the place looked much worse and older than it was. Still, it was old and rambling with the look of a house that was well-used, leaning leeward, and holding. Magaffey would open for GP hours at eight A.M. sharp, see his patients, be out by one for lunch, and then to the morgue by two where he concluded his coroner's duties by five. But all that would not happen today, and people all over Andover would be wondering where the old black doctor was, and what had happened to him. At the downtown offices of City Morgue he'd also be missed.

There were no lights on at Magaffey's. Stroud drove around the block twice with his own lights out before deciding that no one was watching the place. It remained dark, the storm clouds of earlier lingering, the smell of wet leaves and damp earth everywhere. Stroud pulled into the rear where an old garage stood, the door—a side-to-side one—flapping in the breeze, creaking like a wounded animal, invited him into a gaping black hole. He drove in quietly and shut down the motor. A few blocks away he'd seen the lights of a police car, but not a soul otherwise. The city streets were tidy and clean from the rain and the street cleaners, all the shops in neat rows locked against the night, people and vampires in their beds.

The sight of the garage door standing open only disturbed Stroud in that it led him to picture the old man whipping from the garage in an excited state some twenty or twenty-one hours before. He imagined Magaffey tearing off in too much heat to stop and close the door. He thought of Magaffey, alive only that morning. He thought of the spirit conjured up over the fumes of Magaffey's blood, of Magaffey's own spirit that had spoken to him there in the circular chamber.

It all seemed impossible—supernatural—on the one hand, and yet so simple and natural on the other. How else might the ethereal soul of man show itself but amid the lifeblood? Hadn't Christ himself risen from the blood of man in his veins to his final destination?

Somehow, via some unnatural, sinister alchemy, dark forces had appeared in the world, beings that learned the lessons of the vulture, but their aim was not carrion but this same lifeblood. With the stolen lifeblood of the dead, they also stole the soul of a man or woman, like Pamela Carr's soul.

All via the abiding power given them by God's opposite number in the universe. Via satanic genius, nature—or *super nature*—had created a thing like Banaker on the very lifeblood as that which fed mankind. Good and evil, evolution and mutation, and all that lie between the two. . . .

Whether he actually saw and spoke to Magaffey's ghost or not, he knew somehow that here, in Magaffey's lab, was enough S-choline to suffocate and destroy all of Banaker's minions. He also knew that it was too dangerous to get within a hypodermic needle's length of one of them. They needed a more effective weapon than that. In fact, they needed more than one weapon. To this end, Stroud had fashioned a lance that would carry the deadly needle the length of a room. Taking his grandfather's spear-stakes, he intended to fashion such spear-darts. "Aim for the heart," he heard his grandfather's voice roiling around in his head.

He got down from the Jeep and quietly hefted several spear-length stakes taken from the manse. Anyone watching him except a vampire would think him quite mad, he assumed. He made his way as quietly as possible to Magaffey's back door, fumbling with the dead man's keys when he realized this door, too, was left unlocked. He thought again of Magaffey's haste to stop the Bradley embalming, and his haste to rush out to the manse.

Stroud silently entered Magaffey's sensing something was wrong, a sour fear coming over him, like that he'd encountered at the bat cave, a raw, animal fear. One of *them*, if not more, was here!

As if he had his own sonar, Stroud felt the rush of air and force of the creature as it came in the dark at him, like a wall of water or heat. Stroud instantly reacted, dropping all but one of the stakes, dropping to his knees and bracing it against the wall. The monster slammed into Stroud, the stake, and the wall, knocking Stroud near senseless, it was so huge. Stroud rolled out and away from the frigate of the thing bent on killing him when he heard its wail in the dark, a terrifying, sickening, keening sound. His eyes adjusting somewhat to the light, he saw the outline of the vampire as it wreathed and twisted against the enormous stake that'd gone through its chest. Stroud was hit again by the weight of the smelly thing when it rolled onto him, trapping him beneath. He felt the weight as if it would crush him. Then, suddenly, it stopped moving and was dead atop him and decaying over him. The foul stench became acrid and unbearable as the monster's body began to liquify and dissolve, some of its fluids burning a hole in Stroud's shirt and skin.

Stroud heaved to free himself, sending soupy and lumpy parts of the creature in various directions, the odor and shock still sending waves of disgust through Stroud. Barely had he got to his knees when another monster attacked from behind, taking his throat in its talons. This one had dropped from overhead where it had been clinging to the ceiling. Stroud felt the talons lock into his throat like two enormous meat hooks; he felt the blood gush up and out, draining down his back and chest. He was in its clutches, and it had him from the rear. He was unable to find a hold on it as it lifted him from his knees and was about to hang him suspended in air until he should bleed to death when he recalled the hypo of S-choline he'd placed in his shirt pocket inside its leather safety container. Stroud fought for his senses, fought back the pain of the monster's grip, and now the sickening flutter of ice down his spine as the thing bent its mouth to his throat wounds to lick at the geyser of blood.

His hands fought with his mind and emotions to do what they must. He found the hypo case, tore at it, fumbled it, and almost dropped the needle along with the case. At the same instant, his limbs were growing weak and he felt as if he might black out, or go into a peace of uncaring. His hands, however, driven by some power beyond what he felt he had, plunged the hypo straight up and into the private parts of the creature perched on his neck and bent completely over to feed on him.

He had had no idea his feet were off the ground or that he'd been lifted halfway to the second floor when the creature, after a moment's inspection, began a wretched sound from its guttural regions and dropped Stroud hard to the floor. In midair, it burst like a balloon, sending a rain of blood and other bodily fluids down over Stroud and what was left of the first vampire.

That had been the last of his supply of the S-choline. If a third attack came now, he knew he was a dead man. He lay on the floor on his back, the wounds to his neck throbbing, his head pounding. He dared not look at the damage, recalling that such wounds had killed Magaffey. He lay there in the pool of dead beasts on either side when his hand touched something rock solid. He lifted the object and held it up to his eyes. It was a Police Special .38 revolver.

Briggs's men had had the place staked out, and now one of them was exploded, and the other was himself staked out. The pole stake now creepily fell over, having nothing to ground itself in.

The fact the two vampires had guns and could simply have shot him to death as he entered told Stroud a great deal about his enemy. They must enjoy rendering their prey helpless with their venomous attack; they must enjoy the attack itself, not unlike some psycho killers he'd had to deal with. They must enjoy inflicting pain and seeing and smelling and lapping at the blood the way their kindred little cousins in that bloody cave by the river did. They were bats at heart.

"You're okay," he told himself as he lay there still stricken, feeling a numbness down his spine from the pain inflicted by the creature. "You're okay. . . . "

"Much work to do," he heard his grandfather's voice, encouraging him on.

"Come on, son." He heard Magaffey as clearly as if he was standing at the entranceway to his office. "We're counting on you."

But when he tried to get up the intense pain sent him into a faint. His last conscious thought was of being late to the rendezvous point and letting Wilson and Ashyer down.

• • •

When he awoke, Stroud had no idea how long he had been unconscious, but he recalled vividly what he had been thinking the entire time. As a former policeman working his way up to detective status, he'd had to do a lot of reading. For reasons obvious, he had thought anew about a book by Cesare Lombroso, a man some considered the father of modern criminology. It had been his lifelong belief that there existed among the human species the type of born criminal who was a throwback to his primordial ancestors.

Lombroso, who lived between 1836 and 1909, had to have been a vampire hunter, for his description of such types as the "primordial" killer resembled Banaker and his people so closely: low cranial capacity, retreating forehead, a thick-boned skull, tufted, almost crispy hair—animallike—and large ears. The nose was his finest feature, aqualine like the beak of a bird of prey, Lombroso wrote in his famous *Criminal Man*. Lombroso said that the primordial killer's eyebrows tended to be bushy and would meet across the nose. He'd thought again of Banaker and of something Dr. Magaffey had said about Banaker: a man who can kiss a woman's hand even as he counts her pulse ought to raise questions of confidence. Even more so, it ought to raise questions of ancestry. How old was the vampire?

It was obvious that modern times and discoveries had pleased the primordial breed, making the attractive fascination of the monster ever stronger to the unwary. The blood exchange between monster and mankind had over the years, no doubt, poisoned the hearts and minds of the human race as well. If this were the case might not evil reign everywhere on the face of the earth like a disease, spread to all corners? Might this not explain the condition of a world which had never known peace? A world rife with murder, poverty, hunger, hatred, and malice? Would it explain the bizarre: showers of blood and spontaneous combustion of human beings? The supernatural and the preternatural?

As an anthropologist and archeologist the questions raised by the startling conclusion fascinated Stroud, but at the same time he hadn't the time to waste worrying over them. He must rifle through Magaffey's offices for the large jar of S-choline said to be here. He must then race to his second stop before dawn would fully break.

He got to his feet, whoozy and wobbling on his legs. His shoulders and neck where the talons had dug in and lifted him off the ground were still throbbing with pain. He crashed into a wall and held onto his head and his equilibrium, wondering if the beast had injected some sort of stunning venom into him at the point of contact as many creatures in nature were apt to do. He recognized the symptom's of an alcoholic hangover. He tried to shake the grogginess and the headache, and he wondered if a third vampire were anywhere on the premises.

It seemed unlikely, as he would no doubt have been killed where he lay amid the remains of the other two. Just the same, he armed himself with the pointed staff that had destroyed his first attacker before going deeper into the house.

Stroud found the office with no difficulty and he passed through it and into the doctor's workroom and lab. Beneath a cabinet he found the weapon he was looking for, the S-choline, exactly where Magaffey had told him it would be. Magaffey had told him of this after he was dead—it had to have been after Magaffey was dead, because none of them knew of its destructive power against the vampires until Ray Carroll was killed by it, none but Lonnie Wilson who claimed that the notion and the action of striking out at Carroll just "popped" into his head. Later, Magaffey's disembodied spirit had told Stroud where a supply could be located. He'd done so without words. It had been a picture that fired off like a flashbulb in Stroud's mind when he saw Magaffey's apparition before him.

Stroud searched about for a supply of hypos, laid several out side by side, opened the S-choline and began the labor of filling each in succession, his time running out by the minute. He glanced at his watch to learn that he was ten minutes behind schedule. He found a roll of adhesive tape and rushed back for the other spears he'd brought, four in all, and taped a hypo to each end firmly and completely, leaving the mechanism free to be pressed down in the event the lance missed the heart. He somehow knew that, given their strength and the fact their hearts seemed to supply all that power, these creatures could walk, or fly, away from a hit to the stomach, back, or other area that would kill a man.

Stroud then saw a dart gun looking much like a staple gun behind Magaffey's glass case. He found the case locked, broke it, and grabbed up the gun and the darts that went with it, filling each with the S-choline.

Finished and pleased with his finds, Stroud trundled off with half of the large jar of vampire poison under one arm, the dart gun loaded and ready in one hand, the lances balanced in the crook of his other arm. He was behind schedule, and wondered if he should not see to his wounds before racing headlong to the Institute. If he stopped to do so, it would put him a half hour behind instead of the ten or fifteen he had already lost.

Abe Stroud half stumbled, half walked, rushing from Magaffey's and returning to his Jeep. Every ink-blotted corner of the yard and the garage might hold another attacker, every tree and every ceiling for that matter. Stroud had been lucky—he had killed Briggs's two men before they'd gotten a chance to call for help.

He raced for the Institute, reviewing in his mind what he thought he knew about the area where the special bone marrow elixir was produced and packaged for the vampire colony. As he drove for his destination, Stroud wondered what properties in the S-choline were so effective against the vampire. He'd read his grandfather's books and not a word about any special medicines ever having been used effectively against the vampire existed. There were only old herbal medicines to combat the fever and pain of the bite, to stanch the blood flow. His own blood continued to flow, and now he wished he'd taken a few moments to clean and dress the wounds. He recalled some mention of the wild rose having some anti-vampire properties, but there was no explanation as to why, other than the rose's origin and its general association with Christ. He knew that the wild rose was the rarest flower in the Holy Land. Jesus had said that He was the rose and the lily of the valleys in Song of Solomon 2:1.

His grandfather's voice came into his head as clear and as strong as if he were in the backseat of the Jeep, startling him, and making him wonder if he would ever get used to this ghost. His grandfather said, "*Land Beyond the Forest* by Emily Gerard."

What of it? Stroud thought but did not say aloud.

"Page one hundred eighty-six."

Damn it, I don't have the books with me! he shouted in his head, but said nothing aloud.

"Tells of the custom in Transylvania of laying a thorny branch of a wild rosebush across the body during burial."

"For what bloody reason?" Stroud said aloud.

He didn't hear the answer, but he knew it: to prevent the body from leaving the coffin.

Stroud had never thought of himself as a soldier of Christ, and he wasn't certain he wanted to start now. Never had he been a particularly religious sort, never had he maintained even a semblance of ritualistic function in this regard. Yet here he was, carrying the modern equivalent of the wild rose in a test tube, carrying on the modern equivalent of a crusade.

Still, Stroud also knew that the loss of blood he had sustained, and seemed to continue to be sustaining, had not only produced a quicker heartbeat and respiratory rate, but had clouded his judgment as well. Fewer red blood cells to the brain. A normal respiratory rate was fourteen to sixteen breaths per minute. A mental check of his own rate had him up around thirty-five. He was still losing blood, and his wounds continued to throb so that he feared touching them. He feared looking at the wounds, knowing that to see them could be a worse shock to his system than not seeing them.

He fought back the pain, trying desperately to reduce his breathing rate, perspiration coursing down his face as he tried to consciously slow his heartbeat as well. A check of his own pulse where he held onto the wheel revealed that it continued to race— this long after the period in which he had put together the weaponry in Magaffey's office. He could not understand why. He could not understand it and almost instinctively his right hand went up to his shoulder to where one of the gashes seemed to be splitting with pain and opening farther. His hand went into a squirming morass of worms at the wound. Worms, *like a mindless army of ants, keeping the wound open for their dead master*. The shock of this realization, that the nerves about all the wounds were deadened and filled with maggots that kept it both clean and open for the vampire's pleasure, sent Stroud into a spin at the wheel. He and the car came to a screeching halt in the parking lot at Banaker Institute, but not before slamming into a parked car.

–22–

The Jeep tore into the side of a car that looked like an unmarked police car, and the noise caused enough of a stir around the doors to the emergency center to bring out curious, white-coated onlookers. Stroud grabbed all that he needed, his cloth bag filled with plastique explosives, enough to get the job done. He slid out and crouched amid the parked cars, making his way to a service entrance he saw in the distance. As he did so, he saw a small crowd of them inspecting his Jeep, and amid the crowd stood Chief Briggs. Of all the luck, Stroud thought now. He'd run directly into Briggs's unmarked vehicle.

He kept one eye on the curious ones combing his Jeep for clues to his whereabouts, and another on the escape door. Or was it a trap door?

The noise of the crash had brought the pseudo-humans out, some staring down from windows high overhead. One of them might've spotted Stroud; one of them might be Banaker.

Behind him, Briggs, his .38 extended, grabbed hold of the Jeep door and tore it open. All of them were trying to understand the situation and, no doubt, Briggs could not believe the nerve Stroud showed in coming here like this after all that'd gone before.

Stroud quietly sprinted for his objective.

Briggs stood staring at the maggot pool on the seat of the abandoned Jeep, saying, "Can you believe this? The nerve?"

"But look," said one of the white-coated attendants from Emergency, "the worms."

"That must mean . . . maybe he's now one of us," said the other one.

"Don't be stupid," said Briggs. "I mean, if he was one of us, the worms wouldn't be just left here to go unused, to die, would they?" Briggs lifted a handful and popped these into his mouth like popcorn. The others took what was left and did likewise.

"He could still be one of us, if whoever got to him took enough of a bite out of him," ventured the first attendant.

Briggs thought about this. He thought about his two men at Magaffey's, and he wondered who'd been the one to inflict pain on Stroud, and if he'd live to tell about it, and what rewards Banaker would bestow on the one who brought Stroud either down or into the fold.

"Phil could be right, Chief," said the second attendant.

Briggs bit his lower lip and nodded, giving them a noncommittal maybe. Then he said, "I'll just make a call and we'll see. Tell you one thing, whoever gets the son of a bitch's going to please Banaker to no end."

Briggs's time as a policeman wasn't completely wasted. He had learned a thing or two, and one was that physical evidence spoke reams if viewed carefully. While the two attendants were wishfully hoping Banaker's problems with Stroud were over, he reserved judgment for good reason. Some of the worms on the driver's seat of Stroud's Jeep were dead. No pire would willingly kill his parasitic helpers. Briggs also knew that if Stroud were still the enemy, and if he, Briggs, were to bring Stroud down, then there would be an eternal thank you and reward that the high and mighty Dr. Oliver Banaker would be bestowing on him.

Briggs had learned via the Institute grapevine that Dolphin Banaker had not returned from Stroud Manse, and rumor had it that Stroud had tortured the young pire to death using some holy and sanctified torture chamber there. Briggs had to go to the other side of the vehicle to reach inside his car for the police radio. His mind wandered over the immense darkness of the eternal damnation that would now befall Banaker's boy; he wished death on no vampire. He pressed to send his message when just outside he heard the disturbance. Stroud was spotted.

Briggs half rolled, half jumped from his mangled car to get a fleeting glimpse of Stroud as the attendants pointed and shouted.

"There!"

"There he goes!"

"Where?"

"Service bay, see the door?"

Briggs did indeed see the top of the door as it closed slowly behind someone of Stroud's general build. Briggs froze for a
moment, terrified of Stroud, a man capable of killing one of them.
Despite all the bullshit Briggs'd heard about some legendary ones
who opted to lie down and die out of a desire to quit living—so
long had they lived—Briggs couldn't imagine anything so asinine
as that: to lie down and wish oneself to death. He knew every
vampire had it within him to do so, the death wish as it was known,
but he could not imagine such despair.

Some ripples of rumor had it that Banaker was on the verge of
the death wish decision, but he doubted this. Banaker? Never. Not
him. He liked power too much. Cooper, now there was a pire that
could maybe take his own life in this manner, but never a pire like
Banaker.

Briggs raced behind the two attendants who were going up a
flight of stairs. "Is Banaker here, on the premises?" he shouted.

"No, at least, I don't think so."

"He's probably going for Banaker. Probably go right for his
office on the top floor," said Briggs. "Let's take the elevator,
hurry!"

When they came to the next landing, the three vampires caught
the elevator on Briggs's hunch. Briggs was certain that Stroud was
bent on killing Banaker as much as Banaker was bent on killing
Stroud. Just before the elevator was about to close, a nurse raced
toward them, shouting for Briggs, but the doors closed on what
she was saying.

"Your office has been trying to reach you! Two of your
men . . . dead . . . at Doctor Magaffey's!"

After the door closed Briggs felt a hot shiver race along his
spine, and while he nor any other vampire ever perspired, he felt
that uneasy odor that his body exuded whenever he was particularly harried or low on his food supply. He'd been waiting for
his replenishment to begin when Stroud's Jeep had torn up the
parking lot, banging into his own car.

"What was that she said?" Briggs asked the two attendants.

"Something to do with Magaffey," said one.

"No, she said two of your men were dead."

Briggs thought about Whiley and Buttrum over at Dr. Magaffey's offices. Dead? Impossible. But the elevator ride to the top

floor seemed now interminable as his mind kicked over the possibilities. If he added up, Stroud had dispatched three vampires in a matter of hours.

Stroud knew the rules of infiltration and camouflage, and that when in Rome . . .

He'd taken great pains to present himself as just another of the Banaker Institute family. Although it was an ill fit, he'd gotten hold of one of Magaffey's white lab coats, which covered the worst of his wounds until the coat became blood-soaked. He'd located stairwell underpasses and a linen closet to stow his firepower close to his target and diversionary target. Before leaving Banaker Institute he meant to display some of his talents, primarily in explosives. But first he must locate his primary target. He calculated his chances of getting out of this place, but it made him lose heart to do so, so he terminated the calculation. He knew he could not very well destroy the entire hospital complex, that there was too much of a chance that some of the patients in beds here were still as human as he was. The blood bank was their only hope of an effective weapon against the number of vampires here.

He'd wisely chosen the stairs, assuming they'd be used less. He found the floor where he now recalled seeing the blood bank.

Someone was coming down the corridor he stepped into, and the fact he was carrying Magaffey's jar made him even more conspicuous than he already was. He grabbed an unattended gurney, placed the S-choline plainly in view on top, and pushed it along. Two vampire doctors passed him without giving him the least notice. They seemed engaged in a conversation revolving around a technique of surgery one felt to be an improvement over earlier methods. Stroud caught only snatches of their talk, but it was fiendish in its overtones, more by virtue of the fact he knew what they were. He also knew that for what he was contemplating, he could be locked up for life, possibly sent to the electric chair.

He came around a corner and saw the sign over a door that designated this area the blood center. Taking the clear liquid solution, cradling it in his arm as if it were a child, he pushed through the door. There was a *thrum-thrum-thrum* noise on this side of the doors that'd been masked out in the hallway. The churning noise of rhythmic machinery lulled the mind here. It reminded him of being in a downtown laundromat in Chicago when all the machines were in use at once. The place was a maze of outer rooms where "donors" gave willingly of their blood, and labs where the bone marrow was extracted. The corridors between these rooms, labs, and offices led him closer and closer to the source of the humming machinery. If anyone saw him or was watching him, he did not know of it. For a moment, the S-choline firmly in his hands, he forgot his mission and the place he was in as his mind locked on the comforting, seashore sound of the machines ahead.

He very likely passed some white-coated monsters in human form, but he did so with such determination and the look of a man who knew where he must be, that no one questioned him.

It was going too easily, he felt, when the corridor led to a glassed-in area that overlooked an enormously large machine squatting below him in a sunken area. A quick calculation led him to realize that the blood bank area linked up with the morgue. Two and two added up to the fact that when someone died at Banaker Institute and his body was sent to the morgue to be prepped for burial or autopsy, or whatever, that the vital red fluid was not simply washed from the corpse along with all other bodily fluids, but pumped in here, to join with the enormous vat of blood being filtrated and enriched through the bone marrow and vampire gene components.

This was the central food processing plant for them. This was Stroud's primary target.

"What is that you have there?" asked a female voice behind him suddenly.

Stroud only slowly turned from the glass. Fumes like those of dry ice, giving off an eerie, ghastly pink cloud, rose from the square vat at Stroud's back now. He'd witnessed the strange red liquid slushing in one compartment, flushing and cascading through funnel tubes in another section of the vampire still.

"I . . . beg your pardon?" asked Stroud.

"What is that you are carrying into the blood room?" She was a tall, raven-haired woman with piercing black eyes with an accent that might be that of a Rumanian. She was instantly suspicious. "Who sent you here? Who are you?"

"Doctor Banaker . . . he sent me."

"Oh?"

"Additives," said Stroud, hefting the clear liquid in the jar. "Vitamins."

"Really?" She was incredulous. "E, I suppose. You men."

Stroud almost took a breath, when she said, "I'll just call Doctor

Banaker. He said nothing of this. Highly irregular; no paper. Just a moment."

Stroud allowed her to walk back to her office, eyeballing the catwalk over the vat just outside. From there, he could drop the entire jar into the works. A little glass in their diet wouldn't harm the bats any. But a phone call would alert the others to the fact this place, the source of their power, was his target tonight. She mustn't be allowed to make that call.

Stroud placed the S-choline in a corner and followed her, snatching out a hypo as he did so. She had her back to him, and he was about to jam the hypo into her when she wheeled, grabbed his hand with an almost superhuman strength and thrust him across the room. She screeched his name, realizing who he was now. "*Ststrooooouuuuud!* Stroud!"

She next scowled and showed her fangs, her gums crawling with white worms. The hypo had gone flying to another corner of the room, so he snatched out the dart gun. He fired point-blank at the heart as she leaped for his throat, but she'd caused the dart gun to fire to one side, striking the wall, quivering there. She was still struggling with him as they fell through the door that led out into the main corridor on the other side of the blood bank. Here they struggled in an empty corridor before the elevator doors. An elevator was passing and Stroud, still in her clutches, snatched out another hypo and jammed the S-choline solution into her gullet now. At the same instant he slapped the elevator call button, the doors swung open and he shoved her into the car. Inside it, she screeched in banshee alto soprano, but just as the doors closed her white-uniformed chest exploded with blood from within, some of it shooting out into the corridor and onto Stroud's clothing, already encrusted with vampire blood.

Stroud saw his opportunity now, and he returned to the blood bank. Here lay Banaker's blood source, flowing through filtrating tubes and vats, great stores of it for the colony. It gave Stroud the first true belief in himself that he could put an end to Banaker and his kind; it also gave Stroud his first true indicator of exactly how large the enemy force was extrapolating from the size of the supply which was at this moment being run through final stages and packaged in robotic rhythm by the machines in the stainless steel room. Stroud guessed there must be as much as several hundred Andover citizens who were, like Ray Carroll, Banaker, and the others, vampires who'd learned to "be" human, until one of their number decided to do the "inhuman" thing. That meant a lot of blood-sucking leeches, and their number had been quietly growing for years. He shuddered with the thought that *had he chosen not* to return to Andover, then the numbers would've simply multiplied and multiplied as the human population dwindled.

Put up in pods in caves for such festive occasions as the Fourth of July and Labor Day and Thanksgiving.

Stroud's plan would work only if no one knew of his having gotten to this source. Thus far, neither Banaker nor any other fiend knew of the antivampire weapon that they'd stumbled onto. The fiends would not be expecting him to tamper with their food source, unless he triggered their thinking in this regard. The missing blood bank attendant's remains would not identify her soon. He had to make them believe that he had, all along, a different plan in mind—a more noisy, conventional, commando-type raid. It was for this reason he'd planted the charges below, just enough to do some damage to the morgue.

He had to work fast. He looked for the controls to the blood filtration mechanism that cleaned the bone marrow. Watching the red liquid gush about the tubes made him think of Edgar Allan Poe's *The Masque of the Red Death*. He located the control panel, shutting down the filtration system but not the packing system. He then stepped out onto the catwalk and made his way toward the middle to drop in the S-choline. Gaining this vantage, he poured into the large mouth of this giant strainer the entire contents of Dr. Magaffey's S-choline. He'd leave the rest of the work to the natural order of the machines, now that the straining, purifying process was shut down. Now he'd kill vampires via the help of the robotics here, as blood pak after pak was filled with the stuff so deadly to the vampires, and the S-choline unknowingly distributed.

Worried that he could still be discovered here, Abe Stroud knew he must set the diversion in motion. He turned on the catwalk to find himself facing one of them who'd come looking for the female vampire doctor he'd just killed. This one, a bull of a man, simply plowed a huge fist into Stroud's jaw, sending him crashing to the metal grillwork of the catwalk. Stroud was kicked once, again, repeatedly, as he tried to roll away. He then felt himself going over the side, knowing he'd drown in the pool of blood below him. Somehow, miraculously, a hand found a hold and he dangled there as the giant vampire laughed and was readying to stomp on his hand.

The pain from the life-threatening wound to his throat, along with the sheer strain of holding onto the rail, his body weight and gravity tugging him toward the churning vat of blood below him, all conspired to sap Stroud of his last ounce of strength and consciousness. But some inner resolve born of generations of vampire hunters before him, made him fight for his sight and his senses, despite the loss of blood and despite the overwhelming odds allied against him.

I've got to do something, he told himself, and in the wind and whirl of the machines, and in the turmoil, he heard the near buried whisper of Ananias's spirit telling him what to do.

Stroud fished for the reloaded dart gun, brought it up to aim just as the man-thing's foot was descending. The impact of the dart startled him, making him stop and stare at it. The man-thing looked curiously confused and dizzy moments before he stumbled over, his body sending up a splash of blood to where Stroud hung on. Stroud grabbed hold with a second hand and pulled himself to safety.

Beaten, his own white lab coat flecked with both his own and the blood of these things, Stroud tore away the lab clothing and watched it cascade down, following the vampire into the vat, lying atop the mixture for a moment before it was engulfed by the redness. All around him, here in the combining room, the heady fumes from the blood and marrow mix made him slightly dizzy, as if the air were made thin by the stuff. He knew he must get out now, standing here in his army fatigues. He knew he had to carry out the second part of his mission in order to make the first part successful. So he rushed from this place to the stairwell, careful once more not to be seen.

He dropped a flight to the morgue.

Briggs had accumulated more help from the staff as he and the attendants had rushed to Banaker's office, but before finding Dr. Oliver Banaker, Banaker found them. "You fools!" shouted Banaker. "He isn't here!" Banaker had amassed his own army of doctors and nurses. "Try the lower floors! Try the morgue, for bloody hell!"

Just then the elevator across from the one that had carried Briggs and the others pinged and slowly opened. The pires stared in at the bloody remains of one of their own just before the doors creepily closed, as if on cue, as if Stroud were controlling them, as if Stroud were winking in wry humor at Briggs and Banaker.

Suddenly, over the PA system, Stroud's voice rang throughout the building. "I have a little surprise for you, Doctor Banaker. Be patient, as they say, and your patience will be rewarded."

"Bastard!" shouted Banaker. "He's making a mockery of us all! He's killed my son! Now this! Briggs, you get all your men over here, now!"

"I've already alerted them! They're on their way."

"He's killed another of us," moaned one of the white-coated attendants who'd come up with Briggs.

"How? How does he take a perfectly healthy pire and turn him into . . . into what was on that elevator?"

"The man's not human," said Briggs philosophically.

Banaker shouted at them all. "Bullshit! He's no match for our strength and numbers! If we just ban together! There is nothing superhuman or . . . or supernatural about Abraham Stroud! His father and mother were killed by vampires, and so was his grandfather."

"Father and mother?"

"Made to look accidental, but yes, the work of a special team I sent out after them. The boy, too, was reported dead, but as we have learned that was far from the truth," explained Banaker. "My father took too damned much on faith. But bottom line here is that Stroud is mortal; he can be stopped. He must be stopped!"

Briggs remained skeptical, shaking where he stood, feeling a great need for a long gulp of energy and courage. "I . . . I got to get to the bank, get a refill," he mumbled and groggily started back for the elevator he had placed on hold. When he turned at the door to the elevator, he imparted the news that Stroud had somehow killed two other pires left to guard Magaffey's only a half hour earlier. "That's four, counting your boy, Dolph . . ."

"Five if you count Ray Carroll," someone reminded the vampire sheriff.

"Damn it, Briggs, all it takes is one shot from your bloody gun! Why can't you bring this man down?" Banaker wanted to know. All the others stared at Briggs for an answer.

"It's not that simple! Not with this man!"

"He's only human!" shouted Banaker. "Only human. A hundred ways for a human to die."

"I got to have a drink," said Briggs.

Some of the others liked this idea. All of them felt stronger, more invincible after a full meal.

"Find Stroud first! Find him and kill him. I don't care how you do it. Pounce on him together, rip him to shreds."

"He could be anywhere."

Over the PA came a female voice in distress, "At the morgue. He's been seen at the morgue!"

"Get to the morgue, of course, the morgue. I see it now, hurry! You fools!" Banaker believed Stroud had targeted the morgue to locate more incriminating evidence against them.

Some went with Briggs via the elevator. The others didn't wish to take car number two and so they scurried down the stairwells on either side. Banaker held back, biding his time. He spoke into a walkie-talkie that linked him up with Briggs, saying, "Place your men around the blood bank and the morgue. They're the two areas where he can hurt us the most."

"Seems he's hurt us pretty good already," grumbled Briggs just before turning off.

Banaker heaved a sigh. He'd spent hours now going over and over the actions taken against Stroud, the loss of his son, and how high the stakes had become. He'd made mistakes all along the way, sending Pam to do the job he himself might've done; perhaps it would have been wiser to turn Briggs and his police force on Stroud. Perhaps he ought to have listened to Ray Carroll when Carroll proposed that he and his friends be allowed to take Stroud down. So many ifs . . .

Banaker was feeling weak and defeated and in need of a good drink himself. Feeling sorry for himself, he supposed, feeling beaten and frightened by a bloody human.

The building was suddenly rocked by an explosion in her bowels. Banaker knew it was the morgue, and, god forbid, the blood bank! He raced for the lower portions of the building and he ran through crowds backing away from others who'd been scared by the blast. He shouted for information, shouted for Briggs.

Briggs, his face blackened from the explosion, holding onto another whose clothing was burned off him, shouted in return. "It's the morgue! He's fired the morgue! The auto-alarm's called in the fire trucks!"

"The bank! What about the blood bank?"

"It's safe, or at least it was a moment ago! No damage. Seems he didn't place a large enough charge. Damned fool!"

"Surround the bank! Keep that fiend out of there!"

"It is surrounded, now!"

Suddenly, over the PA system, Stroud's voice came booming along the corridors of Banaker Institute. "This is just a taste, Banaker! Just a taste of what is to come!"

"Bastard! Bastard's still here! Find him!"

Fire trucks were entering the hospital lot, sirens screeching. Banaker raced outside to shout orders and directions when he saw Stroud's helicopter lifting off the roof of the Institute, far overhead.

"There! See! There he is!"

The chopper was off and running, and so, too, were a number of the vampires who disappeared into the night sky in pursuit. Stroud shouted for Lonnie to open the throttle full. He was not certain they could make their next destination before the agile bat creatures. Vampire forms outlined in the sky behind them gave rise to fear and perspiration. "Hurry! Hurry!"

"Begging your pardon, sir," said Ashyer from the rear with the still decaying pods, "but what took you so long?"

"A welcoming party at Magaffey's."

"You are quite untidy, if you don't mind my saying so, sir. But did you accomplish the objective? Sir?"

"Yes, yes I did."

"Excellent, sir!"

Lonnie added a resounding, "*Yahooooooo!* Now we'll kick some ass, *ahhh*, sir."

"My sentiments exactly," replied Stroud, laughing.

Behind them the three monsters in pursuit were closing in. Ashyer rushed to the rear, sticking a head out just as one made a dive at the bay door. Ashyer lifted a large wad of cable and shoved it into the creature's talons and slapped down a high voltage electrical charge rigged years before by his first master, Ananias Stroud. The creature was stunned by the charge and hung on by the cable, the electricity passing through its body again and again in waves as it grew limp and finally fell away. Ashyer rushed back to Stroud and Wilson, saying, "They're on us!"

"How many more?"

"Two, sir!"

Stroud climbed back and with the helicopter shaking him from his footing, he crouched and took aim at the next creature who dared strike at the chopper. This one seemed bent on a hari-kari maneuver to throw itself into the propeller blades to hopefully damage the mechanism, sacrificing itself for Banaker's dream for its race. Stroud aimed the dart gun and fired. The impact slowed the creature and stunned it. In another moment the heart burst inside the chest and the chest ballooned until the thing blew into several pieces, the parts flying in all directions. Some of it hit the interior wall of the cargo bay, a portion of its claw and hairy wing which Stroud would have liked to preserve; but these began to liquify and finally changed to red-hued dust which blew about the cabin and into their eyes.

The third vampire fell back, seeing the awful fate of the ones before it, not understanding how Stroud could have found so powerful a weapon against them. It seemed like magic. As this one fell away, Stroud worried, seeing it turn in midair, going off. He shouted orders to Lonnie to turn and give chase. Lonnie balked.

"Do as I say, damn it! Now!"

"Yes, sir!"

Lonnie wheeled the old chopper around until it groaned with the tight turn, and they gave chase, the vampire spinning away. Stroud knew any moment *it* could take on another shape and he'd lose it for good. He took aim. The creature was at some distance. The shot would require all his skill as a marksman and, since it was a dart gun and since they were rocking wildly in an aircraft with debris flying about, the odds were stacked heavily in favor of the vampire.

"Approaching the Institute area, sir!" shouted Ashyer.

Stroud fired, hitting the target. In a matter of seconds, this one exploded in midair. No fire, just a rain of blood and parts.

Lonnie wheeled the machine around once more and tore off for their next destination, Andover Cold Storage. Ashyer said over and over, "Incredible shot, sir, just incredible!"

Stroud hadn't wanted this lone vampire to take the news back to Banaker that they had a secret weapon. So far, so good. The next distribution of the blood paks to Banaker's people would kill them.

In the meantime, Stroud had to get his decaying evidence in storage. And somewhere they must locate more of the S-choline. A pharmacy seemed the logical place.

For now they sped toward Andover Cold Storage through the black sky, a line of light barely visible on the horizon.

—23—

Banaker and the others watched from the top of the Institute as the helicopter wheeled around boldly in midair after destroying first one, and then two, and finally a third vampire. It was evident to all of them now that Abraham Stroud and his companions had found an effective weapon against them, that they could die at Stroud's hand in an instant.

Banaker was shaken in his beliefs. It was as if the natural order of the world had been turned upside down. His face showed his confusion clearly, leading his people to distrust him. All of them were coming unglued. The family was coming asunder. Each was thinking of saving himself.

To this end, the blood bank downstairs was already being overrun by them, each stockpiling a source of the energy-giving food Banaker's Institute provided; each thinking of the long, dry spell ahead when they would make their journeys to somewhere as far from Stroud and Andover as possible. Banaker had to stop the defection. He must act quickly and swiftly. He must regain control of his people, his Institute, his life, his Andover.

He turned to the closest of his people and struck him a powerful blow, sending him to the tarmac. "Get downstairs to Briggs! Tell him I said to alert the Cold Storage group that Stroud is on his way there now! Tell him to hurry! Go!" Banaker then looked at the others standing about the rooftop and he said calmly but firmly, "The rest of you, come with me!"

Banaker tore away his lab coat and clothing, stood on the edge of the building, and changed into the hairy vampire he was. The others followed his example. In moments they all took to the black sky, some thirty in number, vicious birds of prey outlined against the dark clouds.

Chief Briggs downed the first good blood pak he'd had in almost twelve hours. Burping, a little laugh escaped him as he wiped his mouth and rushed out to his car to call ahead to the Cold Storage folk before Stroud should arrive, just as Banaker had asked. Briggs ran amid the firefighters, most of whom were human, going unnoticed in the melee, when suddenly the burp turned into an intolerable heartburn that gripped his heart with unremitting pain. The pain itself seemed like a steel spearpoint that grew larger and larger from deep within his heart until suddenly he felt an instance's relief.

But he also felt the warmth of a liquid splatter on his chest. At first he thought it was a fleshy, bloody piece of one of the pires Stroud had killed in midair, dropping out of the sky onto him like bird shit. Then he realized the flesh of his chest had shredded into jagged edges, his heart was spurting forth blood, and his head was afloat with weakness, dizzying odors, and cold feelings—that he was a dead pire. He desperately tried to deny it with good thoughts, filling his mind with the image of a true Bloody Mary at Jack Tebo's bar where all the pires hung out—cops, paramedics, firemen mostly . . . good pires . . . just there to hoist a few. Then it hit Briggs. The blood! Stroud had contaminated their blood! His shout came out a pitiful wheeze.

He expired just outside his car, his form turning into a gelatinous puddle before becoming ash and being swept away by the wind.

The other side of the hospital, other pires were carrying out Banaker's order to ship and distribute as much of the blood paks as possible to safe storage locations, such as Andover Cold Storage and the mausoleum. A moving van was being filled with the stuff, but from the back of this van pires were grabbing off what they could, taking what they felt belonged rightfully to them, and what they must have to endure should Banaker fall. Vampires trundled off to Volvos and Jaguars, according to their social and economic means, rushing for their homes to make their families safe, all with boxes and armfuls of the bone marrow elixir.

• • •

Abraham Stroud was confident that now they might have a
fighting chance against the hordes of monsters among them.
The contaminated blood source would thin out their numbers
considerably, depending upon how long it went undetected. If
Banaker so much as got near it with a microscope, he'd shut
down all reliance on the food source, and all the vampires would
revert to older methods of finding food by feeding on human prey,
just as Dolph Banaker did for the sport of it. It was a calculated
gamble, and a risky one. It could mean the ruination of the entire
human population of Andover if it should backfire. The trick then
was to keep Dr. Oliver Banaker so busy, his head spinning, that
he would not be looking for the sneak attack of the contaminated
blood. Thus far, it seemed to be working.

Andover Cold Storage was their next stop, and once again a
diversion had been worked out. There was a pharmacy nearby.
They'd break into it and locate more S-choline for the dart gun
and hypos to build their arsenal. Once the contaminated blood
was discovered, all that stood between them and the vampires
was the dart gun and the hypodermic needles.

While Stroud and Lonnie placed the pods in the ice at Andover
Cold Storage, Ashyer would break into the pharmacy. Stroud gave
him a device for silencing the alarm before breaking the window. As
the helicopter touched down in a Little League baseball field beside
the cold storage plant and pharmacy, Stroud shouted a good luck
to Ashyer who dashed for the pharmacy. Ashyer's black clothes
were swallowed up by the dark, and he was gone.

Stroud and Lonnie Wilson began the labor of getting the first
pod, the most damaged one with Pamela Carr's remains, to the
freezers. But the moment they picked it up, the thing crumbled
like ancient cardboard into powder. The powder dusted them,
reminding Stroud of a "Devil's Egg" with its millions of spores.
"Don't breathe the stuff!" Stroud shouted at Wilson who was
coughing amid a cloud of it. "Get out of the bay!"

The two men jumped out, gasping for clean air, the acrid smell
of the bursted pod making Stroud ill and Lonnie retch. From where
he stood, Stroud watched the smoke inside the cargo bay turn to a
brackish, brown cloud before it finally dissipated, allowing them
back to gather up Mrs. Bradley's pod. Pam Carr had been one of
the vampires and since Dolph Banaker had opened the pod, her
remains were unable to withstand the decaying process brought on
by the air and all the microbes it carried with it. Mrs. Bradley's

remains, on the other hand, were those of a human being to begin with, and despite the fact the pod had been damaged by Dolph, the woman's body remained intact, the pod itself undamaged by the body it housed.

Once more Stroud and Lonnie moved toward the bay door and out onto the playing field. They made for the cold storage plant with their vampire evidence. Somewhere across the street Ashyer was, Stroud hoped, doing much better than they.

They'd have to break into Andover Cold Storage as well, but Stroud knew from his own experience that warehouses were relatively lax on security, depending upon what wares they housed. Cold storage places in Chicago went for cheap alarm systems which could typically be cut off from the outside by a burglar who knew what he was doing, and since Stroud had gone through training as a burglar in order to catch burglars, he knew all the tricks.

"We have to go around back," he told Lonnie.

But as they did so, he saw a side door and something told him the side door was unlocked. On this hunch, he had Lonnie hold up as he gave the knob a jiggle. It clicked open. "Luck is changing for the better," he commented as they made their way inside.

Above, on the roof, Banaker and twenty-eight other vampires looked on as the rats stepped into their trap. Two of Banakers people had literally exploded in air during the trip as if a timed-released bomb had been ticking inside them. The ripple effect of fear that spread through his people threatened to send them all flying off at any moment. "Now we kill him, once and for all," he said, "with the help of the cold storage."

Cold storage pires were the blue-collar workers, the less educated among the pires. The mausoleum was too good for their kind. At this time, the truck from the Institute carrying the recently fermented blood paks arrived in the parking lot at Andover Cold Storage, soon to be unloaded. Banaker sent word to have the unloading held until further notice. He didn't want Abe Stroud anywhere near the blood supply.

Stroud thought it odd that a door would be unlocked here, yet it was close to dawn, close to opening, and so one of the owners, or an eager-beaver employee, might be booting up the Xerox or computer in the office, "waking" the place. He and Lonnie inched forward through the dark corridor with their burden. In due time the pod would provide reasons for the nonbeliever and the authorities why a seemingly mad Dr. Abraham Stroud had touched off an explosion at the prestigious Banaker Institute. The pod was their only direct link to the bizarre, irrational facts of this, his most peculiar case. Stroud believed that if he survived this night he'd either be crucified by the authorities or lauded a hero who had put an end to an insidious enemy of the people.

He knew no policeman in Chicago or Springfield would believe a word of his story without concrete evidence, and if they must freeze Mrs. Bradley in her present condition to provide that evidence, then so be it.

Stroud stopped in his tracks. He heard, or sensed, movement in the building. He put a finger to his lips to indicate to Lonnie Wilson that something was amiss. They quietly moved on but with even more caution than when they'd entered. The building even here was cold, the temperature at or below freezing. Signs for canned goods, meat, poultry and vegetables, all surrounded in heaps of ice, lined the walls. They came on a door deep within the confines of the place where rising cold smoke seeped like water through the crevices. Stroud opened it and moved ahead, although his face and figure were suddenly lost in the gas cloud of cold that poured from this room. Inside, visibility was terrible and Stroud walked into a table upon which lay an enormous box, but the box was no box: it was a coffin. And when he bumped the table, the lid slowly began to rise.

Wilson dropped his end of the pod, making Stroud wheel around. Lonnie was struggling in the fog with something that had him by the throat. Stroud, too, dropped the pod and pressed the dart gun against the back of the creature about to rip open Lonnie's throat with its incisors. He fired into the kidney area but the creature sunk its teeth into Lonnie at the same moment, holding firm, as something hit Stroud from behind. Falling, he realized that Andover Cold Storage housed vampires. Falling, he heard and felt and saw pieces of the monster at Lonnie as it exploded from within. The bloody explosion fired the imaginations of the others whom Stroud sensed now and saw outlined amid the icy fog of the freezer. He and Lonnie were shivering unbearably and he felt his grip on the dart gun turning numb.

"We've got to get out of here, now!" shouted Stroud, feeling the awakened vampire crowd backing off, fearful, cowardly at heart. Seeing one of their number explode from within as if staked from within, made *them* shiver. But Stroud couldn't count on this for long. Should they suddenly all attack at once, he knew that he and

Lonnie could not withstand the assault. They'd have to abandon Mrs. Bradley here and now; he could only be thankful that she was dead inside the pod and they could do no more to her.

The evidence lost to them, Stroud now turned his attention to getting Lonnie out of this place safely and efficiently. There was no telling how soon the vampires here would come charging after. They'd surprised them, awakened and stunned the vampires all at once. But once they began in earnest to file out after Stroud, he and Lonnie would become carrion for them.

They raced for the side entrance, the same way as they'd come in. It was blocked by two snarling creatures who showed their incisors, their gums discolored by squirming white worms. These two flapped and keened and spat the worms at them. Behind them the others were rushing from the freezer compartment. Stroud crashed through a glass partition that opened on the offices, and he helped Lonnie through. The vampires raced for them.

Stroud fired the reloaded dart gun catching one in the chest, and this instantly burst his heart before the others, sending them into awe, stopping them in their tracks. It was obvious none of them had ever seen such destructive power used on their kind before. Stroud literally dove through the broken glass, cutting himself as he did so, rolling to an upright position. Another vampire came in atop him, digging its talons into him. Lonnie, a hypodermic at the ready, stabbed this one and the creature began to tremble as if a minor earthquake had hold of its epicenter. In a moment it exploded all over Stroud. Again, the others were stopped cold in their tracks at the sight of one of their number so horribly and quickly disposed of. They began to hold back as Stroud, on his feet now, reloaded the dart gun and backed through the offices of Andover Cold Storage, through a conference room, through an adjacent closet and duplicating room, to a back corridor that opened on another section of the warehouse. All the while, the vampire numbers were increasing as they seemed to step out of every dark corner. The temperature in the warehouse was again beginning to affect the humans badly. Stroud tried to determine a way out as they passed by whole sides of beef on hooks, his mind picturing how he and Lonnie would look alongside the beef, hung here for the vampires' pleasure. Someone, or something slapped a button and the sides of beef began to rotate, causing a deafening, screeching, metallic noise. Stroud and Wilson weaved in and around and out of the moving carcasses, knowing that, like a wheat field, they could not long hide here.

Overhead, some of the vampires took to the air and began diving down toward them. Stroud fired, bringing one down, a direct hit to the heart. Lonnie lashed out at a second that caught his forearm and tore the hypo and much of his flesh away, causing him to scream out.

"You have nowhere to hide, nowhere to go now, Stroud!" shouted Banaker from a catwalk high overhead, his form looking one moment human, one moment monstrous as he willfully controlled his appearance. "Now you are going to pay for the crimes you've committed against my race, the murder of my son, and so many other pires."

Stroud fired the next dart at Banaker but he was not there when the dart pinged harmlessly against the metal of a crossbar on the catwalk. Then Banaker re-formed in exactly the spot he had disappeared. "Your puny weaponry only works on the feeble-minded, the slow and tardy, those we'd just as soon weed out from the gene pool anyway."

"Come on down here and fight me, then! Damn you! Damn you back to the hell from which you came! You filthy, mutant bastard!"

Banaker laughed at the outburst, and his calm and ability in dealing with Stroud gave confidence to the other pires, one of which suddenly leapt over the top of the beef all around Stroud and was atop him, digging at him with his talons, tearing with his teeth. The others raced to overwhelm Stroud at Banaker's order. "Now, now! Get him, now! All of you!"

Stroud felt the creatures all around him, crowding into the confined space he occupied, tearing at him, knowing that he was about to die here, like this, like another slab of frozen meat to be added to cold storage, no one the wiser. Lonnie, too, was being overwhelmed. Each man stabbed out at the creatures with as many hypos as they commanded, but there weren't enough! One pire would fall away, burst to death, only to be replaced by another and another, while each wound they inflicted brought on a new surge of helplessness in Stroud and Wilson. Wilson's cries were horrible and Stroud felt a pang of guilt at having gotten him into this, the final moment before death.

Suddenly a glass container burst beside them, sending up a cloud of acrid smoke in the chamber of ice and fog, turning the meat locker into a green place. The green cloud encircled the twisting torsos of the monsters at combat with the humans. Then the creatures began to drop, grasp at their nostrils and throats, gasping for air. Stroud looked around for the reason why as he stabbed yet another of the creatures with his last S-choline dart, using his hand and weight for the plunger.

Stroud grabbed hold of one of the things that'd attached itself to Wilson, but it held on with a bulldog ferocity at Wilson's neck. Wilson's eyes had rolled back in their sockets and he barely looked alive. Stroud pummeled the creature but it came loose and stumbled away not because of Stroud's beating, but because it, too, had inhaled the green gas all around them now.

Stroud himself was coughing, choking on the gas, but he felt no weakness from it. He lifted Wilson over his shoulders and looked all around for the reason for his and Wilson's salvation. He saw a Freon pipe had been smashed by a fire ax lying nearby, and in a corner he got a glimpse of Ashyer holding up a large crucifix to several creatures moving in on him. The crucifix was absolutely useless against Banaker's new breed of vampire.

Stroud realized now that Ashyer had come in on the scene, saw there was no hope, and reacted by throwing down the jar of S-choline. The liquid in the presence of the Freon had created a dry ice gas of the S-choline, a gas deadly for the pires. Some had, thus far, escaped the effects of the gas, and one now took Ashyer in its mighty grasp as if the man were a rag doll, about to take a bite from him. At a safe distance somewhere overhead, Banaker's angry voice cried out over the tumult and keening of the dying pires. "Stop Stroud! Stop the man!"

But on all sides, the vampire horde raced from the deadly gas billowing around them. Two surrounding Ashyer succumbed to the fumes, and Stroud stepped on these and used them as springboards to get to the other one, hitting it full in its powerful back, knocking it and Ashyer to the frozen, hard-packed floor. Freon caught the pire in the face, making it screech, but the S-choline cloud silenced him.

"Good work, Ashyer!" shouted Stroud, still coughing.

"We must get out," he replied. "This way!"

Stroud helped Lonnie who was the weakest of the trio now. The three men found a back bay door and ran into a loading zone where men who were not men were unloading twenty-pound-bag blood paks from the Institute. Vampires who'd struggled with Stroud's trio had escaped this way, and many were tearing into the blood paks, downing fresh supplies, looking for courage and the strength that Banaker seemed to possess.

Stroud and the others stopped dead in their tracks. The vampires turned and stared at them, and for a long uneasy moment of silence the two sides sized one another up. Wilson was barely capable of standing, and both Stroud and Ashyer had sustained wounds that were openly bleeding, and enticing to the creatures. With so many gashes to his body, Stroud knew he was running on adrenaline, but he was unsure how long he could sustain his strength. The creatures, for their part, were choking and coughing, having come out of the S-choline gas. The gas would take a longer time, but now it seemed to be doing the trick, as one of them keeled over, lay cadaverlike a moment and then erupted as he stared up at his comrades.

The others looked round at one another, wondering who would be next. The fear sent them into a gulping match for who could ingest Banaker's elixir of life the fastest.

"God," moaned Stroud, "I hope that's the right stuff."

The vampires looked like a band of warriors who'd just stumbled onto a cache of liquor. They were jubilant at the sight of so much energy and power at their beck and call. With the rules of fair distribution gone, they tore wildly into the blood paks, swallowing hungrily.

A second vampire burst open where he stood, and then another in firecracker fashion, until the interior explosions sounded off in rhythmic succession. "Cooking good now," said Stroud. "Let's go!"

It was just coming on light when Stroud saw those vampires who had hung closest to Banaker winging off to the south. They'd seen enough. They'd witnessed a full-scale wipeout of their kind at the blood truck from the Institute. Banaker now knew that Stroud had gotten to the blood supply and had tainted it with an antivampire agent. He most assuredly had no idea of the properties of the killing liquid in Stroud's darts and hypos, or in the gas cloud that had magically erupted around Stroud, but unlike the others who now believed Stroud was some sort of god, he knew it had to do with medicine.

Through medicine Banaker had made his great strides for the race; ironically, now medicine would wipe them out, unless . . .

The only clean blood paks were at the mausoleum where Banaker stocked his own personal supply, keeping it close at hand for emergencies of one sort or another. Foresight was a wonderful thing. . . .

He'd thought for a moment of destroying Stroud's helicopter, but he shied off from this decision. He had the pod that encased the Bradley body now. He'd destroy this, but not Stroud's bloody helicopter. He wanted Stroud to follow. It was time he himself killed the bestial human who was so unlike his fellow man.

Stroud sensed the meaning of Banaker's quick retreat, and in the distance he noted the oddly shaped vampire being carried between two others, and he realized it was the pod. He sensed that the helicopter was left undamaged so that he would follow and fall into an even deeper trench than the one they'd just climbed out of. He knew he must do so, but he felt he could no longer endanger Wilson and Ashyer.

"Into the chopper," he ordered Ashyer who climbed in and helped get Lonnie aboard. They were being trailed by pires, but one would suddenly die from within, and this would stop the others, retarding their progress. None of them had put it together with the blood paks; they thought it the after effects of inhaling the gas fumes which continued to plume out of doors and windows at the warehouse. The sound of sirens was in the air as firefighters approached.

Stroud got in behind Ashyer and Lonnie and was about to race for the cockpit when out of nowhere a pire grabbed him and threw him across the cargo bay. Ashyer rushed at the creature with a hypodermic he'd been hording and sunk it deeply into the thing's stomach as it grasped him by the throat and lifted him off the floor. Suddenly the monster burst open in a flood of red liquid, then quickly turned to ash. Stroud didn't bother strapping in or doing flight check. He simply lifted off, several of the pires hanging onto the skids but soon dropping away, bursting in air.

They were away, safe, out of harm's grip. Even Wilson, in great pain, lifted his head and gave him a thumbs-up sign as Ashyer shouted a rousing Rebel yell totally out of character. "If only Mother could see me now," he said.

"Mother?"

"Mrs. Ashyer."

Stroud had never heard her referred to as "Mother" by the man. For a moment, he wondered if Ashyer was an "imposter" planted by Banaker. The man-thing was devious enough to do such a thing.

"Did you and she have children?" asked Stroud.

Ashyer came to the copilot's seat and seemed to deflate as he got comfortable in the ripped leather. "We had a girl, once.

She . . . she didn't survive. Your grandfather did everything in his power, but . . ."

"I see. I see."

Ashyer was crying. Stroud knew he was a man. He said, "I'm going after Banaker alone from here."

"But, sir!"

"No, no buts."

"I want to help."

"You've done enough. Mrs. Ashyer needs you."

"I have something that might help," he said flatly. "It's a pharmacological encyclopedia. I came back to the helicopter with the S-choline and the book, grew fearful when you and Lonnie didn't soon appear, and that is when I found you. I had to use up the S-choline, but in the book are the ingredients, sir, and they are all found around any kitchen. We can prepare our own arsenal."

Stroud smiled at this. "Perfect."

"Where will Banaker be, sir?"

"That's between him and me."

"Do you expect him to attack Stroud Manse again? Tonight?"

"Not if we strike him first."

"Yes, very good, sir, take the offensive."

"We've got to get Lonnie and you looked after. Mrs. Ashyer'll take care of you."

"When Andover awakes to fires and explosions at the Institute and the warehouse, people will want to know what is happening. They'll think we are mad, sir."

"Yes, I know. No help for that at the moment. And now what proof of the existence of this threat do we have? Very little, I'm afraid, unless we can recover that pod."

"But don't you think they've damaged it, burned it, destroyed it by now, sir?"

"Banaker will use it as long as it represents a lure for me. I believe that he believes that if he kills me, things in Andover can and will go back to normal. Normal, that is, by a vampire's definition of the word. At this point, the pod's his bait.

"They'll be puttin' by more pods now . . . Now, since we destroyed their source of food. They'll be killing the innocent," said Stroud. "Unless we stop them now."

Stroud recalled that Magaffey had believed that some of the monsters, while sporting big houses for show, actually lived—or slept—at the mausoleum in Andover's cemetery. He heard

Magaffey's faint voice telling him it was so, telling him now again. The old man's crackling voice filtered through the metal in Stroud's cranium. He knew where Banaker had gone, knew where Banaker wished a final showdown to take place, knew it would be on Banaker's terms.

His only hope lay in a fierce arsenal of the S-choline. He had no idea how many more pires Banaker could amass now. He had no idea of how many of the many hundreds of such beings had this night ingested some bad blood. Banaker had chosen to surround himself with his strongest, sharpest, and fiercest fighters. He'd hand-picked these pires, and he had kept them from the blood paks, thus saving them all a horrible death, and so they owed him. He also kept them from feeding on any other source, and would continue to do so, so that their desire for blood, their frenzy to feed, their hunger hormones would be razor sharp for when Stroud arrived. *He* was to be the main course.

—24—

Dr. Oliver Banaker had done all that Stroud had believed. He also did much more. He'd withheld blood paks free of the contamination even from himself so that the vampire miracle drink might survive, even if not a single one of them did. There were other pires far from here, other colonies. He'd sent it out to one of these colonies, it and the data. They could not ignore the importance of the elixir. He'd sent it by messenger earlier at the Institute.

But the messenger hadn't returned, hadn't checked in, and it began to trouble Banaker. Suppose Stroud had intercepted the message and the sample? Or, had the messenger become fearful, swallowing up the elixir himself for the courage and strength it brought? Or had it been contaminated, like that on the truck? When had Stroud gotten into the blood bank?

He imagined the humiliation and defeat that would accompany his having sent a tainted supply of blood to his fellow beings in another colony far to the north. After he dispensed with Stroud, he meant to carry on the work. There was always the work, and always work to be done. He missed the peace that Stroud had so disrupted; he missed the time before when Dolph had been young and had no greater ambition than to please himself with harmless distractions, and feed on what his father gave him to feed upon. He missed those calm days before all this had begun.

His reverie was demolished by the images of his people in that meat locker bursting into pieces of flesh and blood to decay in

224

rapid succession, even at those temperatures, and turn to nothing more than a fistful of dirt. An eternity as ashen dirt. He knew he must put on a good show for Stroud in order to stop his evil genius bent on the destruction of all vampires, and especially on him, Oliver Banaker. He knew he'd have to provide a stunning display of power and strength and those things the human mind found horrific, if he were to take Stroud down. He knew now he must make Stroud one of them. He knew this in his heart and mind, because his own god had told him as much. His god would find it most pleasing, and he himself would find it a nice, ironic touch to turn the vampire killer into the vampire.

Banaker went about the mausoleum rousing others who had no idea the havoc being wreaked all around them. Only Banaker and his immediate army of body guards knew the full extent of the force they intended to meet head on here. Banaker, nonetheless, ordered his people out of the mausoleum and into the earth, just as in olden times. They must burrow into the graves all around the cemetery and lay in wait for Stroud's arrival.

These pires did as instructed. They'd heard rumors carried back to them about Stroud's powers, but none had seen evidence of it firsthand. All wanted for a fresh, morning cup of the red, life-giving drink, but Banaker had them on rations! They began to disperse among the graves, digging in as small rodents might, shape-changing to accommodate themselves in a kind of hibernation beneath the earth to await a high-frequency screech signal from Banaker. As they were going about this, the caretaker of the cemetery, one of them, saw a car pull up at the gate. A man, the fellow who had come to his wife's gravesite every day for six weeks now, was back again. The caretaker frowned and feared the human would see the disturbed gravesites since he was so bloody meticulous about his wife's, and raise a complaint. He also worried that, as the man had drawn close to the gate, he may well have seen some of the brothers and sisters squirming into their appointed holes in the earth. Some had chosen the good digging form of a large white worm and they had burrowed quickly and efficiently out of sight. But others had adopted foolish methods.

But the caretaker needn't have worried about the secret of Andover Cemetery going abroad, for suddenly several of Banaker's hand-picked guards swooped down over the man and attacked him with a ferocity the caretaker had never seen, even in vampires. The man's limbs were severed, along with his head, as the pires drank of his blood as if they'd never had a meal in their lives, as if they had returned to the old ways. The caretaker didn't understand it, nor did he grasp the reason for Banaker's having them all lie low beneath the earth, another old and out-of-mode custom. But, like everyone who owed so much to Dr. Banaker, the cemetery man found an empty gravesite of his own, shape-changed into the big worm, and burrowed in. Beneath the earth he felt comforted in knowing that he could burrow his way out anytime he wished.

He, with countless others here, dozed a bit as he relaxed to await Banaker's signal.

It could be a long wait.

Nobody seemed to know.

Everybody was confused.

Banaker said.

Simon says . . .

Sunshine blanketed the streets of Andover and a mild bracing breeze felt cool and refreshing on the skin, but the moment people began going about, even to step out to pick up the morning paper, they sensed something was wrong in their town. For one, there was no paper to pick up. Maybe the carrier simply hadn't gotten out of bed, but there were other indications about the little neighborhoods all around the small city that things were not quite right. Down the street the number of lights on, the number of cars pulling from garages, the number of children readying for school had all drastically reduced. Why? Was it one of those school and federal holidays?

TV news had nothing to offer. Tom McEarn's morning broadcast was nothing but a blur on the screen. A check with neighbors showed that half or more of the neighbors were simply missing, gone, their cars, garages, homes, and beds having been untouched. It was as if they'd been beamed from existence by some alien visitors in the night whose selection process was as inscrutable as God's own.

The disturbing morning turned into a much more disturbing day as remnants of ash and an occasional bit of unwholesome and unidentifiable liquid mixture was found amid spectacular arrays of blood-smattered concrete walks, parkways, fences, store entanceways, the interiors of cars and trucks. And the number of the missing among the Andover population steadily grew with each passing hour. A count was organized by the citizenry as the entire police force, too, was missing, along with most of the local media persons, like McEarn. There were many missing firemen. All of the nurses, orderlies, doctors, paramedics, morticians, as well as Dr. Oliver Banaker himself—all missing, gone without a trace.

Old civil service rules were instantly put into place and many lamented the lack of safety shelters below the ground, certain that some bizarre radioactive cloud had passed over Andover, or that something had gotten into the drinking water, or that a kind of Love Canal gas had seeped from the earth to claim its victims.

A few men organized a hastily got up Vigilante Committee that would see to organizing against the unknown. The police department was taken as central headquarters and an alert was sent out to Springfield for help. From the description of the chaos and nature of the disturbance, word was instantly dispatched to the National Environmental Protection Agency. By two in the afternoon the EPA reps out of Chicago and Springfield and St. Louis were on the scene, arguing territory and putting machines and personnel to work on the problem.

Andover was scoured by men in protective wear looking like astronauts far from the moon and quite out of place. Farmers coming in from the surrounding rural areas parked their trucks for hours just to sit and watch the unusual "space men" in their midst. The locals sat on porch chairs, carved wood, spat tobacco, and swapped theories about the catastrophe. Meanwhile, sensing devices were set up at key locations in the search for the cause of the catastrophe which had claimed several hundred of the population of the small city. Banaker's white coats had been replaced by the EPA's. The search went on until dusk without result. By evening, the only sure thing was that people were missing en masse.

News teams from the major surrounding areas flocked to Andover to film it all, but there was really nothing to film, and the footage being sent back to their respective stations drew dull groans.

During the day Stroud had not remained idle. He had sent for his own experts. He had used the ham radio to get through to Chicago and was patched into Cage, who, thank God, was available. When Stroud described his situation, he knew he sounded like a madman, but already Cage and others in Chicago were getting disturbing reports from the previously unheard of rural city of Andover, Illinois—something either to do with UFOs or toxic waste, no one seemed to know what, except that literally hundreds of people had disappeared overnight. Nothing like it in recent history had ever been heard of, and yet there were recorded cases of whole colonies of people who'd seemingly disappeared overnight, leaving food in dishes, doors ajar, animals unfed. Cage agreed to put together a team of scientists who would see Stroud at his manse sometime this evening.

"Can you get the governor?"

"No way."

Static interrupted them.

"Deputy governor, then. A goddamned senator, then . . . FBI, CIA?"

"I'll try but . . . " More static. "Can you give me more to go on?"

"Only that we do have an *alien* race among us here, Cage, but they're not from outer space."

"Where are they from, then?"

"They're from . . . " Static intensified. " . . . from the dead."

"Have you flipped?"

"Wish it were that simple."

"This has to do with that bone field you mentioned?"

"Right! These aliens feed on human blood, Cage."

"Christ, maybe you'd best call out the National Guard."

"They're on their way, but they . . . much help . . . not without the solution."

"Solution? The S-choline you told me about?"

"Right."

"You're out of it?"

"Cage, got to rush. Can I count on you?"

"Sure, sure, Doctor Stroud."

"You're not just humoring me to go along with the sick vet routine, are you?"

"I'll be there. Will you have the bodies for me to examine?"

"I will," he lied, not knowing how he would regain the Bradley woman's body. Knowing Banaker, it was already destroyed, unless he meant to use it as bait for him.

They signed off and Stroud went back to work on his vampire arsenal. Mrs. Ashyer had been of great help, first taking care of Wilson and her husband, getting their wounds cleaned and tied off, seeing they rested. She then began gathering up various household items that would contribute to creating a new batch of S-choline. The homemade brew would be diluted with other chemicals, yet in theory it ought to work. Using the pharmacological encyclopedia

Ashyer had wisely chosen to come away with, they had some notion that while vanilla extract would be of no use to them, Clorox bleach and other routinely used chemicals about the place would. In fact, they were finding the various mixtures they needed at every turn. Before long they had half a drum filled with a substance approximating S-choline. This was loaded onto the chopper.

Stroud opened up some thirty large casings to use in his AK-47 assault rifle which, up until now, had been useless against the creatures. He removed the casings, placed an eye drop of the homemade S-choline into each bullet, reassembled the casing and the lead, and laid each into the chamber.

Using Pepsi bottles and Coke cans, he created Molotov cocktails of larger ingredients that would be touched off in incendiary fashion. He made nine of these and stuffed them into a cloth bag that he could dangle from his shoulder along with the loaded AK-47.

The entire time he used for his preparations against Banaker, he sensed Banaker was also setting up his weaponry and arsenal. In a sense, the monster and the monster-hunter were now so connected that their thought patterns had become entwined. Stroud feared he would be too predictable, that Banaker would know his every maneuver before he did. He must plan his attack wisely. Banaker expected him; Banaker would not be taken by surprise again. Banaker would have scouts watching, waiting . . . there in the cemetery where they would struggle to the death.

Banaker began rationing out the blood supply he'd kept on hand at the mausoleum. He wanted his people hale and fit for battle when Stroud arrived. With the sun going below the lip of the horizon, they needed the marrow mix to keep them whole and strong.

Where the hell was Stroud?

The waiting was driving Banaker crazy.

He wondered if he ought not attack the manse again.

But if he did so, at what cost?

Better to remain here on his own ground.

Better to take the defensive.

"There! There in the west!" shouted one of Banaker's closest bodyguards. "It's Stroud! It's the machine!"

The word machine resounded through Banaker's psyche as "the machine that killed his father, housing the grandson of the man

who'd killed his father." Banaker gave out a wild, animal scream
that turned to silence as its high pitch rose to such a treble that none
but the bat creatures and the bats in surrounding caves could hear.
Whole clouds of small bats stormed from their caves in clouds of
blackness against the late afternoon sky. They moved as if of one
mind, straight for Stroud's machine.

Banaker keened frantically, his own monster form now having
taken full shape. The lesser bats would bring Stroud down to the
earth, if Banaker willed them to.

The cloud of black, keening, sweeping bats blotted out the
image of the chopper as it approached, there were so many
of them.

Stroud saw the moving, living cloud of bats coming and he
knew they were bent on suicide or any other cost to drive him
to the ground and destroy his mobility.

Stroud knew they were honing in on him and his already shaky
craft. Should they dive-bomb the rotars en masse, or cover the
bubble with their blood and bodies, he'd go directly down and
be killed before he even got near Banaker.

In the distance he saw Banaker surrounded by several huge bat
things. He determined to swoop, avoiding the first army of the
bat colony sent to destroy him in midair. He shoved the stick
forward at full throttle at the last possible instant, missing the
bulk of the small bats who nonetheless gave chase. Leveling out,
he was faced with trees directly ahead, but before pulling up, he
threw down three of the cocktails, causing confusion and a gas
cloud to erupt on the ground at the cemetery. He then pulled up
as madly as possible, feeling the skids at the bottom of the chopper
tear away the top limbs of the trees.

He circled around, the bats still in pursuit, enough of them
jamming into the tail rotar to effectively shut it down. It was only
a matter of minutes before they'd do the same to the top rotar.

Stroud cursed to himself. He hadn't expected trouble in the air.
He'd planned to dump the final drum of home-made S-choline out
the back and onto Banaker's party. It was held onto a platform
firmly bolted to the chopper. There was only one way to explode
it. It must be done kamikaze fashion, but Stroud didn't particularly
wish to die.

He instead took the bird straight up over the top of the cemetery
field. He had strapped on a parachute, and now he cut loose from
the straps holding him in the seat, dashed to the rear, holding firm

to the dart gun, hand grenades, Molotovs, plastique, and hypos in the pack lashed to him, and jumped. The bats kept at the dead machine like ants feeding on the carcass of an enormous beetle as Stroud flew down and yanked the chute open. Above him, he saw and felt the powerful aircraft coming at him. It missed by mere feet, sending him off like a feather in its wake. His grandfather's tough old chopper was covered in bat hair and bat blood. Other bats dive-bombed him as he was descending, some trying to rend holes in the fabric of the chute. Stroud used every maneuver he knew to descend as quickly as possible, knowing he'd have a welcoming committee waiting below. As they gathered, he sent down a rain of Molotov cocktails for the beasts.

But the chopper exploded on impact, and while fire and a blast were no match for the enemy, the explosion of chemicals aboard the helicopter sent up a weird mushroom cloud that spread out in a dense blanket all around the graveyard. So dense was the canopy, even sunlight could not filter through.

This Stroud landed in.

He didn't know where Banaker was, but his ears were filled with the agonized, animal cries of the dead and dying. What he saw all around him both amazed and terrified, as the earth over graves began to tremble. He tore himself loose from the parachute, knowing he was helpless buckled to it. He stumbled into a headstone as he did so, and he felt something grab his leg. His eyes fell on the large, bony hand that held his ankle. It was sticking out from a grave. In fact, all around him, things— *corpses*—seemed to be crawling from their graves, shaking off earth, and making their way toward him, the lone living human in all the cemetery. Stroud stepped onto the body of a giant white worm that was cork-screwing from a grave.

Then Stroud saw one of the walking dead snarl in a salty fashion as if he was readying to pounce and bite off Stroud's arm. In the thing's mouth, curled on the gums, Stroud saw the now familiar miniature white worms. *They* were Banaker's *things*, still in their human form, and some were beginning to fall over and quake with the symptoms of the poisonous gas that worked on their nerves, liver, blood pressure and heart, until some began to explode. These exploded with soft, *pop-pulp* sounds. The kitchen mixture of S-choline was taking more time, and was less dramatic in result, but just as effective in the long run. But for now, the one that had him by the ankle

had wisely remained below ground, and the gas had not had
the killing effect as a result, and the grip of the monster was
threatening to break Stroud's ankle bone. He could not pull
loose. Others were moving in to converge on Stroud and rip
him apart with outstretched hands. Stroud fired off one of the
darts, striking the closest of the standing creatures, sending it
into an immediate paroxysm of pain and anguish before it softly
burst open. Still he was held in place by the iron grip of the
hand from the grave. Stroud jammed one of the hypos into the
hand and it opened almost instantly in response, allowing Stroud
escape.

But escape to where?

How many were left in the ground? How many were left in the
fog. Where was Banaker?

Another explosion from the chopper debris rumbled the earth,
toppling headstones. Andover Cemetery was now looking like a
war-torn area. Over his shoulder, Stroud carried the conventional
weapons of war, his AK-47, hand grenades, and plastique. He
was disoriented in the smoke and fog which were causing the
things on all sides of him to gag, cry out like wounded bears,
collapse, and turn to a kind of molten mass of gelatinous flesh
before becoming ash. Stroud tried desperately to find the huge
white brick mausoleum that was at the northern section of the
cemetery. He believed he was heading in the right direction, and
he believed that if Banaker was still alive, he'd be there.

Stroud was hit from atop. One of the vampires had flown above
the killing cloud, but now dived onto him, sending its ghastly
talons into Stroud's back, right between the shoulder blades. It
felt as if the thing were about to take his head off when suddenly
it lifted him, his own weight causing more pain against the lifting
talons. The creature had gotten in and out of the deadly cloud so
quickly that it hadn't taken a breath. They were slow learners, but
the vampires were catching on. This one was flying Stroud to some
strange destination. Stroud felt for the dart gun, but it was gone,
dropped somewhere below as Stroud fought for consciousness.
The power of the being that held him was formidable. It slammed
him face first into the side of the mausoleum, almost knocking
Stroud senseless. Stroud slid down onto the pearly white stone
steps before the closed door of the brick edifice.

Two of them now straddled him. They bent to lift him, their
eyes black and animal-like, fixing him there as if he were a bug,
easy prey. They could have killed him then and there had they

lifted him and together slammed him into the concrete. Stroud acted quickly, however, jamming a hypo into one of them. The other watched in sheer horror at the fate of its fellow being. Stroud ran.

-25-

Abraham Stroud stumbled, got up, ran farther, and then saw it was hopeless—there was nowhere to run to.

They were everywhere, and they had encircled him, hatred for him causing a communal keening noise that pierced the human ear with a painful screech. These were the ones who'd survived the contaminated blood earlier and the initial S-choline bomb that had exploded with the chopper. These were the ones who'd witnessed so many of their kind die at Stroud's hand; these monsters had quickly burrowed back beneath the earth when the S-choline cloud came over the cemetery.

Stroud stared back at their angry, animal faces and watched as their snouts twitched in rage at him, as each locked its sonar on him, fixing him in place. Their dead, black pupils were like the unmoving, closed eyelids of a snake that lived below ground, locating prey by smell and feel. They were closing in on him. He'd be devoured by the horde, just as Banaker had planned all along.

In fact, he could almost hear Banaker's order as if he could pull it out of the air: Destroy the one human who can destroy you.

Stroud instinctively reached for the missing AK-47 automatic assault gun that had been dangling from his shoulder, but it was a futile gesture. It had flown from his grasp when he'd been unceremoniously dumped on the stone steps before Banaker's altar. The bag carrying the Molotov cocktails was empty of these

234

and dangling about him like a loose fold of skin. But deep in its bottom, he'd placed a layer of the sanctified earth from his grandfather's coffins. He lifted out a handful of the dirt and flung it in the faces of the bat people. It rose like sand, catching and refracting the moonlight, turning to miniature stars as it cascaded into the crowd of vampires. Where it fell it burned and seared hair and flesh, causing a ripple of fear to hold them in check. He cast out a second handful of the holy dirt and, like water, it wet the creatures but with a wetness of burning sores. But then even the dirt was gone and Stroud was weaponless, defeated.

He backed toward the mausoleum door, trying desperately to gain entrance, but it remained locked against him. Banaker was inside, he could feel his presence deep within the concrete walls. He was inside, and yet he was out, watching the drama unfold, orchestrating from afar, at a safe distance, cowardly at heart.

Somewhere deep inside the crypt, Stroud realized Banaker had a route out. He was too smart to seal himself up without an escape hatch. He concentrated on Banaker and willed his own thoughts through to the creature that could read his mind, and that of his fellow creatures. He willed Banaker to know that he had killed Dolphin and that he, Stroud, believed Banaker a skulking coward, afraid to face him, afraid to open the door and let him through.

Behind him, Stroud felt the others closing the distance to the mausoleum. Stroud fought back the image of his own body being ravaged, lying on the white steps, a bloodless pulp of flesh. He instead concentrated on challenging Banaker with his mind. The attempt put great strain on him and for a moment he feared he would black out and it would be over; they would then feast on his life's blood.

But then the door he leaned against moved and it came suddenly open, displaying a sheer, clean black gaping hole into which Stroud might run, if he dared. Stroud turned to face the oncoming rush of vampires, knowing he had no choice but to accept Banaker's new challenge now. The army of pires moved ever closer, eerily reaching out for him now, closing in. He had little choice left but to step into Banaker's home.

The smoke pall over the cemetery was dissipated, and Stroud saw that about forty vampires stood around him, all with gleeful snarls on their filthy lips where the occasional worm flashed, reflecting the moonlight. Then a child stepped from the vampire horde and Stroud stared into the eyes of Ray Carroll's boy. He was holding onto Stroud's AK-47, pointing it at Stroud.

"No!" another of the pires shouted. "Doctor Banaker wants him alive."

"He's to die slowly," said another.

"He killed my father!" shouted the boy whose shape was wavy, forming bat features and then human again, and back again.

"Kill him! Kill him now!" shouted a female voice in the crowd, the boy's mother.

But one of Banaker's lieutenants slammed into the boy and snatched the gun away. Stroud rushed this one and took firm hold of the automatic's grip, firing as the monster's hands were still on the barrel. The bullet with the S-choline slammed into Carroll's child who laughed nastily in response before he suddenly went into spasms. The others, including the powerful one who had hold of the AK-47 backed off. Stroud stood over them on the steps to the white mausoleum, its pillars a kind of archway into the hell that lay at his back. He stared down at the things surrounding him, the mutant race of the undead whose human and inhuman genes had for centuries commingled; it was a race of beings that lived off his race like the parasitic worms that lived off them in turn; it was a race spawned by Satan.

His eyes holding them in place as they watched the suffering death of the Carroll boy, Stroud opened fire with the automatic, slicing them down. The more courageous of them flew at Stroud in kamikaze fashion, attempting to slam him down so that the others might devour him quickly as the boy had wanted to do. Stroud nimbly side-stepped such actions and blew holes in these intrepid ones. Others raced to the pits from which they came, Stroud trying desperately to destroy each and every monster, to keep each from escaping. Should any one do so, Andover could be repopulated by the hideous things again.

Stroud then heard automobile, van, and truck engines coming up over the rise, their lights like beacons in the black sea of the cemetery, flashing on the disgusting, horrifying sight of creatures burrowing into gravesites in a mad rush to save themselves from the man at the marblelike mausoleum at the center of the grave-yard. Rushing from the cars, Stroud saw human forms, but he dared not hope it was human help, and he dared not let down his guard. Banaker had thrown up one surprise and hurdle after another. This could be another of his tricks.

Then he heard Lonnie Wilson's voice, followed by Ashyer's. Dr. Cage was with them, along with state and federal officials who stopped dead in their tracks, seeing the Andover horror in the beaming headlights, but unable to calculate the meaning of it all. It was understandable that most of them froze in place while Wilson and Ashyer rushed in with more of the unusual ammunition required to kill the vampires. They'd apparently gotten hold of more dart guns, possibly from Dr. Cage and the others on hand. They went about firing darts of the S-choline into the scurrying bats. Wise enough to fire on anything else that moved as well, they also destroyed a dog that bounded over the fence, and rats and squirrels that dared move. In almost every case, the shape of the bat creature returned before it melted from existence.

Cage, a big, lumbering man with graying black hair and a walrus mustache, finally got control of himself and he rushed in with his sample bag, trying desperately to get and freeze tissue with a fixative spray that he carried in his bag, creating slides on the spot, as ghouls and humans did battle.

Stroud turned his attention to the interior of the mausoleum, sensing that Banaker was inside, waiting for him. Some thing inside his head told Stroud that perhaps he had to die with Banaker, that the two of them should go out of this world together, and that this somehow would ensure that there would be no more vampires ever again, that the vampire line and that of the vampire hunter had come to an end this night. But he didn't care for the idea of dying here in a death struggle with a gargoyle. He didn't accept the notion. It was bull.

Stroud stepped inside, cautiously; he sensed that Banaker was not alone. He'd held back several others with him here in his last retreat, his bomb shelter. The ones who'd fought Abe outside this structure had been powerful, having three and four times Stroud's strength, like Briggs's deputies. That meant they'd had a recent infusion of blood, Banaker's special distillation, but not the contaminated brew back at the Institute. Banaker must keep a supply here somewhere.

It was pitch-dark at the center of the place, the only light coming in at the door where the noise of the struggle and dying going on there filtered through. Stroud could see nothing. He reached for the matches he'd stuffed in his pocket earlier, the same ones he'd used to touch off the Molotov cocktails the bat creatures had so enjoyed. Stroud lit one just as the door behind him slammed, blowing the light out, but not before he saw the army of creatures arrayed against him here. There were seven, maybe eight and they flew at him as the match went out.

"Welcome, Doctor Stroud," came Banaker's voice in mock politeness. "Welcome to my coffin."

Stroud was pinned by the powerful hold on him. He could not move so much as a muscle as the deadly weapon was wrenched from him. At the moment, he was helpless and in Banaker's power, completely.

"Good of you to have me," he said with mock humor.

"Oh, I will have you all right . . . every drop of you, Abraham Stroud."

Neither of them could see one another in the pitch-blackness here, but Banaker's echo-location organs had Stroud in his sight.

"Bring the human bastard along," he told his followers. "We must hurry."

Outside the mausoleum, demolition men used explosives to blow away the door. Wilson, Ashyer, Cage, and the others rushed through with torches, but they found nothing. On inspection, they found there were no bodies in the crypts in the walls, but there was the sure animal smell they'd all come to despise, a smell like bad mildew, wet wool, permeating the concrete coffins.

They brought in lanterns and flashlights and torches. They scoured every inch of the mausoleum for a way out. Everyone had seen Stroud enter. There had to be a way out. They began to dissassemble the place, tearing open every wall drawer. In one a vampire leapt out and latched onto the throat of one of the men in the party, tearing at his neck so viciously as to sever the jugular, killing him instantly before Ashyer's dart drove into the monster, turning it into a gelatinous mass that Cage scooped bits from, splatting it onto a slide, covering it with a fixative moments before the Jell-o on the floor tiles turned to ash before their eyes.

Behind where the creature had crawled from was a sheer drop into a black hole. They'd have to go down one at a time, and it was likely that more guards would be waiting for them. Ashyer pushed forward, prepared to go first. Wilson argued for this honor, holding Ashyer at bay. No one else wanted the job, but Dr. Cage grabbed his bag and said, "I'm with you."

The line of men began to climb single file into the open hole where the slab had been pulled away with the door, and began the descent into the underground passageway. It was rough going. There were no steps, no ladders, and it was tar black inside, and cramped. Flashing lights did not penetrate beyond a foot or so here. The cavernous hole had a slight tilt downward and it seemed to go on forever.

Once on solid footing the passageway opened a bit wider. The tunnels seemed to be bored out by some machine, so smooth and orderly were they. Wilson was suddenly grabbed from behind by Ashyer, sending a quake through him.

"What?"

"Flash your light up and to your left."

Wilson did so. Cage, just behind the other two, followed by others less intrepid, stared at what the light illuminated. In the dirt wall they could make out the visible side and bottom of a coffin.

"My God," said Ashyer.

"We're beneath the graveyard," said Cage.

"We've got to find Doctor Stroud," said Wilson almost tearfully.

As they continued, the sight of bones and coffin parts, several having been broken into, became almost commonplace. It was like being in a haunted house, except for the fact that there was nothing bogus here. This was for real, and any moment one of them could leap out at the men who must pass this way.

But none came . . . until suddenly someone at the far end of the line screamed. One of the monsters had attacked the rear of the line of humans. The terrified cries and the sound of mangling filled the tunnel when suddenly from overhead an upside-down coffin firmly held in the ceiling popped open and a vampire was atop Wilson.

Ashyer pumped two S-choline darts into the creature before it let the trembling, terrified Wilson loose. Wilson leapt to his feet and stomped at the creature but his feet went into a soupy mixture of flesh and dissolving bone as the vampire poison did its work. Wilson screamed obscenities at the mush before him but Ashyer rushed to the rear to determine the extent of damage there. They'd lost two men before someone had the presence of mind to fire one of the S-choline darts that'd been distributed to them.

Ashyer feared that Dr. Stroud was already dead, but knowing this and knowing Stroud, he also knew that they must go on until they were certain that every vampire in the colony was destroyed.

Ashyer returned to the front of the line and told Wilson that he would now lead the way. Wilson, still shaken by the incident, did not argue but allowed Ashyer his way.

"Come along then," he told the others.

"I've never been so frightened and sickened in my life," said the coroner and paleontologist, Dr. Cage.

Stroud had been knocked unconscious and carried off by the pires, and now he awoke to find himself hanging by his ankles from the ceiling of a cave.

He felt blood dribbling from his neck onto his chin and into his mouth. It was his own blood from a wound Banaker had inflicted. Banaker had already fed on him once. How soon before he'd feed on him again?

His feet and ankles were wrapped in a gluey substance two of the vampires were regurgitating from their mouths after feeding on blood paks that lay on the floor here. Abe Stroud's first sight was of the blood paks, his eyes beginning to accustom themselves to the darkness. This place was not, however, as black as the mausoleum. It was a wide, large ceilinged cavern, very much like those Stroud and Magaffey had visited on the Spoon. The two ghouls hovered in midair as they worked to cover Stroud in the gooey substance that had encased Pamela Carr, Cooper, the Bradley woman, the child, and the dog. Now it was Stroud's turn. And turn he did, his helpless body twirling in midair like a side of beef. He cursed his foolhardiness and the wrong decisions that had landed him here in this hopeless situation. He'd known men who died of similar fate in Vietnam. Had he escaped the creatures of war only to die at the hands of the creatures of night?

Stroud tried to think but a pain was building in his head where the blood had rushed to it. The steel plate in his head was swimming in it, he imagined. At any rate, it was doing him no good. He couldn't think clearly. The blood rushing to his head was making what little vision he had blur. Before him, upside down, on an outcropping of rock, his hands on his hips, was Banaker as Banaker really was. It was the same monster who had murdered Magaffey. The markings, the size, the feel of the thing to Stroud's mind, was exact, a duplicate.

"Concentrate, damn you!" Stroud heard a voice deep within him say.

"I am trying to," he told himself. There was something he could still use against Banaker, something he'd held back. He drew on all the strength left to him and he willed for his grandfather's help, his grandfather's interference. It took all of his concentration, but he let it slip because he recalled that he still had a weapon or two at his disposal. He'd taken the precaution for such an event as this, should he no longer have recourse to the S-choline. He had taped to his chest a large crucifix, and strapped to his ankle was a knife in a scabbard which he could feel had gone undetected. The knife could act as a stake.

He must distract Banaker, however. He could feel Banaker's mind pressing in on his own. It was a mind of great power, great ESP. If he were not careful, Banaker would know his plan.

He pulled himself up, holding himself at the mid-section like a marlin jumping in a vain attempt to fight the hook. He desperately needed to clear his mind and he could feel the oxygen level rising, but in an instant, with a sign from Banaker, one of the vampires hit him hard across the face, sending him snapping back into place, twirling and spinning.

Stroud prayed.

Stroud prayed to God.

He prayed to his father, his grandfather, and his great-grandfather. He concentrated on Ananias's features. He willed him to come, to be with him in this, his last hour. He didn't want to die alone.

"You won't die, Stroud," said Banaker, reading his mind. "No, you will live. You, the great progeny of vampire killers . . . you will *become* a vampire. You and I then, we'll be linked like brothers, and between us, we'll have no equal. We'll rebuild the race, and one day, as planned, our race—yours and mine—evil married to evil, will be as one. Peace on earth, goodwill to men . . . and pires."

Stroud fought back the words, trying not to listen, trying to maintain his concentration against the pain in his head and Banaker's smugness. "Grandfather, help . . . help me now in my hour of—"

A luminous apparition whose features coalesced into those of Ananias Stroud appeared before Banaker. Banaker screeched at it and dived into it, slamming into the wall of the cave, knocking himself near senseless. Abe instantly tore open his fatigues to display the cross there, lifting anew to his ankles and pulling the knife free. One of the puking vampires lunged at him, but Stroud's long knife went into the heart up to the hilt and out the thing's back, gushing blood. The other one backed off, fearful, seeing the cross and the long blade. Banaker sent keening orders to this one, but it had had enough and went racing for the nearest tunnel where it disappeared.

"It's you and me Banaker," said Stroud, who was still very much a sitting duck, or rather a hanging one. Still, he taunted Oliver Banaker to come and get him. "Come on, can't you do your own dirty work, Oliver? Or are you afraid? What about Dolph, Oliver? Aren't you going to avenge the boy? Come on, Oliver . . . come and get me."

Banaker rose up high, higher, completely to the ceiling. He moved in circles, closer and closer, narrowing his margin, keeping his trapped prey in sight, biding his time.

"You don't have all day, Oliver. I think I hear the others coming for me. They've got bullets and darts that can kill you, Oliver, instantly. Come on, you're stronger than I am, and I'm hanging by my fucking heels. What more advantage could you want?"

Banaker drew in like a falcon that has spotted its prey and came straight at him, his talons alone capable of tearing Stroud in two. Stroud got a mental picture of half his torso torn away by the time Ashyer and the others found him. But he hadn't time for negative thinking. He again sought his grandfather's assistance, throwing up an image of the old man before the creature, and again temporarily distracting him, just long enough to straight-arm him with the knife. It sunk home, but not at the heart. Banaker was hit, but not mortally wounded. Stroud held firmly to the knife, but it had almost been pulled away by the speed of the pendulum pass the creature had made. Stroud rose up at the waist, trying desperately to again clear his head of the dizzying, pounding, pooling blood at what had become his bottom-most extremity, his brain. The creature made a second pass, slicing out at exactly the spot where his neck would have been had he not chosen that instant to lift.

Banaker was infuriated at his own inability to lop off Stroud's head. Driving at his top speed, he turned and locked on his target with his radar. Stroud sensed this was it. He held firm to the knife as Banaker closed the gap between them. Banaker slammed into him, sending Stroud into the ceiling above, tearing away one ankle from the glue, but his body swung back down and held. He felt like a rubber chicken, the pain of the impact shooting through him, blood rising from a wound to his arm, his hand that had held the knife numb now; he thought he heard a ping against a rock below where the knife fell.

Banaker was coming in for the kill. Stroud dangled, twirled, sent up a cry of pain from the unendurable slice of him the talons had removed.

"The vial," he heard Ananias's voice say.

"Vile, yeah . . . real vile," he answered either himself or the ghost. He really no longer knew if he had ever spoken to Ananias, or simply to himself and the steel in his own head.

"Not vile! Damn it, vial, the vial in your pocket!"

"Vial?"

"Of S-choline!" said Magaffey's voice in his head.

"S-choline?" He'd forgotten the suicide vial. He'd placed it there in the event he was caught by the creatures. He meant to swallow the stuff. It would anesthetize him from the pain and it would kill any of them that chose to feed on his blood. "I . . . I should take it . . . now," he told himself. The situation was hopeless. The cavalry was not coming. This wasn't the goddamned movies and his hunch that he and Banaker must die together appeared fated.

He pulled at his pockets in search of the vial. He poked and searched as Banaker bore down on him. Then his hands located the vial, a mere capsule of the vampire killing substance. He was still swinging when Banaker, seeing now he was harmless, the knife far from his reach, lighted on him and cackled in a kind of bat keening that meant something akin to victory to him. Stroud realized that the cross had no effect on Banaker who ripped it and the tape holding it from Stroud's chest hair. He poked it in Stroud's face and tossed it downward, still keening. Stroud saw the blind eyes up close and the puckering mouth with the worms crawling there, preparing to take Stroud's last blood. Stroud must either swallow the suicide capsule now or . . .

Stroud's fist opened and he shoved the capsule instead into the creature's puckering mouth moments before its teeth sank into Stroud's shoulder. It was as if the thing did not even feel the capsule as it swallowed Stroud's blood, sending Stroud into a swoon as he dangled there by one ankle. With both hands, Stroud pushed at the hairy, clinging thing on him and as he pushed the thing's chest made a soft, *pop-pulp* sound, and the chest heaved open, spilling blood and intestines to the cavern floor as the bones turned soft and dispersed in the death flight to the ground.

Stroud mercifully blacked out. Moments later the vampire that had run from the cavern came screaming through, followed by several others. They were followed by Ashyer, Wilson, Cage, and the others who fired the last of their darts into these creatures who splatted against one another where they died.

"It's Abe!" shouted Cage, unable to take his eyes from the gruesome sight of Stroud's bleeding, torn body, dangling some six or eight feet off the ground by one leg.

"We've got to get him down!" shouted Wilson.

"Every man present, lend a hand!" Ashyer ordered the others who were made to form a pyramid to the top where Ashyer sliced and sliced at the tough, resilient, hemplike material of the vampires.

Stroud was unconscious when they got him down, and was to remain so for days after. Dr. Cage stayed on long after other officials and notables from the EPA, the FBI, and the CIA had left the area. He'd taken samples of the vampire matter, both that of the dissolving bodies and the ropey substance used to create the cocoons. No full cocoon was ever regained—that of the Bradley woman's having been destroyed by Banaker along with the body. All that they had to show for the presence of the vampire colony in Andover, Illinois, was a handful of slides, a jar with a collection of blind white worms, and the unknown, inert matter the vampires created as they regurgitated. The marrowless bones were of little value or importance. The story Stroud and his people told was unacceptable to the federal authorities and the state did not wish to be held up to ridicule. Thus far, all they had was a mass disappearance and a mass hysteria case out at the Andover Cemetery where some madmen had blown away parts of the mausoleum and destroyed all the bodies at rest there.

The worst case of graveyard vandalism anyone in the history of Andover could recall.

Even many of the men who'd joined Cage, Ashyer, and Wilson that night to save Stroud, refused to talk about the incident. Those who did, denied any knowledge of it.

Meanwhile, Stroud slept the sleep of a comatose patient, but doctors assured his friends that it was not a coma, but healing sleep.

EPILOGUE

Two days later...

When Stroud did awake, he was surprised to be alive, hungry and anxious to leave the hospital. He was pleased to find his friend Cage had stayed on, and that the pathologist actually believed his story of the vampires. Cage, in fact, had done a great deal of reading in Stroud's circular chamber during his stay, and he had gotten to know a lot more about Ananias Stroud in this time.

Andover itself had cleaned its wounds and cleaned up the debris, and had carried on with life. Stroud could look out the hospital window and see that Banaker Institute was the only visible symbol of the former unholy situation allowed to flourish here for so long. The Institute still remained an object of curiosity and investigation. Representatives from various agencies worked in consort to determine what Banaker's elixir meant, and why it was being distilled there like liquor in Scotland.

Despite officials being shy to sanction anything at this point, according to Cage it had become apparent that Dr. Abraham Stroud, if not a hero of the people, was now looked upon in the highest circles of Washington as a legitimate occult-crime detector and fighter. Cage informed him of this.

"So, what does that mean, Cage?"

"It means you're going to the Soviet Union."

"The Soviet Union?"

"Yeah, part of glasnost. Seems they have some strange goings-on over there, too, and the President of the United States is asking

for you. Seems he read one of my reports on the Andover affair
and—"

"What kind of goings-on are you talking about in the Soviet
Union?"

"Seems there's some sort of mass murderer and the Ruskies
think he, or it, could be more than human."

"Hey, buddy, I'm not a cop any longer. I'm an archeologist,
remember?"

"Sure, sure . . . that's why the Russian's are giving us permis-
sion to dig in the USSR!"

"Really? Where?"

"Valdai Hills, the highest point in the USSR."

"The Vodlaniski Site? Abandoned in 1917?" This was one of
world archeology's saddest developments. Due to the Russian
Revolution, all scientific endeavor funded and encouraged by the
czar had halted, and many of the scientists had been brutally slain.
The Vodlaniski Site, rumor had it, was eons old, a site where
Neanderthal man had taken up residence in the area of Valdai,
not to mention countless extinct creatures. Information lying in
the earth there for mankind to learn from was like a book on a
shelf locked away in a forbidden library. Talk about curses on
archeological dig sites.

"Some great opportunity, huh?"

"I'll say. But let me get this straight."

"Shoot."

Stroud paced the hospital room. "In return, they want our help
with this murderer?"

"Russians don't know much about serial killers, pal. That's
strictly a modern American phenomenon, although there've been
historical cases elsewhere, lately—"

"Yeah, I know all that. Where are the killings taking place?"

"Not far from Valdai Hills and the dig site.

"I see. Moscow?"

"You got it."

"Red Square?"

"Right under their noses."

"Sounds bizarre."

"Wait till you hear the details."

"Mangled bodies?"

"Eaten bodies."

"Good Christ."

"Can I give the State Department the go-ahead? They want us

as a team, pal," Cage told him matter-of-factly, as if he'd already vouched for Stroud. No doubt people in high places had gone over his record.

"They know about my . . . my stay at the VA, of course?"

"They do." Cage was chomping at the bit.

"How soon?" Abe asked him.

"Yesterday."

"Set it up. I'll make arrangements here, if I can get my damned pants."

Cage laughed at this. "You know, Abe, you may've saved the whole damned country from these vampires."

"Don't you for a moment believe that we got them all, Cage . . . not for a moment. All we know, this killer in the Soviet Union is one of them."

Cage looked thoughtfully into Stroud's eyes and he saw something strange and forboding there, something he'd never seen there before. The man's eyes seemed to have changed with his experience in Andover, they looked, for all the world, like the gray eyes of his grandfather.

"Get us booked, have everything first class. What the State Department won't foot, put on my tab," he told Cage decisively. "Imagine—*my first dig*, and its my show, right? On Soviet soil!"

If you enjoyed *Curse of the Vampire*, then you'll enjoy reading the next Abraham Stroud novel by Geoffrey Caine, *Wake of the Werewolf*, coming from Diamond Books in September.

Following is an excerpt from that book.

He had to be as cunning as an animal. He had to be an animal.

There was a time when the howling in his ears had been stilled, but Kerac couldn't recall how that felt. He'd been hearing the cry of the creature for too long now. What? An hour, a day, two . . . maybe a week, two weeks . . . double that? A month? Many months? Couldn't tell.

The cries told him he had to escape. If he didn't escape, he'd die.

The howls told him what to do. He fell dead away in the cafeteria at Merimac, the state-operated prison for the criminally insane. He had no idea how long he'd been here, or what he had done to deserve being put away, but the cries told him clearly how to faint by restricting his own air supply.

It'd worked and he'd been taken to the infirmiry. There the cries told him even before he'd fully recovered his senses that his disorder must be made more complicated if he was to be taken to a real hospital, outside the great walls that held him here.

Kerac dug for the piece of glass he'd held beneath his tongue, grateful he had neither swallowed nor choked on it. He waited until the prison doctor looked away before he reached down into his pants and slit his penis nearly in two with the glass. He made not a sound, just listened to what the noises inside his head instructed him to do. He lay back and let the blood stain his pants with a dark, purple splotch, a kind of stigmata the buzzing in his mind told him in an indecipherable tongue that somehow was translated into self-mutilation.

He wondered again what he'd done to deserve imprisonment alongside madmen. The pain in his privates was the price he must pay for escape. To keep from thinking about the pain, he concentrated on his laugh. He'd thought a great deal about laughter since coming here, and how important laughter really was. He let out with a laugh now which seemed to percolate in his diaphram and erupt with the force of a volcano. It was a raw, naked laugh. The laughing slowed the cries and the howls and the mournful wails of the animal inside his brain.

When the doctor looked back at him, quaking it seemed from Kerac's laugh, he had a look of horror on his face. Kerac's eyes dimmed over with a thick, gummy substance and suddenly he was seeing everything in a kind of 3-D, everything in clear perspective, angles and depths jutting out and in, nothing hidden in the dark shadow-covered corners. It was like seeing for the first time. It was wild and exciting. It was mind-blowing, like being on a heroin high, but without the color because everything was in grays, blacks and shimmering whites.

His hearing had also become incredibly acute. He could actually hear the orderly's sneakers on the floor as he inched toward the door. He thought he could hear the other man's heartbeat. He could hear someone in the TV room snoring. He could hear a fly breathe. It was a power he'd not ever expected to possess.

All this as well as his intensified sense of smell. In fact, he could smell the other men as never before, and in his brain he distinguished each man by his smell. The orderly sweat heavily and exuded a goatlike stench, he used no deodorant; while the doctor's perspiration was a cold, sweet scent . . . There was the faint scent of anise escaping his pores along with the disinfectant on his hands.

The look on the doctor's face, the look of shock and puzzlement must be due to the cut and the blood, reasoned Kerac. But Kerac then caught sight of his own hands in the now colorless world around him, and he saw the extended claws and the hair and the parasites nestling in the fur covering his limbs. The realization that he was mad only now dawned on him, seeing himself this way.

He lifted himself off the table and the doctor and his orderly backed away in fright. Kerac saw his gray reflection in the doctor's glass cabinet. Like his mind, his body was all a tangle of knotted confusion. His eyes had dropped below the brow into a deep recess of dark circles created by folds of leathery skin from which prickly, whiskerlike hairs sprouted. His nose had enlarged, the nostrils flared. His jaw was snoutlike and the pain that wracked his body made him shout, but the shout came out as an inhuman howl, the cry of a beast that had been raging in his head for as long as he could remember.

The orderly tore open the door in an attempt to race from the room, but Kerac's reaction was quick and instinctive, pouncing on the man in catlike fashion, ripping away at his face to stop the screaming.

"Kerac! Kerac!" shouted the doctor, pleading.

But Kerac's claws came down in rapid-fire fashion, turning the young orderly's features to mincemeat before he slid dead to the floor.

Screaming, the doctor tried to escape, but Kerac's hairy arm caught him about the neck, a deadly claw sinking deep into the man's throat, severing the jugular. Kerac tore a limb from the man as he was bleeding to death. He did so with playful ease, amazed at the strength he possessed. He wanted to try his strength again, but something cunning deep within his mind opted for escape. But not before he ripped apart his prey. He left nothing recognizable as human in a matter of minutes. Kerac lapped at the blood, crawling about the carrion on all fours. But hearing the shouts and footsteps of others, he tore away another limb, and taking his two prizes, he leapt through the window to the sound of sirens and the flash of lights.

One of the guards sighted Kerac, drew a bead on him and hesitated, realizing that the escaping form was some sort of animal. A second guard arrived just in time to see what looked to him like a large dog—maybe a bear—leap over the ten-foot wall, dropping something in its wake. The two men went to inspect what the creature had dropped at the foot of the stone wall. The flashlight told them it was a large man's bloody leg.

"Get the dogs, hurry!" shouted one of the guards to the other.

In an hour guards and dogs were scouring the woods surrounding Merimac, but they found nothing when the dogs refused to cooperate.

The scene in which two men were literally ripped apart by some kind of bloodthirsty animal kept coming back at Abraham Hale Stroud, wanting—*demanding*—clarification from his subconscious.

Twice now it had run on the "silver screen," his playful term for the steel plate in his head which had some years before become a kind of pyschic antenna, somehow combining with what had apparently been in his makeup all along: extrasensory perception. The combination made for something the experts called second sight, but for Stroud there were no words that fit the peculiar "gift" that seemed initially to be inherited, in the genes. In a sense his own body chemistry had been wed to a kind of electromagnetic pole at the cranium that sometimes sent and sometimes received messages from far away. He'd been visited by his grandfather's ghost and others on more than one occasion. Typically, the visits were, while shocking and heart-stopping, benign in nature. Often, they were meant to guide him to answers not readily perceived by any other means. They'd certainly been beneficial in the case of the Andover Devil . . .

Just the same, he was often confused as to the meanings of his visions. He'd once been a soldier hunting the enemy in a tangled jungle in Southeast Asia, and this before the metal plate was in his head. With his abilities he'd located the enemy where nothing mechanical could. In fact, he was so good at locating the enemy that over half his company was killed in an ensuing engagement. He was himself left for dead on the field for two soul-searching days before he was found and brought out. He was then shipped home after a Hanoi hospital stay, where the doctors stabilized the rest of his body but could do very little for the missing shards of his skull. They then packed him off like a mail bag into a cargo plane and got him state-side, where a "real" hospital outside Chicago replaced part of his skull with a metal brace. Curiously, the doctor's name had been Bracewell.

Later, as an officer of the Chicago Police Department for some thirteen years, he became known as the "Psychic Cop." During those years he'd also completed his work on a doctorate in Archeology at the University of Chicago, working nights, weekends, and holidays to do so. He had retired from the arena of the policeman when his grandfather died, leaving him an estate in Andover, Illinois, on the Spoon River, along with full ownership of Stroud Bank of Andover, and the family fortune. It had all seemed like any man's dream—winning the lottery—at first, but now Stroud knew there were stipulations, even a real live "curse" associated with the wealth of Stroud Manse.

He'd had to rid Andover of what the locals had for years whispered about in the pubs and coffeehouses as the Andover Devil. As a result there'd been a great loss of life, including a good friend, Dr. Magaffey. And although the immediate threat of the vampire colony that'd held Andover in its collective grasp for generations had been broken, Stroud knew that he'd be called on again to use his wealth and his gift to fight evil in whatever other form or guise it took. And right now, it seemed to be taking on the form of a ghastly monster of the night that left men lying in flesh heaps the way a lion on the Serengeti left its prey to the vultures, scavengers and maggots.

Just exactly what the creature resembled in appearance, Abraham was unprepared to say. The images and vision that'd come to him of this overwhelming evil gave him the feelings of the monster far more than it gave him the appearance. The creature hungered. It hungered not just for blood and flesh to fill its stomach, but for the exhilaration and adrenaline high of the kill itself. It was a hunter, a predator of the first order, but the purpose of its hunt was love of the kill first, feeding second. Its instincts were those of the jaguar. It was large, ferocious and powerful, and it delighted in its own attributes.

But Stroud had his hands full with his work. The dig at the newly discovered burial mounds at a well-established and well-known Cahokia Indian village here in southern Illinois was disproving some long-held notions about the Cahokias. He was having a wonderful time with it, feeling like a boy in the toy department at Macy's. It was taking up most of his waking hours. The evening hours, however, were being given over to fantastic visions of a creature roaming the countryside. The "disturbance" had not gone unnoticed by colleagues and friends here, including Dr. Cage, the expedition leader.

"You feeling all right?" was a constant question put to him lately down at the dig site.

He had plenty of time to think there on his hands and knees beside students—children—a third his age. He meant to get dirty, to grind the dirt into his jeans, sift it through his fingers and get it under his nails. He meant to learn firsthand what Cahokia meant to its people. He meant to unearth another set of bones for Cage and the others to marvel over. Meantime, he was truly soaking up the field experience and learning the newest techniques. The game of the bone hunter had advanced rapidly in the past few years; so many new toys at the scientists' disposal, like the Earthscan, a device that told the archeologist where his best chance of finding buried earth formations lie. With the help of the Earthscan, time, energy and backaches were saved, not to mention the integrity of the dig itself. Who needed a useless slag heap?

It was all good experience for Dr. Abe Stroud, newly appointed assistant to Dr. Cage. Stroud knew best that he needed the invaluable experience before becoming involved in an overseas dig.

With work and focusing his attention on the artifacts and bones the earth reluctantly gave into his hands, Stroud had felt he could fend off the nagging nightmare that had now returned for a third time like a bad penny. So long as it remained a nightmare, however vivid, Stroud remained uncertain of the meaning of the vicious killing played out in his mind. It might be nothing more than a simple and meaningless nightmare, and yet he knew that he wasn't like other men who had bad dreams and could wake up and forget about them, or blot them out entirely. His dreams sometimes predicted the future, and sometimes were replays of incidents already in the past. That was how he had first met the missing boy, Timmy Meyers, who had eventually led to the discovery of an entire vampire colony that had learned to cohabit with humans by day and night so closely it was impossible to tell them apart. Maybe the dream was trying to tell him something. Maybe the dream was brought to him by his dead grandfather . . .

How did the old Celtic prayer go? *From ghoulies and ghosties and long-leggety beasties . . . And things that go bump in the night . . . deliver us!*

Maybe he was just being foolish, letting his imagination run wild . . . maybe the stress and excitement of the work weaving itself into his nights and turning into a garden worm when it hit the plate in his head. Maybe . . .

Dusk was coming on again, and again Abe feared going to sleep. He had tired of the shaking, heart-gripping scene that'd played out in his tent and in his mind thrice now. He prayed it wouldn't return. He clamored to his feet, his legs numb at first and then shooting with pain, especially the knees. A young fellow named Jack offered him a hand up out of the pit, and he took it gratefully.

"You've been at it since noon nonstop, Dr. Stroud," he said.

"Guess I didn't notice the time. Happens in a flash when you enjoy what you do."

"Everybody in camp's talking about you."

"What?"

"About how you pitch in, how you work, get your hands in . . . not like some I've worked with, believe me. Last guy I worked with, real old, ugly, skinny fart—"

"Dr. Sturdevant?"

"Yeah, sorry . . . didn't know you knew him."

"Only by reputation."

"Reputation, huh. All he was interested in was getting the fresh-man girls into bed with him."

Stroud laughed and said, *"Archeology and Sex."*

"That's right . . . bartered grades for it, the old weasel."

"I meant his book, *Archeology and Sex.*"

"Oh, oh yeah . . . well, I'm off to mess. See you, Dr. Stroud."

"Thanks, Jack, for the hand up and the lesson."

He looked back over his shoulder and said, "Don't mention it to her, but Tammy Wymes thinks you're a hunk, Dr. Stroud. Might help you sleep, you know what I mean?"

Stroud dropped his gaze and shook his head. "Yeah, maybe that'd set things right, all right."

Stroud then wandered off from camp as was his habit, to spend a little time along the brook the Indians had no name for. For the Indians, where the water flowed from and where it went as it moved past their village was of no consequence. It was enough that it was here, and that it gave of itself to them. Stroud wondered how the world had become so complex and difficult.

The night was coming on fast, a chill in the breaking wind. Young saplings twitched and the bugs were chattering. It was the sort of night a man could see forever, the stars flirting with the imagination, a high, near-full moon blinking around a stray cloud; when the moon moved over it flushed the land around Cahokia with a sandy, silvery hue. Then it dawned on Dr. Stroud that he'd stood here in a near catatonic state so long that he'd missed dinner. He was left with the prospect of going to his tent, where he'd log a few notes, catch up on his reading, and try like hell to get some deserved sleep. Maybe tonight it wouldn't elude him.

Nothing disturbed Stroud and he slept through the night to awake to the morning noises of camp. He breathed a deep sigh of relief for the fact that he'd shaken off the nightmare that'd haunted him now for several nights. But his contentment and his thoughts were rudely interrupted by his friend and associate, Dr. Louis Cage. Cage, a burly, lumbering man with spectacles too small for his huge face and a walrus mustache but no hair on his head, burst into Stroud's tent flapping a newspaper.

"Look at this! Abe, look!"

"I came out here to escape newspapers, Lou."

Cage looked momentarily stunned, but then went on. "This is your dream, your nightmare, down to the last detail. It's made page one in *USA Today*."

"What?" Stroud grabbed the paper from Cage's fumbling fingers. He glanced over the cover story, scanning for details below the photo of a Dr. Harold Perotto and a second man. In the before picture the two men were wearing the normal look of medical men standing for a photo, but in the after picture, there was nothing left of either man, save the bloody torso and a scramble of limbs about the floor. The paper said that a criminally insane man named John Kerac had butchered the men with some unknown weapon, leapt through a glass window, and eluded guards to escape the Michigan state facility for the criminally insane near Merimac, Michigan. Kerac remained at large.

"I'm right, aren't I, Abe? Isn't this the nightmare you've been having?"

"Premonition . . . the first time, and the second. Happened last night."

"You couldn't've known it. Now, don't go blaming yourself. You didn't even know the men were medical men, or that the monster you saw was an insane fiend. You didn't know the time, or the place."

"But if I'd let it come, instead of fighting it . . . maybe."

"Damn it, Abe, you're not a sorcerer. You're only human."

"Thanks, that's great comfort, Lou."

Cage took in a great breath of air, seeing a familiar look come over his friend's features. "You're going up there, aren't you?"

Some of the guys at the watering hole outside were laughing over something. In a paranoid moment, he wondered if they were discussing him. If he knew anything about paranoia, he knew it was quite often an early warning device that was often as accurate as a Timex. His instincts marched along the epidermal layer of his skin to alert the brain that was, like a slow cursor on a computer, half a pulse behind this morning.

"Maybe it wouldn't be such a bad idea," he said. "Around here, I seem to be stirring up more curiosity than what's out there in the Indian Mounds."

"That's nonsense."

"Really?"

"Damned straight it is."

"Damn it, Lou, you're the best detail man in the pathology business, and you're an excellent paleontologist, but you've got a hell of a lot to learn about the living."

"I take that as a compliment. What the hell do I really want to know about the living?"

"I'm going, Lou."

"Fine, go! Good riddance, as you say. And what'll you do in Michigan once you get there?"

"I'll offer my help."

"And if they refuse it?"

"Then at least I can say I gave it my best."

"To convince whom? Your dead grandfather, or yourself?"

"Both, maybe."

"Dead set on this, are you?"

"I have to, Lou . . . you know that."

He frowned and slowly nodded. "Get back as quick as you can. Give me a holler if you need me."

"Thanks, and will do."

"Taking your new chopper up?"

"I figure to fly, sure. Sooner I get there, the better. Lou, I think I understand how this madman, Kerac, thinks. It could be helpful to the authorities up there."

"Well, if you should find yourself butting heads with a back-woods geek who thinks he's God, then turn yourself right around and leave them to their own stupidities." Cage stood up and took his hand. "It's been a delight, these past weeks with you here, Abe, you know that."

"All but the past few days and nights, you mean."

All of it, my friend. We'll be here when you've finished in Michigan.

With that Cage left abruptly, not a man for lengthy good-byes.

Kerac awoke naked and bloody, the pain in his penis shooting a searing rod of fire through him. He had blood encrusted over his lips and chin. He had a foul taste in his mouth, coppery and greasy. He felt he might wretch at any moment. He crawled about in the cold, high, dead reeds and grass all around him, trying to determine where he was and how he'd gotten here. He felt numb from the cold, so numb he could hardly think to recall anything. Then he crawled up toward a bone from which some fleshy strings clung; it was cushioned in a nestlike place in the high thatch. He realized he'd stumbled onto the lair or sleeping place of some sort of animal that had been feeding on the large bone. He looked around instinctively for whatever it might be. When he saw nothing, he calmed a bit, going closer to the bone and lifting it as much from curiosity as anything, and yet . . . something about the bone and its smell, and the smell of the flesh clinging there like wet noodle brought on images that made little sense to John Kerac.

He saw himself at a hunting camp, sitting by a warm fire, a few friends without names or faces with him. He saw the flames blind out the image and replace it with his running madly through the woods. He tried desperately to remember, fighting with his mind for the right to his past, to access to more than mere images flashing on and off in the manner of a wino. There was more . . . much more, he knew. If only he could tap into it.

Then he saw the doctor's face at Merimac; he saw it torn from the man, reduced to a gelatinous mass. He saw it being done by a creature of immense power, and as he watched he saw the creature's eyes, and in the eyes he recognized something else. He saw that the eyes of the monster were his eyes.

He found himself cradling the bone again, realizing now what sort of bone it was, and where it had come from. He also realized that the nesting animal had been him, and that it was he who had fed on the flesh of the bone.

He trembled at the cold around him, and he trembled at the power of the *other* within him.

They must be scouring the countryside for him this instant. There must be an APB out on him. He must run and he must hide. But which way? Indecision and fear could get him captured or killed. He'd be crucified for killing the doctor and his orderly. What had he done before this to warrant his being locked up at Merimac, he again wondered. Then he saw the fire and the camp once more, and he saw the dark shape in the nearby trees leap down and run ahead of him, as he and his friends chased after it with guns.

Something had happened out there . . . but what?

Something was drawing him back, too . . . back to where this all started, to where his nameless, faceless friends had . . . had all . . . all dead . . . they were all mutilated by some *thing*. He saw the bone in his lap, and he wondered if it had been him who had killed the others in a brutal spree of madness. He thought he recalled feeding on them as he had on the doctor's arm last night.

He dropped the bone and bent over, vomiting up chunks of the doctor's flesh, crawling to escape the sight and the smell and himself, but he could do none of these things.

Kerac heard a dog's braying. Alert to the danger, he raced away from the thatch lair, searching for something safer. In another direction he heard the call of a cock and he went instinctively for what he prayed would be a farm with an automobile somewhere on the premises.

Something told him he had to go back, back to the area outside Grand Rapids where it had all begun, but he feared it terribly. He had friends in Chicago and he knew the city like the back of his hand. Maybe there he could get straight somehow. Maybe there he could beat this insanity thing.

He fought back the pain in his lower parts, rushing wildly toward his future.

Stroud stepped out of his helicopter to a waiting patrol car driven by Merimac's own sheriff, a lady sheriff named Chief Anna Laughing More. The name alone had intrigued Abe, and he had wondered about its history during his flight to Michigan via his newly acquired Mooney XE6000 chopper. He'd had breakfast in the Cahokia archeological camp, and was now in Merimac, some fifty miles southeast of Grand Rapids, for lunch. But the reception he got from the lady cop was as cutting as the cold wind that rippled across the small airstrip in Merimac, a town founded, it seemed, on the economy created by the state facility from which John Kerac had successfully escaped.

Before the rotar blades on his shiny new helicopter had slowed to a stop, Chief Laughing More indicated with a gesture that he was to get into her patrol car. She was dressed in a tight-fitting, strangely seductive brown and beige uniform that showed off her tall, elegant figure. Her hair was a jet black, severely cut like a man's, perhaps to fit beneath the chief's cap, perhaps to gain acceptance and respect. But this was the only feature that detracted from her femininity, he thought as he got into the vehicle. Without a word, she tore off the tarmac, using no siren, but clearly no one best get in her way. Immediately, Stroud got the feeling she didn't want him here. It was as cold inside the car as out.

The chatter of the car radio buzz recalled his days as a police officer in Chicago. "I'm Dr. Stroud, and you must be Chief Laughing More."

Her Ojibway ancestry showed in the high cheekbones and her proud bearing. She was beautiful to look at. He imagined she'd worn her hair long all her life, up to the point she'd become a police woman. She was as tall as Stroud, and he guessed her to be in her early to mid-thirties. Her skin was a smooth, tight, coppery color and her eyes were as black as the darkness on a blank computer screen, giving up nothing.

"I know who you are, Dr. Stroud."

"You understand why I've come?"

"You've come to . . . " she paused, considering her words carefully, "help out, as I understand it."

She spoke exquisite English, despite her exotic features. "Yes, any way I can."

"You say you saw this man, Kerac, in a dream, kill our Dr. Perotto and Carl Holms?"

"I didn't know their names at the time. Read about it later in the papers, like everyone else."

"But your dream—"

"More a nightmare than a dream, a premonition."

"Premonition, yes . . . well . . . "

"I fully understand your reluctance to believe me, Chief Laughing More."

"You can call me Chief More," she corrected him. "Everyone else does." She didn't appear in a laughing mood, nor, Stroud guessed, did she display laughter very often while in uniform. "Listen, Dr. Stroud, I'm not much of a believer in your . . . in powers of precognition, is it called? Nor do I much hold with psychic investigators. You may as well know it."

"Refreshing," he replied cryptically.

And for a long moment, she tried to decipher his meaning without benefit of explanation. Finally, she repeated the word in puzzlement, "Refreshing?"

"I only wish everyone were as honest around me, Chief."

"Oh, you will find me honest, all right—honest Injun, as they say, Doctor."

He managed a weak smile at this, unsure how to take her remark. "I've fought very hard to get where I am today, Dr. Stroud."

"I can see that you have."

"Can you? Really? You have any idea how entrenched the KKK is in Michigan? The Knights of the Baldies? Ordinary redneck mentality? Any idea how hard it is for an Indian in Michigan to beat the reservation system, the inadequate school system, the poverty, the prejudice? No, I suppose not."

"Perhaps not . . . certainly not firsthand, but I'm here to learn."

"I thought you came to provide us with lavish information on the crime and the killer, Dr. Stroud. I had no idea you were here to gather information. Are you writing a book?" Her sarcasm came full to the surface now.

"I used to be a cop, Chief More. I know how you feel when a outsider steps in, but—"

"Chicago cop. What do you know about Michigan?"

"I know serious crime is on the rise here, like most places, six hundred and eighty-six murders in Detroit alone—"

"This isn't Detroit. This is—"

"Six thousand four hundred and fifty-eight serious crimes reported statewide."

"So, you've done your homework, and now you know how Merimac works?"

He frowned and scratched his ear and moved uneasily in the car seat beside her. "I don't pretend to understand the people or the politics, but I had expected a little common courtesy after flying here at my own expense to look into this matter and offer—at no expense to Merimac—any assistance I can render. What the hell is it, Chief? Election time in Merimac?"

"Why, you are very perceptive at that, Dr. Stroud."

"Election's coming up, huh?"

"It's always election day in Merimac. You may think Michigan is cozy, middle-America, the hunting and fishing paradise in the brochures, and all is beautiful and serene in the Michigan forests, that all's right in the world. What bad could happen in Michigan? How about we begin with a red population that is still treated like animals?"

He could see she had a large chip on her shoulder, and that he wasn't about to dislodge it here and now. He was a white man and she was a red woman; he was an outsider, and she was an insider. He was a civilian while she was a police chief.

"Is Kerac . . . is he Indian?"

"He was."

"What do you mean, was? Has he been shot?"

She looked across at him. "No, he is still at large, but he is also *Ninatoo*; you might call it banished."

"Banished?"

She swallowed hard. "When an Ojibway Indian murders, he is cast out of the race of the *first people*, the Ojibway. Kerac was a guide. He led several men into the Maniste National Forest a month ago. He slaughtered all three of the other men."

"Three white men?"

"On holiday . . . hunters. Anyway, he was apprehended and sent here to await trial. He had been judged completely insane. He'd . . . he had eaten the flesh of the white men."

"Cannibalized them?"

"Yes."

"All three?"

"Yes, like a wild animal might."

Stroud breathed deeply, his skin crawling with the image. "Autopsies were done on the dead men?"

"In Grand Rapids, yes."

"And here, with Dr. Perotto and the other man?"

"Our town, the hospital pathologist performs any autopsy."

"I see." Stroud knew that hospital pathologists were not the most reliable people where autopsy was concerned. "What about Grand Rapids? Do they have a municipal pathologist?"

"Dr. Henry Sands, but he's second rate at best."

"Why do you say so?"

"Let me put it this way; I've worked cases with him before. I know."

"Good enough for me."

She gave him a quick gaze. "What do you hope to find in a pathology report, anyway?"

"Connections, patterns . . . not sure."

"Oh, you'll see patterns all right—patterns on the bodies—gashes. Whatever Kerac used on these men—" she shivered involuntarily. "I've never seen such brutality before, I'll admit that. I'm sure it's nothing to a Chicago cop. Want to swing by the morgue first before going out to the pen?"

"Is it on the way?"

"Have to go through town, then on to the other side."

"Fine, whatever you say, Chief."

"Funny thing about Kerac and me, Stroud . . . "

"Oh, what's that?"

"We grew up together on the same reservation . . . went to the same schools—"

"Ever figure him for this?"

"He was nothing but a shy, sweet boy when I knew him. Big and clumsy and shy, like a bear up here," she pointed to her head. "Not very smart, but keen as a tracker and a guide. We have one other thing in common, Dr. Stroud."

"And what is that?"

"I'm also banished from my tribe."